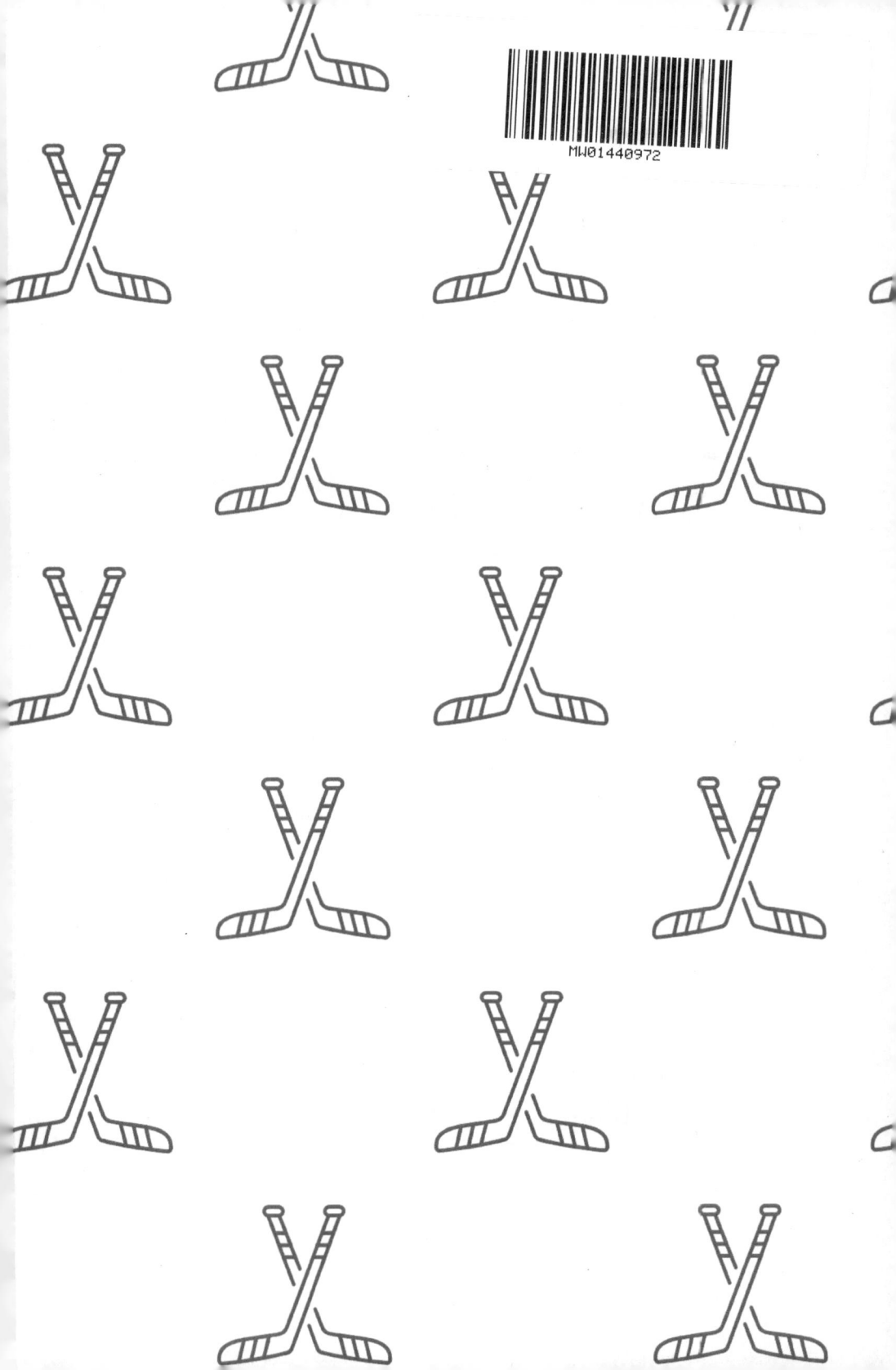

THE DRAFT

ANA SHAY

Cover Illustrations by Elen Bushe

Cover Design by Regan Kindrick

Edits & Proof by Sarah at All Encompassing Books

Copyright © 2024 Ana Shay
All rights reserved. No part of this publication may be reproduced, distributed or transmitted in any form or by any means, including photocopying, recording, or other electronic or mechanical methods, without the prior written consent of the publisher, except in the case of brief quotation embodied in critical reviews and certain other noncommercial uses committed by copyright law.

Resemblance to actual persons, things, living or dead, locales or events is entirely coincidence.

To Stephanie,
Thank you for going against Jay's advice and contacting me…
Best decision ever!

Chapter 1

Dash

"I can't believe I let you talk me into this," I grumbled, wanting to push a hand through my hair but knowing I couldn't because it had gel in it. I shook my head, feeling mildly disappointed that I let Scotty talk me into coming tonight, let alone style my hair.

What the hell was I thinking?

Scotty, my teammate, had a shit-eating grin on his face as he took me in because of course he would find this hilarious. I was sitting on the world's most uncomfortable barstool, wearing his too-tight button-down shirt and a pair of jeans two sizes too small for my meaty ass. I looked ridiculous, and I didn't need Scotty's smug grin confirming it.

"Relax," he drawled out as he clasped a hand on my shoulder, giving it a squeeze. "It's just a little fun. You don't need to take everything in life so seriously, Dash."

Narrowing my eyes, I glared at him with enough fire to burn the entire place down.

Oh, he was loving every single second of this. I could tell.

He laughed again while I tried to think of a reasonable explanation for why a goalie would knock out the star center of his own team with a puck at our next game, but I came up short. Much like these pants.

"A little fun?" I grunted and clutched my beer tightly, pretending it was his throat. "A little fun to me is beating Erik's ass on the Xbox while Alex watches and provides mildly entertaining commentary. A little fun is catching a baseball game with the guys during the offseason. A little fun is beating Southern Collegiate with little to no effort. This is a speed dating event disguised as a sports mixer that you forced me to come to because everyone else on our floor of the hockey dorm was busy."

Scotty took a sharp breath and clutched his shirt in mock shock. He looked around the room and smiled at a few of the freshman players that he'd also managed to drag along before pinning his gaze back on me. "The Draft isn't just a dating event." He leaned in as if anyone could hear our conversation over the incessantly loud, sugary pop music blasting in the campus bar, Covey's Cantina. "It's *the* dating event at Covey U. Any athlete worth their salt would kill to be here because it means that the school is interested in them and their sport. That's important to some people."

I rolled my eyes because even the name of this thing was stupid. The Draft. It may have started out with good intentions twenty years ago, working as a meet and greet for students and players alike, but unfortunately, the event's goals got lost in translation as time passed. Jersey chasers and puck bunnies figured out it was a pretty good way to gain one-on-one access to any athlete they were interested in earning an M.R.S. degree from. That was when the debauchery began. Players caught on pretty quickly and used it to their advantage too. Guys wanted to be part of it just for the easy access to women, but I wanted nothing to do with this mess. Quick lays and drunken nights weren't things I was really into. I'd much rather Netflix and chill with one girl that I like than deal with people who only knew my name because of my NHL draft status. But, unfortunately for me, since I was single, I had no excuse to leave.

"Cade would have been a better choice for this. I'm sure he'd relish the attention. He always does. Even Erik makes a better first impression than me. I hate people."

And I really hated this.

People were watching me, I could feel it, and I didn't like being judged. That was why I was good as a goaltender. My mask was so big that I barely drew attention from girls. Having Mr. Hot Shot in the form of Scotty Hendricks on the team helped, too, because the minute girls found out he was from hockey royalty, they'd swarm to him like flies to shit. Not that he liked the attention.

Scotty dropped his head and shook it before looking back up at me. "Don't you get it? That's exactly why you're the best pick for this." He pointed to himself. "Everyone wants to meet me because they want to speak to the son of a Stanley Cup winner," he said with disdain, and I got it. Everyone knew Scott Hendricks, and therefore the expectation of Scotty to be just as good, if not better than his father, was always there. Scotty flipped his finger over, so he was pointing at me. "You, however, are the biggest mystery of any player on the Covey Crushers. You don't speak to people. You hardly leave the rink, and when you do, your hair is long enough that you can flick your bangs down and hide your face."

"I don't have bangs."

"Would you prefer I call them curtains?" He pointed to the strands of hair at the side of my face, biting back a smile. Granted, my hair was longer than the boy band quiff he had going on, but it was nothing like that freshman quarterback we'd just recruited for next year. What was his name again? It was something that began with a T. Tanner, Tarzan, I didn't know. Anyway, what that guy's name was or what Scotty thought about my hair was beside the point. I was here, and I didn't want to be.

"I'd prefer you never mention my hair again. In fact, if you could lose my number, that would be ideal."

He tried to hide his amusement at just how uncomfortable I was finding all of this, but it didn't work. "You do realize that I have never used your number, right? Kind of unnecessary when we all live on the same floor."

It was the sad reality of my life and the problem with playing hockey at Covey U. We ate, slept, and played together, and any potential privacy was long gone when Cade punched a hole through my door in a rage against a loss to our biggest rival, the St. Michael's Storm, a couple of weeks ago.

The guy had a serious anger problem, but I considered him a brother, so I couldn't stay upset. Next-door neighbors and teammates since we were ten, to say we were close would be an understatement. He was my brother for all intents and purposes.

"Come on, Sasquatch." Scotty shook my shoulders, flashing me his perfect smile again. It was his defense mechanism when he didn't want to get too deep with anyone. "It's not *all* that bad. When was the last time you went on a date with anyone besides your foam roller?"

I glared at him because, yes, my foam roller and I might have had a close relationship since I had to be able to perform the splits at a second's notice in the middle of a game, but that didn't mean I enjoyed being taunted about it.

Scotty was unfazed by my stare and waited for my response, so I thought about it for a second. *Who was the last girl I slept with?* I raised my brows and blew out my breath, remembering that my last relationship was in high school with some hardly memorable chick named Amy. Kind of sad to think about, considering I dated her for two and a half years. She cheated on me because she thought I was too serious. Joke was on her, though. I only dated her because she bared a striking resemblance to…never mind.

"Exactly," Scotty said sharply, as though my facial expression was all the answer he needed. "You've not let a single girl put their hands on you since you arrived at Covey U two years ago. Your dick is probably ready to fall off. Why not loosen up a little and let yourself have some fun?"

Flat-lipped, I responded, "Because I'm not interested in having that kind of fun."

"You won't know you're not interested until you try."

I rolled my eyes at the sentiment, even though he might have had a point. Unfortunately for him, it was lost when he winked at a girl passing by. Shaking my head, I grumbled at his antics. He was always trying to keep up this playboy façade, but it was so easy to see through it when you knew him. "That's rich coming from a guy who's obsessed with some girl he met on the internet before he even started here."

His smile fell. "Laura is not some girl on the internet."

"Maybe not, but she's definitely not interested in you."

"Yet."

The Draft

"If those viral videos of you humping the ice didn't do it for her, I'd expect nothing will."

"I was stretching, and it was taken from the stands, so I'd watch out because I'm pretty sure there are some viral videos of you just waiting to be released." He smoothed down his black button-up, completely unfazed by my surliness.

Ding! Ding! Ding!

"And that's my cue." Scotty smirked and adjusted his tie before standing. "Good luck fending off all those puck bunnies."

"I think that's more your issue than mine." He saluted me and walked over to the table set up for him. There were at least sixty athletes in here, all of whom had their own table with their name and sport listed on a piece of paper in front of them. That was it. The bar didn't need to put any effort in to make this event a success, the jersey chasers did that for them.

Looking down at the only beer I allowed myself to have tonight, I blew out an exasperated breath.

This was going to be a long night.

I hung my head in shame and pulled at my…curtains? Was that really what they were called? If so, I needed to rethink this cut. Then I growled at myself because this whole thing was stupid. I shouldn't be sitting here thinking about my hair. Scotty was already charming some puck bunny, and as the room filled, I knew it wouldn't be long before I had no choice but to engage in conversation with someone. I didn't like to talk at the best of times, and this was possibly the worst.

Screw It. I'm leaving.

My chair screeched across the floor and I winced because it drew the attention of the surrounding tables. Way to be subtle.

"Where do you think you're going, Big Man?"

Big Man?

I stopped moving. My feet touched the ground, but my mind was reeling because that voice had haunted my brain for nearly ten years.

"Madison? What are you doing here?" I tried to sound unbothered, but that was impossible when I was in the presence of Madison Bright. The girl who had no idea she held my heart in a viselike grip.

When I looked up, I swore I was having palpitations because she was dressed to kill, and my initial reaction was to go on a murder spree and slaughter every single man in here for merely being in her presence. I'd start with Scotty because, even though I knew he wasn't interested in his teammate's little sister, he deserved to die for dragging me here and making me see her in that tight, black dress which dipped painfully low at the front.

She flicked her sleek, blonde ponytail over one side and smiled as she lifted her shoulder flirtatiously. Then she winked and blew me a kiss as she sat down. My jaw clenched, and I drew my hands into a fist as I tamed my reaction because this wasn't the first time she'd acted like this. Madison was a heartbreaker. Had been one ever since her first boyfriend cheated on her. From that moment forward, she put on this flirty, dumb blonde persona which she was anything but. The girl was a valedictorian for crying out loud. I could easily see through it. She only did it because she didn't want anyone to think she was hurt by the entire situation. But I saw it. Every time she winked, giggled and shook her shoulders. I could see the hurt hidden behind the act. She didn't notice me watching her though, much like how she had no idea how her flirting specifically affected me.

"Mhm," she hummed out. "I think the more interesting question is, what are *you* doing here? Because I know for a fact, you'd rather be watching Cade scrub his dirty boxers than talking to a bunch of girls about what lurks in yours." Her gaze flicked down to my chest as she rested her chin in her hand. "Although, wearing a shirt that emphasizes your broad shoulders and hulking chest isn't going to make the jersey chasers leave you alone, you know?"

I grumbled out an incoherent response because I didn't like the way her compliment affected me.

Madison brought her hand to her ear, smiling. "What's that, Big Man? I can't hear you over all that discontent."

"Scotty made me do it," I said a little more clearly while adjusting my puck cufflinks. They were a present from Scotty during his freshman year, and I always wore them for good luck.

She dragged her eyes to my teammate who was now animatedly talking to some guy about hockey and the Stanley Cup, no doubt. "Ah, now that I can believe. Scotty's the life of any party without even trying." She pointed her finger at my chest. "You, however. Not so much. I thought you voluntarily coming to a dating event seemed like a stretch."

"It's not a dating event."

"Then what do you call this portion of the night?"

She waved her hand at the rest of the room. Everyone else was laughing and having a good time, drinking away as they got to know each other. As much as I wanted to enjoy myself, this wasn't the place for me to do it.

"Suffering."

"Sounds about right for you." She giggled, and I hated the way it made my chest constrict. She was just so damn cute. "Ooh, is Scotty speaking to that girl he's interested in?" Her perfectly manicured nails came together, and she looked over at him with interest. "What's her name again? Laurie? Lana? Luna?"

"Laura," I corrected. "And I doubt she'd come to something like this. From my understanding, she has no interest in athletes, especially ones who play hockey and happen to be named Scotty."

"That's what they all say," she muttered, and when she noticed I'd heard, she squared her shoulders, owning the response. Unfortunately for me, it also emphasized her perfect breasts, which made it harder to concentrate. "Everyone says they hate an athlete until one with smoldering eyes and abs to kill pays them the smallest ounce of attention. Then it's game over. The athlete's already won."

"Is that why you're here?" I raised a brow and clenched my jaw harder than I liked to admit because even though Madison was off-limits, and she had been since I met her, I still hated the idea of her being interested in anyone else but me. "Because you know Cade will kill you if he finds out his baby sister is at a dating event."

It was a twisted kind of torture I put myself through when it came to Madison. She was the girl I'd always want, but I'd never be allowed to have because her brother was my teammate and had been since we met in middle school. I may be taller than Cade, but I'd seen him take on the biggest motherfuckers in high school, and he'd win every single time. So instead of working against him, I found myself working with him and blocking any guy who tried to date her because if I couldn't have her, then no one else could either.

"Remember what happened with Henry?" I said with warning in my voice.

She groaned and covered her face with her hands. Sure, it felt a little shitty to be bringing up something that happened three years ago, but it was the easiest way to get her to drop her sunshiny, flirty act with me.

"Did you have to mention him?"

I smiled because I felt no remorse for bringing up that asshat. The guy cheated on her with *my* girlfriend. He'd technically done me a favor and given me an excuse to break up with Amy, but that wasn't enough to save him from a broken nose, which I inevitably gave him because he deserved it for cheating on Madison.

"I'm just looking out for you. Cade wouldn't want you here." I didn't want her here either. She was too good for any of the dirty athletes at this school—including me.

"Glad to see you're still doing my big brother's bidding," she joked, but it wasn't funny because we both knew it was kind of true. I would do anything for her brother, and that included doing anything for his little sister. "Honestly, Cade needs to get over himself. I'm nineteen now, which means I can do what and, more importantly, *who* I want."

Don't break the glass. Don't break the glass.

My brain was repeating the mantra as I stared at my beer because if I thought too hard about what she was implying with that statement, I'd probably break the table too.

"And yet you're sitting with me. A guy you've known since you were in braces. I've gotta wonder how that's working for you." I played it cool, like I always did when it came to her, while I eagerly awaited the name of the guy she was trying to impress tonight. Once she told me, I'd warn that idiot off on Cade's behalf because I was a good friend like that.

"Well, thanks for the vote of confidence. If you must know, I just met Brandon Gold from the baseball team." She tipped her head to the dudebro in a hat.

With tanned skin and an incredibly white smile, I could see the appeal. I could also see why he'd now made his way to the top of my kill list. I supposed Scotty could live another day. "He was nice," she drawled out and licked the corners of her lips.

I swallowed hard because there were so many things I wanted to say and do but couldn't.

"Careful," I warned, taking a sip of my beer.

That made her cackle. "Relax, Big Man. I'm not here for him. Or you, for that matter."

I sputtered out my drink and could feel the sweat dripping down my…curtains. "Me?"

She rolled her eyes and surveyed the room. "Don't get me started on my favorite book trope."

"I have no idea what you're talking about."

"Brother's best friend," she said dreamily. "After you knocked Henry's lights out, I always thought something might happen between us." I couldn't tell if she was joking or not. "But alas, my dreams were dashed—no pun intended—the day you looked at me like you'd rather kiss Sidney Williams than be in the same room as me."

"Sidney Williams? The girl in my class who picked her nose and ate it?"

"Yeah, her."

My brows furrowed as this girl who I'd never thought about came to mind. "Wait a minute, are you talking about that time we played Spin the Bottle in high school?"

She nodded her head proudly. "I'm surprised it's not a core memory for you like it is for me."

I blew out a breath, not sure how to answer that. "All I remember about that night is that you were sixteen, and when the bottle landed on you, your brother was staring at me like he was ready to tear my limbs off if I so much as thought about touching you."

"Careful, D. You're making it sound like I still might have hope."

I pursed my lips, and I bit my tongue because I couldn't respond to that. Not without lying to her and to myself.

"Anyway," she continued before I had to answer. "I'm here for them." She pointed her pink-tipped finger at the three football players in the corner.

Wearing their Covey Wildcat jerseys, they had hordes of people waiting to speak to them. I rolled my eyes and held back a groan of annoyance because of course she'd want to shoot her shot with the football team. They were considered the crowning glory of Covey U sports. But I couldn't be angry about that fact. I knew this was a football college before I picked it, and honestly, that was part of the appeal. I kind of thought it meant I could play hockey and get out of stupid things like this. Apparently, I was wrong.

"Aiden Matthews, Adam Hartley, and Devin Walker," Madison said with a dreamy wistfulness in her tone.

Okay, now the football team was on my hit list, too, but I'd have to take them out individually since they'd likely win if I tried it any other way.

"I can't decide which one I want to try my luck with first." With her fingers tickling across her chin, she pursed her lips and smiled as she looked at me. "Mhm. As teammates, they'd be used to sharing, right?" I didn't like where she was going with this. "Maybe I could be the cheese in their why choose sandwich."

"Again, I have no idea what you're talking about."

"Well, I certainly wouldn't be the meat. They'd be the ones bringing that."

"You've got no shot with Aiden Matthews," I said sharply and then tried to tone down my annoyance. "The only thing I know about him is that he called dibs on his next-door neighbor the minute she moved in and he likes to remind everyone of that fact on a weekly basis."

That made her smirk fall and blow out a breath that sounded somewhat similar to a deflating balloon. I didn't mean to crush her dreams, but I couldn't deny I was happy about it.

"Okay. Well, that makes it a little easier, then. Devin or Adam? Adam or Devin?" Madison raised her brow. "Devin *and* Adam."

I closed my eyes, breathing in deeply, cursing Scotty under my breath again for being the reason I was suffering through this conversation. "Madison. Can we please talk about something other than your desire to have a threesome with the football team? It's getting tiresome. No one is going to play into your deluded fantasies, especially not a couple of guys that are roommates."

She dropped her shoulders. "All right. I get it. You still think of me as Cade's kid sister, but you don't have to get shitty about it. I'm just trying to do what any girl in my situation would, and even though you may not think it, I've been told by a few guys that I'm cute."

The Draft

She was a hell of a lot more than cute, and I felt a little bad that she'd taken my words to heart. The reality of seeing a girl I thought was perfect have her confidence throttled by a guy like Henry was rough because he was so undeserving of the status she gave him. She apparently dated that dirtbag for at least six months in secret since Henry was on the hockey team and he convinced her that it was best no one knew about it. What an idiot. If I managed to get a girl like her, I'd be shouting it from the rooftops. The only reason the school found out about them was because I'd broken Henry's nose after catching him with my girlfriend.

I still remember that day like it was yesterday. Henry was slumped against a locker, holding his head while the foam roller I hit him with was lying on the ground next to him. It was only after I heard Madison's meek voice say, "Henry," and I saw her trembling chin and wide eyes, that I knew he'd done something to hurt her. It gutted me because she was so innocent, and perfect. It was in that moment that I'd made a vow to myself that no one would hurt her again.

The satisfaction of hearing his nose crack when I punched him was good, but it wasn't enough to make up for her tears. I might have gotten a one-week suspension out of it, but it didn't really matter for me. I just missed the last few classes of my senior year. That was it. The thing that really got me was that I never got to make Henry pay for his mistake on the ice.

Yet. I should say. I'd heard he'd made an impact at one of our main rivals, Southern Collegiate, in his first few weeks there, which meant there was a possibility I'd finally see him on the ice this year.

"You are cute."

Oh, damn. There it was again. Madison's overeager smile. The one that crushed any barrier I tried to put between us.

"You think so?"

"Yes," I croaked out, immediately regretting it. "But that doesn't mean I think it's a good idea for you to speak to those guys."

I was ready to give her a lecture on athletes and their intentions, but I could already see she was rolling her eyes.

Ding! Ding! Ding!

With a bright smile, Madison jumped from the stool and sang, "Welp, I guess you can't stop me now."

"Madison, wait."

Ignoring me, she made her way to the football team, shaking that pert little ass of hers on the way. Fine. If she wanted to play dirty, I was willing to go over there, drag her out of here, and lock her in her dorm if I had to.

I shut my eyes, trying to stop the thoughts running through my head at the mere idea of locking her in my room.

I pushed back my stool, ready to haul her over my shoulder and kill anyone that got in my way, when a short brunette barged in front of me.

"Dash, it's so nice to finally meet you. My name is Sienna Lawrence."

All of my hopes were crushed when she pushed her hand in my direction because I knew immediately who she was. The communications major who was taking her job as a hockey broadcaster a little too seriously for a freshman.

She was glaring at me from over her black-rimmed glasses, pouting her red-lined lips as though I'd ticked her off because I was breathing. With long, dark hair, Sienna was a beautiful girl, but unlike most of the women here, she wasn't looking for a date.

She wanted a story.

And for some reason, she thought that I was the answer to it.

For weeks, she'd been trying to secure a time for an interview, and I'd spent just as long ignoring her, but she wasn't taking the hint.

As I accepted her hand with a shake, she somehow lulled me back to my table and onto my seat.

"You're a hard man to get a hold of," she said with a flirty edge, but I knew she had no interest in me. This was all business. Sienna pulled out her notebook and clicked her pen on before she scribbled my name across the top line of the paper.

"So, Dash. That's an interesting name. I assume it's not short for Daniel, so where did it come from?"

I glanced over to the football table, and Madison had yet to make her way through the throng of jersey chasers waiting for their chance to talk to the football team. Strangely, the minute she took a step toward them, the crowd parted like the Red Sea as though it were her destiny to have an orgy with them.

Un-fucking-likely.

Her perfect ass did another perfect wiggle, and I was ready to lose my mind.

"Daniel?" Sienna's piqued annoyance brought me back to her.

Sighing, I said, "Don't call me Daniel. No one has since I was ten. Dash is my name, and it started as a joke because I'm the slowest guy on the team."

"Interesting." It was so interesting that she didn't bother to write it down. My plan was working.

Grumbling, I made myself comfortable in my seat because I was almost certain that if I left, Sienna would write about what an asshole I was, and I didn't want that kind of attention. So, I was left with only one option. I had to sit with this woman and talk nonsense while I watched Madison try her luck with the football team.

Dammit.

CHAPTER 2
Madison

With my head held high, I strutted over to the football team with the sole intention of getting some form of male attention tonight.

"You are cute."

Dash's words played in my mind like an endless taunt because if I was so damn cute, then why wouldn't he just kiss me? The way his eyes flickered down my chest and his jaw clenched gave me all the signs that he liked me, but he'd never act on it. Well, if he wanted to keep pretending there wasn't this electric energy firing between us, then that was fine. He could do or say whatever the hell he wanted, but that meant I could too, and I was planning on losing something tonight, even if it was just my sanity from talking to him.

As I stood behind a few jersey chasers, I shimmied my dress down and ignored the urge to look over my shoulder at Dash. What would that gain me except a broken heart and a grudge? He was infuriating and acted like I was still that naïve high school sophomore he left behind after beating the shit out of my boyfriend. I was more than that now, he'd made sure of it and seemingly had no idea of the effect he had on me.

The day after he and Cade were drafted to the Atlanta Anglerfish and they accepted a place at Covey U to study while they developed their skills was the day no guy would talk to me again, let alone ask me on a date. It didn't matter how cute I dressed or how much I flirted, I was untouchable. I'd reached a status no girl wanted to reach—OFF-LIMITS. Because it wasn't bad enough that I was Cade Bright's, future NHL star's, little sister. Daniel "Dash" Bridges, the six foot six behemoth and also future hockey star, had inadvertently become my bodyguard, and unbeknownst to him, my secret obsession.

How could he not become everything I ever wanted?

He was beating up guys for me, and apparently that was something I was into. Okay, maybe beating up the guy wasn't technically for me, as his girlfriend was also involved in the cheating scandal, and that was probably the sole reason that Henry got that broken nose, but a girl could dream.

And my head was firmly in the clouds when it came to Dash Bridges.

"Excuse me!" I yelled as the crowd parted, leaving the heartthrob Adam Hartley free and waiting for me. A small thrill ran up my spine when he took me in with wide, surprised eyes. I smirked because if this didn't get Dash's attention, then nothing would.

And I was always trying to get Dash's attention, whether he'd like to admit it or not.

"Adam," I crooned as I took a seat on the barstool opposite. He immediately pushed his body back and let out an uneasy groan. Great start. "It's nice to meet you. I'm Madison." I flashed him a smile and held out my hand, hoping that would make it better. Unfortunately, he just stared at my palm, dumbfounded.

"Oh, I know exactly who you are." He laughed. "You're Cade Bright's sister."

My whole bravado immediately deflated. Cade Bright's sister. That was all I was to everyone here, and it was my own stupid fault. I knew I should have gone to Southern Collegiate. They had beaches and the same good weather as Covey, but all those rumors about the bullying on campus stopped me, so I decided to come here. And it was all because they had one of the best programs in computer science in the country.

"I'm more than just his little sister, you know?" Why was I bothering to defend myself around a guy I wasn't actually interested in? I didn't want to date a football player, but the idea of not being taken seriously the minute I attempted to flirt irked me in indescribable ways because I desperately wanted to be seen as every other girl. Hell, I spent enough time dressing up this evening for everyone in this entire room to think I meant business, but just like the last table, I was getting shot down.

"I'm sure you are." Adam ran a hand through his spiked blond hair and let out a hesitant chuckle. "You know, if you're looking for a good time, you might have more luck with Devin." He pointed his thumb to the burly guy behind him. Brooding and angry, Devin gave off the same vibes as Dash, and I wasn't sure how I felt about it.

Dash and I...well, we were complicated. Falling slightly in love with him after he became my unintentional knight in shining armor wasn't my wisest decision, but I couldn't help it. In that moment, when I heard the crunch of my boyfriend's nose and felt the blood splatter across my white shirt, it seemed like we were meant to be. I'd always play back the same fantasy in my head that we'd somehow end up together after he got over the fact that Cade was my brother. He'd be a professional hockey player for the Atlanta Anglerfish, and I'd be a software engineer for 180Betting. We'd make the perfect team. Unfortunately, he had always held firm that it was a team he didn't want to be on.

But I knew it was a lie.

Because I saw it. The way he looked at me when I realized Henry cheated on me. The way he stopped any guy from asking me out. The way he stared at me when he thought no one knew he was looking. There was something there, and I guessed he felt conflicted since he was practically attached at the hip to my brother.

Even tonight, his fists clenched when I accidentally brushed my hand across my cleavage. The cleavage I purposely pushed up so I would get that desperate, hungry look from him. I wanted to believe he might have some lingering feelings for me, too, but he was too quiet and reserved to just outright admit them to me. The only way I was going to find out was to pull them out of him.

When I glanced back at Dash, my mood soured. I knew I shouldn't have looked. He was talking away to that reporter girl. The one that everyone seemed to have a crush on, but she didn't give anyone the time of day. Except for Dash, apparently. She was animatedly smiling and flicking her hair in all kinds of directions. It was glossy and perfect just like her figure. Screw her. He looked down at his hands and smiled. *Smiled?!* Dash Bridges was smiling over a girl who wasn't me, and I hated it.

"Wow, I've only been sitting for two minutes and you're already pawning me off to other guys. I guess I should have hiked my boobs up a little higher," I deadpanned, drawing my attention back to Adam to try to calm my anger, or maybe take it out on him. I wasn't sure.

Don't get me wrong, Adam was cute and known for respecting women. Not to mention he was one of the best wide receivers in the country but was most certainly not my type. He had that Labrador vibe about him, and as much as I liked a guy to be loyal, I wanted some fire and passion, too.

Adam let out an awkward breath. "I'm sorry. Look, it's not you. You're gorgeous." The tension in my shoulders eased slightly. "It's just, I guess there's someone back home." I sighed, adjusting my bra because the fit was a little off. It was the only strapless one I could find in my closet before coming here, so I had to make do.

"Ain't it always the case?"

I couldn't even be upset about the admission because it was the truth with every guy I tried my advances on after Henry. There was always someone else that they were more interested in because they had fewer complications. They were probably prettier too. I'd come to the conclusion that "there's someone else" was just the nice guy way of telling me they weren't into me, or they were afraid of my brother. I just hoped one day a guy would think about me as that "someone else." Preferably Dash, but at this point, I'd make do with what I could.

"What's her name?"

"Who?"

I flitted my fingers in front of his face. "The girl that's got you goo goo gaga over there? I can tell you're thinking about her."

"No one. Just a friend from high school."

"A friend? From high school?" I leaned back and crossed my arms. "Damn, I'm competing with girls who don't even go here and I can't win." I shook my head, only mildly annoyed about that fact. "When am I going to find a guy who views me as a friend but can't stop thinking about me?" I huffed out a breath, which only made Adam laugh.

"I, uh, think you might already have that."

I glared at him in confusion. "What are you talking about?"

Adam glanced over my shoulder before bringing his attention back to me. "How well do you know Dash Bridges?"

Well, that piqued my interest. The hairs on the back of my neck rose, and I sat up a little straighter as I leaned in. "Why are you asking?" I whispered more seductively than I intended. I couldn't help it. Dash brought it out of me without trying. With his dark hair and brooding personality, there was so much I wanted to know about him, but he refused to let me in.

"Because he hasn't stopped glaring at me since you sat down, and he's not the kind of guy I want to tick off."

"Really?" I tried to hide my excitement, but I couldn't help myself. The sixteen-year-old who still thought Dash only saw her as the gawky kid with braces was leaping inside my stomach with happiness. Could Dash be jealous?!

Adam smirked. "Oh, is there something going on between you two?"

"I wish. I've had a crush on the guy for as long as I can remember. He, on the other hand"—I pointed my thumb behind me—"has been single since the end of his senior year in high school and hasn't looked at me twice."

Adam smiled and took a sip of his drink. "And you haven't put yourself out there?"

I shook my head with pinched lips. "Nope. What's the point? He's my brother's teammate and clearly doesn't see me as anything other than the girl whose boyfriend he beat up."

Adam's brow crossed. "Wait, he beat up your boyfriend?"

I waved it off, looking to the side. "Yeah, but it was only because *my* boyfriend was making out with *his* girlfriend. Had nothing to do with me, but there was a moment when the blood from my boyfriend's face was dripping off his fist, that I could have sworn he broke his nose just for me."

Adam hummed, taking another moment to look over my shoulder, and then looked back at me with a smile.

"Is he still staring?" I tried to sound cool, but my high-pitched tone was giving me away.

"Yup," Adam popped out. "What's stopping you from telling him?"

I shuffled my shoulders and cracked my neck because this wasn't exactly the conversation I was planning on having tonight. Especially with Adam Hartley of all people, but he seemed genuine enough. Maybe he didn't want to be here as much as Dash. "I'm saving myself from the resounding rejection I will no doubt face. Not only will he be my brother's teammate at the Atlanta Anglerfish, but they're best friends. Always have been. There's no way I can break up that bromance."

"You'll never know if you don't tell him."

"Did you not just hear my list of complications?"

He shrugged. "What relationships aren't complicated? I sure as hell wish I had told the girl I liked in high school just how much she meant to me, but I was too late. Now she's dating some idiot quarterback at Southern Collegiate and doesn't give me a second thought, and here we are."

"Yeah, here we are," I deadpanned. Adam looked over my shoulder and smirked. "What? You can't give me that look and not tell me what's happening."

"Nothing, except Dash is still staring. Well, no. That's putting it politely. He's glaring in a way that doesn't look normal."

"Do you mean that snarly, scowly thing? Where his lip turns up on one side? That's his usual face."

"Nah. It's not that one. It's almost like he's trying to hold back a fart and a burp at the same time."

"Well, that's a new expression. But wait, does that mean he's not looking at Sienna?"

"Is that the girl he's sitting with?" I nodded. "She's talking and making notes, but he doesn't look engaged at all. In fact, he's way more interested in watching me watch him."

Why did that little fact make my heart skip a beat?

Adam looked between me and Dash and then sat up. He gave me a gawky smile, and to anyone that couldn't hear our conversation, it looked like we were having a serious heart-to-heart. Maybe we were.

"Wanna try something out?"

Adam's eyebrows wiggled, and there was a second where I thought maybe, just maybe, he was asking if I wanted to try something out…sexually, because at this point, hell yes. I'd be up for anything. It had been so long since I'd kissed a guy because much like high school, no one at Covey U wanted to take a chance with me. Hell, after the Henry debacle, it felt like someone had put a giant red cross on my forehead, and I was the only one who couldn't see it. Although, if I thought about it, someone did do that—Dash. Which would explain why it didn't matter how flirty I got with guys, no one wanted to come near me. So if Adam wanted to take a chance and try something for fun, why not?

"What were you thinking?" I asked, leaning in a little closer and trying to subtly pout my cherry-glossed lips, hoping it made them look enticing.

"Do you trust me?"

"I've only just met you."

"Yeah, but don't worry, I'm a good guy."

"Said all the bad boys in the world."

He rolled his eyes. "I just want to try something out. These events bore the crap out of me, but Dash is making it mildly entertaining." Adam leaned back and tapped his friend on the shoulder. "Hey, D."

"What?" Devin grumbled back. Surprisingly, the voice sounded familiar. Angry and gruff, he really did remind me of Dash. The only thing that was different was Devin's Southern accent.

"You busy?"

The girl sitting opposite Devin was less than interested. She was staring at her phone, completely ignoring him. I could only assume it was because Devin had already told her she didn't have a chance. Poor girl. Like I said, he seemed broody and angry with the world. Just my type. I just wished my brother's grumpy best friend didn't make everyone else look like mere mortals.

"Nope. Gina's just waiting for Aiden to be free." He dipped his head over in the direction of the dark-haired guy with the piercing blue eyes. I'd heard a lot about Aiden Matthews since I joined Covey U this year, and let's just say, if rumors were true, it wasn't just his eyes that were piercing.

Much like the other guys on the football team, he lacked focus on the girl in front of him, and when I followed his gaze, it was because he was looking at…Scotty's table?

Scotty was grinning at a brunette, and there was a blonde sitting close by, scowling, but that was about it. There was nothing nefarious going on, so why was he so interested in them?

Devin's chair screeched across the floor as he pushed it back and dragged it to our table.

"Oh, is this allowed?" I looked to see if someone was about to yell at us for sitting too close together, but no one was watching.

"I don't think anyone cares," Adam replied, and he poked Devin with his elbow. "Hey, D. What would be your thoughts on if a teammate tried to date your sister?"

Devin's chin dipped. That grumpy look on his face turned to a dark, brooding anger. Okay, I couldn't deny it, it was sexy. "Are you trying to tell me you want to hit on Chloe? Because—"

Adam raised his hands and let out a long, hesitant breath. "No. No. Nothing like that." He then pointed at me. "We're just talking about Madison here."

Devin turned and looked at me for the first time, and I wanted to say he perked up a little, but that wasn't hard considering the baseline was so low. "Oh, yeah?"

"Madison *Bright*." Adam emphasized my last name, and I rolled my eyes.

"Oh. I'm assuming there's some relation to Cade Bright, then?"

"Yup, I'm his sister."

He raised his hands and backed away from the table, so they were resting on his seat. "Then I wouldn't mess with you."

"Why not?"

"Because I've heard things about your brother."

"What kind of things?"

"Well, first, I heard he cage fights."

"False."

"Then how'd he get that scar on the top of his eyebrow?"

"Me. When I was twelve, he pissed me off, so I threw a puck in his face."

"What about the scars on his knuckles?"

"Also me. I accidentally ran over his fingers with my dirt bike when he was fourteen."

"Well, damn. Now I won't go near you for the sole reason that *you* might kill me."

"Don't worry, D. She has no interest in us. She wants Dash Bridges." Adam couldn't be any less subtle if he tried.

I immediately looked down at the table and covered my face in embarrassment. "Could you be any more obvious?!"

Devin laughed, throwing his head back. "Oh wow. Now, this just got good. The goalie?"

"Yup," I grumbled out, feeling like maybe it was a mistake to confide in these guys. I didn't know them after all, but there was no one else to talk to, and maybe it was good to get an athlete's perspective. "But he's not interested."

"Oh, he's interested," Adam interrupted. "Don't look now, but he's currently cracking his knuckles so much, I'm surprised his fingers are still connected to his palm."

"Really?" *Tone it down, M.* "Good to know," I said with less enthusiasm as I pushed my ponytail to the side. I could be cool and calm when I wanted to be.

"Wanna see if we can get him to admit his feelings for you?" Adam asked with a grin sprawled across his face.

"And how do you propose we do that?"

Adam and Devin looked at each other and smiled. "Easy. Like this."

Without another word, Devin slid his chair closer to mine and draped his arm around the back of it. In this position, I could smell his woody cologne. Spicy with a hint of pine, it made me wonder how delicious Dash might smell if I were ever able to get this close to him.

The music cut out in the switch of songs just as Devin dropped to whisper something in my ear. "I think it worked." That was all he said before the loud, booming grumble of my goalie took over.

"That's it," I heard Dash say, but I couldn't see what was going on since

I was facing the wrong direction. Adam's grin dropped.

"What's happening?" I asked, and before he could respond, I had my answer.

Adam held his hand out and stood. "Hey, Dash. Long time, no see. What's up?" Dash took his hand and they bro-hugged for all of two seconds because it was obvious Dash wasn't interested in pleasantries with Adam. His eyes were firmly narrowed in on me.

Dark, beady, and threatening, he was looking at me like I was a bad, bad girl and he wanted to teach me a lesson or two.

God, why did the idea of that send tingles straight to my core?

Adam gave me a side glance and winked. His way of telling me he was right, I assumed.

"Dash," I said, flitting my hand in his direction, pretending not to care. "Everything okay? Looked like you were having a good time with Sienna."

Devin's hand dropped to my side, and all of Dash's attention focused on that paw of a hand. With a pinched expression, he wouldn't stop looking at the fingers resting on my hip, and after a few seconds, when Devin's hand moved, Dash huffed out an annoyed breath.

"Are you coming over for our fantasy football league on Friday?" Adam asked with an amused smile on his face, pretending to be oblivious to the mounting tension between Dash and me. "Missed you last month."

"I'm busy." It was his only response. Curt, but to the point. A lot like him.

Adam leaned over the table and brushed his hand against mine. A move that did not go unnoticed by Dash. "What about you, Madison? You coming?"

I smiled, ready to answer, but Dash spoke first. "You guys know that Madison is Cade Bright's little sister, right?" He emphasized the "little" a little too much for my liking.

"Yeah, she was just telling us about how she smacked him in the face with a puck when they were kids. Wouldn't want to mess with a girl who's so vicious."

Dash's lips twitched as he tried to stop them from curling in a smile.

"Do you remember that, Big Man?" I asked, watching him do his best to hide any emotion. "You were there too." Turning back to the football players, I pointed my thumb at Dash. "Ever the responsible one, he called the ambulance so Cade could get the stitches he needed. Luckily, I hit him right in the spot that makes the split in his eyebrow look intentional."

"She's a badass, isn't she?" Adam goaded, and before long, Aiden Matthews was at our table.

"Devin, where'd Gina go? I thought you were looking after her for me."

"Gina left when she realized you wouldn't stop drooling over Lyss."

Aiden rolled his eyes and cut his gaze to me as if he were trying to prove a point. A grin split across his face, and all of a sudden, it felt like I was all he could focus on. "Maybe I don't need Gina. Who's this enchantress?"

Sexy and seductive, I could see why the entire student body wanted to try their luck with Aiden. There was something about the way he looked at you that made you feel like he wanted to memorize every single inch of your body using only his tongue.

"That's it," Dash interrupted, pushing Aiden to the side. "Madison needs to go home. It's way past her bedtime."

"Oh, sorry, man." Aiden raised his hands and stood at full height. He was tall, but no one could beat Dash. "Did I just walk in on some kinky role-play or something? Are you trying to be her daddy?" Aiden asked with amusement.

"I wish," I mumbled, but Adam was the only one who heard me, and he nearly spit his drink out.

"Well, if it's past your bedtime, my house is only a five-minute walk away. I've got a California king and a soundproof room." Aiden pushed in front of Dash, completely ignoring him as he gave me a wicked grin.

I had to admit, it felt nice talking to guys who were outright matching my energy instead of cowering away from it. Had I been so fixated on hockey players that I didn't notice I was more of a football girl? Was I about to do a Taylor Swift and switch my type to a guy who catches balls for a living? Or maybe he throws them. I didn't know his position.

"I thought you were waiting for Gina?" I retorted, enjoying the sexy smirk Aiden threw my way.

"And I thought Devin had game, but here we are, talking about all the things I could do to keep you warm while his arm is around your shoulder. I'm sorry, Devin has issues when it comes to incredibly hot women. He can't express himself." Aiden winked, and I nearly swooned because the way he was looking at me made me feel like he could see deep into my soul, and I didn't like it.

I took in a sharp breath, staring straight back at Aiden. Was there something happening between us?

No. Aiden was obsessed with some other girl, but being the object of his affections for all of two minutes was fun.

"Aaand...we're done here." Dash pulled my chair out and grabbed my arm, forcing me off the seat. Pinning me to his side, he wrapped his arm around my shoulder. His hard body was pressing against mine as his fingers applied pressure to my arm.

So possessive. So hot. "See you guys around." With that, he moved hastily while I was firmly attached to his side.

"Hey!" I wailed at no one in particular because I really didn't care that Dash was dragging me away. I was happy about it. Where was he going to take me? Home? To my bed? Maybe he'd join me just to tick Aiden off.

I was nearly tripping over my heels because he was pulling me out of the bar so quickly, and the entire room was watching us in shock. For someone who hated making a scene, he was doing a pretty good job at creating one right now.

"Dash." I rushed out because I could barely keep up with his pace. The spikes of my heels were hitting the ground so hard, I was going to have to send him a bill to get them re-heeled.

"Would you mind slowing down a little?" I said in the sweetest voice I could as I huffed out a breath. This was the most exercise I'd done in weeks, and I wasn't prepared to be red-faced and blotchy when I finally got to speak to Dash about my undying love for him. Undying love? Okay, that might have been a little strong, but it was a crush that never seemed to die.

"Nope." Cold and harsh. His tone and words would make it seem like he wasn't interested in me, but his actions were telling me the exact opposite. He dragged me out of a bar because I was harmlessly flirting with a few guys. Talk about overprotective.

"You know, there are people watching."

"Let them. Then they can all tell Cade that I was the one to get you out of this mess."

I forced him to stop, and when he looked down at me annoyed, I said, "Mess? Sorry, talking to a few football players isn't a mess. Some might even describe it as a good time."

"A good time?" he mused in that angry tone he was so good at. "Discussing a threesome with them doesn't sound like a good time."

"To me it does. And besides, it would be a foursome because there were three of them and one of me."

He didn't bother responding, but I knew I was getting to him because his hand gripped my arm just a little tighter.

The bar was starting to take more interest in us, and Dash grumbled. "Fuck it," he said before I had a chance to realize what he was doing.

Bending forward, and without asking, he pulled at my arm until it was past his neck and my side was touching his face. Then, with little effort, he hauled me over his shoulder.

"Dash! What are you doing?" I couldn't hide the thrill in my voice. He was so ticked off that he was picking me up. My hair might have been close to dangling on the floor, but in this position, I got the perfect view of Dash's toned ass. Oh, how I wanted to grab it.

"You're taking too long, and I'm tired of waiting," he said like this was a completely normal thing to do. He was acting deranged, and I was here for it.

"Put me down!" It was a command that I knew he wouldn't follow through on—not that I'd want him to—but I needed it to at least look like I wasn't happy about the predicament I found myself in.

"No."

One of his arms was firmly wrapped around my legs as his hand gripped my thigh so tight, I hoped he'd just raise it the tiniest bit and slip it under my dress. He didn't. That was just a fantasy I'd made up in my head.

Dash pushed the door open with his free hand and just as we slipped out of the bar, I'd managed to push my hair out of my face fast enough to see Adam, Devin and Aiden laughing at me.

Giving them a little wave, I felt the whoosh of the cold air rush up my skirt to the point that goosebumps traveled up my skin. The thrill I got from the sensation was embarrassing, but the way Dash was holding me made me feel like this might be the night to end all the mounting tension between us.

When the door automatically shut, Dash put me down and pushed me against the brick wall. Without warning, he placed his hands on either side of my head, encasing me in.

Breathing heavily, he stared me down. Our lips were inches apart, and in any other circumstance, I would assume that he was going to try to kiss me, but this was Dash we were talking about. There was a better chance of leprechauns popping out of my ass than him admitting he saw me as anything other than Cade's little sister.

"You're infuriating, you know that?" Dash dropped his head and laughed humorlessly. He was pissed, and now he was refusing to look at me.

So I made him because tonight was probably the only night I'd ever get the chance to shoot my shot. At the end of this year, I had no doubts that Cade and Dash would be leaving Covey early to join their team in Atlanta. This was potentially the only time I'd ever be alone with him again, and I wanted to make it count.

Resting my finger under Dash's chin, I gave his day-old stubble a little scratch before pushing it up. Big, brown eyes bore into mine. There was something there hiding under that expression, and I needed to find out what it was. Smiling at him, I said, "So you dragged me out of there. We're alone. What are you going to do now, Big Man?"

He visibly swallowed when I licked my bottom lip, tasting my cherry red lip gloss. How could I ever forget that Cherry Garcia was his favorite ice cream flavor?

Kiss me. Please, just kiss me.

I was repeating the same mantra in my head, hoping that would manifest it into existence, or that he could read my mind and oblige. Either option would do.

Dash's lip curled, and he let out the smallest of groans. He was holding something back, but if I asked him what, he'd say it was constipation. I knew better. It wasn't bowel issues. I could feel the vibrating energy between us whenever we were alone.

And right now, no one was watching.

The tension was palpable as his breath fanned across my collarbone. I was hot for him; he was hot for me. Why couldn't we just admit it?

"What do you want me to do?" he asked, and I could think of so many things, but the main one being throwing me back over his shoulder, spanking my ass, and taking me to his dorm to show me the type of treatment bad girls get. But again, that was all fantasy, not reality. When I didn't answer instantly, he said, "I'm taking you home."

His hand dragged down my arm. I wanted to grab it and waffle my fingers with his, but I didn't. I just let him wrap his hand around my bicep as he contemplated his next move.

Taking a deep breath, I was so ready for something to happen, but all my hopes were dashed when he dropped his hand.

"Come on." He tipped his chin and started to walk away.

Nothing?

That was it.

Absolutely nothing.

Dash wasn't even going to rise to any of my teasing?

I stood there speechless, watching his ass waddle in a pair of black jeans. Damn, I'd never seen him wear pants that tight, and although it was sexy, it did kind of remind me of when he had to walk around wearing his goalie padding off the ice.

"What are you waiting for?" he grumbled, looking at me over his shoulder angrily. He narrowed his eyes and said something inaudible, but I knew it was probably some gripe about me being annoying, so I didn't bother asking him to clarify.

That was Dash, though. If he didn't care, he wouldn't be grumbling.

He was feeling the chemistry between us. I just knew it.

"Dash?" My voice was shaky now because as he took several steps toward me, I knew I was about to do something that I'd only dreamed of. My knees were knocking, my hands were jittery. Did I have the guts to do it?

"What?" he griped back and got annoyed when I didn't answer. He shook his head and raised his hand to his hair but grumbled before flicking it out of his face. "Wait until Cade hears about this."

I rolled my eyes and groaned.

"Madison." Dash bent down so he could see my face clearly. Nose to nose, his eyes searched mine. "What's wrong?" My lips trembled with the things I refused to say, knowing the damage they'd do if I did. "Use your words."

"Words never work."

I swallowed down my nerves as he watched me with interest.

Now or never.

You snooze, you lose.

Make or break.

Strike while the iron's hot.

All these stupid phrases danced through my mind, catapulting me into a decision that would potentially change everything.

Then, I did it.

I stood on my tiptoes, wrapped my arms around Dash's neck, and gave him a moment to let that sink in. His back stiffened, but he didn't push me away, which I thought was a good sign. Being in his arms relaxed me enough to realize that what I was doing was the right thing.

"Madison?"

Urgency laced his eyes, but the only thing I could feel in my chest was a yearning need to get closer to him. Before he could stop me, I did the one thing I'd been thinking about ever since the day I saw Dash beat up Henry.

I kissed my brother's best friend.

Chapter 3
Dash

What the hell is happening?

Madison's lips were sliding across mine. Her hands were clawing at my shirt, and she was kissing me…like she wanted me.

And yet, I didn't want it to end.

Because she felt good.

So. Damn. Good.

Madison's fingers threaded through my hair, and she pulled at the strands with so much force that I almost forgot my name. Her other hand wrapped around my neck as she stood on her tiptoes, desperately trying to keep our connection. Her tongue swiped across my lips before she dipped it into my mouth.

She wanted me, and I was doing nothing to stop it.

I was also doing nothing to encourage it, either. My hands were at my side, too stunned to move, and my lips hadn't quite fathomed that the perfect, pillowy lips kissing them were attached to my best friend's little sister. And her lips...shit. Her lips were already the end of me. *She* was the end of me. Soft, pliable, and plump, they were better than I'd ever imagined. And I'd imagined her lips in many different places over the years. All of which were more inappropriate than the last.

Hungry and lustful, Madison let out a small whimper before her hands disconnected from me and landed on my chest. Then she pushed with enough force to stun a linebacker, making me almost lose my balance.

Her red lip gloss was smudged across her face. Her hair was a mess, but she looked phenomenal, nonetheless. Staring at me, she took a deep breath, making her chest poke out. It took everything in me not to look down at her perfect breasts. The only thing that helped was that I'd already memorized how amazing her rack looked earlier in the night.

Thwack!

A sharp pain radiated down my cheek as my body fell back. My hand immediately went to the side of my face to the stinging pain.

"What the hell was that for, Madison?" When I snapped my gaze to her, she was just standing in front of me with her arms folded and an angry pout across those perfect lips.

"Why didn't you kiss me back?" she yelled. I checked the surroundings, thankful that most people were still inside and weren't witnessing this.

"Why did you kiss me in the first place?" I couldn't help but laugh because this conversation was ridiculous.

"You know why." It sounded more like a threat than anything else.

"No." I chuckled sarcastically. "I really don't."

With her hands covering her face, she threw her head up to the sky and groaned in disappointment. "This is so stupid, Dash."

I was still rubbing my cheek, watching her intently as she dropped her hands and drew her chin down. It was hard to make out her features in the dark, but what was left of her lip gloss was glistening against the streetlight, enticing me to taste her again.

"Tell me, Dash. Why did you just pull me out of there? Didn't like me getting close to the football guys, or was it Brandon Gold that got you hot and bothered?"

With a tense jaw, I unclenched my fists at the mere memory of those guys looking at Madison. She didn't have to dress like a goddess to be one, but today those athletes got her at her best. They wanted her, and all I wanted to do was claim her, even though I knew I couldn't.

"I don't like you getting close to any of them," I gritted out, hating that she managed to get me to admit it out loud. It wasn't my fault. She was poking the bear, and I was answering instinctively.

"I knew it." She had this crazed, smug look on her face, and I was concerned over what she might uncover, so I cut this interaction short.

"Because they're athletes, Madison," I replied sharply. "I know exactly what goes through their minds, and I don't want you anywhere near them."

"Oh, really?! And why do you care so much?" She had a raised brow and a smile on her face, as though she'd just caught me outside with my pants off. Thankfully, she hadn't because otherwise she would have seen the obnoxiously large boner I had due to our impromptu kiss.

"Because Henry was an asshole to you, and I vowed to Cade that I wouldn't let another athlete hurt you like that again."

Thwack.

Another slap, and I grunted in sheer pain. Madison was a small thing, but my goodness, when she slapped, it felt like I was going against Ronda Rousey.

"Why'd you do that?" I groused.

"Because you're an idiot, and I'm tired of trying to pretend that I'm not desperately in love with you."

I hadn't looked up from the floor since her hit, but I felt like her last sentence alone was a punch in the gut. Did she just tell me she was desperately in love with me? Because if she did, we were going to have a serious problem on our hands.

"Is that it?" she chimed out. "You've got nothing to say."

What could I say? Admit that I was in love with her too? Because hell, I loved her from the minute I laid eyes on her in middle school, but even back then I knew that nothing could ever happen between us. The feeling only intensified when I saw her heart breaking over a loser like Henry because she deserved so much better than him.

Madison was looking at me, waiting for me to answer, but I was lost for words. Sure, she loved to flirt, but she'd never taken it this far, and honestly, my brain was still a little fuzzy because I kissed her, so I didn't want to say something I might regret later.

Madison didn't love me. It wasn't possible. That yearning feeling for her was one-sided. She was fucking with me. That was the only explanation for her incoherent ramblings.

Madison laughed bitterly, shaking her head as she looked at me with so much anger, I wished my net was around so I could cower into it. That was my safe space. The only place that I felt truly comfortable because all I had to do when I was in there was focus on the puck. That was it. None of this soft shit where looking at Madison's face made my heart beat in ways that I knew was inappropriate.

"You're a coward, Dash."

She was right. My gaze was still very much focused on the gum on the ground and her gold-pointed shoe right next to it. I knew I was going crazy because it felt like the shoes were looking at me with disappointment. She tipped her toes, and I breathed in, still not ready to talk about it.

Then, before I could look up, she growled in frustration as her feet turned and she walked away. It was only after the clanking of her heels started to fade that I looked up and watched that perfect ass of hers strut into the distance again.

It was getting darker, and in that tight black dress, Madison was getting harder to see. No one was around, but she couldn't run in sneakers, let alone those heels. If someone wanted to attack her, she'd be there for the taking.

Fuck.

I scraped a hand across my face, groaning as I watched her get further away. I couldn't leave her. Cade would kill me. Not to mention, I'd never forgive myself if something happened to her. Not after we kissed. But if she knew I was following her, she'd pester me about my feelings, and I wasn't willing to talk about it. Not until I'd figured out what they were for myself.

So I did what any normal person would do in my situation. I subtly walked behind her with no intention of announcing my presence. With my hands stuffed in my pockets and my head hung low, I silently walked behind her, only looking up occasionally through my…curtains. I was getting my hair cut in the morning.

Madison hadn't noticed me at all, but that could have been because I was using streetlights and bushes to cover myself every time she glanced over her shoulder to check her surroundings. Honestly, her inability to detect the fact that someone was following her frightened me. What if I'd really been a creeper with different intentions? It wasn't like I was a small guy. I was six foot six, which was perfect for guarding the net, but not so good when you were trying to be inconspicuous.

I nearly rushed to help her when she stumbled on her heel, but as she gained her footing, she cursed my name, so I subtly stepped to the side, taking cover in a large bush before she could see me.

Sniffling and grumbling more obscenities, she riffled through her bag and took her phone out. Dipping further into the bush, I ignored the fact that there was a stick poking in my ear and checked my own phone to make sure it was on silent. On the off chance that she was calling me, I didn't want it to give me away.

"Hey, Tiff," she drawled out, wiping her eyes as she did it. I knew exactly who she was talking to, and it only served to rile me up more.

Why couldn't she have waited until she got to her dorm to call her cousin?

"I know it's late. I'm sorry. I didn't wake up Ella, did I? Oh, good. It's just I've had a crappy night, and I need to vent."

My back was nearly breaking in this crouched position, and I tried to subtly stretch but cringed when a stick snapped under my foot.

Dammit.

So much for being inconspicuous. Madison's head whipped in my direction, and I stayed deathly still, hoping she would be too scared to come looking in the bushes and find me.

"Yeah, I'm still here, sorry." She shook her head, turned around, and as she started walking to her dorm, I sighed in relief. "I just thought I heard someone behind me, but it must have been a coyote."

I pushed out a silent snort because she'd have no chance against a coyote, let alone a two-hundred-and-twenty-pound hockey player. Although maybe I'd been underestimating her this whole time since my face was still tingling from those slaps earlier.

"I kissed Dash."

Her voice had all kinds of emotion in it. Hope, excitement, but the main one was sadness, and that didn't make me feel good.

I could have sworn I heard her cousin squeal down the phone, but Madison didn't pull it away, so it was probably just the ringing in my head from the stick piercing my eardrum.

"No. You don't get it. *I* kissed him. He didn't kiss me back." Okay, she was upset. Her sadness was heavy and thick now, and I was almost certain she'd been silently crying as she hobbled across campus. I acted like a dick, and it felt like my stomach was being gutted.

"I know. I know. I should have gotten over him a long time ago, but you don't see the way he looks at me. It's like he wants to eat me, and you know him, he hardly looks at anyone. He even dragged me out of this dating event because he didn't want to see me in there."

She took a long breath, which turned into a snort-slash-sniff at the end. It wasn't the most flattering noise, but Madison could vomit on my shoes, and I'd still marvel at the pretty pattern it made.

"I'm outside. All right, I'll call you later," she huffed before dropping her phone back into her purse and strutting to the dorm. Madison wasn't drunk, but she wasn't steady on her heels either, and I could only assume it was because she was so upset, she couldn't walk straight.

By the time she made it back to her dorm, I sighed in relief. At least she was in there and not fraternizing with the football team. Not that they were bad guys or anything, but they weren't for her. Especially not Aiden.

The only person for Madison Bright was me.

Even if I could never have her.

Checking my phone, I swiped through a bunch of annoyed messages from Scotty for ditching him, which, if I was being honest, I was surprised he'd noticed, and then headed straight to my dorm, which was only a ten-minute walk away.

As I opened the door, I smiled, waved at the girl behind the desk, and headed to the hockey wing.

Unlike the football players, who ended up in the frats and private housing, the hockey team had its own dedicated dorm block. With bathrooms attached to each bedroom, we were the luckiest team on campus because the Hendricks Building was considered the best. Yes, you heard that correctly. The Hendricks Building. The block was purchased and maintained by Scott Hendricks, Scotty's father, when Scotty committed to playing here before joining his father's old team, the Toronto Thrashers. Some would think it was crazy for a father to purchase an entire building for their son, but that was typical of Scott Hendricks. He'd do anything to give Scotty everything he needed to make it as a professional NHL player.

Scotty was lucky. He was rich beyond his wildest desires, better looking than the rest of us, and could play the game like his father. He had everything going for him and more, yet we still had one thing in common: He couldn't get the one girl he wanted, either.

As I trudged up the stairs, I decided to respond to him and let him know I had to bail because I was feeling sick. It wasn't a lie. Seeing Madison with Aiden *had* made me nauseous, and I did need a little alone time to recover from the reality of the situation, which was that I was eventually going to have to watch Madison date someone else and be...happy for her.

I didn't like that idea, but there was no other choice. I couldn't police her life, and she deserved to be happy, even if it wasn't with me. But just like high school, that could wait until I'd left college at the end of the year and officially signed my entry level contract to the Atlanta Anglerfish, so I wasn't here to see it.

"Dash," Cade drawled as I appeared at the top of the steps. He had a hand wrapped around a girl's waist as he tipped his chin and winked. "What are you doing home so early? I thought you were out with Scotty."

"What are you doing here at all? Didn't you tell Scotty you had something to do tonight?"

His eyes gleamed with mischief as he squeezed the hip of the girl he was standing with. "I do. She's right here. Who needs to go to The Draft when you're already guaranteed some puck bunny love?" He nuzzled her neck, and my brows crossed in confusion. Was she okay with being called that? Judging by the soft smile on her face and the way she drew her head back, it seemed so.

I rolled my eyes because Cade was such a pig when it came to women. "Looks like you didn't do too badly, either. Let me guess. Cherry?" He gestured to my face.

"What are you talking about?"

"The flavor of the girl's lip gloss you made out with tonight?"

Fuck.

I clasped my hand over my mouth, and the sticky substance clung to my palm.

Double fuck.

I'd been walking around campus with the evidence of Madison all over my face without realizing it. I licked my lips subconsciously, and surprisingly, I could still taste her, which made that boner that had just calmed down a little more visible. God, that kiss was imprinted in my brain. I'd never forget how good it felt to have her tongue gliding across mine.

"Who was it?" Cade asked, his eyebrows wiggling in amusement.

"Don't remember," I quipped, because any other answer would put me in a direct line for a punch.

"Dash." Cade unwound from the girl so he could push me on the arm. "I had no idea you were such a lothario." He leaned into the girl beside him. "When we were in high school, his girlfriend cheated on him and broke his heart. From then on, he was too shy to speak to anyone else, and the only way he could get over his anxiety was to date on the internet."

"Aww," the girl next to him cooed, and I was about ready to add to the scar Madison put on Cade's eyebrow for the lie, but luckily for him, my phone started buzzing in my jeans pocket. I went to grab it but stopped because I was still standing opposite Cade, and what if it was Madison calling?

"I don't need your pity. I've dated girls. Cade's even met them, he's just too self-absorbed to remember."

"Have I?"

"Yes, I went on dates before you punched a hole in my door." It wasn't a lie. I went on maybe two if you counted that girl I had to work with in one of my classes. However, the timing of Madison arriving on campus and that door punch was convenient because it was such a good excuse for not dating. I hadn't tried very hard the first two years here, but I pretty much stopped looking at any girl once Madison was back in my life.

Cade narrowed his eyes and looked at the girl before turning his attention to me. "Are you sure those girls weren't your cousins? I always thought you looked related."

"No. They definitely weren't." He clearly didn't remember or care, because if he did, he would have questioned why Amy and any other girl I had casually dated had a striking resemblance to his sister.

My phone was still buzzing, and I was itching to see who it was.

"You going to answer that?" Cade raised a brow in challenge. "Whoever it is seems to be desperate to talk to you. Wonder if it's Little Miss Pop My Cherry?"

"I don't know, I can't get the phone out of my pants, Scotty's jeans are too tight."

He scoffed. "So she doesn't have a name?" My hands dropped to my sides.

"I already told you, I don't remember," I responded curtly.

He gave me a lopsided smile. "Don't worry, man. It happens to the best of us. I'm sure she'll come looking for you if she hasn't already found you."

I hoped not, because if Madison did, she'd more than likely find her brother. Shit, I really did need to talk to her about this and how we planned on dealing with it around Cade. Should we tell him? Was one little kiss worth my balls being chopped off? After all, Madison was acting on impulse, and I had no idea how much she'd drunk tonight. She didn't want me. She couldn't. I was the overly grumpy, quiet goalie who kept to myself. Even if she thought she had a crush on me, she'd grow bored in a week because there was no way I could keep a girl like her entertained.

"You know what? I've had a long night. I'm going to bed," I grumbled, walking past Cade and his companion. I jumped when Cade slapped my butt on the way past. Idiot.

"I bet you did, you dirty dog." I could only imagine the pain I'd have felt if he found out it was Madison's lip gloss coating my mouth.

Stupid, stupid mistake.

I trudged into my room, and when the door was shut, I closed my eyes, careful not to growl in annoyance as I thought about Madison because the only thing protecting me from the common room was a giant pizza box taped over the hole in my door, and I had no doubt Cade was eavesdropping.

When my phone buzzed again, after much fidgeting, I was able to pull it out of my pocket, and my chest tightened when I saw who'd messaged me.

Scotty...and Madison.

Scotty: I can't believe you bailed because you're "sick." What ever happened to no man left behind? I'm now stuck talking to some Brooks-obsessed fangirl who is showing me all the compilation videos she made of the guy. As much as I like him, I don't think I'm ever going to recover from seeing his bare chest in a near-professionally edited film montage.

I quickly responded to Scotty, telling him to try pestering Erik because I had some personal stuff to deal with. He may not have liked that answer, but at least he knew I wasn't about to go back there and save him.

Madison: Let's just pretend tonight never happened, m'kay? Thx.

Short and simple, and I wasn't surprised given the content of the conversation I heard her have with Tiff. However, there was just one problem with that request. There was no way I was going to be able to forget her now.

CHAPTER 4
Madison

Big Bro: So, have you transferred out of Covey U or something, because I haven't seen you in weeks. You haven't called. You haven't texted. What's going on, little sis?

I growled, flicking the message off my screen before stuffing my phone in my purse because I didn't want to answer Cade. It had been two weeks since I'd seen him, which was pretty long considering I lived a ten-minute walk away, but there was one very good reason I'd been avoiding him like the plague.

Dash.

I couldn't face what I'd done. Not only had I kissed him and he rejected me, but he didn't bother responding to my text where I asked him to forget about it. I glared down at the floor, not wanting to make eye contact with anyone because I was so embarrassed.

It wasn't like I was expecting a declaration of love or anything, but I had expected a hell of a lot more than nothing. And not to mention the uncomfortable truth that it left me in limbo with Cade.

What had Dash told him? Was Cade being extra concerned about me because he wanted to lure me into a false sense of security, so I'd confide in him? Had Dash described me as a desperate stalker? The thought didn't bear thinking about, but it did mean that I had no idea how to act around my brother. So I did the only thing I could. I avoided him and everyone that knew Cade like the plague, which brought me to the unfortunate realization that I really depended on him because I didn't know anyone else.

Cade helped me settle in by introducing me to all his teammates, and I repaid him by kissing his best friend. That wasn't even what hurt the most to think about because it wasn't just a random teammate like Alex, Erik, or Brooks. It was Dash.

Big, hulking, and a little too broody for his own good, Dash. He'd been loyal to a fault with my brother, and I just went and volunteered him to test those boundaries. It was stupid of me to act on my feelings, and even more stupid to think that Dash might feel something for me too.

Having no one to talk about this mess with on campus meant I was hitting up my cousin, Tiff, constantly, and she didn't have time for my pathetic boy issues. She was dealing with a toddler, for crying out loud. Her only advice to me was to tell Cade and get the whole incident out in the open so we could move on.

Move on? How could I even dream of doing that?

Besides, I was a chicken. Telling Cade anything other than my lunch order always seemed somewhat hard after everything that happened with Henry. He was so angry that I went behind his back and dated his teammate that he hardly spoke to me for a month after. When he finally did, it was to promise I wouldn't go behind his back and date another teammate again. Yet here I was, doing my best to blow that whole promise out of the water.

Come to think of it, I bet the only reason Cade was so nice when I started here was because he'd told his teammates I was off-limits. He probably thought I'd never be interested in another hockey player after everything Henry did. I guess it never crossed his mind that a hockey player defended me too.

Would he hurt Dash if he found out I kissed him? Had I ruined my brother's longest friendship?

Dash and Cade were a package deal. Always had been. You couldn't see one without the other on campus, and I couldn't ignore Cade forever. They chose to go to college together and play on the same team instead of going straight to the NHL. They loved each other like brothers, and here I was putting a wedge right in the middle of that because my love for Dash was far from brotherly.

I pushed the bill of my Carolina Catfish baseball cap down and made sure I could still see the floor as I walked around with my sunglasses on. It was raining and overcast, but I was hoping this disguise would make it harder for anyone to recognize me. The only thing worse than seeing Cade on campus was seeing Dash. I was dreading that conversation even though I knew we needed to have it.

How the hell was I supposed to look him in the eyes again, let alone tell him to forget me kissing him in person? My knees knocked at the mere thought of it, and I wanted to shrivel into my sweatshirt and never come out because I'd never felt smaller in my life. Here I was, remembering how much he tasted like heaven while he viewed me as nothing more than his best friend's little sister.

It wasn't just heartbreaking. It was soul-destroying.

I sounded dramatic, but it was the truth. I'd never had a first kiss like that, and I knew no other experience in the world would match it. Just thinking about it made my toes curl and my fingers dance. I was almost certain my body sprung to life like it had been electrified when I managed to palm a little part of his chest.

Dash felt perfect when his big, bulky body was wrapped around mine, and for the slightest of seconds, I felt whole. Like I could see the future I'd always imagined with him in high school. The one that involved Dash and me running away just to be together.

Not that I could share those plans with anyone. Especially after seeing the shock on Dash's face after I pulled away.

Ugh, this whole thing felt ridiculous.

I wanted to text Cade back, but I didn't know what to say without giving the game away.

"Yeah, I'm still thinking about entering the draft this time instead of waiting until we're seniors next year." My ears prickled when I heard that familiar drawl, and I couldn't help myself, I turned to have a look to see if it was really him.

It sure was. Devin Walker was standing in the middle of the quad. Still broody, but way less mysterious now that I'd spoken to him. Oh, and look at that. I must have done something right in the world, because Adam Hartley was standing right next to him, nodding away like the dutiful best friend he seemed to be. Were they put here just so I could talk to them? Did God know I needed some advice?

"I get it, and I think it makes sense. What's the point in risking a potential injury for free when you could at least be earning something for the pleasure?" Adam replied.

"There's that, and, you know, my sister."

They shared a pointed look and were so engrossed in the conversation that they hadn't noticed me eavesdropping from across the quad, but we were outside. There were a lot of distractions, so I wasn't surprised.

My feet were urging my body to go over to them, but my brain wasn't certain if I should. Sure, we'd talked a few weeks ago, and they helped me rile Dash up, but would they remember me? Would they even *want* to talk to me again?

Just then, another message from Cade came through.

Cade: If I don't see you soon, I might have to send out a search party.

I pursed my lips because a search party would definitely include Dash. No, thank you.

"How do you think Coach will take it?"

Adam and Devin were still oblivious to me, or anyone else in the quad, for that matter, because if they had noticed anyone else's existence, then they wouldn't be talking so loudly.

Screw it.

I was just going to go over there to say hi. It'd be like old friends catching up. If they asked about me, then I might casually mention it, but nothing more.

"Hey guys!" I said brightly as I tipped on my toes and waved like an obsessed fangirl. At this point, I probably was.

"Uh, hey, Madison." Adam was the first one to respond, and his eyes shifted from me to Devin with unease.

I nodded, and some might say I was a little overeager and desperate, but I couldn't help it. I was excited they remembered me. After all that bonding we did at The Draft, you could say these guys felt a little like family. To me, at least.

"You got it." I pointed my finger with a grin and ignored the obvious awkwardness. "How are you guys?"

They hesitated before Adam finally answered. "We're good, but I guess neither one of us thought we'd see you alive again."

I pushed out an obnoxious breath and folded my arms, desperately trying to look nonchalant. "Bit dramatic, don't you think? Why do you say that?"

"Did you forget Dash dragged you out of Covey's Cantina like you were his next hunting victim?" He raised his brows, hiding his grin. "I thought he was going to maul you to death out there."

"Oh, he gave me a mauling, all right," I muttered under my breath. "But not the type I was hoping for."

Adam tilted his head, studying me with intrigue. "Care to elaborate?"

I jumped, surprised that I'd apparently said that out loud. "It was nothing," I quipped. "Just a joke."

"Sure," Devin drawled with his usual Southern cadence. I looked between the two men as they stared at me blankly. I guessed it was because they were waiting for me to explain why I interrupted them.

"So, since we're here and friends now, I was hoping I could ask you guys for some advice about Dash." A knowing look passed between them, and Adam let out a low, uneasy breath.

"I'm, uh, not sure that's the best idea," he replied.

"Why not?"

"Because we don't know Dash, and even though he and Devin are both built like trains, I'd rather not jump in front of one for no apparent reason."

THE DRAFT

I laughed sarcastically. "Dash wouldn't hurt a fly. That's why they made him a goaltender in high school. He got into the least amount of fights. Hell, he's slow as a snail, too. That's why his nickname is Dash. It's ironic."

"Neither of those things would stop him from bashing my head in with a hockey stick over you, though."

"Pu-lease." I waved him off. "All I want to know is what he was thinking after hauling me out of The Draft in front of everyone."

"And why do you think we'd know the answer to that? We barely know him."

"But you're athletes. He's an athlete, too. Aren't you all wired the same?"

"Not exactly. You'd be surprised to learn that we're all different."

"You sure about that? Because, Dev, I can call you Dev, right? You seem to be all up in your feelings the same way Dash is." I looked him up and down. His body was wide like a brick house, but I believed I could break through his hard exterior if I was given enough time. Devin didn't answer me, but he did grumble in annoyance. At least I was getting somewhere.

With flat lips, he stared at me like he hoped the glare alone would make me wither into nothing and die. Okay, so I wasn't going to get an answer out of him. I turned back to Adam, who seemed to be the people-pleaser of the football team and gave him a smile.

"I think your answer lies in the fact that you're Cade's sister," Adam answered, as if that should explain everything.

"I'm more than that, though."

"I'm sure you are. But that's the answer you're looking for. You're his teammate's sister, and you'd have to be stupid to think that your brother would be okay with you dating Dash."

"Why? I don't get it. Dash is Cade's best friend. He's kind and serious and knows where he wants to go in life. Wouldn't he want me to end up with someone like that?"

"Wait. They're best friends, too?" Devin's brows rose, and when I nodded, he whistled. "That's not good."

Adam butted in. "As someone with a sister, I can tell you, as much as I love Devin like a brother, I would want to rip his heart out if he ever attempted to date Molly." Adam rolled his head and looked at Devin, seemingly waiting for confirmation.

"Ditto." A short and sweet response from Devin. Just what I expected from that brooding hunk of man meat.

"Are you telling me he views me like a sister?"

Their non-response was enough. *Sister?* I cringed because the word hit like a heavy stone in my stomach, making me want to vomit. Was that why he recoiled from my touch? Was he imagining Cade when I kissed him?

"What happened after Dash dragged you out of the bar?" Devin asked curiously.

I pursed my lips, wincing at the memory. Did I want to admit it to them? I guessed I had no choice at this point. I was the one who had brought them into this in the first place. Swallowing, I said, "I kissed him."

Devin took in a sharp breath just as Adam let out a surprised, "Oh."

"But he didn't kiss me back." Both guys grimaced, and Adam whistled. "I know it's bad. I didn't want to do it, but I couldn't stop myself." I raised my hands, flailing them around to explain. "His lips were just there, looking all perfect and kissable, and I'd been thinking about kissing him for the longest time. So, I just did it."

"Yup, he's going to get a black eye," Devin said.

"Black eye?" I looked to Adam for confirmation, and he nodded. *That's it?* "Well, that's not so bad."

Black eyes were a normal thing in hockey, and Cade had at least one a week, but as I looked over at the two footballers' perfect faces, I guessed they were more sensitive souls. Probably explained why they had shorter seasons. They couldn't handle the pressure like hockey players.

"So, you think I should talk to Cade? Because technically, I was the one that jumped Dash. I don't want him getting a black eye for my mistake."

"Have you talked to Cade since you kissed his best friend?" Adam asked.

"Nope."

"What about Dash? You talk to him?"

I was squirming in my shoes now, feeling somewhat guilty. "No." Another wince from the two of them, and I threw my arms in the air in aggravation. "What am I supposed to do? Talk to him about the kiss he didn't want? He didn't respond to my text, and he only ever hangs out at the hockey dorm or the rink with my brother. It's not like there are many chances to get him alone."

"I think you're going to have to find a way to speak to him," Adam answered. "You can't leave it to fester like this because otherwise it will grow into a bigger problem. You need to deal with it."

I nodded in agreement. It was the same advice Tiff had given me, and I supposed there was no point avoiding this anymore. I needed to do something.

"And for the love of all things sports-related, talk to him in person. Don't try to sort this out over text. It will only end in disaster."

"Did Dash tell your brother?"

"I have absolutely no idea. He won't talk to me, remember? But Cade is texting me, wondering why I haven't been around, so I'm assuming not."

Adam thought about it for a second. "Yeah, but he could be pretending just to get you to go over there. So, the first thing you need to do is figure that out. Speak to Cade. Feel him out by seeing how angry he is. Granted, he always seems angry, but you catch my drift. If he doesn't know about it, then speak to Dash and come up with a plan on how to address it."

"Good idea. I like it." I raised my hands for high fives, and they both looked at each other uneasily before reluctantly slapping my palms with theirs. "We make a great team."

"If you say so," Devin mumbled under his breath.

CHAPTER 5

Dash

"Here we go again," I sighed as I stared at the cocky player gliding toward me, crisscrossing around the ice while he toyed with the puck. Cade had such precision when he was skating that I had to concentrate on his every move because I didn't know what he was going to do next. That ability was impressive for a defender, but it wasn't the only reason Coach Henson favored playing him in tough games. Cade had a secret talent. He was one of the best long-distance shooters on the team and liked to test it out on me any chance he got, which was fine. I was used to that. Today, however, things felt different.

He'd been testing me more than usual, hitting me harder, throwing endless taunts my way, and using the excuse of making sure I had no weak spots for his newfound vigor. Hit after hit, I was slowly getting pummeled by pucks, and although I was wearing enough padding to stop the blows from bruising, I couldn't help but feel like the hits were personal. Cade wasn't an unassuming, relaxed kind of guy on a good day, and this was supposed to be his warm-up. I knew better.

He knew about the kiss.

How could he not?

Madison practically mauled me in the street after I dragged her out of The Draft. It didn't matter how drunk the surrounding student body was, someone had to have seen it. Besides, if the rumor mill hadn't gotten to him yet, his sister would have. Madison was a blabbermouth, and there was no way she could keep a secret as big as kissing me from her brother. She just wouldn't feel right about it. I was certain this was Cade's way of tormenting me over the whole thing because he had to find out through her instead of me. His teammate. His apparent best friend.

"Let's see if you can get this one, Bridges," Cade mocked from the center line. I kept my eye on the puck even though he was doing everything in his power to make it nearly impossible to.

A puck flew past my right side, hitting the back of the net. I missed it again.

Dammit.

"Come on, Bridges," Cade hollered, elbowing Alex in the stomach as he grinned with pride. I gripped my hockey stick tighter, stopping myself from losing it. "You're going to have to do better than that."

Funny. It felt like he was trying to be supportive by riling me up because I hadn't played my best today, which wasn't due to the lack of commitment. It was because I was too in my head, and I needed to be fluid. Whenever Cade came close, my body stiffened up at the mere thought of telling him that Madison kissed me. Shit. Madison kissed me, and that wasn't the worst part. The worst part was that I liked it, and I wanted to do it over and over again.

How the hell was I supposed to tell Cade that?

Alex whacked a puck in my direction, and I caught it without trying. See. I could do it, I just seemed to have a block when it came to Cade, and that was catching me off guard.

"Bridges," Cade sang, his voice echoing through the rink. Thank fuck he couldn't see my face through the mask, because otherwise, he'd see that I was wincing. I didn't wince. It was pretty much a requirement if you were going to be in the net. Cade dipped his chin and glared at me with mischief. He drew back his stick, and I fully prepared myself for what was coming. A puck in the head.

"Hey, Bright."

I opened my eyes to see that Erik had taken me out of my misery. With his helmet half on, he slowed his sprints to a gentle skate before turning with ease. The guy should have been a figure skater with how effortless he made it look. He smiled and pointed to the crowd. "Your sister is here."

Well, shit.

As if things couldn't get any worse today.

The hairs on the back of my neck rose, and when I'd finally managed to convince myself to look at the other side of the plexiglass, I froze, because, yup, there she was. Wide-eyed and beautiful. Only now I knew that she had feelings for me, and I had no idea what the hell to do about it.

What was she doing here?

It wasn't uncommon for people to come and watch our practices, but Madison hadn't done it in a while. Not since she kissed me, so why was today different? Maybe Cade invited her to come so she could watch him pulverize me to a pulp.

Cade waved at his sister for a couple of seconds, but it wasn't long before he focused his attention back on me. I crouched into position, and glared back at him, but as much as I tried to keep my focus on him, my mind had other ideas.

Was Madison smiling because she could finally see me? Was she snarling at me because I hadn't responded to her text?

I needed to know everything that was going on in her head, so I tried to subtly flick my gaze to her. Even if it was for only a second.

With her hands stuffed in her sweatshirt to keep her warm, she was jumping on the spot, wearing her Carolina Catfish baseball hat so low that I couldn't see her facial expression. I could tell she was looking in Cade's direction, though, acting like nothing happened between us and we were all good.

She hadn't told him if their interaction was anything to go by. But when I really thought about it, why would it be different for them? Cade would never blame his sweet, innocent little sister for trying to seduce me. It would be all my fault because, despite my best efforts, I would have clearly led her on.

Thwack!

"Dammit."

I dropped my stick and threw my hand up to the sharp pain radiating from the side of my head. Pulling my helmet off, I checked to see if Cade's puck had done any damage and then with my other hand; I pulled one glove off with my teeth.

When my hand was free, I flicked back my sweat-soaked hair, annoyed that I still hadn't cut it, and patted my head, making sure I wasn't bleeding. It was unlikely, but I needed a minute before I got back in the net anyway, so I might as well check. My ears were ringing, and I knew I'd have a throbbing headache in the morning, but that pain was only temporary. The need to look at Madison and gauge her reaction seemed to be a permanent fixture, however. Would she be concerned about me? Maybe she'd revel in my pain? Or worse, she might be completely unaffected by my injury, because the only thing worse than hate is indifference.

"I told you to keep your eyes on the puck, Bridges." Cade's tone combined with the hit made it sound like a threat. Eyes on the puck, not his sister. I got it.

"Are you okay?" Brooks asked as he skated over to me. Although he was an excellent skater, he always had this tiny bit of clunkiness about him, which was one of his only faults. I was told the strange skate gait had something to do with how he unintentionally walked on his tiptoes-something he didn't like to talk about.

"Yeah, I'm fine."

Scotty, Alex, and Erik joined, creating a barrier around me and blocking Madison's view. Great. I'd made a scene. Something I'd been doing a lot of recently.

"Not sure why the defense is getting so many shots in today," I griped under my breath, glaring at my best friend as he sprinted toward me.

Cade was by my side in an instant, pulling me into a side hug and squeezed. "This is exactly why." There was a lilt of humor in his voice, and I just couldn't work him the fuck out. "You've got to be ready for the unexpected. Clearly, you weren't, and it's better you found that out against me than some angry guy from an opposing team. They would have knocked you unconscious, and that dream of us signing our contracts with Atlanta together would have flown right out the window." He hit my back so hard, I balked forward. "Luckily, I went easy on you."

"You still hit him in the head, though." Alex pointed at me with his hockey stick.

"Yes, but I aimed for the top side, knowing it would only skim him instead of directly at his face so he could see it coming. That's called being a good friend."

I rolled my eyes, lifting my shoulder enough to shunt him away from me. "Thank you, oh, so powerful Cade," I replied sarcastically. Pushing my hair back, I shoved my helmet and gloves on and then took my position back in the net. While the rest of the team slowly went back to their practice routines, I took a moment to glance over at Madison and was not prepared for what I saw.

Flat-lipped with furrowed brows, Madison was watching me. Thankfully, she couldn't see I was looking at her with my helmet on, but when she bit down on her bottom lip with concern, I noticed her lip gloss shimmer under the rink lights.

Did it taste like Cherry Garcia?

I shifted on my skates, thankful that I looked like a marshmallow in my padding because it made it hard for anyone to see the half-mast erection I got from just thinking about kissing her again.

Focus.

I closed my eyes and forced myself to look back at the ice. I was met with the hard faces of my teammates—a sight that was nowhere near as interesting as Madison's bouncing form. The girl was like a walking distraction, making it hard to concentrate. I couldn't help it. Those big blue eyes, that unmistakable pout. She was by far the most beautiful girl I'd ever seen, and it was getting harder to stop myself from looking.

Beep.

What the?

A puck hit the back of my net, drawing my attention to the hockey player in front.

"You need to concentrate, D," Scotty warned, lining up his next puck, ready to attack me again.

Right. Concentrate.

It wasn't like playing hockey in front of Madison was new to me. She'd watched us for years, so this should be no different. Except now it was because all those other times she'd watched before, I hadn't known what it felt like to kiss her. What it felt like to have her clawing at my shirt because she wanted more from me. What it felt like to have her body leaning into mine.

"Shit," I whispered sharply. "Get it together, Bridges."

Shaking my head, I squatted back into position and focused all my attention on Scotty's puck. Dancing it around with his stick, he was doing his best to distract me, and I was determined to prove I could remain focused.

But then I heard a giggle, and my chest constricted because I knew who it was and I wanted to know what, or more importantly, who she found so funny.

Scotty slapped the puck, aiming between my legs, and I butterflied down to catch it. With my knees on the ice, I heard the beep of the puck hitting the net and cursed under my breath. The sad reality of today was that I'd missed more opportunities than I'd saved, and that wasn't like me at all.

Shaking my head, I punched the top of my net, sending a few curse words to the hockey gods before taking one final glance at Madison.

She was still staring at me. Not her brother doing drills around the ice, but me.

The fuck-up who fucked up.

She was wearing a sweatshirt and jeans, and I knew I was in trouble, because for some asinine reason, I thought she looked even better than at The Draft. Something about her being all cozy and warm under there made me want to slide my hands across her taut stomach so I could feel what was underneath.

I crushed my eyes shut because I wasn't helping myself. Her body. Her smooth skin. Those perfect tits that I'd forced myself to never think about were there in the forefront of my mind and it seemed like every time I looked at her, it was all I could imagine.

When I opened my eyes, Madison was licking her lips and a rush of cherry filled my mouth. Instinctively, I swiped my tongue across my own lips, almost certain I could still taste her.

Sweet cherry perfection. I wondered if that was how she tasted everywhere.

Argh, I needed to stop. This was Cade's sister I was thinking about. Cade's *baby* sister.

But man, had she grown up in all the right places.

Another puck flew past. This time it was at my side, and I hadn't even attempted to save it. I'd accepted the fact that I'd pretty much failed in practice today, so what was another puck?

When Coach's whistle blew, I looked at the door, and he was pointing at me. Tipping his chin in my direction, he said, "Bridges, you're off."

Even with his disappointed face, I was relieved, happy that he'd finally seen enough sense to take me out of practice. I wasn't myself today, and I needed to get out. Off the ice and away from Madison.

"Gunman, you're up." Coach gestured to our second-string goalie, and as I pushed through the gate, I knocked his shoulder, tipping my head in acknowledgment as I made my way to the locker room.

Was Madison still looking at me?

I cut a quick glance behind me, only to see Madison talking with Alex and Scotty. What was that feeling burning inside me? Why did all those thoughts from the other night come rushing back? Why did I want to murder every single man for even smiling at her?

Did I have a crush on Madison? I knew I liked her and thought she was hot, but the way I was starting to think felt like somewhere down the line, it had turned into an obsession.

Shit. We really did need to talk before I took this too far. I couldn't stop thinking about her and we needed to figure out what was going on between us before her brother found out. Not that anything could happen no matter how much I wanted her. That was a line I'd drawn in the sand way back in high school when Cade first told me how betrayed he felt after Henry. I wasn't willing to go back on that now just because her presence was driving me insane.

As I stepped onto the rubber floor, I put my skate guards on and made my way to the locker room. Out of Madison's sight and away from my teammates, surely it would be easier to figure out what to do about our situation with no one throwing pucks in my face.

"Hey," Scotty said as he opened the locker next to me and hung his skates up.

I cursed under my breath because I didn't realize practice had already finished. All that time to think, and it had done absolutely nothing to clear up my Madison dilemma. In fact, I'd made it worse because the more I thought about it, the more I realized I was screwed no matter what I did. If I agreed with Madison that I'd forget about the kiss, then I'd only be hurting myself, because I couldn't forget it. Thus, I'd then be sentencing myself to continual torture for the rest of the year, watching as she flirted with every guy on campus. However, if I told Cade I had feelings for his little sister, I probably wouldn't live to kiss Madison again. See. No upside.

Stuffing my padding into my bag, I cursed under my breath and let everyone think it was because I was angry about my performance today. It was partly right. That had annoyed me, but the bigger annoyance was that I'd let a girl screw with my game, something that had never happened before. Frankly, I'd never cared enough about one to let it break my concentration, but Madison was different. I'd always known that, and the fact that she was my best friend's little sister had made it easy to push her to the back of my mind. Now that she'd voluntarily broken through that barrier, opening the floodgates right along with it, she was all I could think about.

"So, uh, there's something I've been meaning to ask you," Scotty said with his head hung low inside his locker. He looked shady as fuck, so I figured he wanted to talk to me about something important and he didn't want anyone else to hear it. It was probably related to Laura.

Standing, I turned so my back was to the rest of the team. "What's up?" I asked, with my head dipped into my locker as I unwrapped the bandages on my hand, pretending that was all I was focusing on. If he wanted this to be discreet, I could be discreet.

Scotty glanced over his shoulder to look at the other players. When he confirmed it was just the two of us within earshot, he asked, "What's going on with you and Madison?"

I stopped unwrapping my bandage, surprised that he'd outright asked me that here.

"There's nothing going on," I gritted out, throwing the used tape into my locker in annoyance.

Scotty blew out his breath and leaned his head against his locker door. "Didn't look like nothing to me when you skipped out on your speed date so you could throw her over your shoulder and take her home."

"It wasn't a speed date. I was talking to Sienna, who was just looking for a story on the hockey guys. Madison had no right being there, and I was doing Cade a favor by keeping her away from those football horndogs." Even I didn't believe my excuse. *She had no right being there?* Pfft. That was a lie, but one I'd keep pandering to if it meant she'd be far away from the football team and Aiden Matthews.

"You know those guys live next to Laura, right? As far as football players go, they're pretty decent. I doubt they were trying anything with Baby Bright. Besides, I hear they're all interested in other people, anyway."

I gave him a side glance.

"How do you know all this?"

"Heard them talking about it once when I was at Laura's house."

That made me pause for thought, and I whipped my head in his direction, studying his face. Nope, his nose wasn't twitching, which was a usual sign of him lying. His lips were flat, and he was completely serious, which made no sense.

"Scotty, when have you ever willingly been invited to Laura's house? I thought she hated you."

His jaw tensed, and he stood up a little straighter because I'd caught him outright.

"She doesn't hate me, and I haven't exactly been to her house. I was just in that neck of the woods because I went to one of those football parties Aiden throws. Happened to walk past her as I was leaving."

I narrowed my eyes, scrutinizing him with a side glare, but as per usual, he held still, never once faltering from what was clearly a lie. I needed to take notes because, apparently, he was much better at keeping secrets than I thought.

"Anyway, we aren't talking about my terrible luck with Laura right now. We're talking about what the hell is going on with you and Baby Bright."

"And much like you avoiding the last question, I refuse to answer this one because there's nothing going on."

"You sure about that? Because it didn't look like nothing when you lost all focus the minute she stepped into the arena just now."

"Fuck. You noticed?"

"Everyone in practice noticed. We were shooting penalties at you. Why do you think Cade whacked you in the head with the puck? He wanted to get your attention on practice and off his little sister."

"Fuck!" I said loud enough that the rest of the locker room quieted down. So much for being discreet. "Do you really think Cade noticed?" I asked with my head hung low as I cursed under my breath. Scotty nodded, and I desperately wanted to slam my locker shut, but I knew that would cause a scene, and I didn't want to draw any more attention to myself.

"Shit. I bet Madison told him about the other night, too." I mumbled more to myself than anything, but Scotty heard it.

"Oh no, Dash." He dropped his head, pinching the bridge of his nose before he looked at me with disappointment. "Please don't tell me you slept with Baby Bright?" His words were a sharp whisper because the room started to fill with the rest of the team. "Because that's not a secret I want to have to keep."

Scotty's reaction was enough to confirm that my instincts were right. This entire thing was a bad idea.

He was still looking at me, waiting for a response but I immediately clamped my lips shut when I heard Cade's booming voice filling the room. Scotty glared at me with urgency now, so I responded with a clenched jaw and a slow, steady shake of my head. It was the truth. I hadn't slept with Madison. Had I thought about it? Multiple times and in multiple positions, but I liked to keep other people on a need-to-know basis.

"Whatcha' guys talking about?" Cade snuck up on us, planting himself firmly between our shoulders. His eyes gleamed with amusement as he looked between Scotty and me, probably thinking we were talking about

Laura.

"Nothing," we both said too quickly to make it sound convincing.

"Ahh, don't hold out on me." He pointed his finger at me as a smile danced on his lips. "You've got that dazed look on your face that you used to get when you got a new hockey stick. Are you guys talking about the girl Dash hooked up with after The Draft?"

Scotty nearly choked on his own spit. His brows rose as he glared at me in shock and betrayal. "You brought a girl home?" I knew his mind was reeling because I just told him I hadn't slept with Madison, but Cade's response was giving him second thoughts.

"Nah, I was kidding. You know Dash. He's too private to do anything in our dorms. He just walked into the common room with a delirious look in his eyes and cherry red lip gloss all over his face. I'm guessing most of the stuff went down at her place."

"You went to a girl's house?" Scotty replied more high-pitched and animated than necessary. I rolled my eyes, not sure how to answer any of this. "Is that the real reason you ditched me?"

"No."

"Then whose lipstick were you wearing?" Cade asked.

Pressure was building in my chest because I had no idea what to do. Scotty was about ready to blow this secret out of the water, and I wasn't ready to tell Cade the truth. So, I did the only thing I could think of.

"Party at ours!" I yelled, throwing a glance at the rest of the locker room.

Welp, that wasn't entirely thought out. Everyone was looking at me. Mostly in confusion, because I wasn't the type of guy to just suddenly initiate a party, especially since I had a broken door, but if a party was the only way to get me out of admitting anything happened with Madison, then we needed to have one.

Cade laughed. "Guess someone didn't get his fill the other night. Invite your girl over, we want to meet her. Then we can talk strategy with the rest of the team for our next game."

I swallowed, and Scotty shook his head, holding back the smile on his face as Cade strolled to his locker.

"Party at ours? Smooth, D. Real smooth," he said through gritted teeth.

"What else was I supposed to do?"

"Oh, I don't know. Maybe tell him the truth."

"Soon," I quipped.

"It better be."

Scotty slammed his locker shut as he trudged to the showers. Luckily for me, I had almost double the padding to put away, so there was always an excuse for me to lag behind everyone else.

I didn't bother going to the showers because, unlike the other guys, I needed to do a few off-the-ice post-game stretches before I was done for the night. Shoving on a pair of black sweats and a T-shirt, I grabbed my foam roller and headed for the little gym attached to the rink, enjoying the fact that it was only me in there. Living with the guys meant there wasn't a lot of alone time, so I always relished the quiet. This was my time to focus.

Stretching for a goalie was imperative, but some might say I took it a little too far. I needed to, though. If I wanted my body to move like liquid on the ice and block shots, I had to be supple; and after trying everything else, I found Pilates and post-practice stretching were the only ways to accomplish that.

Dropping the foam roller on the mat, I decided to start with my quads and relaxed my thigh against the firm foam, rolling my hips back and forth as I held myself up in a press-up position. With every roll, my mind went deeper into thoughts it shouldn't. The main one being what it would be like to have Madison underneath me instead of this equipment.

Her blonde hair would be splayed out across the mat. Her hips would be rolling in time to mine. Her fingers would be digging into my shoulders, and she'd no doubt be letting out these soft, breathy moans.

And I was hard.

This needed to stop.

For the first time in my life, I quit my foam roller stretching and moved to the mat. I had to get Madison off my mind and focus on something else. But after spending twenty minutes in solitude, attempting to stretch my muscles, and over-analyzing the shit out of my performance today, I finally quit. I knew why I failed so badly. I kissed my best friend's sister, and she was in the crowd watching. It wasn't rocket science. Fixing it, though, felt like a messed-up Rubik's Cube, and I'd never been good at solving those.

By the time I finished, the locker room was empty. Throwing my towel across the bench, I took my time with getting ready. The party had no doubt already started, and although I was technically the host, I was hoping I'd be able to sneak into my room before I had to talk to anyone.

I walked out of the doors of the arena, and just as they shut, I immediately stopped in my tracks. What was she doing here?

Adjusting the bill of her hat, Madison was sitting on the bench outside the rink, looking around like she was waiting for someone. It was getting dark, and the place was too quiet for my liking. The campus was safe, but I didn't like seeing her out here alone, potentially putting herself in danger, so I immediately walked over.

"Madison," I said, and she jumped in surprise before looking up at me with those bright blue eyes of hers. The tiniest of smiles pulled across her lips as her gaze drifted down my body.

Still so hot. Still *not* mine.

"Are you waiting for Cade? Because I think he left already."

She shook her head and pursed her lips. "No. I, uh, came to see you."

I swallowed, committing those words to memory because, as much as I didn't want to admit it, I liked the way it sounded. "Me? Why?"

"You know why, and it has nothing to do with your unhealthy thigh-stretching obsession." Her gaze dropped to the trusty black foam roller tucked under my arm, and the tiniest quirk of a smile grazed her lips.

"What's so funny?"

"Nothing." She shook her head and pushed whatever thoughts she had to the side. "We need to talk."

And those words just killed the mood because they had so many implications, and I didn't want to be part of any one of them. "Are you sure you want to do that?"

She sighed, tucking her hands into her Covey Crushers sweatshirt. "We don't have a choice. You're my brother's teammate and one of his best friends. We need to figure things out."

"Have you talked to Cade?"

She tilted her head, holding back an amused smile. "I think we both know that you wouldn't be walking straight if I had."

Something that felt a lot like relief washed through me, because then I

THE DRAFT

knew his odd behavior today at practice was just him being a dick.

"But that's beside the point." She waved her hand dismissively in my direction. "We're going to be around each other a lot these next few months with your games, so we need to play nice, and the only way we're going to do that is if we come up with a strategy."

Strategy? She kissed the living daylights out of me the other week, and all she wanted to do was talk *strategy*. It was my fault. I was too stunned and stilted to really give her my best stuff, but wow, the feedback was real.

Maybe she didn't like me as much as she said. Maybe that kiss cured her of any feelings.

"MB." Cade's loud, gruff voice made Madison jump, and I took a few steps away to ease any suspicions. "Glad you could finally make it to practice." He rolled a hand over my shoulder, squeezing tightly before making his way to Madison and hauling her into a hug. "Did you enjoy watching me nearly decapitate Dash today?"

"Can't say it was the highlight of my evening, but if it makes you happy, then yes."

He chuckled, and I glared at him because he should have been at the party already. "What are you still doing here?" I certainly wouldn't have taken the risk of talking to Madison right now if I knew he was still lurking around the place.

"I had a call to take, but I guess you were too busy fucking your foam roller to notice." He pointed at my arm. "I see you're still holding Bertha, so I'm guessing it went well," Cade joked.

"Did you name your foam roller?" Madison asked, holding back a laugh. I was glad she was enjoying this, but it annoyed me that she was so cute when she was giggling.

"No, and I don't fuck my foam roller." I pushed him off me and cracked my neck. Usually. Today, however, there was potential because I was thinking about his sister.

Cade raised his brows and looked at Madison. "Whatever you say, but honestly, you need to take a long, hard—no pun intended—look at your life when you've sweet-talked your foam roller more than any girls at college."

"You don't know what you're talking about," I sniped, so badly wanting to throw the fact that I kissed his sister in his face, but I held back because that was like throwing a grenade on our friendship.

"Ah, you're right. I don't." With his arm over Madison's shoulder, Cade leaned toward her and said, "MB, did you know that our friend over here got some a couple of weeks ago?" Madison's eyes grew wide and she blushed.

"He did?" Her voice had gone up a few octaves, but Cade hadn't noticed.

"Yeah. He won't tell me who the girl is, but he came sauntering up the stairs like he was some big man on campus with a delirious smile and lip gloss smeared all over his face."

"Gross." She curled her lip in disgust. Why did she look so freaked out? Did she think he was talking about someone else?

I stayed silent, not bothering to deny it because I wanted a change in subject.

"Are you coming over for the party?" I asked Madison because apparently it was the only way I knew how to distract anyone these days.

"Yeah, MB, are you coming to ours for a little fun? The guys haven't seen you in a while, and we're getting sushi. Your favorite."

For a split second, she glanced over her shoulder and then back to me. "Uh, yeah, sure," she replied hesitantly.

"Perfect." Cade threw an arm over his sister's shoulder, dragging her along to this party. So much for going to my room and thinking about things. "So tell me, MB, what happened in that dating show you've been watching? What's it called again?"

The Baseball Bachelor.

"Sounds riveting," I said from behind them because I needed to keep up the façade that I didn't care, when really, I wanted to know as much about her as possible. Madison glanced at me from over her shoulder with a tentative smile. I gave her my usual look of discontent, so she turned back around. I kept walking behind them, subtly glancing at her ass whenever I got the opportunity. One thing was for certain: I needed to talk to her, and it needed to happen tonight.

When we were close enough to the house, and Cade was listening to Madison explain the storyline behind that asinine TV show, I sent her a quick text.

Dash: Meet me in my room after you've had your sushi. We need to talk.

She jumped when the vibration of the message went off on her phone, and it was only when we were in the elevator and she was far enough away from Cade that she read the message, responding with a thumbs-up emoji.

I had no idea how things were going to go tonight, but I hoped we'd at least be able to clear the air.

When the doors opened to our dorm, the party was already in full swing. Brooks had his usual line of fangirls waiting to get a picture with him, while Scotty was talking to a bunch of hockey fans in the corner. It was like any other night we'd have here, and I felt like enough people had forgotten that I was the one to initiate the party to question me. Maybe I could sneak out of here sooner than I hoped.

A couple of hours and several awkward conversations later, I concluded that it was naïve of me to think that I could get out of here unnoticed. I was the tallest one here for crying out loud. Subtlety wasn't my best quality. However, the party had slowed now, and as I got myself another water from the fridge, I saw the opportunity to get away this time.

Walking past the couch, I took a subtle look at Madison, who was still sitting and talking to her brother. It would probably be a while until she was free, but that was fine. I was willing to wait because we needed to clear the air. Madison wanted me to forget it, and I desperately wanted to as well, but that wasn't going to happen without her telling me that I was a mistake because she was drunk and couldn't think straight. I needed to be a mistake, otherwise I didn't know where this would end.

I sighed in relief when I opened my door. Alone at last.

"Daniel."

My eyes popped open and I nearly lost my shit when I saw what was going on inside my dorm.

"What the hell are you doing in here?"

CHAPTER 6

Madison

"So, are you ever going to tell me what's wrong, MB?" Cade asked with such sincerity that it surprised me. Sitting next to me on the couch in his team's common room, Cade was watching me, waiting for my answer expectantly. This was weird. He'd never attempted a heart-to-heart before, and was that what he was doing right now? Didn't showing up at his practice give him enough reassurance that I was alive?

I shuffled in my seat, trying to ease the tension because I must have been acting shifty. "What are you talking about?" I feigned ignorance, thinking that was the best course of action.

He dipped his chin, glaring at me with narrowed eyes. "Come on, MB. I know you. You're not normally this jittery." He pointed to my leg, and it was then I noticed it was bouncing. I immediately forced it to a halt.

"I'm fine."

"Then why aren't you outrageously flirting with every hockey player here?" His gaze dragged over to Brooks, the very personification of a Disney prince with the personality to match. Brooks was the heartthrob of the team, and when Scotty's hockey dynasty didn't cut it, Brooks's good looks did. He wasn't for me, though. I had only ever been interested in the grumpy, particularly bendy, introverted goalie who liked to keep his net to himself.

"I don't flirt." That was a lie. The entire college knew I flirted, but for Cade to have the audacity to come out and say it was just rude. Cade's lips quirked. "Okay, fine. I flirt, but not outrageously."

"Are you seeing someone?"

I answered his question with an eye roll and took another swig of my beer.

"Something's up, and if I don't know, I can't help you."

"I think your form of helping might be the thing stopping me from telling you," I said pointedly as I tried to subtly look around the room for Dash. He'd been talking to a few people for an hour or so, and I was just waiting for him to go to his room so I could follow behind.

The place was starting to calm down, but for some weird reason, Cade was clinging to me like a bad smell tonight. I guessed it would be understandable if he thought I was upset, but it would be *really* helpful for him to leave for just a few minutes so I could sneak away and talk to Dash.

Cade stood a little straighter and cracked his knuckles. "That sounds like you're confirming something's wrong. Who is it? Which guy do I need to give a nose job to?"

I narrowed my eyes and glared at him. "Why is your immediate response to every problem a punch in the nose?"

He shrugged. "It's the fastest way of letting people know you're upset with their behavior."

I rolled my eyes and shook my head. No wonder I hadn't told him about Dash yet—I liked his nose placement.

"But seriously. If someone has hurt you, I'm more than willing to hurt them back."

"Cade, I'm nineteen. I don't need you fighting my battles for me."

He raised his hands and laughed. "Hey, it's only an offer, and I can't remember ever fighting a battle for you before."

"Henry." That was all I needed to say. One name, and my brother let out an uncertain chuckle as he looked to the side.

"I mean, I did nothing there. That was all Dash's doing."

"You sure about that?"

"I'm not gonna deny that I would have helped if I was present, but Dash had it covered. Where is the big guy, anyway? He'll corroborate my version of events." He looked over his shoulder, but I knew he wouldn't find him because I just saw Dash go into his room. Now all I had to do was sneak in there myself with no one noticing.

"I think I saw him go to bed," I replied, half-heartedly pointing to his door, which had half a pizza box stuck to the middle of it with silver duct tape holding it up.

Cade dragged his gaze to the door, and a smile drew on his lips. "Bet he's in there thinking about Little Miss Pop My Cherry."

There he was, mentioning the girl Dash apparently kissed a few weeks ago, or me. I still hadn't completely figured it out yet. God, Cade would hate himself if he knew he was referring to me as that. "Who?" I once again feigned ignorance because I was getting so good at it.

Cade shook his head. "Doesn't matter, but I have a theory that our goaltender has a girlfriend."

"Oh, really?" My heart beat a little faster, and my self-doubt got the better of me. What if Dash had started dating someone *before* The Draft, and I mauled him at it? What if he was already happily in love with someone else and that was why he hadn't told Cade about the kiss? What if he didn't want it getting out because he was trying to impress someone else?

It was like my little heart had just been trampled on and there was no way I could come back from it. Dash with another girl. The last time I saw it was in high school before I really considered Dash my knight in shining armor. Was the reason I'd never seen it because he was hiding her?

"Yup. He kissed some girl a couple of weeks ago, and he hasn't been acting the same since. You know, he's being shifty. He doesn't want to talk to me or get any advice, which makes me wonder what the hell he's doing on those dates."

The timeline immediately sent red alerts through my brain because that surely had to be me, right? I so badly wanted it to be me, but there was something irking in the back of my mind, stopping me from being so confident in the assumption. My stomach churned, and I felt like I might throw up. I wanted to speak to Dash and get this entire conversation over with, but I needed to get Cade to leave me alone first. So I did the thing that usually worked.

"Dash is being shifty. What about you?" Talk about him. Cade hated telling me anything private because he knew I had a hard time keeping things to myself. He'd clam up any minute now, and I'd be able to sneak into his best friend's room with no one suspecting a thing.

"What about me?" he replied defensively. "I've been acting perfectly normal."

"Exactly. You're anything but normal. You haven't had a girlfriend for a while, which is new for you. What's stopping you?" Granted, I didn't want to know about his sex life, but Cade was the kind of guy who always had his eye on someone, and I hadn't been introduced to anyone since I got here, which now that I thought about it, was almost as odd as me kissing his best friend in a parking lot.

Cade's hard features immediately softened, and that was when I knew I'd made the right move on changing the subject. I loved my brother, but concentration wasn't his best asset, especially if his love life was involved.

"There's a girl, isn't there?"

"I don't know." He looked at me and then waved me off. "There's someone, but she's made it pretty clear that she's not interested, despite smiling every time she sees me at the bar." His lips were tight, and he clenched his teeth in what looked like an attempt to stop showing any emotion. Oh, Cadey, I knew that face. He had a crush but wasn't willing to tell me or anyone else about her because...well, the great Cade Bright didn't do crushes or love interests, or anything romantic for that matter. "However, this isn't something I should be talking to my little sister about."

"But you're perfectly okay to talk about *my* love life?"

"Madison." The fact that he used my full name meant he was serious and wanted to make a point. "I'm not interested in your love life, but you don't make things easy on your big brother." He blew out a breath, and my heart was beating wildly because I could almost feel the tension building between us. Cade knew something, and he was going to confront me about it. Buckle up. "Look, I didn't want to say anything, but I heard something."

I heard something.

Those three words were just that. Words. But they cut through me like a knife because what the fuck had he heard?

"You did?" My voice was squeaky again, and I was looking around the room, taking names, wondering who ratted me and Dash out.

He pushed my shoulder to the side. "I heard a little rumor that you were flirting with some of the guys from the football team."

My eyes bugged out, and I was rendered speechless for the first time in my life. So, he'd heard about my conversations at The Draft, but not the way it ended? With his best friend essentially dragging me out of the place? Weird.

"I flirted with them, yes, but isn't that what you're supposed to do at an event like that?"

"Madison," he drawled out with pointed annoyance as he looked at me in warning.

"Cadence."

He balked. "You know that's not my full name."

"Yeah, but what am I supposed to do when you're about to give me some overbearing lecture about how I should never date again?"

"Good. So we've agreed on your correct course of action," Cade replied with a chuckle.

"I was just talking to them. There's nothing going on."

"Okay, and you're right, it's not for me to decide who or how you date."

"Really? Because that's not what you said in high school. Didn't you put a team-wide ban on me after Henry? Bet you did the same thing here, too."

"Team-wide ban?" He thought about it for a minute then shook his head. "That's not where I was going with this. You didn't let me finish."

"Oh."

"*But* dating an athlete will do absolutely nothing for you. Especially one on the football team, or one of my teammates, for that matter. I know what these guys talk about in the locker room, and none of them would be right for you."

That felt a lot like he was trying to control who I was dating, but when it came to the hockey team, I got it. That was his team, and last time I messed with it, their flow was screwed up for the rest of the season. Really, I should have respected that his teammates were a hard boundary for my brother, but I had a hard time with rules, and Henry was persistent. As for Dash, well, he was just too tempting. Brooding, older, and my brother's best friend. Yeah, he never had a chance when it came to my advances.

Narrowing his eyes, Cade gave me a hooded glare. "I also know for a fact that the football team is even worse when it comes to women. Especially Aiden Matthews. If you go anywhere near him..." He drawled out the warning but didn't finish his sentence.

"I only spoke to Aiden for a few minutes. I barely got to know the guy." I raised my hands in defense, and he looked at me in disbelief. "Trust me, I'm just friends with Adam and Devin."

"You know guys can't just be friends with girls, right?"

"You know that's an outdated thought, right?" I said, sassing him right back. I checked my phone, noting that I hadn't received anything from Dash. He'd been in his room for ten minutes now, and I was still stuck out here talking to my bro, so I needed to do something. "Anyway...I should probably go." And by go, I meant that I needed to pretend I was leaving so I could sneak into Dash's room.

"Let me drive you home. I've got some things to do, anyway. I can drop you off on the way."

Well, that didn't work. "Cade, I'm only a block away. I don't need to be chauffeur driven home. I'll be fine."

He lifted one eyebrow and stared me down.

"No. It's late."

"And I'm on campus. There's security."

"Hard no."

"Would you feel better if I called Todd?" Todd was the nearly seven-foot, gentle giant that acted as a security guard for our dorms when he wasn't in class. He was quiet, and kept himself to himself, and had that kind of looming presence that meant no one would mess with him.

I took my phone out of my sweatshirt pocket, and wrote out a text, showing Cade. "See. I'll be fine. Todd said he'll come and pick me up in a minute." I put my phone back in my pocket, happy that Cade didn't look close enough at the text that he'd realize I was showing him a conversation from a few weeks ago.

"Fine," he sighed out. "At least let me walk you to the door."

"You mean the one that's right there." I pointed to the exit, which was behind their living room, and held back a laugh. "Relax, there's no need to worry about me. I'm fine."

"I'll always worry about you. You're my baby sister."

I stood from my seat, grabbed my bag, scuffed my brother's short, light brown hair, and pursed my lips. "And you're my slightly unhinged big brother that I'll always love."

"Unhinged?"

I shrugged. "You chose hockey over football because you wanted to break Graham Fischel's nose and fight without getting in trouble. The wrestling team wouldn't even have you. That's unhinged if you ask me."

He flashed me a wry smile. "Yeah…all right. Well, message me when you get home, MB."

"Sure thing, C. Night. Night." I saluted Cade as he got up and headed to his dorm room.

"Night."

When I was at the elevator, I pressed the call button and subtly watched Cade open his door. As he took a step into his room, the elevator dinged open, and I pretended to take a step in. When Cade's door was firmly shut, I jumped out of the elevator and snuck behind a column so he couldn't see me. Even when I heard the click of the lock, it took a few minutes for me to gain enough courage to poke my head around the column because I wasn't sure who was still out there. Luckily for me, the coast was clear. Everyone was gone, giving me the perfect opportunity to sneak over to Dash's room.

CHAPTER 7

Madison

I padded across the carpet to the door in the corner, far away from the others. The pizza box was still proudly displayed in the center. Why that hadn't been fixed yet was beyond me. Didn't Scotty's dad pay for this place? Surely a replacement wasn't that expensive.

Staring at the door, my heart was beating wildly because I knew this conversation was do-or-die for Dash and me. I just wished we lived in an alternate universe where Dash wasn't Cade's best friend, and we could be together. Hell, at this point, I'd settle for one night with the guy just to see if it would help get him off my mind.

I raised my fist but hovered it over the door for a few seconds. Where do I even knock with all the cardboard in the way? I chose a spot under the box and bit my bottom lip, trying to suppress a nervous giggle because I'd somehow managed to get to Dash's dorm undetected.

Knock. Knock. Knock.

I rocked on my toes, hoping that would get rid of the anxiety building in my bones. Then I played with my hands, crossing and uncrossing my legs like I needed to pee. I couldn't stand still, knowing that Dash was just on the other side, waiting for me.

I was being ridiculous. For all I knew, he just wanted me over so he could tell me he wasn't interested. It wasn't like I was coming here to get something from him. That would never happen, and the sooner I got on board with that, the easier my life would be.

When he opened the door, I immediately smiled. I couldn't help it. It was a side effect of being around him.

"Dash," I whispered sharply. "Can I come in before anyone sees me?"

He looked surprised, almost like he forgot that we'd agreed to meet. Granted, it was nearing midnight, so maybe he thought I chickened out and wasn't coming.

When I heard footsteps shuffling behind him, I peered over his shoulder and could have sworn my heart broke so loudly that everyone in the dorm heard it shattering on the floor.

Right behind Dash's wide frame was a girl.

Not just any girl.

Sienna.

The same girl he was speaking to at The Draft. She flicked her perfectly curled dark hair out of her leather jacket before adjusting the front, so it sat straight. I hated how beautiful she was because it made me feel so inferior. Of course, he was secretly seeing *her*. I was nothing compared to a confident, sexy, and vivacious girl like Sienna.

I tipped on my toes before saying, "You know what? You look busy. I think I'm going to head out." I used my thumb to point behind my shoulder and offered him a smile. It was forced and awkward, but it was the best I could do under the circumstances.

"Madison. Wait," he said before I could get more than a few steps through the common room, and I immediately stopped at his command. "Can we talk?"

Oh, so now he wanted to talk. When he had the upper hand and a girl in his room. I bit my bottom lip because it suddenly hit me. Dash must have *wanted* me to see them together. He did have a secret girlfriend and he thought this was his way of letting me down gently. Oh, how I yearned for my bedroom where I could cower under my covers and not see anyone for the next three weeks.

"Sienna was just leaving," he said with enough gruffness to sound angry. But then again, maybe it was me he was angry with since I technically ruined his booty call.

Sienna nodded and skipped out, only looking up at me for a split second before shuffling past.

I couldn't help myself; I watched her go the whole way, analyzing her every move, her every breath, just to figure out what she had that I didn't.

Everything.

She was everything.

Tall. Perfect legs, perfect body, great style.

"Madison?" When I finally brought my attention back to Dash, his brows were lowered, and he watched me with intent. "Did you want to come in?"

Ha. What a loaded question. Did I want to come in? Of course. But what for? I had no idea. So, I set myself up for the notion that it would be so I could apologize for kissing him when he clearly had a girlfriend, and then I could somehow get around his crushing rejection.

Dash stepped back, allowing me space to enter his room. The minute I walked beyond the threshold, I was immediately hit by his woody cologne, which wrapped around me the same way I'd wish he would.

His dorm room wasn't huge, but it was bigger than mine, and he was one of the lucky ones who had an adjoining bathroom. So at least he didn't have to share a shower with forty other hockey players. I guessed that was a privilege he earned because he was an upperclassman.

"Take a seat."

I looked around, slightly bemused, because the only two places to sit were either his bed or his desk chair. Did I want to sit on the scene of the crime? Although, the bed was still made and there wasn't a crinkle in sight. I must have interrupted them before they'd had a chance to sleep together.

I pointed at his black bed cover and asked, "Is here okay?"

He nodded.

It felt awkward, but to be honest, that wasn't new. There was always this weird tension brewing between us, which I'd taken to be sexual tension, but now I was much less confident in that assessment. My luck, it was just an unrequited crush that I should have let go of a long time ago.

As I sat on the bed, Dash took a seat in his desk chair a few feet away and placed his hands over his stomach. Watching him twiddle his thumbs, I decided to break the silence. "So, you and Sienna?" I raised my brow because she had suddenly become the most important topic of conversation for me.

Dash rolled his eyes, huffing out a breath as he looked at his door in annoyance. "Sienna's just a reporter after a story, and I'm not willing to help her find one."

"You sure about that? She looked pretty cozy in here, like she'd been here before."

"That's because apparently, she had. She was snooping. Unfortunately for me, the lock on my door is fucked, and somehow, she knew. She's looking for dirt and seems to believe I'm hiding something."

"You are. Me," I said with a grin. It was supposed to be a joke, but the way he looked at me made me realize it wasn't funny. "Although she saw me walk in here. Do you think she'd say anything?"

"Sienna is trying to become a bona fide reporter. She's not going to write about idle gossip. She wants juice. A story that's never been seen before, and she's not getting one from me."

My smile quickly faded, and I nodded. Dash had always been the no-nonsense kind of guy, and I used to tease him about it, but right now, nothing felt particularly funny.

"But Sienna wasn't what you came to talk about, was it?"

"No. You're right." I raised my hands and pressed my lips together because I was the one making a fool of myself here. Sienna and Dash didn't matter. Dash didn't want me. He made that clear, so now I had to say my peace to move on. If that was even possible at this point. "About the other night."

"What about it?" He was looking at me as though he was bored and this conversation meant nothing. I shouldn't be offended, as that was his normal facial expression, but it was making me feel tiny in this context.

"I kissed you."

"And you slapped me. Twice."

"And you don't think that's something we should talk about?"

"Nope," he quipped. "Not really."

I chuckled bitterly. "Are you serious?" When he didn't answer, I knew he was. I played with the ends of my hair, thinking about how to word my next sentence. Finally, I dropped my shoulders and said, "I think I need to apologize. I let my schoolgirl feelings get the better of me. I guess I was just running on adrenaline, and I took some bad advice from those football players. I was wrong, and I'm sorry."

There. Getting it out wasn't so bad. In fact, it felt a little relieving.

"What did they say?" His voice startled me. It was so low he was nearly growling.

"Huh?"

"Do I really have to ask again? What did those football players say to you?"

"Nothing."

"It was clearly something if it gave you the courage to kiss me."

So, this was how it was going to go? I could feel my face flushing with embarrassment because I didn't want to tell him that the football team convinced me that he might actually like me.

"It wasn't them. They didn't say anything. I'd had too much to drink." He was still glaring at me, and I'd lost my nerve. Talking to him wasn't erasing any of my feelings. It was only highlighting them. "You know what? I've had too much to drink right now too."

I stood without thinking, and headed straight for the door, because I would die of embarrassment if Dash told me the football team was wrong about his crush on me. Like literally, I would expire on the floor, right now, and then there would be an awkward conversation with my brother as to why I was sprawled out on the carpet, dead for no apparent reason except embarrassment.

"Madison," I heard him drawl out in annoyance as I skittered past. I couldn't look back. Not after everything.

"I know, I know. I'm just the embarrassing little sister." I tried my best to sound lighthearted, like I was laughing it off, but I was certain Dash knew me better than that. Instead of worrying about it, I focused on the blue lettering of the pizza box taped on the door. I was getting out of here if it was the last thing I did.

"Madison." He spoke again, but I was too off in my own rambles to really take heed of what he was saying.

When I got to the door, I turned around, thinking one final apology might make me feel better. "It's stupid. I should remember that I'm always going to just be the little sister. And that should be fine."

"Madison," he said much louder now, which made me jump, and when I glanced up to look at him, I realized just how close he'd gotten. My knees were knocking against him, and he was staring down at me, all brooding and angry. It was hot and terrifying at the same time. "Will you listen to me?"

"O-Okay."

Dash watched me for the longest time before letting out a long, slow sigh. "Madison," he drawled out my name again, and I wasn't afraid to admit how much I liked it. It was like audio porn.

"Yes, Dash." I swallowed, staring into his deep brown eyes, already feeling like I was drowning in his mere presence.

"I don't know how to say this."

"Then don't say it."

I leaned onto the back of the door, annoyed that I brought all of this on myself. How was I ever going to look at Dash again without thinking about this moment? Without knowing that I embarrassed myself in front of him? He would be in my life forever because he was Cade's best friend, and I would always be the girl who had a little crush on him. Humiliation flared through my body, and I could feel my cheeks heating. This was really it. Dash and I were never meant to be, and this was the end of that dream.

"Don't break my heart. Please." My voice was a soft whimper, and I closed my eyes, bracing for the impact like it was a knife about to stab me.

I felt him shuffling forward, his body brushing against mine, and I could already tell what was about to happen. He was going to try to comfort me. *Comfort me.* Was there anything more mortifying than being consoled by the guy you loved who didn't love you back?

His hand rested on my shoulder, and it was then I realized that I was sobbing silently to myself because this had all become too much.

This couldn't be happening.

I was more embarrassed now than I'd ever been with Henry, and he'd cheated on me in front of the entire school. Now, it was just me and Dash, and yet, it hurt so much more because he meant so much more to me.

Dash's hand stroked my arm, his thumb making small circles by my elbow. There, we had it. The consoling had commenced, and I was almost certain my heart was on the floor decimated by the impact.

"Madison," he said more forcefully this time, and I'd prepared myself for the worst. He was going to tell me that I never had a chance with him, and that he just finished getting his dick sucked by the most beautiful girl in this college, or something like that. I sure was a glutton for punishment, wasn't I? Maybe I should just leave before he could say anything. Wouldn't that be better?

"You know what?" My voice was croaky, and I couldn't bear to look at him. "I think I'm just going to go."

I stepped to the side, but Dash held on to my arm a little tighter. "Madison."

I raised my hand. "Shh. It's okay. I get it."

"No, you clearly don't."

I slunk out of his hold and turned so I could leave. As I opened the door, Dash's hand slapped the wood above me, slamming it shut.

I stared at the cardboard taped to the door, still too afraid to look at him, so I started talking to myself. If I got close enough to the old pizza box, would I be able to smell the cheese from it? How long ago did they have this pizza? Did cardboard that thin hold any kind of soundproofing qualities? My stomach bottomed out, and my eyes grew wide because I suddenly realized that anyone outside could hear us.

"Do you ever listen, Madison?" Anger dripped from his tone, and I couldn't figure out why he wanted to add to my torture. I just wanted to go and cry in a corner, but he wasn't going to let me do that, was he? "Turn around."

The command sent the tiniest of sparks through my spine because even though I knew there was no hope for us, my body couldn't help but respond to his growl. It was just so hot.

I dropped my back onto the wood and stared at Dash's wide chest. He was breathing heavily, and his arm was still on the door, caging me in.

"Look at me, Madison."

"I don't want to." I sniffled, knowing I sounded pathetic, but I couldn't help it. I felt like I was fifteen again with no chest and braces, trying to get the attention of my brother's best friend, knowing deep down that it would never happen.

With his hand still against the wood, he used his other to tip my chin up. When I finally looked at him, a single tear rolled down my cheek, and I bit my lip, hoping the pain would stop the heartache of him crushing my soul when he rejected me.

Dash watched the tear trickle down my face and cupped my cheek, wiping it away with his thumb. He stared at me for what felt like hours, but it was probably only a few seconds. Either way, I was in agony.

"I'm sorry, Dash."

"Do you ever stop talking?"

"Not when—"

Then something wholly unexpected happened.

Dash kissed me.

I repeat, Dash kissed me.

Not like a friendly goodbye peck, either. It was a full-on, angry kiss. Almost like he was letting his frustration out on me. It felt like I'd been struck by lightning because my body had never been so shocked. His arm was looming over me, balancing against the door as his large hand cupped my cheek, holding me in place while his lips crashed against mine.

Obviously, I didn't let this opportunity go to waste. Pushing myself onto my tiptoes, I threaded my hands through his hair and pulled a little. He groaned into our kiss, urging me to open up for him.

I wanted to giggle with excitement, but that was hard to do when Dash's tongue was pushing into my mouth. The tingling feeling it sent to my core made me dizzy, and I felt like I might burst when his tongue flicked against mine. Would it feel like that if he was licking me down there? I was getting ahead of myself, but how could I not? Dash Bridges was kissing me like I was his only oxygen.

I fell back against the door, too weak to hold myself up, and Dash followed suit, relaxing his entire body against mine. The weight of him felt so good. I groaned as my head fell back onto the cardboard, probably making my hair smell like pizza, but I didn't care because not only was Dash Bridges kissing me, but I could feel something very hard and long rubbing against my stomach, and I was more than certain it wasn't his cell phone.

Sprawling his expansive body over mine, the kiss became feral. A hot hunger and an angry heat was coursing through the both of us.

I knew it.

I KNEW IT.

Dash felt the tension between us, too, and he was trying to fight it as much as I was trying to force it out of him.

I didn't know where this was going to end, but as his hand dropped from my cheek to my hip, and he dragged his lips down my neck, I was more than a little excited to find out.

"Dash," I whispered because it was the only thing I could get out.

He brought his mouth back to mine and nipped at my bottom lip before soothing it better with a few soft kisses. He was so assertive. Taking everything he wanted from me, and I was letting him. I'd only ever dreamed about seeing this side of Dash, so I was making a conscious effort to commit the entire thing to memory just in case it never happened again.

"Madison," he growled out, his lips still sealed across mine. My legs were trembling, and when his fingers pressed into my hips, I was almost certain I was going to have an orgasm right then and there.

Biting his bottom lip, I pulled my head back until it knocked against the door and took his lip with me. Then I popped it out with a smile, admiring my handiwork. Plump and red, his lips were addictive, and I wanted to dive right back in.

"Madison," he whispered a little more clearly this time.

"Yes, Dash?" I heaved out because in the heat of the moment I'd almost forgotten to breathe.

His eyes looked at every point of my face, almost as if he was trying to memorize it. "Your brother's going to kill me."

Groaning, I pushed him, but only slightly because I didn't want him going too far. "Don't bring him up now."

I snaked my hands down to his chest and gripped his black T-shirt, drawing him back to me so I could kiss him the way I always wanted to. I wasn't the most experienced when it came to following through with a make-out session, but being here with Dash was giving me a crash course in just how good a man could make you feel if he wanted to; and he was making sure I'd ace this class.

His hands roamed my body, searing me with burning heat at every point they touched. My cheeks were flushed, and I was hornier than I'd ever been, acting on instinct since my brain was so foggy with arousal.

My hips rolled against Dash's thigh, and he knew I needed relief, but he seemed reluctant to put his hands where I needed them most. That didn't stop him from teasing me, though. His fingers gripped my hips, his kisses became savage. It felt like he was releasing ten years of pent-up frustration on me right now.

And I was here for it.

Hard muscles against soft curves never felt so good.

Tipping my head back, I closed my eyes and did everything in my power not to moan, but I couldn't help it. If it wasn't my voice, my body was reacting to him. He was just so good with his hands, which were now cupping my ass as he pushed me up the door, so my center was aligned with his.

Again, I nearly giggled in excitement when he dropped his hips so I could feel the hard bulge in his jeans. It was wild and feral and so not Dash.

"Don't stop," I urged, feeling my climax building just through dry humping alone.

"I'm only just getting started," he said as his lips skated across my collarbone. I pulled at his hair, venting my own frustration that it took all these years for him to touch me like this because, clearly, we both needed it.

His hand stilled at the end of my sweatshirt. His kisses stopped before he brought his mouth to my ear and whispered, "Is this okay?"

"More than."

As his fingers tickled under my sweatshirt, I could hardly breathe, and any chance of gaining my composure was lost when he sealed his mouth against mine. His hand landed on my lace bra, and small sparks of pleasure danced across my body because his cock was rubbing against my jeans, hitting me in just the right spot.

His huge hands explored my chest before he brushed his thumb across my nipple. I wanted to take in a breath, but Dash's tongue pushed into my mouth before I could. As his thumb tweaked my nipple over and over, I thought I was losing my mind because it was the most pleasure I'd ever felt.

I couldn't hold it back anymore. There was too much stimulation, so I tipped my toes, trying to outrun the feeling burning in my core. I was getting so turned on that there was a very huge possibility I could come from this alone. I couldn't do that. Not when girls as hot as Sienna were sniffing around him.

But then he did something so unholy that I had no chance of recovering. He dropped his other hand to my hip, skating it across the apex of my jeans, right over my center. I couldn't feel much except for his warm heat and tickles against the jean stitching, but it was enough.

With every little push, I was screaming for more in my head but trying my best to keep it together, hoping he couldn't see just how close I was to climaxing. He'd barely touched me, yet I felt like I was falling into oblivion.

Maybe I was.

"Dash, that feels so…"

Closer. Closer. Closer.

I winced, ready for the inevitable crash, unsure how we would move forward after this.

BANG! BANG! BANG!

Dash pulled his hand from my center and smothered my mouth, quieting my moans. I opened my eyes in shock because the bang reverberated through my entire body, dowsing the tension like a fire hose.

"What the hell are you guys doing in there?"

I crushed my eyes shut.

No. No. No.

This couldn't be happening.

Cade's voice wasn't even muffled through the cardboard, and it immediately killed the mood. Any high that I was riding was well and truly gone. Dash had stilled a while ago, but his other hand remained on my nipple because he was too afraid to move it. Hell, there was a very real possibility that Cade would hear the ruffling of my bra if we weren't careful.

"It sounds like you're individually plucking each hair out of your ball sack. How many times do I have to tell you? Wax every time, dude. The ladies will thank you."

I cringed because this couldn't be happening. Did my brother really just ruin my first sexual encounter? Of course he did. He was the thorn in my side when it came to Dash. He was always going to be right there. Getting in the way.

Dash didn't respond to Cade. He just stared down at me, his eyes getting wider and breathing heavier by the second. It was as though everything he'd just done had finally hit him. When no one responded, Cade mumbled something before I assumed walking away, leaving Dash and me on the other side of the door, silently staring at each other.

After a good five minutes of what felt like not breathing, Dash finally stepped back, removing his hand and body from me. He was caught up in his own thoughts, and I knew I'd lost him. So close. I was so close to getting what I wanted. My body ached for him, but I couldn't figure out a way to make this work.

"It was only a kiss."

"It wasn't just a kiss, Madison. You know that." That sentiment was supposed to be in my head, but apparently, he heard it.

The way he said my name, all gloomy and angry, made me feel hot all over again, and it was then that I decided that I might need therapy to discuss this obsession. It wasn't normal.

"What was it, then?" Yeah, I put it out there because I didn't want to be caught with the wrong idea again.

"It was everything."

That was it. His short and sweet answer to our kissing dilemma.

"And…" I closed my eyes because I could feel the weight of his crushing blow about to come down. *And it can't happen again.* I was waiting for those words, but he didn't say anything. I opened one eye just to make sure he hadn't left the room, and then the other.

Dash was only a few feet away, but it felt like the Grand Canyon was between us. What could I say? I wanted him, that much was obvious, but he wasn't willing to take the chance to be with me because of my last name, and I couldn't think of any way around it.

"And?" I prompted, pushing Dash out of his own thoughts.

Dash watched the door in case more noise from the party penetrated into the room. It was getting late. It would be quiet soon, but that didn't stop the fact that he'd come to his senses about me. Any sliver of hope that we could be together was blocked by my brother.

He shook his head, taking a step toward me. Placing his hand on my arm, I whimpered because I suspected he was going to take us outside and admit everything to Cade. He was just that kind of guy. Too noble for his own good.

"I can't talk to you in this room when everyone and their mother can hear," he grumbled before guiding me into his bathroom, and once we were both in there, he shut the door.

Okay, the bathroom was nice. Clean for a hockey player, but it wasn't a space for two people to be hanging out in. Especially when you were about to get your heart broken.

Dash's hands skated over my hips, and he lifted me, perching me on the vanity unit before he dropped the lid of the toilet and took a seat.

I wet my lips, looking anywhere in the room except at Dash. I wasn't going to speak first because if he didn't want this, then he was going to have to confirm it himself.

Dash rested his elbows on his knees, bringing his hands together in a clap as he blew out a long breath. "Madison, I like you, but—"

There it was again. The unease in his voice. I may not have had a guy break up with me before, but I'd seen enough TV shows to know when he was letting you down gently.

I didn't want this.

I was almost ninety-nine percent certain Dash didn't want this either.

So why was he doing it?

Cade.

It was ridiculous. He was willing to ignore the chemistry between us for the rest of his life just because he didn't want to upset my brother. The same brother who slept with half of Connecticut when he was in high school. Seriously, there were rumors about him sleeping with our friend's mom, but I digress. I had no business knowing Cade's sex life, just like he had no business knowing mine.

Not that mine existed.

But the point was that I should be allowed to have one that he didn't know about. I should be allowed to sleep with the one guy I've been fantasizing about and not feel guilty over it. Why couldn't I get what I so badly wanted this one time?

What if there was another way?

"One night."

Shit. Shit. Shit.

I winced because the echo from the bathroom confirmed that I said that out loud. It was just an idea that had been flittering through my head since reading it in a novel last week. A little spark of something that when I went to sleep at night and my hand drifted south that I thought about. If Dash and I only had one night, maybe that would solve everything. We'd either get each other out of our systems, realize we aren't compatible, or he'd fall desperately in love with me.

Sure, that last one might seem a little optimistic, but why couldn't it work? One night might be just what I need to dull the desperate ache between my thighs when Dash crossed my mind. The more I thought about it, the more I convinced myself that this was the right thing.

"One night?" Dash repeated, confused.

Well, he hadn't kicked me out at the mere mention of it, so that was a good thing. I could drop it now, and play it off as some random thought, but I didn't want to. I wanted to feel him out and get his opinion on it. I'd managed to get him to kiss me after all. What else could I convince him to do with just a little push? "Give me just one night."

"Of?"

I wet my lips and stiffened my back, in disbelief that I was about to say this but feeling confident that I should. "Us. You and me. Together. For one night."

I knew it sounded crazy, but it really wasn't *that* bad when you thought about it. We both needed this. I needed this, because even if nothing else came from it, at least I tried.

Dash was a quiet guy, but it seemed that I'd stunned him into silence. Stewing in his own broodiness, I watched him lean back and shake his head. "Madison. I can't do that."

I couldn't deny that I was feeling deflated, but it was obvious that was going to be his first reaction. I needed to make the offer more enticing.

"Why not? You just kissed the crap out of me against your door."

"I did, and that was a mistake."

"A mistake you're no doubt going to tell my brother about, right? Well, if you're going to get punished for something, you might as well go all the way with it." My logic was flawed. It was like saying you'd already beaten someone up, why not kill them? But it seemed Dash was contemplating the idea, so he might have been as drunk on arousal as me. He took a sharp breath and slowed the rubbing of his hands.

I was getting so jittery and nervous; I was about to pee my pants because, on top of trying to convince Dash, I was low key trying to convince myself that this was a good idea. He just had a girl in his room for crying out loud, and I was desperately trying to convince him to sleep with me because I couldn't stop thinking about him. Not to mention the tiny fact that I was a virgin.

Was I getting myself in too deep?

Maybe, but it wasn't like Dash was going to be easy to convince, anyway. Besides, I'd already come to terms with the fact that I'd throw out all my logic just for one night with him. Even if it was the biggest mistake of my life and he broke my heart after. I needed to know what it felt like to be with him. I needed Dash to be my first regret if that was what he ended up being.

"No," Dash lamented.

"Yes."

He chuckled humorlessly. "I'm not going to sit in my bathroom and barter over whether or not I'm going to sleep with you, Madison."

"Then what do you call this?"

"Trying to stop your delusional thinking."

"Delusional thinking?" I pouted my bottom lip out, pretending to be stronger in my conviction than I was. This was right. We both needed this. Dash just needed a little push, and I was more than happy to provide one. "Maybe you need to think outside of the net for once."

"What's that supposed to mean?"

"Delusional thinking is at ten years old imagining you can make it to the NHL against so many other people. Delusional thinking is believing that you and your best friend will be able to play for the same team for the rest of your lives. Delusional thinking has gotten you further in life than you think. Do you really call the chemistry between us delusional? Because the way your hand gripped me earlier says otherwise. You feel it. I know you do."

Dash made an incoherent noise. Not unusual for him, but the way his lips were pressed together made me think I might have been winning him over.

"One night, Dash. Get me out of your system. I'll get you out of mine, and we can move on with our lives. No one has to know. Not even Cade. You can go on like normal because all of that tension between us will disappear."

"How much did you drink with Cade before you came in here?"

"Nothing. I'm sober as a nun, and I think it's the best idea I've ever had."

Dash stood. I was losing him, but I was a fighter, and I wasn't going to give up. Not when what I wanted was in reach. He wanted me. I felt it in that kiss.

I just needed this. For my own sanity.

Pushing myself off the vanity, I jumped in front of the bathroom door before he could get to it. Dash nearly stumbled into me when I created a human-sized barrier to this conversation ending. In this position, he was towering over me, watching me in disbelief. I was lost for words. "Dash. Please."

He was silent, but when his hands swept across my shoulders and I felt tingles, there was a tiny bit of hope that he was about to make all my dreams come true.

He bent down, his face coming closer to mine. I was losing my breath and my sanity the longer he made me wait.

"Madison. This isn't happening. You're Cade's sister."

His eyes softened as my chest heaved.

Cade. Cade. Cade.

He was always talking about Cade, but when was he going to shut up and finally talk about me?

I glared at him, trying to silently communicate that, but he didn't get it. I was losing hope, but I just had to try one more time.

"If that's your only excuse for not going through with it, then it's pathetic." He moved back, almost surprised at my outburst. I seemed to be doing that a lot with him recently. Maybe I was just tired of sitting around, waiting for something to happen with him. "That feeling in the pit of your chest whenever you think about me, I have it too."

Dash trained his eyes to the floor, and that was when I knew I was going in the right direction.

"This tension won't end between us unless we get it out of our system."

"So you keep saying."

Dash could easily pick me up and move me out of the way if he wanted to, but he hadn't. He chose to stand, hovering over me, giving me that sexy, snarly scowl and expecting my panties not to get wet over it.

"You're his best friend. His teammate. You're going to be around him forever. Therefore, you're going to be around *me* forever. What's worse? Having to explain why there's all this sexual tension between us, or getting rid of it, so we can be normal with each other?" His jaw was tight, and I felt his fingers flex against my shoulders, almost like he agreed.

"Let me think about it over the next few days."

"No." I was adamant it had to happen tonight, otherwise it wouldn't happen at all. I wasn't stupid. I knew that Dash was acting on instinct and with his dick right now. If his brain got involved and started thinking about the consequences, nothing would happen, and I'd forever wonder what could have been.

"Tonight. Give us one night. Get me out of your system."

His breath was labored now, but I let it sink in because my logic was starting to make sense. So much so that even I believed it was the best course of action. If we got it out of the way, then maybe we could both move on from it. Not that I wanted to move on, but again, if all I was supposed to be was a 'hit and quit' then I'd take it.

Dash's hands were still curled around my arms, and I laughed to myself because here I was again, pinned to a door, waiting for him to make a move. It wasn't going to happen, so I needed to take destiny into my own hands. Cupping his cheeks, I stood on my toes and brushed my nose against his. "You've already kissed me."

Slowly, I swept my nose across his face until I got to his cheek, then I kissed the corner of his lips. His body tensed, but he didn't move me away.

Again, a good sign. Moving to his other side, I kissed the corner of his mouth. Still no movement, but I persevered. "It will be our little secret," I whispered before swiping my tongue across my lips, preparing to kiss Dash one final time.

Only I didn't get a chance.

CHAPTER 8

Madison

Dash growled, pushing me against the bathroom door, kissing me passionately before I could even let out a squeak.

My hands dropped to his wrists as his large palms held me in place, controlling the kiss. He was showing me how he liked it, and I was putty in his hands, going with it. My brain was frying, and I was doing my best not to hyperventilate because it worked. All that talking got me to where I wanted to be.

"One night." His lips were essentially on mine as he spoke, almost like he couldn't bear to be away from me. It was hot. His tongue dipped into my mouth, swallowing any hope of a verbal response.

I drew my head back, whimpering into the kiss as I let him take me wherever he wanted to go. Dash's hands were at my hips as he slipped them under my sweatshirt, before pulling it off. I helped to push it over my head and dropped it to the floor.

Breathing out, I adjusted my wrinkled white T-shirt as I felt his gaze roam my body. Goose bumps flared across my arms because he was silent, and I thought he might be having second thoughts.

"You okay, Big Man?" I asked with a hard swallow.

"One night," he reconfirmed like he was a broken computer. "That's it. Just one night." It sounded more like a threat than anything else.

"Exactly."

"Are you sure you can handle something like that?" There was unease in his voice. The real answer for me was that I wasn't sure. I'd never had sex, so I didn't know how it would affect our relationship, but now that Dash was on offer to be my first, there was no way I would back down.

"I can. Can you?"

He quietly contemplated, and again, I knew Dash. The quieter he was, the more likely he was thinking himself out of doing anything. So I did something that I knew would prove my commitment. I showed him my pinkie finger, and he glared at it with surprise. The significance wasn't lost on either of us. Cade and Dash pinkie promised on everything when they were younger. They did it when they were deciding which high school to go to, which friends to hang out with. They even pinkie promised on going to Covey U together and getting on the same team. How they managed to make that come true was beyond me, but I had some theories it had to do with the power of the promise.

This promise was just as important as the others.

He dropped his hand, sliding it down my arm, and when his pinkie wrapped around mine, I nearly fainted.

Not only was it a behemoth of a pinkie because it was the size of a normal person's index finger, but he'd agreed to sleep with me. It was all there, set in stone. Or flesh if you wanted to be pedantic.

"One night just between you and me," he said lowly, but I could hear the determination in his voice.

"No one has to know."

"No one has to know," he repeated, and as our fingers stayed wrapped around each other, I felt our fate sealing in that one moment.

My body shivered, and I hoped to everything holy that I hadn't just broken out in hives because there was no way I was wasting this one opportunity. Dash Bridges and I were going to fool around, and if that was all I could get, then I'd take it.

"This is going to be one hell of a night," he said, his eyes firmly on my breasts. I poked them out, wanting to feel sexy for the first time in my life, but also not wanting to give away that I was a virgin because I knew Dash. He was the righteous, chivalrous type and would suggest I save it for the guy I loved. He wouldn't want us to go through with it. What he didn't realize was that it was him I wanted.

Stepping back from me, he reached down and pulled open a drawer beside the sink where there were several new toothbrushes and an undeniably large pack of condoms.

Seriously, how many did one guy need?

"Got enough in there?" I blurted before thinking. When he looked at me with furrowed brows, my mind thought it would be good to keep talking. "Because, you know, you have enough condoms and toothbrushes in there to have a new girl over once a night."

He glanced down at the drawer and took the box of condoms out. Sighing, he placed it on the vanity beside us. My gaze had dropped to my hands because I suddenly felt like I was in over my head in this situation. I thought finally getting the guy I always wanted would make me feel less insecure, not more.

Wrapping his hands in mine, he brought them to his chest and waited for me to look at him. It took some time, but when I gained the courage to tip my chin up, Dash was watching me with intent.

"Do you really think that I have girls here all the time?"

"I didn't, but that drawer…"

"Is full because I've never used any of the stuff in there. Erik bought enough condoms for the entire team when we moved in two years ago. I found all that stuff in there before I'd even unpacked on my first day. Come to think of it, they've been sitting there so long, they've probably expired."

He picked up the box, flipped it over, laughed, then showed me. "Someone is looking down on us because they're expiring in a week."

I crinkled my nose, looking at the still-sealed pack, and huffed out a nervous laugh because it made sense. Dash hadn't brought any other girls home since he started college, and he didn't like people on the best of days.

He wasn't like other hockey players. He was quiet and broody. I'd seen the way he reacted to those girls at The Draft. The only one he was interested in was me. He wasn't sleeping with girls every night, and I knew it. My brain just had a momentary freak out similar to when I saw Sienna.

"Why would Erik buy you condoms in bulk?"

"Because he's addicted to Costco. Have you ever been in his room?" I shook my head. "Last Christmas, he brought back two six-foot nutcrackers and planned on displaying them in the common room, but see, Alex hates clowns, and a nutcracker is essentially their creepy Christmas cousin. Alex freaked out so much when he saw them, he slept on Scotty's floor for a week."

"Did Erik return them?"

"Nope. He has to keep them in his room year-round. They sit at the end of his bed like they're guarding the place. I'm surprised any girls walk out in the morning, considering how freaky they are."

I let out a breath, but my face must have looked off because he asked, "Are you sure you're okay with doing this?"

"Yes," I said meekly, feeling foolish for calling him out because someone more experienced wouldn't be accidentally shaming their potential partner.

Dash didn't let me sit on that feeling for long. He tipped my chin up so I could look him in the eye, and watched me expectantly, waiting for a better answer because he knew something was up.

"Look, I know you've had sex. Haven't we all?" Did I sound believable? He didn't balk, so I hoped so. "I'm just not a guy on the hockey team, so my roster might be a little shorter than yours, but that's not a problem, is it? If it's only for one night?"

Dash bent down. "First, I think you're vastly overestimating my numbers. But either way, it doesn't bother me, and I want you to know that I'm not going to push you into anything. You tell me, and we can stop whenever you want."

I almost snorted at his response because, like I would ever ask him to stop.

"Then what are you waiting for? Let's open that box and get started." I rubbed my hands together, doing my best to rid myself of any nervous energy. "How many do you think we can get through tonight? Seven?

Eight?" Again, if this was the only time I could have with Dash, then I was going to make it count.

He chuckled as he opened the box and pulled out one lone condom.

My face fell. One time? Well, that was mildly disappointing.

"Without getting too clinical over this, I'll leave these here so we can come back for more, but let's see how things go the first time before we commit to anything else."

I nodded, swallowing down my nervousness. I didn't need to be anxious because I knew Dash would take care of me even if he didn't know this was my first time.

Putting the condom in his jeans pocket, he leaned down to give me another kiss, and as he pulled away, he smiled, taking my face in thoroughly. "You have no idea how long I've wanted to kiss you like that."

"Probably not as long as I've wanted you to."

His fingers tickled against my jeans, skirting around the back until he was holding my thighs. Then he picked me up, forcing me to wrap my legs around his waist. Kissing my collarbone, he managed to kick open the bathroom door and walk us back into his bedroom.

"Now, Madison, remember. The guys are probably asleep, and this room doesn't have the best soundproof qualities. You're going to have to be quiet."

"Then you're going to have to shut me up."

He paused and looked at me with surprise. I would too, because did I just say that? Well, maybe I was feeling more confident than I thought.

A smirk pulled at one side of his face. "I can think of plenty of ways to do that."

I giggled as he carried me over to his bed, deliriously happy that he accepted my deal. When he dropped me onto his sheets, I fell back, ready for whatever he wanted to do. Oh, all the possibilities were running through my head, and I wasn't sure what I wanted him to start with. Judging by the look in his eyes, he didn't know either.

My feet were teetering at the end of the mattress, and Dash silently dropped to his knees as he got onto the bed, prowling forward until a hand was resting on either side of my head. His deep brown eyes stared into me before he kissed me again. Long and full, as though he was conveying a message with it.

As I ran a hand through Dash's hair, I turned my face to give him better access to my neck. Kissing and nipping his way down to my collarbone, I was already lost in him.

But then he pulled away and looked down at me. "Can I ask you something?"

I nodded.

"Has a guy ever made you come with just his fingers?"

"Umm."

"It's not a hard answer, Madison. Has a guy ever made you so dripping wet from his mere touch that you couldn't stop yourself from clenching around his fingers?"

I gulped because I wasn't expecting Dash to talk like that. The guy who barely liked to talk at all, wanted to whisper dirty things into my ear, and I loved it.

"Madison," he growled. I felt this burst of confidence as I arched my back because I didn't want him to stop touching me. He was treating me like any other girl. Not like I was his best friend's sister. Or that I was a virgin. He was treating me like a regular hookup. Dirty and illicit. Exactly the way I wanted to see Dash. I bit down on my bottom lip, flicking my gaze to his with a challenging glare. "I'm the only one that has ever been able to get me off."

Was that a white lie since no one else had tried?

"Then let's see if I can change that."

With his lips pursed, he let his hands glide under my shirt again. Only this time, they kept pushing the fabric up until I had to raise my arms and shuck it over my head. Dash's hands rubbed against my sides, warming me up, but I didn't need it. The heat from his glare was more than enough to keep me warm.

With just a white cotton lace bra on, I felt a little self-conscious. We were definitely teetering into unchartered territory now.

"You are the most beautiful woman I've ever seen." Dash dropped a kiss to the center of my breasts, and I sucked in a harsh breath. They weren't huge, and I'd always been a little self-conscious of that fact, but when Dash's hand smothered them, I felt like a goddess.

His fingers dragged over the fabric, flipping the cup down to expose my nipples. "And I've been thinking about doing this for the longest time." He licked his lips, his mouth on me before I could think. My back arched and I could hardly breathe because, even though I'd thought about what it might feel like to have Dash do this to me, I'd never imagined it quite like this.

My body was shaking, my hips were bucking of their own accord because Dash was flicking his warm tongue across my nipple like it was my clit. After the intense buildup earlier, there was no way I wasn't going to come from this.

His free hand dropped to my hip as he gently tapered down any movement, which only made the buildup more intense. I was hot, longing to feel him completely against me, but he was hell-bent on lavishing my breasts in attention before anything else could happen.

Leaving a trail of kisses up my body, he kissed me fully when he got to my mouth. "Are you wet for me, Madison?" he asked against my mouth, his body now smothering mine. At some point, my legs had fallen all the way open, making it easy for him to rub his jean-covered crotch against my center.

We might have been fully dressed below, but the friction and his hands were more than enough to get me off if he wanted to.

I gulped. "Yes."

"Will you come if I keep doing this?"

"Y-Yes."

"Good." He kissed me one more time before bringing himself back down to my nipples.

Nipping, licking, biting. Nothing was out of bounds when it came to my chest, and with every kiss and scrape, I was getting closer and closer to the precipice.

Right on the edge, and I'd hardly been touched where I needed it most.

I gripped the back of his arms, digging my nails in to try to ease the pleasure slowly simmering to a boiling point. When his tongue flicked across my nipple in just the right way, there was no stopping my climax now.

"Dash!" I cried out, louder than I'd intended, but I couldn't believe what was happening. My hips were bucking wildly, but he held them down with his thigh, letting me ride my orgasm out against it.

Breathing heavily, it took me a second to regain my composure. Unfortunately, when I did, shame replaced any of my euphoria.

Dash wasn't looking at me, his head was buried between my neck and shoulder, and I was left staring at his ceiling, feeling drained.

My jeans were still on, my panties were wet, and I felt like I needed a long nap to recover from that.

"What's wrong?" he asked as he pushed himself up with his arms. "Did that not feel good?"

"It felt great."

"Then why do you look like you're about to throw up?" he asked and looked genuinely curious for the answer.

"I, uh, just wanted to know what it felt like to have you touch me. You know, without jeans and all that stuff in the way."

"Did you think we were done?" he whispered as he shucked his own shirt off, throwing it across the room. Then he stood from the bed and swiftly removed his jeans. I nearly choked because, wow. I was not prepared to see Dash in just a pair of tight black boxers. Sure, I'd seen him swimming with my brother when we were younger, but in the last two years, he'd bulked up. He was cut to the point that I wanted to count every muscle on his stomach.

My entire body felt like jelly, so when he made his way back to the bed, I let him do his thing and pull my jeans and thong off in one go. I helped him along by shrugging off the straps of my bra and unclasping it. Then, I threw it to the side. What was supposed to happen after that evaded me. I was naked. Did I open my legs wide for him? That seemed a little presumptuous, but did keeping them closed make it seem like I was having second thoughts?

Dash decided for me. His hands skated up my bare legs until he got to my knees, then he pushed them up, so my legs were bent. Kneeling in front of me, he opened them wide enough so that he could fit in between them.

I felt the cold air against my center and closed my eyes because it almost felt like a pelvic exam. Damn, I wished I'd prepared myself. I kept it neat down there, but if I had known Dash would be anywhere near me, then I would have gotten a wax or something.

Dash was silent for far too long, so I opened one eye and saw him just studying my center.

"Fuck," he drew out. "I wanted to take my time, but I think I might come just looking at you."

"Then get inside me."

He chuckled lightly and shook his head. "So eager."

"Can't help it. I've been thinking about this for a long time." Not to mention that I really didn't want him to stop.

"All right." He pushed his thumb under the waistband of his boxers, and I looked up to the ceiling as he pulled them down. The reality was, I'd seen the outline of Dash's dick through those boxers, and if I saw the real thing, I wasn't sure I'd be able to go through with actually sleeping with him.

When the mattress dipped, my heart raced because this was it. I was about to lose my virginity to Dash, and I was excited but scared to death at the same time.

When he climbed on top of me, I shivered, feeling his naked skin caress mine. It felt nice as he left kisses across my collarbone. While I was trying to decipher if that giant rod-like thing brushing across my thigh was Dash's dick or leg, his hand descended to my center.

My pulse was so high, I couldn't think straight, and breathing became tough because he was about to touch me. This was happening. I was about to lose my virginity to my high school crush.

Oh my god.

Don't hyperventilate.

Swallowing, I closed my eyes and did my best to relax. Dash was still kissing my neck, oblivious to the fact that I was mildly freaking out over one of my biggest dreams coming true, even though I wasn't sure I was ready for it.

I let out a satisfied sigh as his fingers touched my clit. It was just a whisper of a touch, but I'd never known what that felt like before. It was exciting and hot, and I didn't want it to stop.

"What a good girl. Already so wet for me," he breathed out with satisfaction as he drew lazy circles around my clit. Was I supposed to lose my vision? Because all I wanted to do was roll my eyes to the back of my head.

He dropped his fingers, exploring the rest of my pussy, but then I had a thought. What if he put his fingers inside me? Would he realize I was a virgin? I didn't know, but I wasn't going to find out tonight.

"Please, Dash. Just fuck me already," I quipped.

He drew back and looked at me with surprise, but I pulled him in for a kiss before he could ask questions. His shoulder muscles relaxed, and his body lay on top of mine.

That was when I felt it again. It wasn't his leg. It was apparently his giant cock that was supposed to fit inside me. Every time his dick brushed against my thigh, a shiver ran through my bones because I was nervous. I was so close to it actually happening or having the entire thing blow up in my face.

I pulled away from his mouth to say, "I've waited so long for this, I just want to feel you inside me."

A hint of a smile pulled across his lips. "Whatever you want, Madison."

He reached over to the bedside table, grabbed the condom that he'd apparently taken out of his jeans, and opened the packet. I arched my back and closed my eyes as I glared at the ceiling, willing myself not to look down.

"Everything okay?" Dash asked.

"Yup, everything's fine. I'm just aware that we need to be quiet, and I've been told I'm a screamer before." It wasn't a lie. I had been told that, just not in this context.

He let out a chuckle before laying his body on top of mine.

"I guess that means I'm going to have to keep you quiet?"

I opened my eyes once again, happy that I could only see Dash's face. His hand dipped between us, and he ran his fingers across my slit, gathering the wetness before teasing my clit for a few seconds. Then he kissed me, and the motion immediately made me relax. It was as though he knew I was nervous and could figure out the right way to calm me down.

He relaxed his forehead against mine just as I felt the head of his cock nudging at my center.

This was it.

There was no backing out now.

Not that I wanted to.

I couldn't wait to feel him, but wow. It almost felt like there should be a marching band ready to celebrate.

"You're so beautiful," he whispered. "Are you sure you're okay with this?"

I nodded and took a sharp breath the minute he pushed in ever so slightly. I guessed that maybe he was in less than an inch, but the feeling was enough to make me moan involuntarily because it felt odd. The noise was loud enough that it forced Dash to smother my mouth with his hand.

"Shhh. If you can't be quiet, I'm going to have to stop. Do you want that?"

With wide eyes, I shook my head. "Then be a good girl and don't make a sound. Bite down on my palm if you need to. Whatever, but I don't want to stop this. You're so fucking tight."

This time, I nodded, and he pushed himself in further. It was faster than I would have liked, but he had no idea this was my first time, so why would he be careful?

"Fuck, Madison," he growled, and I held my breath, trying to ignore that pinch of pain radiating at my core. It would pass. I knew that, but it didn't stop tears prickling from my eyes as he pushed in further.

He was huge.

I gripped on to his shoulders and crushed my eyes shut, biting down on his palm, which made me taste my own arousal.

When was this going to feel good?

He suddenly stopped, stilling inside me. "Madison," he gritted out as he moved his hand from my mouth.

"Are you inside me yet?" I asked with my eyes still closed.

"Not completely."

Not completely?! How much more did he have to put in there?

"Is there something you forgot to tell me?" he asked with pointed annoyance, but it was hard to take him seriously when he was inside me. We both knew what I neglected to tell him, but I figured I could play dumb for a little longer.

"Nope. Nothing," I squeaked out. I had to admit that this little interlude had stopped him from moving, which helped me adjust to his size. So much so that my hips started to wiggle to try to take more of him in. Maybe I was about to enjoy this.

"Madison, are you a virgin?"

I huffed out a laugh. "You're having sex with me right now, so the answer is no."

"Fuck," he whispered sharply, banging the mattress next to me. "I thought you lost your virginity to Henry in high school?"

I gulped, looking anywhere but at the man who had his penis inside me. "Umm, funny story. That was the plan, but you found him cheating on me hours before that could happen."

"Fuck. Fuck. Fuck. I can't do this. What was I thinking?"

He was about to pull out, but I didn't let him. I clamped my legs around his waist and braced the back of his neck with my hands. "Please. Don't stop. I want this. I wanted it to be you. You wouldn't stop with anyone else, so don't make me the exception. You agreed to one night, and this is the one night I want."

His lips were pressed together, and he studied me intently. In that moment, I knew. I'd lost him. I shouldn't have lied. He was going to stop because he was regretting it, and he was going to leave me as a half-virgin since he wasn't technically all the way in.

I closed my eyes, and this time the tears falling were from the sad reality that I couldn't even do a one-night hookup right.

Surprisingly, Dash's lips met mine, and he kissed me slowly. Almost like he was savoring it. It was enough to coax me out of my thoughts and open my eyes. All I saw was Dash. Towering above me, unmoving, but watching me with an emotion I couldn't decipher.

"Why haven't you left yet?"

"Because I'm not going to."

"You're not?"

"No." I couldn't figure out if he was happy or sad about it. "But I am going to make sure it feels good for you. I mean, fuck, Madison. Why the hell didn't you say anything?" He started moving ever so slightly, and my legs quivered but automatically opened for him.

"I didn't think you'd go through with our deal if you knew."

"You got that right." He muttered something else under his breath, but I couldn't make it out.

Then, he kissed me again, and this time there was a gentleness behind it. It didn't just warm my body, it warmed my soul, and my bones melted in relief.

"Has it been hurting?" He was lightly pulsing inside me now, watching my face for any sign of pain.

"A little." I bit my bottom lip, embarrassed at the confession because I wanted it so badly, but now that I had it, I felt guilty that I forced Dash to take it.

"Okay, well, I'm sorry, but this might hurt a little more."

"I understand, but please don't stop."

He slid his lips across mine as he pushed himself further in, swallowing my whimper. I felt his fingers skate across my clit, and he gently caressed me as he continued thrusting. There was another pinch of pain, but it went away a lot quicker with Dash's hand working on me.

"Almost there," he whispered, and with another push, that was it. "Good girl." The pain subsided to the point that it started to feel almost pleasurable.

"Keep moving." I squeezed his arms, wanting to feel it all. My hips rocked against his as he started to develop a rhythm. One that I was matching. Each and every thrust.

Dash's hot breath skated down my chest as he thrust into me. I couldn't help but watch him. With his eyes closed, his breathing was labored, and his skin was red from the heat.

"So. Fucking. Good," he whispered, looking down at me. "Look at you. Taking me all in that tight little pussy of yours."

I scraped my nails across his chest, painting his pecs with scratches, which only pushed him to go harder.

He kissed me again, our bodies connected in every possible way, and I felt something deep in me burn bright. It wasn't my pending orgasm, which had somehow managed to build after all that pain, but something else. Something a little deeper. Something harder to describe.

Dash's hand pulled at my thigh, changing the angle, and as I whimpered, he covered it with a kiss.

His body was hitting me in just the right spot now, and I was right on the edge again.

"Just one night," Dash said in barely a whisper against my lips as I came.

Stars burst in my vision, and my back arched, trying to get as much of him as possible.

That was it.

I fell back onto the bed, with Dash on top of me. I couldn't move. My legs were tingling, and my heart was pounding. That was the best experience of my life.

Dash stayed inside me for a few seconds, letting our sticky bodies come down from our highs. He kissed my shoulder, then gently eased out of me.

Nothing was said as he rolled off the bed and disposed of the condom in the bathroom. I had to admit, that wasn't exactly how I imagined things ending.

When he came out of the bathroom with a washcloth, I was confused. Pushing the sheets back, Dash sat on the edge of the bed, next to my hips. He gently opened my legs and to my surprise, he put the warm washcloth against my center.

I closed my eyes, enjoying the heat as it eased my pain.

"I've got some acetaminophen in the bedside table. I'll get you some water when I'm done here."

His hands continued massaging me, and would it be weird to tell him that it was kind of turning me on again? Was it normal to be this insatiable after the first time?

After cleaning me up, he made his way back to the bathroom and came out with a drink, placing it by my side.

"Thank you," I said in barely a whisper.

He rounded the bed, getting in on the other side and dragged me into his still naked body.

"Just one night." He spoke so softly that if it weren't so quiet, I wouldn't have heard it.

I knew he'd start repeating that to himself, but how could he really think that was possible now? That connection. It wasn't just sex. That was a life-altering experience, and I needed more.

"How are you feeling?" Dash kissed just behind my ear as his fingers

THE DRAFT

pressed into my hips.

"Good." I swallowed, knowing that something needed to be said. "I'm sorry. I should have told you that I was a virgin."

"You should have."

"I was just worried you wouldn't go through with it." I was about to go into a tirade about why and apologize again, but Dash started talking before I could.

"You're right, I wouldn't have. You should have told me, but I'm so damn happy you didn't."

It took me a minute to really take in what he was saying. I blamed the post-orgasmic haze, but when I realized that was his way of telling me he didn't regret it, I smiled, burrowing my body even further into his giant frame.

He held me tighter, leaving the smallest of kisses across my head, making my heart skip a beat.

Tonight was perfect. It was everything I wanted, and as Dash whispered sweet nothings into my ear, I felt myself drifting off to sleep.

CHAPTER 9

Madison

Twiddling my thumbs, I stared at the ceiling as I tried to stop my mind from thinking. My legs were aching, my core was hurting, and I felt like I was going to be sick. I'd only managed to sleep for fifteen minutes before my mind decided to wake me up, leaving me with just my thoughts and worries about what was going to happen between Dash and me after all of this.

I rolled my head to the side and looked at Dash. He was sleeping soundly, and even with the little light that was available in the room, he looked beautiful. I had an urge to snuggle into him and wake him up for another round, but I knew that was only prolonging the inevitable heartbreak that was going to come my way.

I slept with Dash, and I already knew that no one could compare to him. Even when he found out I was a virgin, he didn't stop because he wanted to make it good for me. I felt cared for. It might be a little foolish, but I felt loved. My chest was heating as I pushed a hair out of his face, admiring his long lashes. It was strange seeing him sleeping like this. Without that permanent scowl, he seemed peaceful, and I only hoped that I was part of the reason for it. He was everything I ever wanted, but I knew deep down that the minute he woke up, he'd come to his senses and push me away.

Before having sex with him, I was confident I could handle that, but I didn't have as much certainty in myself now.

Biting my bottom lip, I looked at him one last time before rolling off the bed and tiptoeing around the room to find my clothes. Once I came out of the bathroom, the harsh reality of what I'd done came crashing down. Looking at Dash still snuggled in the sheets, I felt my heart breaking a little. One night with my dream guy wasn't enough. I wanted forever, and even suggesting the idea was a rookie error on my part. One brought on from desperation.

Dash was everything, but could he see past my brother enough to give me a chance? I didn't think so. Sometimes I wished I was just another uncomplicated girl at Covey U. One that he met at The Draft with no history. I rolled my eyes because I was basically wishing to be Sienna. She probably had one-night situationships all the time. I doubted there was a guy in this college who could keep her interest for longer than a few hours. If she were me right now, she'd take the emotion away and just walk out on the guy. That was what probably kept them interested.

I took a sharp breath, thinking about my own situationship, and as I looked at Dash nuzzling into a pillow, thinking it was me, a thought came to mind.

What would Dash do if he woke up and I wasn't here?

I smiled just thinking about his reaction. He'd be pissed because that wasn't something I'd do. I was his 'good girl', but what if I turned bad and left? He'd probably text me, annoyed, and he'd have to come to my dorm to check out where I'd gone. Either way, his attention would still be on me. Exactly where I wanted it.

I started smiling because it was all coming together in my head. That was precisely what I needed to do.

Leave.

He knew that I had liked him for years, so he'd totally expect me to stay here and most likely try to convince him for at least one more round. Honestly, that was pretty much my plan before we slept together, but what if I tried something different? What if I tried something unexpected? A different strategy worked at The Draft. Kissing Dash made him loosen up and kiss me back. A different strategy got him to sleep with me. If it wasn't obvious he wanted me before that, it was damn obvious now. He just wasn't ready to deal with the guilt of betraying his best friend that dating me brought along with it.

If Dash and I were going to have any chance of taking our relationship to the next level, I needed to play a different game. I needed to be the confident, sexy, experienced girl who chewed men up and spat them out.

What would Sienna do?

It could be my new motto. Sienna would play it cool because she knew she had the guy by the balls. So that was exactly what I was going to do, too. Take his balls out with me. Figuratively speaking, of course.

Let him worry and have to find me.

Grinning so widely, I could feel my cheeks aching. I grabbed my jeans and shucked them on, sans underwear, since I figured Dash would find them somewhere in the room, which would be his first positive reminder of me.

I slowly opened his drawer, careful not to make any noise, and pulled out a gray T-shirt with our high school logo on it and put it on. I immediately melted at the smell of him surrounding me, and I was fighting the urge to go back to bed and snuggle with him. If I had Dash by the balls, then he had me by the soul.

It was cold out, but I decided to leave my sweatshirt here since it meant Dash would have to see me to return it.

Blowing out a breath, I grabbed my purse and phone and headed to the door. Taking one last glance at Dash, who was still wiped out and looking gorgeous, I blew him a kiss and snuck out of his room, ready to see how far I could push this.

Turning my phone flashlight on, I nearly screamed when I saw a body asleep out on the couch. The guy's butt wiggled a little, the blanket covering him fell off. It was then I saw the back of his shirt and realized it was Erik. I didn't know why he'd passed out on the couch instead of walking those two extra feet to his room, but I wasn't going to wake him up to find out.

I carefully snuck through the lounge, straight to the elevator, and as my finger hovered over the button, I stopped myself. If I pressed that, the ding might wake Erik, so I crept past the elevator doors, over to the stairs, and skipped out of the hockey dorm.

Shuffling down the steps, I was holding back a giggle because I got away with it. It was three a.m., and I was sneaking out of a one-night stand. When I made it out of the building, I started jogging to my dorm block, giggling the entire way. I felt naughty. Not only was I running around campus in the middle of the night, but I was leaving Dash behind, and I could only imagine his reaction when he didn't find me in bed with him in the morning.

Would he text me or come running to my dorm?

Either way, I was ready for his next move.

CHAPTER 10

Dash

Traitor. Traitor. Traitor.

I woke up to the fresh scent of strawberries stuck to my sheets, stirring memories of last night and giving me a boner that only one person could fix.

Traitor. Traitor. Traitor.

Cade's voice was swirling in my head, reminding me that what I did last night was wrong. It was the only reason I was able to keep my hands to myself while sleeping for the rest of the night.

But damn. What a hell of a night that was. Madison and I only had sex once, but I already knew nothing would compare to it. How could it? I unknowingly took her virginity, and I was berating myself for not checking. It should have been the first thing I asked, but the thought didn't pass my mind. I'd always assumed she'd lost it with Henry, which was why I thought she was so upset over finding him cheating. But I was wrong, and it was the first time in my life I was happy about that fact. Happy because she hadn't lost her virginity to that fuckwit. Happy that I was the only person who knew what she felt like from the inside. Happy to know the feeling of her clenching around me when she came.

Traitor. Traitor. Traitor.

Cade's voice was another reminder that I wasn't much better than Henry. I was just more successful at sleeping with her. I still couldn't give her what she deserved, no matter how much I wanted to. She deserved a guy that could fawn over her in public and make her happy all the time. I couldn't do that. Not without screwing up other aspects of both of our lives.

Fuck.

Was last night the worst decision of my life? If it meant Cade's voice was in my head for the rest of it whispering 'traitor,' then the answer was a resounding yes. I was a traitor. No, wait. I was worse than a traitor because I was hiding in plain sight.

I took a deep breath, trying to center myself, and immediately calmed down when another waft of strawberries hit my nostrils. My muscles relaxed, and I felt a strange sense of peace when I thought about Madison.

She grounded me.

Being inside her was even better than I'd imagined, and all I could think about were those short, breathy whimpers that I managed to calm once I slowed down and helped her enjoy it. Slow and steady was good for her, but damn near torture for me. There was a stone in my stomach because I felt something I never did with Amy. It wasn't just sex. The connection was stronger, which made my climax ten times better. I wanted more, but I could never admit it out loud. Not without facing serious repercussions.

A growl emanated from my throat as I thought about Madison because no one else would compare.

How could they?

She shone brighter than the damn sun.

One night.

I reminded myself. We agreed to one night, and I had to abide by it for both of our sakes. Thinking about it like this was only going to drive me crazy. But then a little thought wormed its way through my brain. When did one night end? We only really had a few hours together, and in one night I could do a hell of a lot more than one time. The sun was starting to pour into my room, which I supposed meant the night was over, but if

I wanted to get technical, one night could be twelve hours of fun. Nine of which we hadn't had yet.

I ignored the little voice in my head, pointing out what a bad idea all of this was, and rolled over, ready to pull Madison into my arms so she'd be able to feel my already-erect dick and see if she thought the same way I did. Only, when I stretched my arm out, there was nothing to grab. Just a pile of pillows smothered in her scent.

Propping myself up, I checked to see if maybe she'd gone to the bathroom, but with the door wide open and the lights off, it was obvious she wasn't in there either.

"Madison?" I whispered sharply into the semi-darkness. Was I really expecting a response? There was no one in the room but me. My brows furrowed, and I felt like I was trying to solve an impossible riddle because Madison had gone, but where the fuck did she go?

Had I been obsessing so much over the kiss that I dreamed about taking her virginity? At this point, it was a very serious possibility because I was starting to believe that I was borderline obsessed with her, but a dream wouldn't explain her perfume drifting in the air. She'd been here. There was no question in my mind. I just hadn't figured out where she'd gone.

Getting up, I pulled on a pair of sweats and looked around the room one more time because I wouldn't put it past her to hide in my closet for several hours just to scare the crap out of me as a joke. Thankfully, she wasn't in there, and as I moved around the room, I found her bra and underwear, but there was still no sign of her.

What the hell?

So, not only had she left me, but she'd left me and was running around with no clothes on somewhere. I growled, annoyed that thinking about her naked was making me hard all over again. Walking over to my door, I opened it and stuck my head out to check that she wasn't outside talking to the guys. There was a blanket strewn over the couch, but apart from that, the place was completely empty. Madison wasn't here, but that begged the question: Where the hell did she go?

I felt numb as I walked over to the elevator for no other reason than not knowing what else to do with myself and clicked the call button. She wouldn't still be in there, but as I watched the number climb to our floor, my chest constricted because I really hoped she was.

Traitor. Traitor. Traitor.

There it was again. The guilt bubbling in my gut, causing the stomach ulcer of a lifetime, no doubt. I was a traitor, but it was the only bad thing I'd ever done in my life, so could it really be *that* bad?

When the elevator doors opened and all I saw was my pathetic reflection in the mirror at the back, my body slumped. Madison left me. After I took her virginity, Madison didn't even have the decency to stay long enough to say goodbye.

I lingered at the elevator for a little longer than necessary because trying to process what just happened was taking most of my brain cells. I'd just had the best sex of my life with the girl of my dreams and woke up to an empty bed and the need to talk to her. My ego was bruised, but my heart was in a worse condition.

I groaned at my own thoughts. Calling Madison my dream girl and claiming a broken heart would never end well because my best friend's little sister shouldn't have that kind of hold on me.

But apparently, life was cruel like that, and it was the truth.

We fucked up.

That summarized our encounter. Yes, it was amazing, and I would have totally been up for another round if she hadn't left, but we fucked everything up. Our friendship. My friendship with Cade. One night was such a lie because how the hell was I supposed to look at Madison again without remembering what it felt like to be inside her? How the hell was I supposed to stop my heart from beating like it was trying to punch its way out of my chest every time I looked at her?

"Dash." His voice was like a splash of ice-cold water. "What are you doing out here? Oh, did reporter girl just leave?" Cade teased. I tried to remain cool as I looked down the hall to find him fully dressed and ready for practice. "What's her name again?" The only good thing about Madison leaving was that she didn't need to hide away from Cade at least.

"Sienna, and yes, she did," I quipped, lying out of my ass to save my face. Unfortunately, when Cade smiled at me eagerly, all the guilt I was ignoring came back to the forefront like a tidal wave because the reality of the situation was that I was willingly betraying him.

Traitor. Traitor. Traitor.
Shut up, brain!

I was fooling around with his sister behind his back and lying about it. What kind of shitty best friend did that?

Me, apparently.

After everything I'd been through, he was always there for me. The guy was like my brother, and lying to him felt impossible when he was standing in front of me, rooting for me and the girl I slept with last night.

"It was a mistake," I added in my own frustration. Yes, it was a shitty thing to say, but I wasn't thinking straight. This wasn't how I wanted Madison. Hidden and illicit. She deserved to be more than a girl I snuck around with. She deserved to be front and center because that was just who she was. It was why she deserved someone who wasn't me.

"Didn't sound like a mistake when you were banging her against the door last night. Not to mention how much your bed shook the entire dorm. Did you know it did that? Probably not. She's the first girl you've had over since we moved in."

Fuck.

He was talking about his sister. I deserved the death penalty for this.

"Funny, Sienna doesn't strike me as the type to be so vocal, either."

"Oh, really?" I cleared my throat. "Because I think the noise goes with that angry reporter vibe she's got going on."

He huffed out a laugh and elbowed me. "You dirty dog. You never bring girls home. That must mean she's something special."

"She's sure special, all right. Now, if you don't mind, I need to shower before we go to practice." I didn't want to wash the memory of Madison off my body, but I needed to if I was going to regain any of my sanity. She left without leaving a note, which was so unlike Madison. The girl was so unsubtle, I was almost surprised she hadn't left my dorm singing and dancing to a routine from *The Greatest Showman*.

As I walked past Cade toward my room, he clasped my arm.

"Before you go...." I stopped in my tracks and looked over my shoulder at my friend. His eyes were downcast, and he was frowning. The expression alone was enough to catch my attention.

"What's up, C?"

The Draft

"I know this is going to sound crazy, but have you, uh, spoken to Madison recently?"

I stopped, not sure what to say. Was he fucking with me? Did he know she was just in my room, and this was his way of playing with his meal before he killed me for touching his sweet, innocent baby sister? Wait a minute. What if she left me to go to Cade's room to cry it all out? What if he already knew I was a traitor and I was making it worse by not coming clean?

"Not much. Why?" My tongue was burning with all the lies as I swallowed down the guilt of lying to Cade yet again. I was gambling here, hoping that Madison had stayed true to her pinkie promise and not told Cade, but could I really blame her? She'd just lost her virginity, which I assumed might make her feel vulnerable. Not to mention that I didn't exactly take it easy on her at the start because I didn't know.

"There's something going on with her."

I swallowed. "Is there?" Did my voice just go up three octaves? I cleared my throat. "I mean, is there?"

"Yeah, but she's being stubborn and won't tell me what it is."

Losing her V-card to your best friend might have something to do with the stonewalling, I thought.

"No offense, but if I were Madison, I wouldn't tell you anything either. You have a tendency to overreact."

He smirked and raised his palms. "I get it. She doesn't want to talk to me, but the only other friends she's made here are those football guys, and I sure as hell don't trust them. What if there's something major going on with her and she has no one to talk to about it?"

Poor Cade. As much as he liked to believe he was all hard edges, he was a real marshmallow when it came to his sister. Or any woman that he chose to have in his life, for that matter. I patted him on the shoulder in a feeble attempt to bring him some comfort. Little did he know I was the reason he was concerned.

"You know what? I'm sure she's fine. She's probably got a lot of stuff going on. It's early in the semester, and she wants to make a good impression with her professors. You know her, she overdoses on caffeinated soda when she's studying a lot. Jitters like a chihuahua. Could just be that."

"Maybe you're right." I felt my heart slow because at least I'd managed to get him off her back for a little while. "Will you talk to her?"

My head shot up. "Me?"

"Yeah. I've tried, and she completely ignores me every time, but she'll talk to you."

"And how do you know that?"

He sighed. "Because she's always had a soft spot for you, and that only solidified when you beat her cheating ass boyfriend to a pulp."

My jaw hung open as I tried to figure out what to say. Was that his way of telling me he knew his sister had a crush on me or was I reading too much into it? I was most definitely overthinking things, and I wasn't an overthinker. As a goalie, I didn't have time to. I had to work on instinct, and as I looked at my best friend, everything in me was telling me to stop lying. Tell him the truth and get the beatdown I deserved over with. But would Madison really want Cade to know about her sex life?

Her tiny little pinkie came to mind. We made a promise, and I wasn't willing to break it.

"She views you as her protector now, so if there is something wrong, I bet she'd tell you."

"I-I can try." It came out lackluster, and I was certain he picked up on that tone, but I hoped he assumed I was nervous since it wasn't like I was the natural choice to spill your guts to.

"If you don't, I'm just going to have to stalk my sister to find out, because if that idiot Aiden Matthews got her pregnant, I'm going to kill him."

Aiden Matthews? Pregnant? How the hell did he get there?

"Dude, there's no need to do that," I piped out quickly. "I'll talk to her. See what I can find out." He looked at me with a smile, completely unaware that I was only offering because I was saving myself.

Fuck. The more I thought about it, the worse it felt.

"Thanks, D. I always know I can count on you." He slapped me on the shoulder and gave me a smile. Guilt slithered through my veins again because if only he knew what I did.

Thankfully, Cade's phone buzzed, ruining our bro moment, and giving me an out before I gave myself away.

"Dammit," he cursed when he saw the text on his phone.

"Anyone important?" I asked, eager to change the subject.

He shook his head. "Just a new study group for one of my classes. They all hate hockey, and I think they're scheduling our sessions during training or games just to fuck with me."

"Sucks, man. Could you cut them loose and work solo?"

He glanced up at me before looking down at his phone with a lazy smile. "I could, but there's a girl I'm trying to figure out."

"Oh, really?" I asked, happy to be talking about him.

"Yeah, but it's nothing. I don't know anything just yet. I'm just testing out a theory, and I can only do that if I'm around her."

"Good to know. I hope it works out for you." I raised my brows and tipped my head to the inside of my bedroom. "I'm going to take a shower so I'm not late for practice."

"Okay, I'm going to skip weight training this morning so I can go to their stupid study group. Can you let Coach know I'll get a session in before the end of the day?"

I nodded, and just as I was about to go into my room, Cade said, "Oh, and Dash? Thanks for your help."

"With what?"

"Madison." It felt like one final dagger to my heart. "I appreciate how you've always had her back throughout the years, and even now, when she doesn't really need anyone to look after her, you're always here, willing to help."

Yup. I was definitely going to hell for this.

"No problem."

I turned on my heel, too caught up in my own thoughts to let it show. When I got into my room, I shut the door and leaned against it. Closing my eyes, I stopped myself from growling in frustration.

What the fuck did I do with his sister? My best friend's sister. *Baby Bright.* He was loyal to me, yet here I was, breaking his trust and potentially setting fire to our relationship. I'd royally fucked up, and there was nothing I could do about it because the worst part about this entire thing was that I'd do it all over again if I had the chance, and that was a problem.

I wanted Madison. Not just on every single surface of my dorm room, but I wanted her in my life as more than my best friend's sister. I just didn't think that was possible.

However, there was an even bigger issue that I needed to deal with that didn't involve asking Madison if she liked me enough to take a chance on me. It was that I had no idea where Madison had gone or if she was wearing any clothes.

CHAPTER 11

Dash

Dash: Are you alive?

After countless rewrites and a couple of hours of thinking over what to send to Madison, that was all I came up with. *Are you alive?* At least it sounded better than my original, mildly threatening message of: *If you don't tell me where you are in the next ten seconds, I'm going to break the nose of every guy you've uttered a word to on campus until you get back in my bed.*

Madison apparently made me unhinged.

Madison: Good morning, Big Man. Did you have a good sleep? I know I did. I believe this text answers your question.

Even through texts, she was just so…chipper. Wasn't her brain frying over what happened between us like mine? Was she just going to go back and pretend like nothing happened? Yes, we agreed to one night, but she was the last person I'd actually expect to go through with the promise. I should be happy about it, but something about her aloofness was ticking me off.

Dash: Where did you go?
Madison: When?
Dash: Really? You're going to play it like you don't know what I'm talking about. After everything that happened between us last night?
Madison: What's so different about last night?
Dash: You know perfectly well.
Madison: I'm just keeping to the rules. One night just between us, right?

My jaw clenched as I clutched my phone, angry with how this was going. In all honesty, not having her in my bed this morning pissed me off, and the fact that she was so happily toying with me now just soured my mood further.

Dash: What's gotten into you?

This wasn't like Madison. She was eager. She was a teacher's pet. If she enjoyed herself, she'd be all over me, trying to get another round in and convincing me we could keep a relationship between us a secret. But she wasn't, which was starting to make me question my performance.

Madison: If you want to get technical, you got into me.
Dash: Madison.
Madison: Dash.
Dash: You're being ridiculous.
Madison: Am I? We said one night, right? What's the problem? We had one night. Did you want me to thank you for it?
Dash: No.
Madison: Thank you, Sir Dash-a-lot. I appreciate you sharpening your sword on me. I think we can both agree it broke through plenty

of barriers. *wink* *wink*
Madison: How was that? Is that what you were looking for?

I rolled my eyes because she was driving me insane. I mean, shit. She made me feel like I was overreacting about the entire thing. Like she did this with other guys all the time. I couldn't figure out where to go next with her.

I ran a hand through my hair in aggravation because all I could think about was Madison. Kissing her was my first mistake, falling for her twisted logic was my second. I could say it wasn't my fault because there were two things blurring my decision: my dick and her perfume, but that would be a lie.

I'd been thinking about her so much that I was willing to fuck everything up for that one night. I knew it was a bad decision, but I also knew that it would be the best bad decision of my life, so I did it anyway. Having Madison right there for the taking, telling me she wanted me, was too much of a temptation. And yes, I'd love another round, but damn, I'd never imagined I'd be the one trying to feel out if she was interested in it too.

Traitor. Traitor. Traitor.

Cade's voice was haunting me like when I had a funky smell in my hockey bag, only to find out there was an old banana in there. I knew what I did last night was bad, yet it wasn't stopping me from talking to his sister this morning. I could lie to myself and say it was because I wanted to make sure she got home safe, but what good would that do now? I'd already slept with her and tasted the forbidden fruit.

I wanted more, and I knew it was wrong. So, so wrong.

Without responding to Madison, I shoved my phone in my pocket as I made my way through the locker room and did the thing I should have done last night. I ignored the temptation.

Most of the team were already ready for practice, but my shower at home took longer than necessary, which was mainly down to the fact that I had a huge boner, and every time I tried to do something about it, all I heard was Cade's voice in my head.

Traitor. Traitor. Traitor.

The guilt was dripping from my sweat at this point, and I could only hope the feeling would subside the further I got from the event. However, if my feelings today were anything to go by, I was screwed. And not in the good way.

By the time I got to my locker, another message from Madison had come through. The right thing to do would be to shove my phone in my bag and forget about it, but when it came to Madison, the temptation was too great.

Madison: Oh, by the way, did you find my panties? I couldn't find them, so I had to walk home commando.

My eye twitched, and I did my best to maintain my composure because now all I could think about was how much I regretted not taking more time to taste her and commit her beautifully naked body to memory.

Madison: I hope they aren't too wet.

I coughed loudly, choking on my own spit, and Erik slapped my back as he walked past me, toward his locker.

"You okay, man?"

"I'm good." It was strained and a little lackluster, but I was thankful that he hadn't looked at my phone screen and seen why I was so choked up. When he walked away, I quickly texted her back.

Dash: Can we talk about this later? I need to get on the rink for practice.
Madison: Practice, eh? Are you going to hump the ice, and then stretch your thighs out with your foam roller after?
Dash: Yes?
Madison: The images in my mind right now are obscene.

I shook my head, letting out a hint of laughter before knocking shoulders with one of my teammates. "Sorry," I mumbled, only looking up when the guy in front wouldn't move.

Fuck.

I immediately dropped my phone because there was no way he could see what was on my screen. I winced as it crashed to the ground. My only saving grace was that it had an unbreakable waterproof case on it.

"Cade."

Cade's wide, grinning face was looking at me like he knew something I didn't. "Gosh, D. I've never seen you like this. Is this because of Reporter Girl?"

"Sure," I quipped as I dropped to pick up my phone, staring at the blank screen.

"You better watch yourself. You've had one night with her, and she's already got your balls in a vise. Your hair's a mess, you aren't dressed for practice, and you're staring at your phone like a zombie. I get it, she's probably great in the sack and you don't exactly get around much, but is she worth screwing up your pretty much guaranteed contract with Atlanta for?" I pressed my lips shut, and Cade's eyes widened. "Oh, she is. Well, unless she's sleeping with the rest of us, she's definitely not worth the extra drills we'll have to do for your tardiness, so get your ass in gear and let's go."

He gestured to my lack of pads, and I rolled my eyes.

"I'm not late. It only takes me thirty seconds to get my padding on, and then I'm done."

"Thirty seconds? I don't have much to worry about then. Sounds like Reporter Girl might be disappointed soon, anyway."

I pushed past him and mumbled, "Trust me, she wasn't disappointed." Dumping my phone in my locker, I pulled out my padding and started to put it on.

Cade dropped next to me and shunted my shoulder. "I was just joking. In all seriousness, I'm happy for you, man. I've never seen you this happy and disgruntled at the same time. It must mean she's something special."

I gulped, because how the hell was I supposed to keep this secret from him for the rest of my life? How could I look my best friend in the eye and not hear 'traitor' in the back of my head every single time he smiled at me? What the hell was I supposed to do when Madison and Cade were in the same vicinity?

Cade leaned in. "Word on the street is something big is happening on the ice today. Any ideas on what it is?"

"Nope."

"Figured. You're too drunk on pussy to be concentrating on the fact that the entire locker room has been talking about something while you've been glued to your phone."

"They have?" Sure enough, when I glanced at the rest of the team, they were all in huddles, whispering as they strolled out to the rink. Just as they were leaving, Scotty looked over his shoulder and gave me an uneasy glare.

"Hey, Hendricks. What's going on?" I called out.

"New guy," Erik responded for Scotty.

"New guy?" With furrowed brows, Cade looked at me with confusion. We were only a few weeks into the season, so it made no sense that new transfers were already being recruited.

"I guess we should go and find out." I turned to my locker, pulled out my skates, and started to lace them up. Cade waited, and we made our way to the rink together. Since no one was moving, I pushed my way to the boards and stood next to Scotty, surprised to see a player already on the ice in all black, skating lengths.

With a stick in one hand, he was handling the puck with ease, and as much as I hated to admit it, he was good. Really good. How he was able to transfer here without it becoming headline news was beyond me because he must have been a starter for another D1 team.

Even after scoring from halfway across the rink, he didn't let the fact he had an audience break his concentration. He was focused and took another puck, ran it up to the other goal, and scored from an almost impossible angle. The guy had accuracy, that was for sure.

Erik let out a low whistle as he looked at Alex with concern. His face was a little paler than usual, which could have been because he was cold on the ice, but I doubted it. He was used to the temperature. No, I assumed Erik looked like he wanted to vomit because the guy was good, and with skills like that, I could only assume he was an attacker, so there was a very real possibility that Erik could get replaced.

When the new guy finally decided to stop showing off, he made his way over to us and let his blades slide across the ice as he came to a stop in front of the door.

His eyes looked familiar, and it was only after he pulled his helmet off that I recognized his off-center nose.

The one *I* broke.

Henry Newman.

One by one, the team entered the rink, giving the new guy a high-five and a bro hug. Oh, how easy it was for them to accept him, but no one knew what he was really like.

A lying cheater.

Standing shoulder to shoulder, it was just Cade and me left on the side, and we glanced at each other knowingly. Neither one of us wanted to get on that ice with him, but we knew we'd have to.

"I'm Henry." He had this forced, fake smile on his face as he waved his gloved hand to the rest of the players he hadn't said hello to yet. "And I'm looking forward to being on the team."

He sounded almost nice, but I knew his game. I was pretty sure that was how he convinced Madison that he wasn't a cheating asshole in high school.

I blew out an annoyed breath because I thought we had gotten rid of this guy. We'd made sure that the rest of the team gave him a hard time in high school after we left, so why would he come here? The college that he knew we attended.

Looking at my teammates, I was surprised at how happy they were. Yes, he was a good player, but how were we going to break it to them that we had a traitor amongst us?

Or at least another one, since I was currently the biggest traitor this team had ever seen.

As Henry talked to a couple of our teammates, Cade pushed past me and skated toward him. When he got close enough, he barged through our other teammates, taking Henry by surprise.

"Oh, Cade. Hi," Henry said as Cade skated closer. So close that Henry had to skate backward and ended up hitting the board.

"What the fuck are you doing here?" Cade gritted out. Scotty was by Cade's side and pushed in front of him, making himself a physical barrier between the two players.

"What the fuck are you doing, Bright?" Scotty glared at Cade in disappointment. Cade was breathing so heavily, I could see his shoulders moving under the padding, and he was gripping his stick like he was trying to hold himself back.

Henry rounded his shoulders and adjusted his jersey before cracking his neck. He was shaken, but as he stood taller in his skates, I could tell he was trying to hide it with bravado. "We're old teammates," he answered to the group.

"Guessing it didn't end well," Scotty mumbled.

Henry ignored Cade's snarls and slid forward, holding his stick with more confidence now. "He hates me because I dated his sister a few years ago. Don't see what the big deal is. It was just a couple of dates. She's over it. I'm over it. It was nothing special." He shrugged it off, and I couldn't think straight. All I could see was red, because now it wasn't just Cade who wanted to kill him.

It was me.

Nothing special? Madison was extraordinary, and no one got away with talking about her like that. I hadn't really registered what I was doing until Henry let out a strangled groan as his body slammed against the plexiglass.

"Whoa," Erik breathed out, and I turned to see everyone glaring at me.

Whoops, did I do that? Well, shit. Now I needed to come up with a plausible explanation for why I held a grudge against him too.

"He slept with my girlfriend in high school," I quickly said to no one in particular.

It was then that the whole rink took a simultaneous intake of breath. "Ouch," Erik muttered with his hand over his mouth. Leaning in, he elbowed Alex and whispered, "Dude, this shit is better than *The Baseball Bachelor*." Did he really think we couldn't hear that in a quiet, echoey rink?

"Sleeping with is a little dramatic, don't you think?" Henry retorted.

Why was this kid not scared of us? Had he grown some balls since we last saw him?

"I was a gawky sixteen-year-old, and a popular senior girl asked me to kiss her under the stairs. I only realized she was your girlfriend after you broke my nose. You didn't exactly show her off."

"He broke your nose?" Erik asked in shock. Really? Was it that surprising? We'd done worse on the ice last week.

Henry nodded and pointed to his rearranged snout, giving me a moment to admire my handiwork. I didn't usually take pride in giving guys deviated septums, but he deserved it, and I really liked that it knocked off the symmetry of his face.

"Please don't tell me this is something I'm going to have to tell Coach about." Scotty sighed. "Because we're a team, not a reality show."

"You don't need to tell Coach Hansen anything. It's fine. Nothing we can't get over," I replied curtly.

"We can be friends, I promise." Henry's words sounded like a taunt, but I'd give him the benefit of the doubt for now.

"Why are you here, Newman?" Cade sneered.

Henry wasn't riled by Cade. Apparently, he'd grown a backbone since we last saw him. "I'm here for the same reason as everyone else. I want to play hockey and win games."

Scotty pulled Cade back, giving Henry space to stand on his own two skates. "But weren't you at Southern Collegiate? They win all the time. Why would you transfer here?"

"Because, unlike most of you, I wasn't eligible for the draft in high school. I don't have four years to build up a camaraderie with my teammates. I need to prove myself this year, and if I want to do that, I need to find the right team."

"And you thought a team with me and Cade was your best bet?"

"Believe me, you're better than the assholes over at Southern Collegiate. We might not be besties, but you can't deny that we played well together."

Although his reasoning made sense, I didn't believe him. How could I? He was a cheat and would have fit right in with those idiots at SoCol. In fact, I had no doubts that he probably arranged this with that college just to fuck with our team dynamic.

Well, he had another thing coming if he thought he could do that.

But then another thought passed through my mind. Did he know Madison attended Covey U? Was he here to try to get her back? That wasn't going to happen. I'd kill him if he fucked with her.

"Bright! Off the ice," Coach hollered. "If you can't play nice, then you can't play at all."

"But—"

"Don't 'but' me." Then he pointed to me. "You too, Bridges. I think you both need to cool down."

"What did I do?" I snarled.

"You pushed the new guy into the wall. As much as I'd like to see that hot head of yours come out more during games, I don't want you using force against teammates. *Teammates.* Remember that word. Nothing comes before your team."

I shook my head and skated beside Cade as we made our way off the ice to our punishment. Cade didn't have a problem bumping shoulders with Coach as we skated past. "If you don't want a reaction like that, then maybe next time you should consult team members before you change the roster. Where's he going to go? All the lines are full."

Cade had balls, I'd give him that.

Coach sighed. "Coaching by committee is not a thing here. You need to get your head out of your ass and remember that I get paid to make decisions about the team. Not you. You play for as long as I allow you to, and if you keep acting like a petulant child, you'll be off the ice until next semester."

Cade grumbled as he put his guards on and stomped through the locker room before whacking his stick against the bench and breaking it in two.

"Calm down, C," I said, sitting on the bench in front of my locker.

"How the fuck do you expect me to be calm when that asshole is out there playing on our team while we've been relegated to the weight room?"

I closed my eyes and leaned my head against the locker, trying not to think about it.

"He fucked your girl in the school hallway, and you're acting like it was nothing."

"They weren't fucking, and he was right. He did me a favor," I replied, thinking about Madison. The only good thing about catching them was that she found out he wasn't all that into her. Oh, and I suppose it also gave me a reason to threaten guys with murder if they hurt Madison. "Amy's out of my life, chasing someone else's jersey."

"And he's right back in ours, being the worst teammate possible."

"It's going to be fine, Cade."

"I want to murder the guy, so I'm not sure how you can say that it's going to be fine."

The Draft

"Murder? Really? Don't you think that's a little overdramatic? Maybe he's right. Maybe we need to forget everything that happened in high school."

Cade glared at me, shaking his head. "He broke my trust by dating my sister behind my back, and then he cheated on her with your girlfriend. Do you know how many nights I had to listen to Madison thinking she was sobbing so quietly I couldn't hear her because of that guy? He deserves more than that broken nose you gave him."

My fists clenched because Cade had never mentioned that to me before. I had no idea Madison was so upset over that idiot. Sure, she cried when she found him cheating, but I thought that broken nose had made her feel better.

"I agree," I replied without question and swallowed down the lump in my throat. If Henry deserved more than a broken nose, then I deserved to burn in the pits of hell for all eternity.

Traitor. Traitor. Traitor.

Guilt riddled my bones because what made me better than Henry in all of this? Arguably, I'd done worse, and not because I'd slept with Madison, but because Cade wasn't just my teammate. He was my best friend. Why the hell did I let my dick do all the thinking last night?

"But if we want to take Henry down, then we've got to be smart about it. Beating him up is exactly what he wants. That gets us benched, and then he's got the higher ground. Think about it."

"I don't want to think about it. I just want to punch him in the nose." Cade glared and pointed at my face. "He better not live with us."

I nodded. "He won't. There's no room on our floor, but I'll speak to Scotty when he's off the ice, just in case."

Cade shook his head, pulling his skates and the rest of his gear off before heading to the showers, muttering annoyances to himself. I leaned my head against my locker and closed my eyes.

Henry wasn't here to play games. Not on the ice, at least. I would figure out what made him transfer, but that wasn't my top priority right now. Madison was. She'd been hurt by Henry before, and now he was back. Someone had to tell her that he was here, and it felt like I was the only appropriate person to do it. Cade thought she trusted me after all and wanted me to see what was up with her, giving me the perfect excuse to see her without suspicion.

So I was going to do it. I'd see Madison, warn her about Henry, and then leave. What was the worst that could happen? I inwardly laughed because I knew damn well I was only making up these excuses in my head because I wanted to see Madison again. Even if it was for just a minute.

I had it bad. I knew that, and even though I wasn't sure how this was going to end, I couldn't stop myself from finding out.

CHAPTER 12

Madison

As I packed my laptop and notes away, I let the other students filter out of the lecture hall before I even attempted to make my way down the steps. With every move of my body, I felt an ache that I didn't think was normal. Sure, I expected a little soreness after my first time, especially with someone of Dash's size, but this felt different. My core clenched at the mere thought of him, and I couldn't move without a yearning I'd never felt before.

The only logical conclusion I could think of was that my vagina was pining over Dash. She missed him. How could she not? He was the perfect fit, and I couldn't blame her. Everything about last night felt right. The connection was more than I could ever ask for, and I knew he felt it too. We were meant to be together, but I wasn't going to chase him. Not anymore. I'd done enough. It was his turn to make a move.

"Is everything okay, Ms. Bright?" the TA, Kinsey, asked, concerned. It was only then I realized that I'd sat there so long that the next class had already started to filter in.

"Yes, I'm fine," I hummed, and stood, shuffling through the chairs until I made it to the stairs. "Sorry, I got lost in my own thoughts there." I smiled, flicking my ponytail to the side as I descended the stairs. Little sharp pains shot up my center, but I hid my wince with a skip.

The pain wasn't that bad, but it was serving as a constant reminder that I'd slept with Dash, which was making it hard to concentrate on anything but him. I couldn't figure out if leaving him was the gutsiest or stupidest move I'd made to date. He was right in the palm of my hands, and I snuck out with the sole belief that Dash would chase me. He'd sent me a few angry texts, but he didn't run to my dorm like I'd expected. I was upset with what seemed to be nonchalance and didn't know what to do next.

As I passed by a few students talking, a pair of muscular hands wrapped around my waist, and when I looked down, I knew exactly who they belonged to.

Dash.

Don't pee your pants, Madison.

My heart was beating fast with all the implications, and I wanted to squeal, but I didn't get the opportunity to because Dash's paw smothered my mouth.

"Shh. It's just me," he whispered as though I didn't already know. My vagina was doing a happy dance, and my toes would be too if they were on the floor. I was feeling light-headed because the way he huffed as he dragged me away from the crowd was making me more aroused than I should be in the computer science building. My back slacked against his chest because I was happy for him to take me wherever he wanted to go.

Turning, Dash dropped me, so my back was against the wall and slapped his palms against the brick, caging me in. Memories of last night ran through my mind, and I did my best to stave off the excitement. I scanned his body, noting that he didn't have a bag with him, which meant he didn't have my clothes. He wasn't here to give them back, which could only mean one thing: He was here to see me. Maybe he wanted to tell me that one night wasn't enough. That time was a linear concept, and we should break these archaic rules. I couldn't wait to hear his excuse.

I waited a good two minutes before clearing my throat and adjusting my sweater in order to hide the smug smile that was threatening to cross my face. He hadn't spoken. He just stared at me like a long-lost puppy waiting for my reaction. That was when I knew I really *did* have him by the balls.

"Was dragging me out of my class like a caveman really necessary?" I finally looked up at him, his eyes were dark and brooding. Strands of hair swept across his forehead in perfect spikes. Was that gel in his hair? Surely not. It must be wet from a shower or something.

"Just didn't want you leaving before we had time to talk about a few things."

A few things? That was the understatement of the century, but hey, I couldn't knock him. He scouted me out, and that was impressive in itself since he didn't know my schedule.

"Oh, yeah? What do we need to talk about, Big Man?" I enunciated in a way that made his eye twitch. Oh, this was getting good. I had him right where I wanted him.

"I came to tell you that, uh." He was stuttering, looking anywhere but at me. Was he trying to think of an excuse to see me, or was I thinking too much about this?

He dropped his head, closed his eyes, and took a deep breath. I had known Dash for nearly ten years now, and I'd never seen him like this with anyone. Taming a smile was the hardest thing I'd ever had to do because, when he looked back up at me, I could see it. The same want in his eyes that I had for him, but I wasn't done making him work for it.

I wanted him feral. I wanted him so desperate for me that he couldn't keep his hands off my body.

I raised my brow and said, in the most serious tone I could muster, "Oh, wait. Let me guess. Did you find my panties?" I scrunched my nose and bit my bottom lip. "They weren't still wet, were they?"

A growl emanated from his chest, and even though we weren't touching at any point, I could feel it through my body, all the way down to my toes. Turned out, I absolutely loved teasing Dash, and I could do it all I wanted now. We'd taken our relationship to a different level. One where we didn't have to skirt around awkward subjects. He'd been inside me. How much more intimate could you get than that?

"You make it awfully difficult to concentrate," he griped. Oh, how much I loved that sexy, snarly growl of his.

"And you make my legs sore. We've all got our strengths and weaknesses, I suppose."

That one got him. His arm flexed above me, and I couldn't deny just being around Dash made me feel a little horny. His smell. His unabashed masculinity. His smile. Everything about him made me want to rip his shirt off and let him take me any way he wanted.

Maybe this was just something that happened after you had sex with someone. Maybe you couldn't just hang out with them anymore. I wouldn't know, and I didn't exactly have anyone to ask.

"Why did you leave?"

"Leave? When?"

"Don't act dumb, Madison. You left my bed without a note or anything." He dropped one of his hands, and just as he was about to push it through his hair, he grumbled something, but the only word I could make out was "gel." So he *did* style it.

"I was only acting on our agreement. One night."

His eye twitched again, and it was obvious he was holding something back. Maybe he was just as annoyed about the whole agreement as I was.

"Yes, but you left in the middle of it."

"Did I? Because I distinctly remember you passed out next to me before I snuck out. What did you want me to do? Play with myself while I waited for you to wake up? Because, frankly, I was too sore for that."

He crushed his eyes shut and grumbled again, but I was still no closer to understanding why he was here, which led me to my own conclusion that it was because, as much as he didn't want to admit it to himself, he needed to see me.

"Madison. Why do you make it so hard?"

"What do I make hard, Big Man?" My gaze drifted down to his crotch, surprised that he was wearing jeans. He was more of a sweats kind of guy. In fact, the only time I'd ever seen him in jeans before was when he was…I took a sharp breath because jeans and hair gel. The only other time I'd seen him like that was at The Draft when he was trying to make a good impression.

Was he trying to make a good impression with me right now?

He pushed his hips back when he noticed my glare but didn't step away. He couldn't. I couldn't either. It almost felt like there was some force pulling us together whenever we were in close proximity.

"Do you ever not joke, Madison?"

I shrugged. "Having sex doesn't change who I am."

He looked over his shoulder just to make sure no one was listening. They weren't. I'd already checked. He turned back, dropping his shoulders on a sigh, before looking at me with pain in his eyes.

"You know, I came here to tell you something, but the minute I saw you, I completely forgot what it was." It was the most honest thing Dash had ever said to me, and for a guy who was usually discontented, he looked pretty distressed today. His eyes were skating over every point of my face, like he was trying to memorize it. Maybe he was. Maybe his intention was to come here and tell me we had to pretend last night never happened.

I couldn't deny that line of thinking was disappointing, but he hadn't said it yet, so I wasn't going to act differently until he asked me to. Instead, I pushed my chest out and smiled. "I've been forgetting a lot too recently. Little hard to concentrate when all I can think about is how good it felt to have you inside me."

"Madison." Dash's voice boomed so loudly that I heard it echo across the hall. He stepped back, knowing he'd drawn attention and bumped into his friend.

"Hey, guys." Alex, Dash's teammate and all-around bro, stood beside us with a big-ass grin on his face, completely oblivious to the fact that he was interrupting.

"Alex," Dash grumbled in his usual tenor, trying to act nonchalant as if he wasn't just caught encasing his best friend's little sister in a dark, quiet corner. I couldn't help but also notice the little adjustment Dash made to his pants. I'd affected him. Good. It was about time he started to feel the same yearning I had.

"What are you guys doing here? Alone?"

Huh. I underestimated Alex. I didn't think he'd have the balls or suspicion to ask that, but he had both, apparently. His eyes shifted between Dash and me, waiting for one of us to answer.

Dash's face went pale, and I knew what he was thinking. Alex wouldn't be able to keep anything a secret. He was too nice, and nice guys couldn't lie. That was a fact. Dash cleared his throat, ready to respond, but I took matters into my own hands.

"Alex," I cooed in my usual flirty drawl, opening my arms wide and engulfing him in a hug. One that I admitted lasted way longer than it should have. What better way to throw him off than to be extra flirty today? He would just think I was messing around. "It's so good to see you," I said, finally pulling out of the hug, and then I did something even I didn't expect. I threaded my hands through his dirty blond hair and messed it up like I was talking to a kid. "How you been, old sport?"

I could almost feel Dash's annoyance. Okay, I might have gone a little too far in the opposite direction, but I was here now, so I needed to keep going with it. Alex pushed my hand out of his hair lightly and chuckled, but there was uneasiness in his laughter. Not surprised. I'd be freaked out by my behavior too. We weren't that close.

"It's good to see you too, Baby B, but, uh, didn't we just see each other the other day? You're acting like you haven't seen me in years."

"Yeah, but you were on the ice, so it doesn't count. I didn't get to talk to you at the party, either." I pouted my bottom lip out, swaying my shoulders. "What are you doing in my neck of the woods? Shouldn't you be in the English department?"

With his mouth parted, his thick brow was still furrowed, but he seemed to relax when I smiled at him.

Swallowing, he said, "Yeah, I'm here because I just had a tutoring session." His cheeks blushed, and I wasn't sure why.

"A tutoring session? With a girl?"

"Yup," he popped out, and I threw a look at Dash from over his shoulder. It was the first time I'd looked at him since I went on the overdramatic attack, and it was obvious he was pissed. At least to me. I bet few people knew the differences in his facial expressions since they only ranged from a snarly scowl to a hooded glare.

"Isn't that sweet, Big Man?" I asked as I scrunched my nose, trying to look cute.

His only addition to the conversation was a grunt.

"It's not like that. I don't have a crush on my tutor," Alex replied flatly.

"Hear that, Big Man? I might still have a chance," I joked, elbowing Dash, but judging by his clenched fists, I was still skating on thin ice.

"So you didn't answer my question? What are you guys doing here, hiding in a dark corner, having secret conversations?"

Well, darn it. I really thought the overacting would have made him forget. I had to think fast.

I pointed my thumb back at Dash. "Dash just met me after class."

"He did?" Alex tilted his head and smiled, and he looked at Dash knowingly. What he knew, I didn't know, but whatever it was, Dash hadn't denied it. In fact, he almost seemed paralyzed in thought. "What kind of business have you got with your best friend's little sister, D?"

The smirk. The raised eyebrows. Yup, he was putting two and two together to make four, but I needed him to believe it was six.

"It's because we've been planning a party for Cade's birthday," I said quickly, trying to get him off the trail, but seriously, what the hell was I talking about? A birthday party? For my brother. It was ridiculous, but Alex's face lit up with curiosity, so I went with it. "Because you know, in the summer, Dash and Cade are probably going to sign their contracts with Atlanta, and I won't see them much, so I wanted to throw Cade the most epic birthday party he's ever been to." I opened my palm and pointed at Dash casually. "Can't throw Cade the perfect birthday party without his best friend involved, obviously."

Alex was nodding, and strangely, I thought he might believe me. Crap. Maybe this worked. Maybe I wasn't as bad a liar as I thought.

"But, and it's a really big but… You can't tell Cade because it's a surprise."

Alex raised his hand, doing some kind of salute. "Scout's honor."

I chuckled because, of course, Alex was a Boy Scout. With light stubble and perfectly cut hair, he was immaculate.

"Explains the secrecy. Don't want any of the guys telling Cade."

"Exactly," I replied brightly. I loved it when people inadvertently helped with my lies. "We don't want any of the guys accidentally ruining the surprise. You know, because Scotty can't keep a secret to save his life. But we can trust you, can't we, Alex?" I rolled the "x" in his name so much that it sounded like I said sex. Another grumble from Dash. I guessed he didn't like me flirting anymore. Interesting. Because this wasn't different from how I was before.

"Well, I'm sure he'll love whatever you have planned. You two know him better than anyone." Yeah, we did, but Dash knew me a hell of a lot better now. Was I getting territorial against my brother? I guessed so. I flittered my gaze to Dash, giving him a quick wink.

"Dash and I were just about to go to Covey's Cantina for lunch. Did you want to come? Maybe help us out with the party planning?"

Dash frowned, but I had to do it. If I wanted to keep us a secret, and I desperately wanted to do that right now because I didn't want any outside forces changing Dash's mind, then we needed to act like we normally would.

"Sure, why not?" Alex said with a shrug. "I need to up my carbs before the game tonight, anyway."

"Sounds great," Dash said through gritted teeth, and I knew it most certainly wasn't great. At all. But what was he going to do now? He wasn't going to leave me with Alex. There were too many things he wanted to talk to me about. So, he was just going to have to deal with it. If the burritos didn't convince Dash he couldn't live without me, then maybe teasing him with a game of footsie under the table would.

Chapter 13
Dash

"Dash also said no to laser tag," Madison said with her mouth dropped in mock shock.

Well, this wasn't going to plan at all. Here I was, sitting next to Alex, spitting with anger because of the way Madison was flirting with him, and I couldn't do a damn thing about it. I wasn't sure what had gotten into me, but I'd screwed this up badly.

I was supposed to meet Madison after class to warn her about Henry, but the minute I saw her, with her hair pulled back, looking fresh-faced and just showered after we'd been together the night before, I couldn't think straight, because all I wanted to do was mess her up all over again.

Suffice it to say, I still hadn't warned her about that idiot's presence because I was too busy monitoring her interaction with another teammate. Honestly, Alex hadn't done anything wrong, but I was so close to giving him a broken nose because she was giving him more attention than me. Madison should be solely focused on me. Preferably without a shirt on so

I could tweak her nipples, but I'd take her any way I could.

Sitting in a booth, Madison was on the other side of us, describing the most ridiculous birthday party I'd ever heard of. I couldn't believe this was happening. Not only was she flirting with the guy next to me, but she'd now essentially forced me to throw a birthday party for Cade. And as we'd already established, I hated parties and people, so my quiet time before joining Atlanta was looking to be completely taken over by this monstrosity of an event.

Madison laughed at something Alex said, and my breath caught.

The girl was driving me insane. I couldn't have her. I knew that. I'd told myself countless times that we needed to be friends. Hell, I even wrote out an apology on my phone to Cade, but when it came down to actually implementing any of my plans, I seemed to be stalling.

"Crazy, right? How could anyone say no to laser tag?" With her hands out to emphasize her disbelief, she had Alex engrossed in her fake plans. Her foot dug deeper into my thigh. Oh, did I also mention that she'd been playing footsie with me under the table this entire time, and I was supposed to keep a straight face?

Torture. It was absolute torture that Madison was putting me through because not only was her foot caressing my dick, but I wanted more. With every new item added to the birthday list, her foot would go progressively higher, so close to my cock that it was straining just to feel her.

Grumbling into my burrito, I took another bite, hoping that would hide my discontent. Thankfully, I was a grumpy asshole on the best of days, so Alex hadn't noticed much of a difference.

Sitting next to me, Alex had eaten his entire burrito and was watching Madison intently. So intently that he hadn't noticed the toes of her shoes were peeking out from under the checkered tablecloth right on my crotch.

I gave her a look of warning, but she didn't heed it. Instead, she pressed her foot down, caressing my cock more. Should I be surprised? She never did listen. She had to have been some kind of contortionist, because how the hell was she able to sit up even though she was toying with me like that? Seriously, her back was straight as a rod, and she had this unaffected smile on her face. There was no way anyone would believe that she was fondling a dick with her foot right now.

"Laser tag?" Alex glared at me with an upturned lip. "I know you have no idea how to have fun, but laser tag?"

Madison rolled her eyes. "Agreed. Dash is the king of all party poopers." That was it. I grabbed her foot and pressed my thumb into her ankle as a warning. If she was going to continue to taunt me, then I was going to get my own back. Madison's eyes widened in surprise, but she quickly masked it with over animated fake shock.

"He even said no to a dinosaur bounce house."

"Madison," I growled in warning as I pushed her foot away and dropped it as far from my body as I could. It was the first time I noticed Alex side-eyeing me, and I realized it was probably because I looked like I was jacking myself off under the table.

"I didn't say no to laser tag. I wasn't aware that it was an option." She'd taken this too far and gotten so detailed into this party planning lie that I already knew this was going to happen.

She raised a brow. "But you said no to the bounce house."

"That's because it's a bounce house, and there will be a bunch of hockey-playing men there. It will be ripped to shreds in minutes."

Madison raised a brow, her lip quirking in amusement. "Men? You really think highly of yourselves, don't you?"

I'd show her exactly what kind of man I was once we got out of this stupid lunch with my teammate.

"Honestly, you're missing out. This bounce house is not just any bounce house. It's awesome." She turned to Alex, knowing full well she'd get a better reception. "Like I said, it's the shape of a dinosaur, and you have to enter it via his mouth. Then, you go through an inflatable assault course in his stomach until you reach the tail, where you get pooped out."

"Sounds perfect for the king of party poopers." Alex elbowed me on the side, and I grumbled in annoyance. It didn't matter that this party was fake, I wasn't going to be attending it. It sounded awful.

"Cade's turning twenty-one. Not five."

"Anyone who doesn't want to relive their youth needs an injection of happiness," she said, and I stopped myself from smiling because I agreed. I needed her. She was the sunshine to my rain and didn't even appreciate it.

"Still, I think the whole thing sounds awesome," Alex said, looking over at Madison with approval. She smiled back, and the only positive thing I could think was that at least Alex was so focused on this imaginary party that he stopped putting the pieces together and working out what was really going on between Madison and me.

"Thank you. You know what? Alex, you're invited."

Alex raised his hand for a high-five, and Madison eagerly accepted. "You can be my date," he said jokingly as they dropped their hands. Madison laughed, subtly glancing over at me and winking.

"Well, that's great. We've got at least three people coming now." I rolled my eyes, wondering how much a pooping dinosaur bounce house would cost because that would no doubt come out of my signing bonus.

Alex took a sip of his drink but quickly drew it away because he started choking. I patted his back while he brought a fist to his chest, heaving in air. When his breathing finally steadied, he looked over at me with bugged-out eyes and red cheeks. The guy looked like a fish out of water.

"Everything okay?"

His eyes were frozen on me, and he nodded quickly. "I'm, I'm good." He didn't sound good, and his eyes kept shifting to the other side of the table like there was a giant spider on the booth that he was too afraid to tell anyone about. Even though his breathing had returned to normal, his cheeks were flaming with heat.

I looked to the side, trying to catch Madison's eye, but she seemed oblivious to my friend's sudden change in demeanor. She touched her phone, watching it brighten up, and her shoulders straightened. "Is that the time? Oh, whoops, I've got to get to my next class. I enjoyed this. Let's get together next week and plan this thing."

"Yup. See you soon," Alex squeaked out. Was he still choking?

Seemingly oblivious, Madison smiled. "See you guys later."

She slid out of the booth, and as she left, she brushed her hand across mine. My dick twitched. Damn it. I knew it was a bad decision to have sex with Madison, but I didn't realize that every time she'd touch me thereafter, I'd instantly get a boner. By the time she'd walked out and I'd stopped discreetly staring at her ass, I turned my attention to Alex, who was still red-faced and flustered.

"Alex, are you having an allergic reaction to the burrito? Your face is still blotchy and red. Can you breathe?"

He huffed out a breath and shook his head before swallowing. "No, it's not that. It's that." He pointed at the exit as though that was enough of an answer.

I looked at the door, then back to him, and realized that he must have figured it all out. How could he not? There was something going on with Madison and me. He could tell. Or he saw her caressing my dick with her foot because that was an obvious giveaway. "It's what?" I played dumb.

"Madison."

Well, that didn't work.

He turned his knees, so we were face-to-face and glared at me, waiting for an explanation. I scratched my hand across my neck, trying to figure out the best way to frame this thing with Madison that would ensure he didn't say anything to Cade before I had the chance to. "Yeah, about Madison."

"Did you know?"

"Know what?"

"Oh, god. How do I say this?" He scraped a hand across his face and then through his hair. He looked like he'd walked through a bush backward, but clearly whatever he needed to tell me was really causing him some turmoil, so I should try to treat it with seriousness.

"Just say it." I closed my eyes, waiting for the words, *are you sleeping with Madison* to come out of his mouth, knowing that I could deny that since technically we weren't sleeping together. Not anymore, anyway.

"I think I accidentally asked Madison out."

I popped open my eyes and stared at his guilt-ridden face. Biting back a laugh, I asked, "What?"

"Madison. I think she likes me, and I accidentally led her on with the jokey date comment."

Don't laugh.

He thought Madison was into him? Holding back my smirk was hard, and I crossed my brows, feigning concern because I had absolutely no idea where that came from. "Oh, really? What makes you think that?"

"She was flirting with me all day."

"Yeah, but she flirts with everyone. You know her. I wouldn't get yourself worked up over it." I slapped him on the shoulder, thinking that would slap some sense into him, but he looked just as worried as when Madison walked out. "What makes you think she's into you?"

He shuffled in his seat uncomfortably. "Well, you know when I saw you guys today?" I nodded. "She gave me an extra-long hug."

"Okay," I drawled out, remembering the raised brows he gave me while he was hugging her, but to be honest, I was too pissed off that she was touching him to really care. "Is that the extent of your evidence? An extra-long hug? Because I've got to be honest, I'm probably guilty of giving you those at some point, too. And as cute as I think you are, I don't have a crush on you."

"No. It wasn't just that." He took a breath in and pointed at the table. "Just now, after I made the joke about taking her as my date to the party, she, she, she played footsie with me under the table."

I completely froze because what the fuck did he just say? Madison playing footsie with Alex? That made no sense. Sure, she liked to say a few suggestive things every now and again, but play footsie? No. That wasn't like her, especially since she'd just been playing footsie with me. Unless…no. Surely, she couldn't have. But what if she'd gotten the wrong leg?

"Are you sure?"

"Sorry, Dash. Are you trying to get me to believe that you somehow managed to shrink your size fuckteen feet into a pair of cute teal Converses, so you could dig your foot into my dick from beside me? Because I find that hard to believe."

Double fuck.

"She rubbed your dick?"

He swallowed, closed his eyes, and nodded like he was admitting he had committed a murder. "She did, but I didn't do anything to encourage it. In fact, I just froze until she realized she was late for something."

"Oh." I was speechless, which didn't happen often.

"Yeah, oh. What the hell do I do? Should I tell Cade? Shit, he's going to kill me. The dude loves to fight, he just needs an excuse."

I needed to think fast. "Why would you need to? Nothing happened, just a little innocent flirting."

"Because when Henry cheated on her, he got a broken nose. Imagine if it came out that I asked her out and then let her rub my dick under the table."

I sat up with a tense jaw. He was right about being worried, but he was worried about the wrong person. It was me that was angry because Madison had no right stroking anyone's dick but mine.

Shit. Did I just think that? I had a serious problem on my hands.

"First, I was the one that gave Henry that broken nose. Cade had nothing to do with it. Remember that. Second, you didn't touch her or kiss her or anything. It was all a joke. What are you going to tell Cade? You think she brushed her shoe against your dick? Do you know how weird that sounds?"

He nodded, taking it all in for a second. "I guess you're right."

"I know I'm right. Wait it out. If any more weird things happen, then maybe you should speak to Cade, but until then, there's no point putting yourself in the firing line for no reason."

"Yeah. You're right. Thanks, man."

"Anytime. Now, I've got to get something in the dorm before practice. I'll catch you later?"

"Mhmm."

Alex waved me off, and I started jogging to the dorm for no other reason than I needed to let off some steam. Madison fondled my friend's dick, and it was making me rage in ways I couldn't describe. Was this how it was going to be with us from now on? Madison flirting with every teammate while I had to sit on the side and watch? It was more than I could handle and making it hard to think straight.

Dash: What the hell was that?

I texted her. There was nothing else I could do because she needed to know that there had to be limits. I had no idea how she was able to function after last night, but I didn't like how things were playing out.

Madison: Not sure what you're talking about, Big Man. I was just

having a little fun.
Dash: **By playing with Alex's dick?**
Madison: **What are you talking about? The only dick I've played with is yours, and let's be honest. I didn't get the opportunity to play with anything. I didn't even see it.**

She had no idea what I was talking about. My shoulders relaxed, and I blew out the breath that I'd been holding.

Dash: **Sorry to tell you, but you may have molested Alex at lunch. That was his thigh you were playing with at the end, not mine.**
Madison: ***Skull Emoji* *Skull Emoji* *Skull Emoji***

She didn't send another message for over a minute, so I sent her one.

Dash: **Now the guy thinks you're in love with him, and your first date is going to be at Cade's birthday.**
Madison: **Maybe I am.**
Dash: **I know you're not.**
Madison: **What should I wear? Do you think one of those inflatable dinosaur suits is too much? Might not show off my curves on our date.**
Dash: **You're not going on a date with Alex.**
Madison: **Aw, Big Man. You're not jealous, are you? Don't worry, your eggplant is still the only one I've experimented any recipes on.**
Dash: **I'm going to block you soon if you keep sending me messages like that.**
Madison: **You're no fun.**
Dash: **And you're driving me insane.**
Madison: **By the way, have you figured out why you came and manhandled me in the computer science department yet? You told me you had something to tell me but forgot. Had any epiphanies since?**

I shook my head because she was calling me out. She knew what I didn't want to admit to myself. What I still wouldn't admit to myself, because if

I did, what would that say about me? I came to tell her about Henry. I left fuming about her flirting with Alex, and I'm walking around with a boner that I can't get rid of because I can't touch her.

Without answering, I stuffed my phone in my jeans, grumbling when I couldn't shove it down far enough. That was another stupid thing I did today. Jeans and hair gel. I dressed up to tell Madison that her ex joined Covey U, because even though I was supposed to be telling her about him, I wanted her thinking about me. I wanted her to beg me for another round. I was holding myself back, yet she seemed completely fine with our arrangement.

This entire thing was a monumental fuckup, and the only thing I could do to tame any of my guilt or stop thinking about her was to go cold turkey. If I stopped talking to her, then maybe there'd be a chance that my dick wouldn't get hard at the mere thought of her.

Maybe letting her move on would be the best course of action. Then maybe she'd stop teasing me, and we could go back to the way things were before we had sex.

Fat chance of that happening.

Chapter 14

Dash

Madison: So, Big Man, I was thinking about you last night. Do you want to know what I was doing?

I shook my head, refusing to dignify Madison with a response. She was taunting me, and I was going to be forever goaded by her messages because I refused to engage. Two weeks had gone by since I slept with her, and although the world seemed darker because I knew I'd never experience something quite so good as her again, she was still somehow coloring my thoughts with visuals that I couldn't get out of my head.

Madison: Well, since you're shy to respond, I'll give you a hint. It involved a shower head and imagining what it would have been like if you'd used your mouth instead of your fingers on me that fateful night.
Madison: Too bad we never got that wet.

Case in point. Another day and another NSFW visual that would crop up in my mind at the most inappropriate time, giving me a boner incredibly hard to ignore.

Grumbling, I shoved my phone in my pocket and adjusted my pants so my half-mast erection wasn't on show when I left my room. This one-night deal was seemingly biting me in the ass at every opportunity.

My phone buzzed, but this time I ignored it. Giving any indication that her goading was working would make her worse. I knew her better than she thought, and I'd always admired her persistence, but she forgot that I was patient. She was the one that left me that night and was insisting we follow the rules of the pinkie promise.

When I stepped out of my dorm room, I immediately stopped in surprise. What the fuck was going on?

All twenty-two teammates were sitting in our living room watching a baseball game. I knew we were having everyone over today because that was what we did on our weekends off, but right in the middle of the horde of men was Madison. Nestled right in the center, she was eating popcorn, watching the Catfish game like she was their biggest fan.

"Guys?" I said to everyone, but my gaze was firmly on Madison and she knew it. A whisper of a smile played across her lips as she snuggled between Scotty and Alex. As per usual, Alex looked like a frightened deer caught in headlights, which Madison seemed to enjoy bringing out of him.

"Oh, hey, D. You're finally up. You ready to watch the game? Looks like it's going to be a good one." Erik raised his pizza slice from his slumped position on the floor. "We've got more in the kitchen."

He tipped his chin to the boxes of pizzas, but I walked straight past them, more interested in the blonde bombshell in the middle of the pack.

"I'm good," I quipped.

"Aw, is it because you're still holding a grudge against pizza because Cade made your room smell like a pizza oven for two weeks? The smell's gone now, I promise." Erik barked out a laugh at his own joke. Good for him, since everyone else seemed to find it as funny as me, which wasn't at all.

Cade was chomping on his own slice across the room and raised his hands in defense. "Hey, I thought it was helping him out. Who doesn't like to make out to the smell of old cheese? Besides, it clearly worked for you the last time you had Reporter Girl over." Cade's eyes bore into mine and his eyebrows wiggled. "That sounded like one hell of a time." I clenched my jaw, annoyed that he had to bring up Sienna again. "Come to think of it, Reporter Girl hasn't been around much. Have you been sneaking off to hers to get a little privacy?"

Instincts took over, and I couldn't stop myself from taking a quick glance at Madison. Yeah, she was pissed at that reference. Well, she could join the club, considering I was pissed that she was sitting in between my teammates whilst sending me dirty texts. What the hell was she thinking? Scotty already knew there was something going on, but what if Alex saw the texts?

Flat-lipped, I waved him off and found a spot at the end of the sofa beside Brooks. "That's not why I don't want pizza. None of us should be eating that kind of stuff during the season."

I was well aware that I hadn't outright rejected the idea I was sleeping with Sienna, but that was because I couldn't. If I did, Cade would then ask who I was about to finger against the wall, and I assumed the real answer could get me killed.

The reality was, I'd pretty much forgotten Sienna's name the minute Madison kissed me at The Draft. Madison clearly hadn't forgotten, though, and she might have enjoyed taunting me, but she didn't enjoy hearing about potential flings, no matter how fictitious they were.

"But we need the carbs."

I tried to play it cool and watch the game, but with Madison sitting next to Alex, and cozying up to him, I couldn't help but feel something in the pit of my stomach. Anger? Jealousy? Maybe a little frustration that she was still flirting with him now that we'd had sex, but what did I expect her to do? Become a nun after I fu-

"Home run!" Brooks, the only one of us that actually watched baseball, stood and clapped as Tate Sorenson rounded the bases.

"Look at him run," Madison crooned, bringing my attention right back to her. It wasn't like I didn't think about her almost every second of the day. What were a few more? "I swear those baseball pants are so see-through, it's obscene."

"Madison," Cade warned with a mouth stuffed full of pizza. He didn't look at her because he was too busy dipping his crust into some nacho cheese.

She thew her hand in the air, pointing at the TV accusingly as she glared at her brother from across the room. "What? You expect me to sit here and not comment on the fact that I can see every muscle of Sorenson's glutes? I know Dash has thighs of steel, but Sorenson is about ready to bust out of the seams."

There it was again. That pit in my stomach. That hot anger because Madison was focusing her boy-crazy attention on another guy. What was worse, she was comparing him to me. Her lips curved slightly, suggesting she was holding back a smile.

And that answered everything I needed to know. She was still taunting me. Even though we were in the same room with more people than I could count, she was openly goading me to see if she could get a reaction.

And I was concerned she was about to get one.

This was so wrong on so many levels.

Scotty leaned back so he could look her in the eye. "So, it's not just football guys you have a thing for now? It's baseball too?"

That made her slump her shoulders as her lips quirked into a smile.

"When they look like that, how could I not consider my options?"

"He's married," I deadpanned, drawing the attention of the entire room. Well, shit. That wasn't how that was supposed to go. Scotty rolled his eyes, leaning back onto the couch and shook his head. Okay, maybe that was a little too obvious. When I glanced at Cade, he wasn't paying much attention, seemingly more interested in his pepperoni slice than my anger over Madison's non-existent affair with a too old and taken baseball player.

"No, he's not," Brooks said, correcting me. "He's got twins with a woman that works in the Catfish marketing department, but they aren't technically married."

"Oooh," Madison cooed playfully. "Guess that means I've got a chance. Now the question is, do I want to be a stepmom this young?"

"Considering you live in California and he's full time in North Carolina, you might have trouble getting his attention," Scotty answered saving me from any potential embarrassment, I presumed. "Besides, you switched allegiances fast. I doubt he'll dump his baby mama for someone as fickle as you."

"Fickle?" Madison's mouth hung open as she stared at him in shock and disappointment. "Et tu, Brute?"

Cade hummed out his disapproval but didn't say much else. Instead, he stuffed his mouth with more nachofied pizza.

Madison nodded, conceding. "I know. I know. I just find it hard to focus when there are so many guys around." She elbowed Alex on her other side and winked when he gave her a weary look. The poor guy had no idea what he got himself into. "But let's be real, the hockey team will always be number one in my heart." She drew a heart in the air with her fingers and shimmied her shoulder against Alex's side, who was doing his best to pretend he didn't notice.

Wait a minute, was that sweat dripping down his temple?

"Can't a girl just appreciate the hours and dedication it takes to look like that?"

"I think I'm going to throw up." Cade hopped off the sofa and walked to his room without another word. With that combination of food, I wasn't surprised.

Scotty raised his brows and blew out a breath. "I don't know how your brother deals with you. If Amelia was this extra, I think I'd have a heart attack."

"Get with the times, Hendricks. I'm a young, independent woman, and I'm going to enjoy my youth while I can." She raised her nose in the air, subtly checking my reaction. I was just watching this conversation play out with annoyance but refusing to show it.

It took everything in me to turn my head away from her and watch the game instead of gazing at her beautiful face. Yeah, I was becoming a stalker.

"In fact, I'm going to enjoy my youth so much that I'm going to the football game tonight." The smug satisfaction in her voice immediately piqued my interest.

"No, you're not," I replied sternly and without thinking. All the guys looked at me with confusion. All of them except Scotty who was clearly bored with this cat-and-mouse game Madison and I were playing. He'd be having another conversation with me soon; I just knew it.

I ignored everyone else and kept my focus on Madison.

Her mouth was open, and she was doing her best to look upset, but she wasn't the best actress. "What do you mean I'm not going? You guys aren't playing, so I don't need to cheer Cade on. I might as well cheer on the Wildcats instead. Especially since they invited me as a special guest."

My lip curled because who the hell was inviting her to a football game as a special guest?

Was she still speaking to Adam and Devin? Or worse, had she decided to give Aiden a shot?

I couldn't stop myself from thinking about all the different things I was going to do to Aiden, and they were all ten times worse than a broken nose. "Does Cade know you're going?"

"Cade isn't my father, and I can do what I want." She waved her hand flippantly.

"Guess we'll see you there, then."

"Wha— Wait, who's we? All of you?" She pointed to the rest of the guys sitting around her. Most were ignoring her antics now since they were used to her, but I was watching. I was always watching.

"No. Me and Scotty. If someone's giving you special seats, then I'm sure they'll be able to wrangle a couple of extra for us."

"Oh, no," Scotty rolled out before falling back onto the sofa.

She looked between me and Scotty a few times, her mouth hung open like a fish. "You're not coming. This is my thing. I'm going on my own without chaperones."

"We aren't chaperoning you. We'll just be there."

Madison narrowed her eyes, and she finally got it. If she wanted to play games, I could too.

"Fine. I'll speak to my friend and see if he can get any extra tickets, but I'm not promising anything."

Friend? She wasn't willing to give up a name.

I glared at her in disbelief because I knew she was lying. "Great. I'm sure if he can't wrangle up the tickets, then we can use Scotty's name to get them."

"Great," Scotty said sarcastically. "Just throw me into this mess."

Madison knew she was losing, and I was going to cock block any attempt to make me jealous with the football team. So she scooted a little closer to

Alex, tapping him on the knee. When he met her gaze, she lifted her shoulder and batted her eyelashes at him. "Are you coming too, Alex? It'd be nice to have you there."

"I'll see," he replied hesitantly, and I shook my head, getting up and going straight to my dorm room.

"Wait, where are you going, Big Man?"

"To get ready. We're going in an hour," I reluctantly replied. Watching football on my only weekend off sounded like a nightmare, but I wasn't about to let Madison hang out with those football idiots alone. "Want to give your friend time to get those good seats."

When I opened the door to my room, I jumped back in surprise. "Why the hell are there always people in my room?"

Cade was sitting at my desk, cracking his knuckles like he'd been waiting for hours. It wasn't unusual for him to be in here, but that didn't mean I was happy about it. Cade watched as I made my way to my bed, grumbling about my lack of privacy.

"Please don't tell me you were using my bathroom to get through your nacho/pizza combo?"

"No." He laughed. "I'm here because I want to know if you've found anything out yet?"

"Anything out?" I raised my brows, trying to remember any conversation between us that involved homework. I'd been so focused on trying to stop Madison from teasing me that I hadn't thought about much else.

Cade lifted his chin to the door. "My sister. Have you found out who she's dating on the football team yet?"

Oh, shit. How did I forget about that?

"No," I said, thinking fast. "But I'm going with her to the game tonight. I'll be able to see for myself just how close she is to these guys."

"You are?" His brows raised in surprise. "Thought you hated football."

"It's not my favorite."

"But you're going for me." I nodded, letting him believe it. Then, he walked over to me and clasped my shoulder. "Appreciate it, man. I always know you'll have my back."

I gulped down the disappointment I had in myself.

Traitor.

It was a constant low whisper in my brain now.

This thing between Madison and me had to stop. It was like a slow hit of poison every time I thought about her. She'd be my downfall; it was just impossible to admit it out loud with her brother standing in the room.

"Why don't you come with us?"

Cade's brows furrowed, but it made perfect sense to have him there. It also blocked any possibility of me touching Madison. "Why?"

I shrugged. "Fun night out. Scotty's going. Alex might too."

He mulled it over. "What time are you leaving?"

"Soon," I replied curtly as he walked to the door.

"Fine, but it's only because I don't have anything better to do tonight."

Just as Cade's hand touched the doorknob, something came over me.

Traitor. Traitor. Traitor.

"Hey, Cade."

I was just about to admit it. Tell him the truth that I'd slept with Madison, and it would never happen again, but just as I tried, I couldn't.

There was more to the story than just sleeping with his sister.

I'd taken Madison's virginity. She told me she wanted it to be me. In telling my secret, I was also telling hers, and I wasn't sure that was fair. Not until I got her consent.

Fuck me.

I did this all wrong. Thinking with my dick instead of my head put me right in the place I never wanted to be.

"Are you sure she's with a football player? Have you ever thought that this was all a decoy and that she might be dating one of those guys out there?"

It was the closest I was going to get to outing myself, but a pretty damn big hint if he was willing to take it.

Cade pursed his lips and silently assessed me. Then he threw his head back and barked out a laugh. "Really? You think one of those guys is stupid enough to try something with Madison?"

"Why would you say that?"

He blew out his breath and laughed. "Isn't it obvious? That's the worst move any one of them could make. There are at least twenty thousand other people on this campus, and they'd choose *my* sister to date?"

"Why not?"

"Really? Do I have to explain it to you? You were there in high school when Henry did it. He was outed as a traitor then, and it's not surprising to me that he's had issues on his team since. It also helps that everyone's now seen what you did to his nose after, so I know for a fact that no one on the team is going to mess with her."

No one but me.

"Besides, they've seen firsthand how it fucked the team dynamic when Henry came on board, and we've only just gotten back on track. We all want to get into the Frozen Four, and the only way that's going to happen is if we focus on the task at hand—winning games. Sneaking around with my sister goes directly against that."

I nodded, silently taking in everything he said.

He was right. This was screwing with the team dynamic. Scotty knew about it and was so close to spilling the beans. Alex had somehow been drawn into this mess, which could potentially create a bigger problem. Telling Cade the truth felt insurmountable in the moment because I wasn't the type of guy that caused trouble. That wasn't who my mother raised me to be.

But as much as I tried to ignore it, my feelings for Madison were getting in the way of everything else.

"Good point."

"I'll go and get my stuff." With that, Cade left the room, unbeknownst to him, leaving me to fester in my own thoughts.

I fell back onto my bed and stared at the ceiling. My bedding was fresh, but the memory of Madison wrapped naked in my sheets would stain this room forever.

How the hell could I forget a night like that?

Why was it that every time I vowed to do the right thing, I ended up going against it?

Traitor. Traitor. Traitor.

I growled in frustration, covering my face with my palms and cursing myself for ever thinking I could just play it off as one night.

I needed to get Madison off my mind. But first, I needed to make sure she wasn't on any football players' minds either.

CHAPTER 15

Madison

"These are interesting seats for someone who's apparently the special guest of the football team."

Pursing my lips, I held off screaming at Dash because what use would that do? He caught me in a lie and was now gloating over it.

With his thick brow raised, he was waiting for me to answer. My lip curled and I was two steps away from growling at him. This entire situation was my own fault. I shouldn't have goaded him into a reaction at the hockey dorm, but I couldn't help myself. Watching him grumble was one of my favorite hobbies.

"Are they worried that if you sit too close, you'll be a distraction, or did you only get relegated to these seats after you told them you were bringing the hockey team? Are *we* too much of a distraction for *them*?"

Was Dash trying to be funny? Wow, things had gotten really bad for me if Dash was smug enough to think he could crack a joke.

I folded my arms in a vain attempt to stop from snarling, but it was hopeless. He knew he'd gotten to me, and if I didn't want to sit on his face so badly, I'd choke him out right now.

Tonight was not going to plan. I was supposed to be in my dorm right now. Relaxing and watching The Baseball Bachelor while I texted Dash obscene things, assuming he'd come to his senses and barge through my door and claim me as his, like in those old-fashioned romance novels. I was not supposed to be freezing my ass off at a football game, and I certainly was not supposed to be at this game with Dash.

"I can't believe you're here," I grumbled under my breath as I looked to the ground and scuffed the concrete with my sneaker. A chill ran up my spine and it wasn't because Dash's arm brushed against mine. It was because it was a little breezy tonight, but I refused to wear my sweatshirt since I was wearing the free T-shirt I got with the ticket purchase.

What could I say? I'd paid an extortionate amount for nosebleed tickets for everyone so that I didn't have to come clean and admit no one invited me.

"You and me both," he grumbled, back to his old ways. The only saving grace of this entire thing was that at least I wasn't the only one having a miserable time.

Cade barked out a laugh from the other side of Scotty, which only served to annoy me more.

"I also can't believe you brought my brother along."

That was an extra sixty bucks down the drain that I could have used on a manicure.

"That had nothing to do with me. He invited himself. He thinks you're sleeping with one of the guys on the football team. Although, I'm guessing these seats have made him realize what a ridiculous assumption that was."

I was going to kill him. Straight after having sex with him one more time, I was going to wrangle his neck and make sure no one could look into his pretty brown eyes ever again.

I sounded as unhinged as I felt.

"Did it ever occur to you that I might have agreed to a little fun with them? That maybe I was here to surprise them, and that you ruined that with your giant ego and not so giant nether regions?"

I glanced down at his sweatpants, lying through my teeth because I knew how big he felt when he was inside me; and although I hadn't been brave enough to look at the time, I could clearly see the bulge in his pants from here.

"Them?"

"Well, I do have more than one hole, don't I? Figured I'd make use of them all."

Thank goodness Scotty was in between me and Cade, so he didn't hear that, but honestly, Dash's reaction would have almost made it worth scarring my brother for the rest of his life.

Even though his jaw was clenched, and he was doing everything possible to tame his reaction, his face was turning red. Almost like he was going to explode.

"Stop it, Madison."

"Stop what?" I replied innocently. "My sexual awakening? Because I guess I should be saying thank you, Dash. You opened me up to new things, literally. Now, I'm ready to explore."

Stone-faced, he didn't find me funny, but that was good. He wasn't supposed to.

"Speaking of exploring." I leaned forward, looking between the three hockey players that came, surprised that I didn't also see another with dirty-blonde hair. "Where's Alex?"

"You scared him off last time," Dash replied bluntly.

"Did I? He seemed absolutely fine sitting next to me earlier."

"I'm guessing he didn't have a choice in seats." He'd be right. I plopped myself right next to Alex the minute I saw him in the hockey dorm, knowing full well it would annoy Dash the most.

Dash could be cold when he wanted to be, but I could see through it. He was going to keep pushing me away, and I was going to keep teasing him until he came to his senses.

"Besides, do you really think a guy like Alex could handle a girl like you?" He was staring at his phone, barely paying attention to me as he flicked through the *Chally Sports* app.

"What does that mean?"

"It means you're too good for any asshole in this college, and the sooner you understand that, the better my blood pressure will be."

It was the most casual declaration of love I'd ever heard. Okay, declaration of love might be a little strong, but it did sound like he was giving a coffee order instead of telling me I was too good for anyone else here.

Blowing out a breath, I subtly glanced over my shoulder to Cade. I wanted to push Dash more, but I didn't know how far I could take it with my brother around. I respected him enough not to kiss his friend in public, but that didn't mean I could get away with some other things.

"Dash." I purposely drew out the 'a' in his name because that was what I did when we were in bed together. Then, I looked back at him and batted my eyelashes.

That got his attention. So, with my back to Cade and Scotty, I gripped my neck and let my nails dig in ever so slightly. Taking in a sharp, almost moaning, breath, I said, "I'm so thirsty."

Dash's eye flicked to my throat, and his jaw tensed, but he refused to act like I was getting to him.

"Tell me about it."

Oh, he could act like I wasn't getting to him all he wanted, but his eyes gave him away. He was staring at my hand like it was wrapped around something else. Granted, it was a heck of a lot girthier than a dick, but Dash was getting the point loud and clear. So, I pressed the pads of my fingers down and let out the softest of whimpers. One I knew only Dash could hear.

His Adam's apple bobbed, but again, there was no change in his facial expression.

"Are you thirsty too, Big Man? Maybe you could get us a drink."

"What are you doing?"

"Nothing," I said innocently while stroking my neck. Up and down. Down and up.

"I'm just so thirsty," I said again, licking the corners of my mouth before biting at my bottom lip.

"Fine," he grumbled, and I stopped myself from smirking because I could hear it in his tone. I'd definitely gotten to him. "But I'm only doing it so I don't have to suffer through the boredom of watching Aiden continually miss throwing a ball to Adam."

"I doubt he misses much. I've heard some stories about him. Have you?"

"Yes, and he misses all the time. Particularly with the one girl he's actually interested in." Those words. Why did they sound so menacing, and more importantly why was I getting a little aroused at his surliness? "What do you want to drink?"

"A Crushie Slushy please."

"Those are only available at the rink."

"What? Why?"

"Clue is in the name, sweetheart. Crushie. They're the Covey Crusher's drink."

"But we're in California. It's always hot outside. Wouldn't it make sense to have them available?"

"I'm not standing here and debating Covey U's marketing strategy with you. You either tell me what you want right now, or I'll choose."

I raised my hand flippantly. "Fine. You can choose because if there isn't something to turn my tongue a different color, then I don't want it."

"I've got something that could do that for you."

His eyes were dark, and he hadn't stopped looking at my neck. My fingers were still clutching the skin there, and I frowned because I wasn't sure how to take that. Was he flirting? I must have been dreaming because this was Dash. He didn't flirt. But, then again, he was dressed, and that rarely happened in my dreams.

With his brows creased, he was still glaring at me, so I looked to my other side noting that Scotty and Cade were still in their own conversation, completely uninterested in ours.

Well, I guessed we could keep playing this game, then.

"Oh, yeah? Have you got something that could paint my tongue, Big Man?" I swiped my bottom lip and tucked it under my teeth.

"Yup. It's same stuff that could quench your thirst."

Did I just wet my panties?

"Uhh." Shit. I wasn't used to this. Yes, I was asking for it with all the flirting, but I had no idea what to do once Dash started flirting back, and in front of my brother, no less. It was so un-Dash-like.

"Are you propositioning me?" The thoughts going through my mind were obscene and I was finding it hard keeping it cool when all I wanted to do was jump his bones.

"No," he said plainly. "I'm merely suggesting that you get a Wildcat juice drink. It's purple, so will do the same thing that slushie thing does. Change the color of your tongue."

My shoulders slumped. Was I really this much of a horn dog that Dash could say anything, and I'd take it as a sexual innuendo?

His gaze swept over me, stopping at my crossed arms just below my chest. "You cold? Do you need my jacket?"

My nipples were no doubt poking out because I was freezing, but I was also stubborn and refused to get any help from a guy who was teasing me.

"I'm good," I quipped, and turned my attention back to the field. I hadn't been watching the game, but even if I had, it wouldn't have mattered. It wasn't like I knew anything about football.

"Great. So, Wildcat juice for you. Does anyone want anything from the snack bar?" Dash asked, getting Scotty and Cade's attention. I glared at the floor, too embarrassed at how riled Dash got me to look at my brother.

"I want something, but I don't know what. Let me come with you," Cade said before taking Scotty's drink order.

When they left, it was just me and Scotty. Scotty and me. I'd never been alone with him like this before, and it wasn't a bad thing. He was a nice guy, after all. It was just kind of weird. Something about being around him made me feel unsettled. It was probably because he was perceptive, and I had a feeling he knew there was something going on with me.

As we sat there, the quiet began to eat away at me. I was a nervous kind of girl. I didn't like sitting silently with someone I knew well, let alone a guy that was considered the star of Covey U. Why did he even come to this tonight?

Blowing out a breath, I leaned into Scotty, brushing his arm, and asked, "Got any idea what's happening down there?"

He turned to me, the first time since we got here, and looked confused. "With what?"

My smile was still forced, and I tilted my head toward the game below me. Was I supposed to be able to read names from here because it felt like I was watching an army of purple ants take on some red ones.

"You can't be serious."

"Yes, I can. I've been hanging around ice rinks my entire life. I've never had time to stand by a field and watch people in spandex grunting while throwing balls." I crinkled my nose, knowing full well that this answered the eternal question in my mind. *Hockey or Football.* I definitely wasn't a football girl. That much was clear. There was just too much stopping.

"Why are you trying to date a football player if you know nothing about the sport?"

"Do I need to know how to sing to enjoy music?"

"What does that even mean?"

I shrugged, acting casually. "Just making an observation."

"That makes no—"

"Um, excuse me. I'm sorry to bother you, but are you Scotty Hendricks?"

As if on cue, Scotty's smile widened, and he was ready to talk to this fan as if it didn't bother him that he couldn't leave his dorm without being recognized.

"Yes, I am."

The girl's face lit up and she elbowed the friend next to her. "I told you it was him. Can we get a picture with you?"

"Sure," he said, and I could almost hear the frustration in his voice, but they didn't notice. They didn't know him well enough.

"I'm happy to take it for you," I offered, and for the slightest of seconds, Scotty's smile dropped. He quickly pulled it back into a smile.

"You sure?"

I nodded.

"Thank you." She turned to Scotty and grinned. "Your girlfriend is so pretty."

"She's not his girlfriend."

A spike of pleasure ran through me when that grouchy voice filled my ears, and I instantly relaxed. Feeling his presence behind me, I tried not to swoon in front of these girls. Then, I felt him raise his arm, and it was getting harder to hold back my excitement. He was going to wrap his arm around me and claim me in front of everyone.

Only, that didn't happen. His arm went above my head, and he pointed to Scotty's other side. "She's that guy's sister."

Urgh. All those swoony thoughts went away with that one sentence. Relegated to Cade's sister again. Not the girl he slept with the other week.

After helping the girl with the Scotty selfie, I turned to Dash, refusing to look at him. I plucked the Wildcat juice out of his hand and slouched into my seat.

I hated it here. I couldn't speak to Dash. I couldn't concentrate on the game below, and as I took a sip of my drink, I realized that also tasted terrible.

When Dash took his seat, I immediately pulled my phone out, hoping I'd see some *Baseball Wives* spoilers so I could get lost for the rest of the night in an online forum.

"What are you looking up?" Dash asked, and although his face was staring straight ahead, his eyes were glaring down at my phone.

I brought it to my chest, clutching it tightly. "Why are you so obsessed with me?"

"Why are you always teasing me?" he muttered under his breath.

"Ooh, am I getting to you, Big Man?"

"No. One night, remember?"

Did I remember? Ha. It was all I'd been thinking about since it happened, but I was seemingly getting further and further away from my goal of making it happen again. Like Icarus, I'd played too close to the sun and got found out. Dash now knew I wasn't being chased by the football team, so why did he need to chase me? I was essentially there for the taking if he wanted it, and I hated that for me.

I wanted to make Dash feral. Like he couldn't live without me. I wanted him to realize that he didn't want anyone else but me.

Suddenly, the fans around us started to stand, and I breathed out a sigh of relief. "Oh, thank goodness. It's finished." Two hours had gone by and I'd learned nothing about football except that I hated it. Even sitting next to Dash the entire time hadn't made the experience worth it.

Cade, Scotty, and Dash all laughed at me.

"It's only halftime," Scotty informed me with a wince.

"Halftime? We've only watched half of the game? Does that mean I have to watch the same thing for another two hours?" I waved my hands at the field as I felt disappointment slither through my veins. This couldn't be happening, could it?

Another two hours?

With Dash gloating.

Not going to happen.

I was tired. I had no idea who was winning, not that I cared, and I was cold. So very cold. I didn't want to do this, so I needed to come up with an excuse to leave. The guys wouldn't care. They had each other, and they got the tickets free, so they should be thanking me.

"You know what? I didn't realize the game was going to be so long. I completely forgot that I have an essay to finish tonight."

"Really?" Cade threw me a questioning brow, and I didn't blame him. It was completely out of character for me. I pretty much got my work done the night I was given it, but excuses needed to be made.

I nodded vehemently. "Yes, I completely forgot about it until just now."

"That's convenient," Dash said under his breath. I stepped on his toe in retaliation. He didn't seem bothered. "I guess I'll have to walk you home." The reluctance in his voice irked me, and frankly, as much as I liked Dash, I didn't want him gloating the entire time.

"You're good. It's still early." I then turned to Cade. "If you need to see where I am, just check the app."

That seemed to be enough to get Cade off my back, and as I stood, I purposely brushed the side of my body against Dash.

"See you guys later." I gave Dash an extra-long look, knowing full well that I was going to get him back, and into my bed, if it was the last thing I did.

CHAPTER 16

Madison

Staring down at the most uninspiring nachos the cafeteria had to offer, I pouted my bottom lip out, feeling as lost and broken as the tortilla chips in front of me, because not only had I not slept in the last two days, but I was completely and utterly confused about what I should do next.

Dash stopped responding to my texts, and it was kind of hard to tease the guy you were interested in when you were almost certain he'd blocked you.

It was my own fault. I got too cocky and showed my hand. I'd embarrassed myself and now he had no reason to chase me when he knew I was right there, waiting for him to come back to me.

My head was hurting, my brain was too confused to keep thinking about it, and what made it worse was that there was no one here to get advice from. I couldn't keep hitting up Tiff with my every problem, she had more important things to worry about. All I could do was replay the memories of my one night with Dash together over and over again in my head. All the things he said, all the ways he made me feel special. It was all there, and if I put the pieces together in my brain, we fit, so why wasn't the puzzle making any sense?

Picking at the nachos, I grunted when the wind picked up, sending a chill through my Covey Wildcat T-shirt. The temperature wasn't too bad for November but sitting outside in voluntary exile sucked. I was hiding out. Avoiding the hockey team at all costs since I didn't want to see Dash and start babbling like an incoherent giraffe.

No one was around, but my face was heating because merely thinking about all the things I did to impress Dash was embarrassing. It was my first semester at college, and I was chasing my high school crush hard instead of focusing on being a strong, independent woman. I should be enjoying myself and meeting new guys, making new friends, and learning how to live life on my own. Instead, I was hiding out and letting myself be shackled to a goaltender who seemed to not be *that* into me after all.

I bit down on a soggy chip harder than I should have, biting my tongue in the process and cursing at the pain it left behind.

Dash's caring eyes came to mind, and I shook my head angrily because I wanted to stop thinking about him, but I couldn't. Was I like those werewolves in *Twilight*? Had having sex with a hockey player once made me imprint on him for the rest of my life? At least, I thought that was what happened in that movie. I was too distracted by all the abs to follow the plot closely enough. But either way, Dash seemed to be the only guy my silly heart wanted, and as much as I tried to entice him, it felt like he just wasn't that interested.

Nothing more was ever going to happen between us, and I needed to accept that. We kissed and had sex, but it was all part of an agreement. One no one else would ever know about. I was Dash's dirty little secret, and I needed to be okay with that.

My eyes were burning from the lack of sleep, and my stomach was churning from drinking too many caffeinated sodas. I checked my phone so often, that I received an alert asking if I was okay. I didn't even know it did that.

Out of habit, I glanced at my phone again, disappointed that the only unread message was from Tiff, asking me about the weather. Nothing from Dash. It was never from Dash, and the only way my little heart was getting through this was to tell myself that he was busy with hockey, because the reality of him blocking me was more than I could handle.

I shoved a nacho in my mouth, letting the burst of spice numb my thoughts for all of two seconds since my head was so fuzzy from tiredness and the sheer number of thoughts running through it.

Dash was trouble. The hockey team was trouble. Even more so for me because my brother was on it. I needed to let them go. Hockey boys were poison, and the only antidote was to stay far, far away from their asses…even if they were the tightest ones I'd ever seen.

"Madison? What are you doing out here? It's freezing." I dropped the nacho chip and looked up. The sun was shining, so I had to squint to see Adam's haloed head in the sunlight.

With his purple and white letterman jacket on, he had his hands in his pockets, clearly shivering from the cold.

"Adam?" I breathed out his name on a sigh because, was this a sign? I'd just affirmed that I needed to stay away from hockey boys, and out walked a *football player*. Not just any football player, one that looked like a literal angel with his blond hair and perfect features.

Shaking my head, I huffed out a breath because this was typical of me. Always jumping on my next boy crush to try to forget about the last guy who broke my heart. Although, if I was honest, the only one that really broke it was Dash. Henry was just something to pass the time, but Dash, well, I'd thought about Dash for years. I'd slept with him, and it was the best moment I'd ever experienced. Hell, I'd made up an entire life for us in my head, and the realization that it wasn't going to happen was the thing hurting me the most.

"You're wearing a Wildcat shirt?" He glared at the purple and white fabric with confusion.

I waved it off. "Yeah, I, uh, went to watch your game last week."

"You did?"

"Yeah," I drawled out, leaving out the fact that I was pretending to be sleeping with one of them.

"Should have told me. I could have gotten you some tickets."

"Too late for that now," I responded sarcastically. Not that he knew what I was referring to.

"Not gonna lie, you look a little down."

"Pfft." I pushed out a pout, trying to make my current situation funny to

THE DRAFT

ease the tension. "That's an understatement if I've ever heard one. Did you know I haven't washed my hair in two days?"

His brows creased, but he didn't balk at the admission, which was surprising because most people did when I started rambling like this.

"Okay. Any particular reason why you've been ignoring your hygiene?"

"Dash and I broke up." I could have told the truth, that I'd slept with Dash, and even though I was trying to win him over with my feminine wiles, it didn't work, but that was too long-winded. The outcome was the same whichever way you looked at it, so why not say that we broke up? It was how I felt, anyway.

Adam drew in a sharp breath and winced like I wounded him. "I'm sorry. That sucks. I know you really liked him."

Yeah, I did. "It's life. Should have known hockey boys weren't for me, I guess."

"Probably didn't help that he was your brother's best friend, either."

"Nope," I popped out, glaring at him with annoyance. "I guess you were right."

"I won't gloat," he said with such a straight face that I believed him. "Look, I've got to meet Aiden for lunch, but I don't feel comfortable leaving you out here when it's so cold. Do you want to come?"

Shaking my head, I pushed the nachos away from me and raised my hands. "Oh no, I couldn't impose." I also couldn't just hop from one athletic team to another, could I?

"You wouldn't be." He tipped his chin toward my nachos. "We're going to Covey's Cantina. The Mexican food there is a lot better than what you're eating now. Is that even considered real cheese?"

My nostrils flared as I glared down at my lunch and thought about it. "Probably not."

"Then come on. It looks like you need some cheering up."

He offered me his arm, and I stared at it for a few seconds. Hang out with a couple of guys talking football, or hang out here, wallowing in my own misery? Without another thought, I threaded my hand through his arm and let him help me up.

"Let's go," I said when I was fully standing. He nodded, leading me to the bar.

If anything, hanging out with them would be a good distraction from all the other stuff going on in my life. Maybe I'd even be able to stop thinking about Dash for a few minutes.

By the time we met Aiden and had food at Covey's Cantina, I could admit that I was having fun. So much so that I had to wipe the tears from my eyes because I was laughing so hard. Turned out, football guys were pretty fun when you gave them a chance. That was when Adam wasn't ragging on Aiden for having loud, hot tub sex, of course.

I was having fun, and for the first time in a long time, I hadn't thought about Dash. Wait, did thinking about not thinking about Dash count as thinking about him? Because if it did, then I was lying to myself because I'd done that a lot. But at least I wasn't in my room crying to Tiff, which was an improvement from last night. I was out; I was eating Mexican food, and I was laughing, which had to count for something.

"So, Madison. Are you joining us tonight?" Aiden asked, raising his brows mischievously. After hearing about all the pranks they'd been pulling on their next-door neighbors for the last hour, I wasn't sure I wanted to know what they were up to.

Adam leaned back and shunted Aiden on the shoulder. "No. She's not."

I might not have been sure if I wanted to go with them, but I didn't want that choice taken away from me.

"Where are you guys going? I might want to come." I sat up a little more confidently.

Aiden held his fisted hand over the table, and when I fist-bumped him, he said, "That's my girl."

"She's not your girl," Adam replied, flat-lipped and annoyed. "And when she finds out where we're going, she's not going to want to come."

"*She* can speak for herself," I replied with sass, because the more time I spent with them, the more at ease I felt. Sure, I was confused about Dash, but these guys made me feel like things were easy. Like I hadn't just potentially screwed up my brother's friendship for a quick lay. "So, where are you guys going?"

"To the Crushers game."

My smile dropped, and all that bravado disappeared. "Oh."

Aiden looked over at me with curiosity. "What's wrong? Thought your brother was on the team."

My brother and his best friend, who also secretly took my virginity. Not complicated at all.

"Doesn't mean she wants to watch him play every single game."

I couldn't help but give Adam an amused smile because it was nice how he was trying to make me sound less pathetic than I felt, but this conversation highlighted a huge issue for me. I would eventually have to go back and watch my brother play.

"Does this have something to do with the disgruntled goalie?" Aiden asked.

"I, uh." Shit. Was it that obvious? "How did you know?"

Aiden's lips curved. "Pretty clear if you look close enough."

"Says the guy who's told everyone Lyss is off-limits."

My gaze was ping-ponging between the two football players as they spoke. "Wait, who's Lyss?"

"Alyssa," Aiden drawled out pointedly, "is the neighbor who keeps pulling pranks on us."

Adam rolled his eyes. "Pretty sure the only reason this prank war started was because you wanted an excuse to rifle through her underwear drawer."

"That's just a perk of the job."

"So, do you like her?"

He didn't answer, but his pressed lips and clenched jaw did. "Never said that."

He was holding back, just like Dash.

"Didn't have to."

"Hey, Madison. I heard that Lyss was getting cozy with one of the hockey players at The Draft. Maybe you could help me reintroduce them." Adam had a glint in his eye, and he flicked his gaze to Aiden.

Tight-lipped, Aiden was doing his best to remain calm, but I could see the anger bubbling up in his jaw.

"Did you see who she was talking to, A?" Adam elbowed his friend but got no response. "Ah, you know what? I remember. His name is Scotty Hendricks. Do you know him?"

I smiled brightly. "Oh, yeah, I know him. He's a great guy—"

"—that Alyssa will never know because she's mine." Aiden said the words so flatly and casually that if you weren't looking at his face, you'd think he was joking. He wasn't, and an icy chill ran through my blood just seeing how protective he was of her.

It was kind of sexy, if I was being honest, and something about it reminded me of Dash. I just wished Dash would act like that with me. The only time he acted nearly as possessive was at the football game.

Suddenly, an idea popped into my head, and I looked between Adam and Aiden with a brighter smile than before.

Dash ignored all my flirting with the hockey team because he knew I wasn't being serious with them. But when I flirted with these guys at The Draft, he was completely different. He was feral and riled up to the hilt. Even just mentioning that I was attending the football game ticked him off enough to escort me, even if the outcome ended up being a shit-show.

Tonight would be different though, because this time, I'd actually be with the football players again. Would he be just as wild if he saw me with them? On *his* turf. It was just too tempting to not find out.

Oh, it was a delicious kind of torture that I was planning on putting my reluctant beau through, and I had to bite my bottom lip just to stop myself from smiling too hard.

"I want to go to the game." Adam looked at me with surprise. "What? I want to watch my brother." *And see Dash's reaction when I show up with you guys*, but I kept that tidbit to myself.

"You sure?" Adam looked at me with unease.

"Yup. I've got to go and watch my brother again sometime. At least you guys can make me feel better about being there. Let's do this," I said confidently because this was going to be even more fun than The Draft.

"Go Crushers!" I hollered and clapped, feeling, for the first time in my life, a little out of place. My shoulders knocked against the football players on either side of me while my brother skated around the rink for his warm-up. If I wanted to make an impression with the hockey team tonight, I certainly did that.

Cade did nothing to hide his snarl when he saw me walking in with the two athletes. I couldn't help but smile because if I could so easily convince my brother that I was dating one of these guys, I could only imagine the kinds of thoughts that would run through Dash's mind.

"Hey!" I hollered when some fabric landed on my head, messing up my hair. Grumbling in annoyance, I pulled it off only to realize it was my brother's practice jersey.

"Madison." Cade's voice took me by surprise, and when I saw him glaring at me from the board, he pointed to his jersey. "Put that on right now."

I laughed off his annoyance and flitted my hand. "Why would I do that?"

He flicked his gaze at Aiden and then to Adam. "They know why. You're a Bright. Don't let anyone take that away from you."

Then he just glared. Really. He glared at them for just standing next to me. Over-protective asshole.

Adam scoffed, and Aiden mumbled, "Challenge accepted," before Cade skated off, scowling at the guys as he did it. It was official. My brother needed to get a life.

"You're not accepting any challenge," Adam said, and I was lucky I was short enough that they could have an argument over my head that I didn't need to participate in. I stopped listening the minute the grumpy goaltender entered the ice because all my focus was on him.

Skating to the side, Dash hadn't noticed me yet, and I wasn't sure how I felt about it. I held my brother's jersey to my stomach, hoping that no one could hear the incessantly loud grumblings coming from it. I wasn't hungry. I was nervous as hell because I couldn't imagine how I'd feel if this didn't work. It was my last attempt at getting Dash, and I wasn't sure I was ready to accept that.

When Dash dropped to the ice and started stretching his legs, all those nerves in my stomach started to subside because I remembered what it was like to be under him when he did that move. Oh, how I dreamed about being that ice and to feel him pushing into me again. When we had sex, he was gentle, but I could tell by the way he spoke that he liked some things dirty, and I wanted to experience more.

Cade banged against the glass, making me jump, but I shouldn't have been surprised. He'd been stopping to wave at me every two minutes and point at his jersey because I still hadn't bothered to put it on. He'd never been this persistent before, so again, I could only put it down to him trying to intimidate the guys on either side of me.

I waved back at him dismissively, hoping he'd stop soon because it was getting mildly embarrassing. I was nineteen, for crying out loud. If I wanted to sleep with these guys, it was my choice. Not my overprotective brother who would rather I become a nun because he doesn't like to see me cry.

"Jersey on."

I gave him a placating smile as I watched him skate away. Lucky for me, he skated around Dash, who was still stretching. My core clenched as I watched him like some kind of voyeur on the internet. I swallowed, wondering if Cade's jersey would stop anyone from seeing me sweating because I was feeling hot and bothered by Dash's display. As I pulled the jersey over my head, I closed my eyes, hoping that little interlude would stop all the naughty thoughts running through my mind. But when I poked my head out and saw Dash now talking to Scotty, I realized it didn't matter what position Dash was in, I'd never be able to look at him again without thinking about what it felt like to have him inside me.

"Are you sure you're okay with being here?" Adam asked, glancing down at my fidgeting hands. To him, I looked nervous because I was worried about seeing my apparent ex-boyfriend, but in reality, I was nervous about what Dash would do when he saw me. He was broody at the best of times, but would this throw him over the edge?

"I'm fine. Why wouldn't I be?"

Adam raised a brow and then glanced over at the rink. "Because your secret boyfriend that you had an argument with is on the ice, doing some mildly erotic stretches."

"He's not my boyfriend." I played it cool, pretending I hadn't been watching him. I subtly glanced over again, surprised that he went back to those stretches. I thought he'd finished.

"Made you look," Adam teased, elbowing me in the ribs.

Rolling my eyes, I pushed his shoulder, but he was so solid I ended up pushing myself into Aiden, who lifted his drink up and out of the way, careful not to spill any on me.

"Sorry," I mumbled, gaining my footing.

Aiden brought his drink down, taking a sip as he raised a brow at me.

"Trying to make your little goaltender jealous again?"

"He's not little. He's six foot six."

"He can join the club. We're all six foot six here."

Adam groaned and rolled his eyes. Leaning over the front of me, he said, "Shall I get the tape measure out? We can check."

"No need. I'm not as precious as you, Mr. Five Foot Eleven."

"I'm six feet."

"That one inch is really important to you, isn't it, Adam? Guess when you don't have many, you've got to cherish the few inches that you do have."

Grunting, I asked, "Is this really how guys talk to each other?"

"Yes," they said simultaneously.

I rolled my eyes and sat down because these guys were making the hockey team look like intellectuals, and I was tired of listening to their macho babble.

Thankfully, the music quieted down and the game started, which meant I could have a little time to myself. Dash's helmet was down now, and he was focused on the game, so getting his attention would be hard. Should I even try? Distracting a player wasn't normally my style, but if that was the only way I was going to get him to notice me, then what else could I do?

Following the crowd, I took my seat and leaned into Adam. He looked down with interest.

I cleared my throat before adjusting my jersey. "If I, uh, wanted to make a certain someone jealous, would you be able to help me?"

Adam narrowed his eyes, looking uncertain. "But they're playing—"

"I'll do it," Aiden said cheerfully from my other side, and when I turned to him, he was grinning eagerly. "Might tick off your annoying brother, too."

"It's your funeral," Adam mumbled, sinking into his seat while he took a sip of his drink.

What was Adam so scared of? He acted like it was wrong of me to poke the proverbial bear. As though Dash would do something crazy, but what was the worst that could happen? He was on the ice, and we were out here. It wasn't like he was going to break through the plexiglass to get to me. He couldn't without making a scene and outing us to my brother, breaking the pinkie promise.

No. He was going to have to watch and see how it felt when he thought I'd apparently moved on from him.

Licking my lips, I relaxed into my seat and smiled because it wasn't going to be long until Dash noticed me here.

CHAPTER 17

Dash

Gripping my stick, I watched the puck intently as it moved from player to player. We were two minutes into the second period, and I'd barely had to defend the goal because my team was on the attack today. Scotty and Erik had scored twice already, making this a potentially easy win if I could continue to keep any of Brighton U's attempts out.

But just as Erik passed the puck to Scotty, a Brighton U player intercepted it and skated toward me with ease, knocking off Cade and Brooks on his way.

I was up. Squatting into position, watching the puck closely, ready to stop any goal attempt.

As it was passed from player to player, I lost my focus when Cade bashed one of the opposing team against the boards. The boards right above...wait a minute.

What the fuck was she doing here?

Buzz.

I closed my eyes and clenched my jaw in anger because they just scored. I took my eye off the puck for one second, and it ended up in the back of my net.

Grumbling, that wasn't even the thing annoying me most.

"Dude, what happened?" Scotty asked, but I wasn't concentrating enough to answer. I was furious, and ready to break the plexiglass to get into the crowd.

Mine.

That was all I could hear in my brain, blaring like it was being shouted through a megaphone because what the fuck was Madison doing here with Adam Hartley?

Scotty gave me a push, forcing me to look at him. When I did, he pointed in Madison's direction with his stick. "Is this about Baby Bright and the fact she's got a new boyfriend?" He yelled loud enough that if Cade was near us, he would have heard it.

Something emanated from my chest. Something I couldn't stop, and something that sounded a lot like an overprotective growl. Madison was not dating Adam.

Madison was mine.

Sure, the guy had been sniffing around her since that stupid Draft event, but if he thought he could just take her, he was vastly mistaken.

"He's not her boyfriend." I was just as loud back, almost hoping Madison could hear it from her seat, but she wasn't even looking at me. She didn't care that I was down here, playing a game, *losing* the game because she was here with someone else.

"Neither are you."

Scotty's words should have been the dose of reality I needed to get my head back in the game, but it wasn't working. Not today. Not after everything. After the way she acted at the football game, I genuinely thought she was bluffing about her friendship with Adam. But here she was, rubbing it in my face.

I pushed my face mask up because I wanted a better look at her.

Madison was smiling, laughing at something Adam said. I kept staring, unable to stop myself from watching her. It was like a car crash and worse than before. When our eyes connected, she froze, and that pretty smile of hers dropped. I stared at her for longer than necessary, trying to prove a point. What that point was, I wasn't sure yet, but I was definitely making it.

Scotty shoved me. "Dude. You're making it obvious."

He skated away, but I couldn't stop myself. I was still staring at her, trying to convey a message that I hoped she'd be able to interpret. Oh, what a dangerous line she was walking with her choice of companion.

Madison eased into her seat, smirking as she smiled at Adam. She knew she was getting to me, and I was powerless to stop her from doing anything. When she looked over her shoulder to her other side, I frowned because she was smiling at Aiden.

When did he get here?

Was she here with *both* of them?

A football sandwich. Wasn't that what she said she wanted before? I swallowed down my anger because all I could think about was them having a threesome after the game in Aiden's infamous soundproof bedroom.

Okay, I was at the point where I was going to break my hockey stick with how hard I was gripping it through my gloves.

Madison's eyes widened when she seemingly confirmed it was her I was staring at. Should have been obvious, really. She was the only thing worth looking at in this entire rink.

She masked her surprise by licking her lips, and then I could have sworn she cuddled up to Adam.

I fully expected Adam to wrap his arm around her and kiss her on the forehead, but something even more disturbing happened.

Aiden tugged at her Crushers jersey, making her fall into his hold. She laughed, slapped his chest, and snuggled in.

What the actual fuck was going on?

I had to be dreaming because this was a nightmare that I couldn't believe Cade was allowing. His sister and the biggest lothario on campus were snuggling, acting like they were on a date. As her nails scratched against Aiden's shirt, Madison kept her gaze on me, challenging me to do something about it.

But what could I do?

My jaw clenched and I dropped my stick in frustration, accidentally hitting the player who just scored.

"Need glasses or something? It might help you actually see the puck next time," he taunted as he skated past.

Not one to let that slide, I pushed him to the ice before he knew what was coming. I was the unassuming player on the team because people expected the goalie to guard the goal with their life and stay out of fights, but I wasn't in the mood for that today. Today, I refused to ignore his taunts because I wanted to hurt something, and he just so happened to be there.

He crumbled to the floor, groaning out in surprise, and as he lay on the ice, I ignored his flailing form because I was still staring at Madison.

"I fell on my stick, you moron."

Was he talking to me? I didn't care. He'd soon learn that the only reason he scored was because my girl was in the crowd, trying to act like she wasn't my girl.

I didn't have time to think about the fact that I was calling Madison my girl in my head because someone pushed me so hard into the top of the net, we dislodged it and hit the boards behind. My side bent unnaturally against the pole, but before I could even finish bouncing off it, another Brighton U player pushed me from behind.

I threw my stick in the air, knowing I was in trouble. When two more players shoved me, I realized I was surrounded. Guess I shouldn't have taken so much joy in knocking over their asshole teammate. After a few more shunts, I dropped to the floor, letting them think they pushed me to the ground, and ended up at the bottom of a dog pile while players tried to land blows that didn't hurt.

At some point, my helmet came off, so I stayed still just in case a rogue skate came my way. Blow after blow, I took the hits because I had no other option. It wasn't that painful, but the more time I spent in this pile, the less time I had to watch Madison.

The pile started to get lighter, and I heard the whistle blow, so I knew it was only a matter of time until I was out of here.

"Don't you ever fucking touch our goalie again!" Cade yelled, pushing two of the guys off me and forcing them to the ground.

The refs had blown the whistle a while ago, but no one had listened. Cade offered me his hand to help me on my feet, and as I got back up, I realized that Scotty, Erik, Brooks, and Alex had all been relegated to the sin bin for apparently fighting the rest of the team.

Cade tossed me my helmet and I caught it with ease. "You okay?" he asked, skating around me.

"I'm fine," I gritted out because it just had to be Cade that saved me, didn't it? The one guy who was always there for me. Even in my darkest hours, he was the one who unknowingly saved me. And yet, I was more than willing to betray him at the drop of his sister's bra.

"Okay, then let's stay focused and make sure we beat these assholes." With tight, flat lips, I nodded.

Stay focused.

He was right. That was what I needed to do. Too bad his sister was so damn distracting. She'd done this on purpose just to taunt me or maybe prove to me that I wanted her. I didn't know. It didn't matter because it got the reaction she wanted.

She was mine, and right after finishing this game, I was going to prove that to her.

I tossed my gloves into my locker, stewing in my own anger because that was the worst game I'd ever played. Frankly, I couldn't believe Coach kept me on the ice. My teammates were congratulating each other over the win as they walked out of the locker room, ready to celebrate at Covey's Cantina, but I was in no mood for celebrating. I'd nearly blown it for us by letting Brighton U score another two points. Thankfully, Scotty and Alex were on fire tonight and managed to keep us ahead, but the game was close. Too close, and it was all because I lost my focus over a girl.

It was pathetic. *I* was pathetic. I'd never let anyone break my concentration like that during a game, but I couldn't think straight. I still couldn't. Just remembering the way Aiden's arm clasped around her shoulder made me want to kiss the shit out of her and claim her in front of everyone. Even Cade.

What the fuck was Madison doing to me?

Blowing out a breath, I took my jersey off in an attempt to remain calm. When that did nothing, I removed the chest padding and placed it on the bench. Nope. Still nothing. I still had that hot heat sitting on my lungs, getting warmer with every inhale.

She was fucking mine, and I vowed that I wouldn't let her attend another game without her wearing my jersey because everyone needed to know that fact.

Mine. Mine. Mine. Mine. Mine.

Pulling my gloves off, I gripped the fabric before tossing them into my locker because that was the only way I could vent my frustration.

Scotty walked into the room and stopped in surprise when he saw me. With his hair slicked back, in his casual gear, he looked ready to celebrate or go on a date.

"What are you still doing here?" I'd ask him the same thing, but that would make him think I cared, and I didn't. I really didn't.

I turned my attention back to my locker, looking at the pile of pads as though they'd somehow give me the meaning of life.

Scotty took a few steps toward me. "Dude, don't beat yourself up over those goals you let in. It's just one game. You'll bounce back," Scotty said with a pat on my shoulder. When I looked up at him, he backed away and laughed nervously. "Umm. I'm guessing this has nothing to do with the game if your face is anything to go by."

"I missed a few pucks, but we still won, didn't we?" I griped before turning and sitting on the bench so I could take the shin pads off.

Scotty raised his hands. "Okay. Well, sorry I asked."

"Where's Cade?" I looked around the locker room for that asshole. I needed to talk to him because he was still blissfully unaware that I was so infatuated with his sister that I was thinking of all the ways I could claim her as mine in the rink. Most were indecent and had broken a resolve in me. It was high time I let her brother know what my intentions were because this feeling wasn't going away anytime soon.

"Oh. Is this still about Baby Bright?"

I pinned him with a glare because he was loud enough for anyone to hear if they were walking in. He winced, looking around before mouthing, "sorry." My facial expression was enough of an answer for him.

"Dammit. I'm a bad friend. I guess I assumed she'd gotten bored with your brooding and dumped your ass in favor of the brooding asshole on the football team. I thought that's why you were annoyed today."

"Madison's still mine."

"Might want to tell her that," he mumbled before wrapping his arm around my shoulder. "In fact, maybe you should come to Covey's tonight and tell her. Pretty sure that's where she's heading with Aiden and Adam."

"I'm not going there."

"Why not?"

"I hate going out, and I hate people."

"Oh, we're back to that again. Angry and menacing under your curtains."

"They aren't curtains." I threw the rest of my pads in my locker. I needed to get out of here. I needed to think, and it wasn't happening in this place. The rink had too many memories associated with Madison, and it was making my brain fry. "And I'm not going to the bar because if I see anyone on the football team, I'm going to punch their lights out."

Scotty drew in a sharp breath. "Yeah, please don't do that. That will get you at least a semester suspension, and you're the best goaltender we got. Save for the last few games, but we all have a few off streaks."

I quickly shoved on my clothes, not caring that I stunk because I hadn't showered yet. I needed to get out of here. Stuffing everything except my phone and wallet in my locker, I slammed it shut and locked it before pushing past Scotty.

"Where are you going?"

I glared at my friend, pinning him with a look that surely made it obvious. "To find Madison. I need to talk to her."

Scotty threw his head back, barking out a laugh. "Good luck with that. I hope you catch her before you find her making out with a football player."

Mine. Mine. Mine. Mine.

I had a one track mind when it came to Madison, and I bit my tongue, tasting blood at the mere thought of Madison kissing one of those guys. I sunk my teeth in further when I thought about them touching.

Madison wasn't going to be with anyone but me. That girl was so mine. She knew it. I knew it. I'd just been fooling myself, thinking that I could get over her by telling her I wasn't interested and ignoring her. That was a mistake. That just made her push me harder.

"Just remember, we're getting on a bus at four a.m. for the airport tomorrow. Hockeyfest waits for no one."

I waved him off but didn't look back because I only had one thing on my mind. Find Madison. Pulling out my phone, I opened the same app I used before to check her location. It was the app Cade forced me to download when we were in high school that let me know exactly where she was at any moment. I wasn't sure how I'd gained permission to have Madison's location, but I assumed it had something to do with Cade granting me access just in case Madison blocked him or her parents. Like she'd ever do that. She loved her family and had nothing to hide.

Except for me, of course. Now, she had to hide because there was no going back. I wanted her, and she just needed to get on board with it. I smiled and pinched the screen to zoom in on that little pin. It was still in the building, and when I zoomed in further, I knew exactly where she was.

I pushed open the door, grinning to myself because it was the first time in weeks I felt like I had a purpose and knew what I was doing. I was approaching the pin, and when I heard two familiar voices, I immediately looked up.

When I saw what was going on in front of me, I was ready to kill him.

CHAPTER 18

Madison

I gnawed on my bottom lip as I walked down the now-familiar hallway. My stomach was churning, and it wasn't because of the overly soggy nachos. Although they *might* have played a tiny part in it.

Was I doing the right thing by coming behind the rink uninvited?

When the game ended, Dash grumbled his way out to the locker room without a second glance at me. I couldn't deny I was disappointed. It felt like all that anger and frustration he was throwing my way the entire game had completely dissipated. My stomach fluttered at the mere thought of his face when he realized I was sitting with a couple of football players. The same players he mocked me about last week. From that point on, he watched me intently. It was like he wanted to kill me. Or eat me. I couldn't figure which it was. That scowly face always made it hard to decipher his emotions since he used it for pretty much all of his expressions.

It was funny. I'd always thought of Dash as focused and determined when it came to hockey. I'd never seen anything hinder his performance, but it was fair to say, that something *was* hindering his performance.

"Dash was watching you more than the puck."

Adam's words rang through my mind, giving me the confidence to walk through this hall like I owned it. Ever the gentleman, he offered to walk me home after the game, but I declined, deciding that my efforts would be better utilized here. Plus, I wanted to see Dash.

How could I not want to see my brooding goaltender?

Honestly, I also figured if I didn't show up back here, he'd likely follow me and make a scene. As much as I wanted him to claim me like that in front of everyone at Covey's Cantina, I knew it wasn't the right move. Dash would eventually freak out because he hadn't told Cade first, and it could ruin any potential long-term plans I had with him.

I slowed my steps and cursed myself because I couldn't shake off this nervous energy. I was going to see Dash, and I needed to act like it didn't bother me. At least, that was what I thought Sienna would do in my position, and since I'd gone this far with that motto, I figured I should keep going because I didn't want to look like a fool.

"Madison, hey."

That voice made me stop. Why did it sound so familiar?

Stunned. I shut my hanging mouth and gulped when I saw my high school ex standing in front of me with a wry smile on his face.

I tripped on my own feet even though I was standing still, and my face bloomed, but I wasn't sure why. It wasn't like I was still pining for him, but maybe it was because I wasn't expecting to see him while I was trying to act like someone who was super confident.

"H-Henry. What are you doing here?"

A heads-up that Henry had transferred here from Dash or Cade would have been nice. He tugged at the purple bag over his shoulder and chuckled as he flicked his wet hair out of his face. Blinking, I swiped away the sprinkles of water that splashed across my cheeks. "I was sitting on the bench waiting for Coach to call me up. Guess I'll have to wait until our next game."

"No, I didn't mean that. I figured that you somehow made it onto the Covey U hockey team." I pointed to the floor as if that would explain the question. "I meant, what are you doing here at Covey? I thought you went to SoCol?"

He scratched the back of his head, letting out an uneasy groan.

"Yeah, I tried it out for a couple of months, but, uh, I just realized I'd made a mistake." A smile tugged at the end of his lips as he took me in. "You know, I've been trying to talk to you since I got here. You're studying computer science, right?" I nodded, and he let out a soft chuckle. "I am, too. Thought I saw you the other day in the lecture hall. I wanted to say hi, but you looked a little busy, so I figured I'd probably catch you at a game."

"You wanted to speak to me?" My voice was high-pitched in surprise. "We didn't talk the last two years of high school. Why would you want to speak to me now?"

"Just thought it would be nice to have a friendly face around."

I raised a brow. "If you think my face is friendly, then your team must hate you."

His smile dropped, but I didn't feel bad about saying it. It was true. It might have been a while since anything happened between us, but he never apologized for what he did. This was the most he'd talked to me since the whole incident, which I assumed was because Dash and Cade had warned him off, but it didn't make it any easier to get over being humiliated so publicly by him.

Henry pulled a strained smile, masking the uncertainty of my reaction. "It's early days with the team. Once I gain their trust, it will be better. Some players have it in their head that I'm trying to mess up their line."

"Gee. I wonder where they got that idea from."

"What do you mean?"

"Isn't that the only reason you 'dated' me in high school?" I didn't like mentioning the complete fiasco that was my love life because, honestly, it just embarrassed me, but he was here, seemingly oblivious to why the Crushers might be less than happy about it. So I'd point it out, loud and clear.

Henry tilted his head, looking at me with confusion. "Is that what you think? That I dated you because I was trying to tick off Cade?"

I pursed my lips, not needing to respond. He could see the answer across my face.

He shook his head, laughing humorlessly. "Wow. People really do have a low opinion of me, don't they? I didn't want to screw up my team. Why would I do that when the dynamic directly affected my future career prospects?"

Now it was my smile that dropped because I hadn't thought about that.

"Might be hard to believe, but I liked you. I thought you were hot, and I asked you out thinking you'd laugh in my face. The hockey team and Cade were the last things on my mind when you said yes. I just wanted to impress you."

"Then why'd you..." I couldn't finish the sentence because we were still in the middle of the hallway, and anyone could hear. However, I doubted there were many players that didn't know about this already.

"Cheat?" He raised his brows, saying it more confidently than I ever could. Sighing out, he looked to the side before bringing his attention back to me. "This wasn't the way I wanted to have this conversation, but honestly, between Cade and Dash, I think this might be the only time I get with you." He scratched the back of his head, taking his time. "Look, I probably should have said this before, but I'm sorry. When I look back on that time in my life, I'm embarrassed. I cheated on you because I was an insecure, scared little boy. Back in high school, you were this perfect girl. The one everyone liked, who was off-limits because of her brother. But here's the thing, that wasn't all you were about. You were smart and kind, and when I started talking to you, I never thought you'd actually like me back, much less agree to secretly date me."

My heart was racing, and I could feel my ears burning as I listened to everything he was saying.

"Honestly, I didn't think I was worth your time. I'm not worth anyone's time. I'm not even sure I'll be able to get drafted this year, which sucks."

"Henry," I breathed out. "Don't think like that. The draft isn't the only way to make it in the NHL. There are so many other opportunities."

He laughed bitterly. "I hope so, but that's not where I was going with this. For a very long time, I felt like I wasn't worthy of anything. It didn't matter how hard I tried, I would always be destined to fail, you know? Even at Southern Collegiate. I tried my hardest for that team, but did you know that everyone who attends that school is pretty much a grade A asshole?" I shook my head, surprised at just how candid he was being in the middle of the hallway.

"Honestly, after just three weeks, I knew it wasn't the right fit. That was when I realized that I was the owner of my own destiny, and if I wanted a shot at being a professional NHL player, I needed to get out of there and play better. Where better to play than their division rivals? Must admit, I look forward to taking them out this year." A wry smile grew on his face, and he almost seemed lost in thought.

"So that's why you're here? Because you want to get better prospects?"

"Yup. Nothing as scandalous as Dash or Cade would have you believe. I'm just here, trying to make it like everyone else. But that's my point. I have a habit of self-sabotaging and I think that's what happened with me and you."

My ears prickled because it seemed like he thought about this a lot when I genuinely thought he didn't care about me at all.

"I always knew you were out of my league, and it would never end with a happily ever after, so I self-sabotaged. Why not act a certain way to prove you're not worthy than have someone else tell you?"

I laughed awkwardly. "I think you put me on quite a high pedestal there." I was being honest, not fishing for more compliments, but something about hearing Henry's explanation made me feel better about how things went down.

"Everyone did. You're Madison Bright. Beautiful, sweet, and smart Madison Bright."

Oh no.

Now things were starting to feel weird. His gaze was locked on me and he had this goofy smile sprawled across his lips. Was he about to declare his undying love for me?

I took the tiniest of steps back, easing away slowly to not draw attention to myself. Henry seemed like a nice guy who'd learned his lesson, but I would never go back there. Not when I had the possibility of Dash at my fingertips.

"Madison."

My blood ran cold, and my stomach pitted out when I heard Dash's emotionless, dark voice say my name. I leaned to the side and stood on my tiptoes so I could look over Henry's shoulder, and sure enough, Dash was a few feet behind him. Angry and brooding, his chest was heaving, and as hot as it was, I didn't want to have the conversation we needed to in front of my ex.

Holding my finger up to Henry, I narrowed my eyes and said, "You know what? Can we talk about this later? I've got a goldfish I need to feed."

Just like that, I was walking fast—okay, I was jogging—down the hallway, away from Dash. If he wanted to talk to me, then he was going to have to chase me. I rounded the corner, looking for somewhere to hide, but all I found were more concrete hallways.

"Madison. Stop." Dash's voice wasn't far behind me, and I huffed out an angry breath. I should have known I couldn't outrun him. He might have been slow for a hockey player, but he was quick compared to me.

As I turned the corner, I caught his eye and realized just how close he was to catching me. I ran as fast as I could, thankful that I was wearing sneakers.

"Thought you were ignoring me, Big Man," I teased from over my shoulder, my pace turning into a quick jog because his stride was so much longer than mine.

"Hard to ignore you when you're everywhere I look."

I scrunched my nose because that statement wasn't true. I wasn't *everywhere*. He was the one that followed me to a game the other day.

"Why are you running?" he groused.

"Because I'm a catch," I sassed, flicking my hair over my shoulder, only to realize I could feel his looming frame getting closer.

When I felt Dash's hand wrap around my torso, I yelped. A flurry of mixed emotions swirled through my body. Excitement. Lust. Trepidation. It felt like I'd been caught by the big bad wolf and there was no way of getting out of his clutches without giving him all my baked goods.

"Will you calm down?" Dash was walking backward, holding me as though my struggling was nothing more than a mild inconvenience for him. My feet barely touched the ground, and I was tripping on my own shoes. He didn't care. He was just grumbling away, as per usual.

"Dash," I whispered sharply, but it wasn't getting through. I looked over my shoulder, thankful that Cade wasn't around to see this since I'd already gotten a lecture about Adam, and I figured he'd freak out if he found out who I was truly interested in.

"Dash." I tried to get through to him one more time, but before I could speak again, he covered my mouth with his palm.

As the voices of his coaches echoed in the distance, Dash drew my body closer to his, and, without another word, he opened a door close by and dragged me through it. I heard the lock click before he turned the light on and looked around in awe at all the hockey equipment. Pucks upon pucks were packaged and stacked next to brand new gloves and padding. We were in the supply closet, and when I glanced over at Dash, he was just staring at me with narrowed eyes and a beady expression.

"What was that about, Madison?" It was a silly question because surely that had to be obvious, but with his hooded gaze, I wasn't willing to backtalk him this time.

He took a step forward. I took a step back. We kept doing this little dance until my back hit the equipment racks, and then I felt his presence all over me. With hands gripping the shelves on either side of my face, he glared down, waiting for me to answer.

So, I did the only thing that I could think of. I smiled and said, "What are you talking about, Big Man? I was just doing what everyone else was. Watching the Covey Crushers crush the competition. Go team." I lifted my fist, pretending I was holding a glow stick, and shook it between us.

He didn't look amused, but that wasn't new for Dash. He didn't have a sense of humor at the best of times, let alone right now.

"Madison." It was a warning and a growl bundled into one, and unsurprisingly, it sent tingles straight to my core. I shivered but tried to hide it. "What were you doing here with Aiden?"

"You mean A-Rizzle?" I joked because it felt like the only appropriate thing to do when you had a broody hockey player glaring at you. "We were just having a good time. Hanging out in public. You know, something you and I can't do," I said just to goad Dash, because what did I have to lose at this point? If I was going down, it was going to be like watching *Titanic*. Long, heartbreaking, and a little confusing because Jack could have totally fit on that damn door.

Dash's hands gripped the shelf behind me tighter, making it shake against my back. His body leaned into mine, and I turned my face so I was looking to the side because I didn't want him to know just how much this entire scenario was turning me on. Yup. I was a lost cause. No one would get me as hot as this smoldering hockey player, and I was just going to have to accept that as fact now.

Dash was breathing heavily but still hadn't spoken.

"What's wrong, Big Man? You seem stressed."

"And you seem hell-bent on giving me an aneurysm."

"No problem. If you dragged me in here just to tell me that I couldn't have you, that's good to know, because I think Henry was just about to admit his undying love for me. Surprised you didn't warn me he was here. Was it because you were worried I'd go back to him?" I pouted my lips out and toyed with that thought. "You know what? Maybe I need to go and see my old friend."

As I tried to slink under his arm, Dash pushed his body onto me, stopping me from moving. Chest to chest, Dash was glaring down at me but saying nothing useful. His eyes were telling me to go, but his body wasn't letting me. See. He was the king of mixed messages, and I was his wench waiting to become his queen.

With my hands rested on Dash's chest, I tried to push him away, but I couldn't; he was too heavy.

He wasn't backing away either.

The only way I was going to get out of this would be to lean into his touch. My body pressed against his, but I was frustrated that my heavy sweatshirt and brother's jersey were dulling the sensation of finally having him this close.

"Do you really think any other guy is going to make you feel the way I do?"

Wetting my lips, I gained the courage to say, "Don't know. Haven't tried yet."

I smiled, ready to tease him for his silence, but before I could say anything, he stole my breath with a searing kiss. Punishing and hot, he kissed me to prove his point, pouring everything into it. Teeth clashed against teeth. Tongues fought with tongues. He was kissing me with so much force it almost hurt. I could feel it. He was grappling with the feelings he had for me and didn't know what to do with them.

"Guess I'm going to have to show you, then." He laughed bitterly, and his lips were back on mine before I could even take in what he said.

His large hands roamed my body, completely unbothered by the minor inconvenience of my clothing, seemingly too lost in kissing me to really care. When his warm palm slipped under my hoodie and grazed my skin, I tried to take in a sharp breath, but Dash wouldn't let me.

His lips were feasting on mine, and my brain went fuzzy when his hand traced the line of my jeans and started to play with the button on the front. As he teased the opening of my jeans, I couldn't take it anymore. I pulled away from him, throwing my head back onto the shelf behind me.

His hand didn't undo the button like I expected. Instead, he flattened his palm and brought it all the way up my torso, under my sweatshirt. It dragged over the front of my bra, and when he found my nipple, he pinched it, sending shockwaves of pleasure straight to my core. My mind was reeling because I knew there were players still loitering outside, not to mention all the coaches out there too. What if someone needed something from in here and then found us?

"Did you really think Aiden Matthews could do this?" he asked so smugly that I almost wanted to slap him away for being so rude about my friend, but I couldn't. His hand was toying with my nipple, while his hardness was pushing against my core. He was putting so much pressure on me that I had to grab on to the shelves just to stay standing.

"Dash," I husked out, trying to get some air, but he was being less than helpful with that. "We can't do anything. Not in here."

"You sure about that?" he challenged, his hand now caressing my breast. I was melting in his arms, and I hated how much control he had over me. I also hated how much he knew it. "Because we've done worse."

I lost my breath when his hand moved from my chest back down to my waist, and then I squeaked a little when he unbuttoned my jeans. Kissing me, he made my body feel like jelly, molding into whatever he wanted me to be. Before I could protest—not that I would—he pushed his palm down the front of my jeans, heading straight for my panties.

I gasped when his thick, warm fingers touched the top of my mound because it felt so good. Dash didn't respond to that, he just used two of his fingers to play with my clit round and round, over and over. He knew how to get me off with such little effort; it was getting annoying.

Laughing into our kiss, he said, "You're already so wet for me, babe. You can't deny that you're mine now."

I winced because I hated how obvious it was that I was desperately in love with him, so I decided to tease him a little. "How can you be so sure it's you I'm wet for?"

His fingers stopped moving, and he pulled away, cutting a look at me.

I licked my lips, making sure I didn't waste an ounce of his taste, and said, "I was just in the stands hanging out with a few football guys, after all. Who knows, maybe we had a ménage à trois planned after this."

Straight-faced, Dash didn't move. He was just glaring at me, wondering how far I would take this.

So, I kept going. "Let's not forget that Henry was looking for a second chance too." His eye twitched. "Maybe I could bring him in on the action."

Still not moving, Dash stared at me for a little longer than what would seem normal when you took into account that his fingers were on my clit. He pushed them down, sending a thrill straight to the back of my spine before moving his hand off me. I stopped the moan emanating from the back of my throat because I didn't want to give him the satisfaction of knowing I yearned for his touch.

I waited for him to pull his hand out of my jeans and give me the inevitable lecture about how we couldn't be together. Only that didn't happen. What happened was even more shocking. He dipped his hand further into my pants and pushed two fingers inside me with ease. My fingers clawed at his arms because I was worried I might lose my balance. He didn't stop at my yelp or the fact that my feet were nearly tipping off the floor because he was pushing me up. He didn't need to. He was making his point loud and clear. My hips were bucking wildly, and if he kept up the pace, I was going to come just from his fingers being inside me. My body couldn't help but react to Dash.

As I was just about to moan out his name, he took his hand away, leaving me wrecked. I opened my eyes lazily, confused over what just happened. Raising his hand between us, he shoved the two fingers that were inside me into my mouth, causing me to taste my own arousal.

"Lick them clean," he commanded.

So I did.

Using my tongue, I stared at Dash while I licked every last crevice of his fingers until I couldn't taste myself anymore. Swirling his fingers around, he pushed them down the back of my throat before pulling them out entirely and giving me a wicked grin. "Just remember, it's me that makes you taste like that."

I was speechless. Was this Dash? The same Dash who was usually quiet and brooding. Ugh. Why did I like this confident and commanding side of him?

Then he stepped back, gesturing for me to leave. He couldn't be serious, could he? My jeans were still unbuttoned, and my panties were soaked, and he was going to leave me like this.

My chest heaved, my clothes were rumpled, and all I could think about was how I was going to have to get myself off against the hockey equipment if Dash didn't come back over here and finish the job himself.

"Dash." My word was short, drawn out, and barely audible because I was disappointed. I was so close to coming, and now it was all wasted. The euphoria building was for nothing because he took it away.

"What do you want, Madison?"

I hated the way he was talking to me in what felt like riddles. My brain was too fuzzy, and I couldn't concentrate.

"To finish what you started," I challenged, knowing Dash couldn't back down from it.

He stalked toward me, encasing me in again, and kissing me even harder than before. Without hesitation, his hand went straight into my panties, and I was almost embarrassed at how easy it was for him to slip his fingers inside me. Thankfully, I was too aroused to think straight.

His thumb swiped across my clit in the little space he had as he moved down and kissed my neck. I closed my eyes and leaned onto the shelves for balance while he used his fingers to get me off.

"Does that feel good?" he asked. I didn't immediately answer, too caught up in a mountain of pleasure to care.

"Yes." He kissed the answer off my lips and pushed my jeans down to the middle of my thighs. Then he dropped to his knees.

A shock of pleasure ran up my spine when Dash looked up at me, grinning. He wasn't about to go down on me, was he?

His face was in line with my pussy, and when he kissed the top of my mound, I shivered, unable to move much because my jeans were holding me in a viselike grip. He knew what he was doing. "Tell me, Madison. Has anyone ever tasted you before?"

He was taunting me. A tit for tat, but for some messed up reason, I liked it. I liked that he was getting so riled up in his own thoughts about what I'd potentially done with other guys because, in a fucked-up way, it showed me how much I meant to him and that this attraction wasn't just in my head.

"Not yet."

Short and simple, it seemed to be all the confirmation Dash needed. He edged my panties to the side, and when his tongue licked my clit, I cried out before quickly clamping my mouth shut with my hand. I desperately wanted to scream at the sensation, but we were in a public place and there was no way I was going to let this stop.

Dash grabbed an ass cheek in each of his hands to bring my center closer to his mouth. It didn't matter that my legs were being held together by my jeans; he was going to make sure I jutted my hips out enough so that he could lavish my clit with attention.

I could hardly breathe, and as every second passed, I felt like I was flying. His touch was something I'd never experienced before, but it was everything. Wet and warm with a little feather-like caress, it was enough to have me begging for release.

People walked by. I could hear their footsteps and muffled voices over Dash's moaning whilst he ate me out. Cringing, I was almost certain someone jiggled the door handle, but that wasn't going to stop my goalie. He was making his point and he wasn't going to stop until I came all over his face.

As my hips moved against his tongue, I choked on my own cry, hoping he couldn't tell how much I was enjoying this. Who was I kidding? I was so wet, my pussy was making noises while I unabashedly rode against his tongue.

As his fingers eased inside me, I gasped because they were so thick, it almost felt like he was going to split me in half. The painful pinch lasted a second before it was replaced with indescribable pleasure as he rolled my clit against his tongue.

His tongue worked faster, and I was holding on to anything I could just to stay standing. I grabbed a box of pucks, accidentally sending the boxes above it to the floor, hitting my shoulder on the way. The pain from that wasn't enough to stop the pleasure that I was trying to hold back.

I couldn't anymore. It just felt too good. Then it happened.

My world came crashing down in a beautiful mess. My hips were chasing the end of the high as Dash held his fingers in place, letting me ride them until I was exhausted.

As I was coming down from my orgasm, Dash stood but didn't back away. Instead, he kissed me, teasing his tongue across my lips, making me taste myself again. Then he rested his forehead against mine as we both breathed heavily. His fingers were the last thing to leave me, and I sighed when they did, disappointed at how empty I felt.

With one final kiss, he casually pushed my sweatshirt down, pulled my jeans up, and buttoned them. Soaking wet and exhausted, it was the first time I might actually need help to walk home because my entire lower half felt like jelly.

"What are we doing, Dash?" I resigned myself to ask the question.

His eyes were still dark, and I could tell there was something on his mind. I just wish I knew what.

"You tell me."

"Well, I guess we'll need to reconsider the definition of one night," I glanced down at my tingling core, waiting to see his reaction. Would he freak out like last time?

Dash sighed in resignation. "What are you doing Friday night, Madison?"

"Friday night? What's happening Friday night?"

"I would very much like to take you out on a date."

I gulped, suddenly feeling nervous and confused at the same time. "A date?"

"Yup. I've come to the conclusion that this is the next logical step for us."

"And why do you think that?"

Don't get me wrong. I was ecstatic that he came to that conclusion, but I needed to act cool about it. His eyes drifted up until he was looking me in the eye, then he licked his lips before smiling. My body tingled because

I could tell he was tasting me with every swipe.

He sighed, moving off me to give us both a little space. "Look, Madison, I like you. I always have, but seeing you hanging out with other guys has made me want to murder everyone, and I'm sure you can imagine how inconvenient a prison sentence would be for me right now. You are mine." I took a sharp breath, doing my best not to show him how long I'd waited to hear him say that. "That's at least how I feel and the direction I've resigned myself to. I can't ignore it anymore. But I need to make sure you want this, too."

"What do you mean? I've made it pretty clear how much I want you."

"No, you told me you've been crushing on me since high school and wanted me to be your first time."

I raised a brow, looking at him in confusion because wasn't that the same thing?

"I just need to make sure it's not the *idea* of me that's making you want this. I want to know that you want me for me."

"You can't be serious?"

"Yes. You yourself talked about that weird brother's best friend obsession. Not to mention how you've been acting since we had sex."

"That was to make you jealous. I'm not interested in any of those guys."

"What about Henry? You told me back in high school that you only dated him because he was the only guy that had ever said you were beautiful. What if the same thing is happening here?"

"It's not. Give me some credit, Big Man. I'm not sixteen anymore. I know what I want now."

"Still, I'm not willing to blow up one of my longest friendships if you're only interested in fucking me. I need to know there's something serious between us before I tell Cade."

I should have known that my own words and actions would be used against me. But how was I to know I'd end up in a supply closet discussing the possibility of dating Dash after he ate me out?

I raised my hand and shook my head. "I don't know what to say, Dash. You're not a fetish to me, if that's what you think. I've had a crush on you since before I even knew what it meant. Ever since the day you taught me how to hit a puck, I always thought you were the coolest guy on the planet.

I couldn't stop thinking about you after you broke Henry's nose, and I wanted you to be my first the minute I saw you grumbling at The Draft. It's always been you."

He didn't say anything at first, and I didn't like the silence, so I dropped my gaze to the floor, feeling a little too exposed. Maybe I came on too strong or said too much but my words were the truth, and I felt like he deserved to know that.

Dash took my hand, making it feel tiny against his. Then he brought it up and rested it on his chest, right over his heart. I only looked at our intertwined hands, yearning for him in so many more ways than I would like to admit.

"Thank you for telling me," he husked out, giving me the courage to look up at him. His thumb rubbed across the top of my palm, and then he dropped down to kiss me on the lips.

It was a different kind of kiss than all the other ones, and as crazy as it sounded, this felt like our first kiss. It wasn't rushed. It wasn't heated with so much lust that we couldn't think straight. It was just a special kiss conveying something words never could, and I loved that.

As he pulled away, threats of a smile pulled on his lips. "I guess if we're confessing crushes, I should probably tell you about the fact that I was obsessed with you in high school, and the only reason I dated Amy was because I thought she'd be a good distraction from you."

"Wh-What do you mean?"

"Come on, Madison. Didn't you find it strange that Amy looked just like you?"

"I, uh, hadn't noticed."

"Really? Because I had...all the time, and as an idiot teenager, I thought that would mean I'd stop thinking about what it would be like to kiss you. It didn't. It just made me want you more. You were the forbidden fruit, and I was almost thankful that I left for college just so I wouldn't be in the same vicinity as you."

I couldn't deny I was taken aback because I only thought the attraction started after Henry.

"The fact that we're here talking about dating is something I never thought would happen, and I need to make sure that you're one hundred percent in this before we get too deep."

"Don't you think we already are?"

He shrugged. "All I'm saying is, you should walk away right now if you don't want this."

The way he was looking at me made me finally realize just how serious this was to him. "Okay. So, you want me to prove I want you?"

He nodded.

"Fine. Then I'd love to go on a date."

A smile grew across his lips, and my heart immediately warmed because I didn't see that often. I took a step toward him and wrapped my arms around his neck, feeling good that I could do this without anxiety riddling my stomach. Dash wasn't going to push me away. He wanted this just as much as me. He just wanted me to prove it to him.

"I know I want you, Big Man, but clearly, you've still got doubts about my intentions, and you know what? That's understandable. I have been acting a little off-kilter recently." I'd say I almost regretted throwing other guys in his face, but we wouldn't be here if I hadn't. "I don't want you to have any doubts when it comes to telling my brother that you're madly in love with me, so I'm happy to do whatever you want to prove that."

He narrowed his eyes, trying his best to tame an amused smirk, but he couldn't hide it. There was something blooming between us and it was all I could ask for.

Dash relaxed his forehead against mine as his fingers gripped my hips, pulling me closer. Was I dreaming because it was impossible for reality to be this good. There was no way Dash was here, spilling his guts to me like this. I never thought making him jealous would lead to him confessing he'd always had a crush on me, but I was living for it. This was the most Dash had talked in years, and to be honest, I loved that it brought us to the same place.

"Great. So, Friday, I'm taking you out," he reconfirmed more to himself than me.

I nodded like an overeager teenager. "I'd like that," I said with a meek smile, pushing some of my wayward hair behind my ear. "But does that mean whatever's happening between us right now has to end?"

Yes, I asked because I was still horny, and I could. The guy just gave me

THE DRAFT

the best orgasm of my life, and all I wanted was another one.

Smiling wickedly, he dropped his chin.

"Is that your way of saying you want to come home with me?" I bit my bottom lip, looking over to the shelves with hockey sticks hanging from them. It didn't matter that we'd had sex before, or he'd just licked my most intimate parts. I still felt a little shy and awkward about asking for what I wanted.

"Maybe you could come to mine since it offers a little more privacy than the two pizza boxes you have."

He seemed like he was ready to say yes, but then he dropped his head, and I knew he was going to reject my offer.

"I wish I could, but we're going to Hockeyfest in the morning, so I've got to be up early."

"Hockeyfest?" I tried to mask my frown with a smile, but Dash knew me. He could see I was disappointed. Hockeyfest. With my brother.

"There are plenty of things we could do before leaving here, then. Door's locked."

He chuckled humorlessly. "Not if I want this boner to go down before anyone sees it and wonders why I'm getting hard over a box of pucks."

He grabbed a box behind me, moved it to the side and shook it. I didn't care about the pucks. I was more interested in what was going on in his pants and if there was any way that I could have a look at it.

Squealing, I dropped my hands to his sweats. "Can I see it?" I didn't care that I sounded overly eager. I'd seen the bulge plenty of times, even felt it inside me, but I'd never actually seen him.

"Can you see what?"

"Your boner." I bit my bottom lip, holding off a giggle as my face flushed. "I've never seen one that wasn't online."

"What are you talking about? We had sex a month ago."

"I know, but I didn't look at it in fear that the sheer size of it would make me want to stop the entire thing. The only ones I've actually seen were online, and they didn't look real. They're all shaved and perfect. It looked so staged."

Dash paused, really taking in what I was saying. "Madison, are you trying to tell me you watch porn online?"

I shrugged my shoulders because being honest with him felt right at this point. He had just tasted the most intimate part of me, after all. "Not much, but every now and again, I find myself going down the rabbit hole. I have needs like everyone else."

Dash crushed his eyes shut, silently cursing to himself. "Of course, you look at porn."

"The porn I watch is tame, really. It's just straightforward sex and doesn't really get me off on its own. I think it's because it's not really catered to women, you know? And I'm always questioning the ethicalness of it, so it really takes me out of the zone." Dash wasn't talking, but he was breathing heavily with his eyes closed, so I thought I'd try to soften the admission. "It's nothing compared to the dick pics that find their way into my DMs."

He growled and pinched the bridge of his nose as he sighed. "Guys send you dick pics, too?"

"Daily. I don't get why they think that will make a girl want to date them, though. I mean, seriously. This one guy covered his little friend in glitter and laid it out on his kitchen counter. Told me he was a unicorn and asked if I wanted a ride." Dash's face looked as disgusted as I felt when I first received the message. "All I could think about was how unhygienic the whole thing was, and also, what's he going to do after he's taken the picture? Glitter is a bitch to get off at the best of times, and surely, that's a one-way route to a UTI."

"How did he stick the glitter on?"

I crinkled my forehead, surprised he was interested. "You don't want to know what he told me." I shivered in his arms, and I could tell Dash was really thinking about everything I'd just admitted.

"Anyway, besides agreeing that you will block every account that's sent you dick pics, I really do need to take you home."

Leaving him when we'd just made this progress felt like torture, so I took his shirt and pulled him back toward me.

"You sure I can't tempt you with a kiss goodbye?" I gently kissed his lips. "One where I'm on my knees?" I raised my brows, throwing him a flirty smile.

"Don't tempt me with a good time." Growling, he grabbed my ass and pulled me up so high that I was forced to wrap my legs around his waist.

He dropped his forehead to mine and closed his eyes as if he was in agony. "As much as I've thought about all the things I want to do to you, they're going to have to wait. I can't risk missing this bus."

"Wait until *after* our date?"

"After," he said lightly. "Before. During. We'll have to see how good of a girl you are while I'm away."

"Good girl?" I raised my brow, remembering last time he said that. Was Dash into that? I tried to suppress as smile when I said, "I can be your good girl."

Bending me backward, Dash grinned and kissed me. Long and slow. I felt like a damn near princess in his arms. He swallowed my sigh with another kiss, and I felt dizzy knowing that this was only the beginning. Finally, Dash and I were able to be comfortable and real with each other.

As we pulled away, knowing that we were going to have to eventually leave, he squeezed my hand. "Come on, I should walk you home before it gets too late, and we blow our cover."

I giggled, enjoying the way my hand was swallowed by his a little too much. This was real, and I couldn't wait to see where Dash and I would go.

CHAPTER 19

Dash

Madison: Can you guess what these are?

I squinted, trying my best to make out the picture, but as per usual, it was blurry and pink. The same as pretty much every photo Madison had sent me since I dropped her off at her dorm last night. Last night. I still couldn't believe that happened. Somehow, it had gone from being the worst night of my life, to the best.

Madison: Have you given up?

I zoomed in, trying to figure out what she'd sent, but just like the last few attempts of this guessing game, I had no idea what I was looking at. Let me think. She's already sent me a close-up picture of her garbage can, her class notes, her laptop. What else could be in her dorm?

I inwardly laughed to myself because if it were any other person trying to play this ridiculous game with me, I would have blocked them, but not

Madison. She could send me a blank screenshot and I'd still stay up all night, eagerly awaiting the next one.

I was obsessed, and it wasn't just because I'd had the luxury of tasting her. It was because the girl I'd always thought I could never have wanted to be with me. I just needed to make sure she felt the same way and I wasn't just a passing trend so I could figure out how to tell her brother about us.

Dash: I have no idea. Your desk chair?

Honestly, I was running out of ideas over what could be in her room. I hadn't even seen it yet, but I was looking forward to it. The mere thought of her sitting on her bed, texting me in just my jersey was making me harder than I should be in an airport line.

Madison: No. Silly. Look a little closer.
Dash: I've looked as close as I can.
Madison: Are you admitting defeat, Big Man?
Dash: Yes.
Madison: You're so bad at this game. It's the panties I was wearing when you ate me out in the equipment room.

I coughed loudly, holding back my surprise because if I thought about it hard enough, I could still taste her on the tip of my tongue. Erik knocked past me as he walked through the tunnel to the plane, and my eyes darted as other teammates followed suit, pushing past me to get to their seats. They were all lost in their own worlds while mine was burning to the ground, and I was blissfully watching it happen. I did dirty things to Madison Bright, and I planned on doing it all over again if given the chance.

I needed to get some privacy so I could text Madison back without the fear of my teammates seeing. I gave the overly preppy air hostess a curt nod as I walked past her and stepped to the side. Standing in the food preparation area, I had more space to quickly text Madison back.

Dash: Are you trying to get me into trouble? I'm with the guys.

Madison: And it's just a blurry picture, so what does it matter?

Dash: It matters because if anyone finds out that you're sending me pictures of your panties, we're screwed. Didn't we agree that we were going to make sure we both really wanted this before outing ourselves?

Madison: You know, I don't remember the conversation going down like that. I think we both agreed that we liked each other. We've known each other since middle school, so what more do you need? My medical records? Is that it? If you must know, I had my gallbladder removed when I was sixteen, but you already knew that, didn't you, Big Man?

I inwardly laughed because she had a point. I was in the hospital, standing right next to Cade when they wheeled her out, but how long we knew each other didn't matter. I needed to make sure she was fully in this and I wasn't just a passing fad for her.

Madison: You said you wanted me to make sure I knew what I was getting into and if this was right for me. I've thought about it, and I want this. I want you.

Why weren't those words as comforting as I thought they'd be?

Madison: It's fine if you're having second thoughts. Just let me know so I can send my wet panty pics to glitter dick instead.

Dash: I swear to God, Madison. If you go anywhere near glitter dick, I will find him and chop his dick off, leaving it to rot in its own glittered glory.

Madison: Possessive much?

Dash: You know I want you. You don't need to tease it out of me like this, but like I said, I will not potentially blow up my relationship with Cade and my team before you're certain.

Madison: I'm certain. I promise.

The Draft

Dash: Let's talk about this on Friday. I'm getting on the plane now.

Hauling my bag over my shoulder, I sidestepped my way down the narrow aisle because it was the only way I could fit. When my phone buzzed in my pocket, I played it cool and fought the urge to check it as I passed the rest of the team. When I felt like I had enough privacy, I pulled my phone out.

"What are you waiting for, D? Our seats are just there." Cade pushed my shoulder, pointing down the aisle at our usual seats. Even with his sunglasses on, I could see his raised eyebrows, questioning me.

I quickly tucked my phone back into my pocket and shuffled down the aisle to our seats. As I looked over the seats, Cade let out a noise like a deflated balloon.

He pushed my back playfully. "Oh. Is that what's holding you up? Trying to see if you can switch seats? Dirty, dirty dog. Am I not enough?"

He pulled me close, wrapping his arm around my neck while he rubbed his fist into my hair. Idiot.

"What are you talking about?" I swatted his hands away and wrestled out of his hold. When I realized who he was looking at, my stomach dropped.

Sienna. How did I forget that she traveled with the team? Narrowing her eyes at me, she was feeding into the false, secret dating narrative that I'd fed to Cade.

"Are you trying to see if you can sit next to your girl on the flight? Maybe have a little double-digit fun under the blanket."

I clenched my jaw and gripped my bag strap tightly because even thinking about a girl other than Madison felt wrong now. "No. I was just texting my mom," I replied curtly as I shuffled down the aisle and straight to our usual seats. For the first time in my life, I was cursing myself and the fact that we had such similar last names. How was I supposed to sit next to my best friend for an entire flight and not mention Madison?

Cade threw his bag in the overhead compartment and sat next to me. "Sorry, D. Did I strike a nerve? Are you and Sienna having problems?"

"Something like that," I muttered while I cracked my knuckles in a lame attempt to reduce my stress.

Traitor. Traitor. Traitor.

It was like a whisper trickling in my brain, and I was waiting for the dam to burst. Fuck. I ate his sister out, and I was just sitting right next to him, pretending everything would always be the same between us.

Cade took me in, then laughed as he got himself comfortable. "I told you."

"Told me what?"

"To watch out. You're drunk on pussy and acting like a clown." I cut my gaze to him, and he was just watching me with a tight jaw. Cade wasn't afraid to speak his mind, and I had a feeling I was about to get lectured. "Your play yesterday was atrocious. Ever since The Draft, you've been playing worse than my blind seventy-year-old uncle. Your performance has never been this terrible, but it has given me insight over why you've never had a girl in your life that you actually like. You're a terrible player when you have one."

He was right about one thing: I had sucked over the last couple of games. But it wasn't Madison causing it. It was trying to hide her from Cade that was my problem.

"I would be grateful if you could figure your shit out before the end of the season because I'd like a spot in the Frozen Four."

When Cade pulled his sunglasses off, I was taken aback. I thought he was trying to glare at me, but I couldn't tell because his eyes were so swollen that I doubted he could see much. "Cade. Your face?"

"Is beautiful. I know." He waved me off, unfazed. Yes, we were hockey players, so a black eye and lost teeth weren't anything new to us, but this made no sense.

"Did that happen while you were defending me at the game last night?"

"Nope," he said nonchalantly as he pulled out the in-flight magazine and began to casually flick through the pages. Cade wasn't reading, he was just milking it because he liked having information that I wanted. "You should see the other guy."

As if on cue, I noticed Henry shuffle past us with his head down. He was trying to be inconspicuous, but much like Cade, he couldn't hide his bruised face. Henry didn't go on the ice last night, and as much as I wanted to pulverize him when I saw him talking to Madison, I didn't.

"Did you beat up Henry?"

"Henry?" Cade raised his brows, and he tamed down the subtlest of grins as Henry walked by. Something passed between them, but I had no idea what. "Nah, I didn't beat him up but he was there."

"Where?"

Cade poked his head out into the aisle, looking back and forth, then he leaned in. *"Behind Closed Doors."*

The flight attendant announced that it was time for takeoff, giving me no time to question Cade, so I buckled my seat belt and leaned forward to take my shoes off. Cade followed suit, and while we were leaning forward, I discreetly asked, "Did you arrange another fight?"

Glaring at him pointedly, we both knew what it would mean if he'd started fighting again and someone found out.

Cade shook his head before forcefully pushing himself back onto the seat in annoyance. "I know I regularly come out unscathed in those fights, but do you really think I'd have time to prepare for a fight, and get on a bus without my bones aching?"

"Well, if it wasn't for a fight, then what were you doing at *Behind Closed Doors*?"

"Celebrating our win." He shrugged.

"You went to a strip club to celebrate our less-than-elegant win against a mediocre team?"

"Burlesque club," Cade corrected. "It's not a strip club. The girls don't strip there. They're dancers, and it's all very professional. You'd know the difference if you ever bothered to attend one of our socials."

"You're acting like you've got a stake in the business or something."

"Maybe I do."

"Did you get beaten up because you got a little too frisky with one of the dancers?"

"Kind of the opposite, actually," he said with his chin pointed up as he put his sunglasses back on.

"That's not cryptic at all," I said with a sarcastic laugh. "What kind of business do you have to deal with that ends with you looking like that?"

"Nothing that anyone else needs to worry about. But while I have you here, locked in a seat, I wanted to talk to you."

"About?"

"Madison. Heard you walked her home after the game."

I swallowed but my mouth was dry. He knew, didn't he? "Cade, I-"

As if the world wanted to torture me, the plane started to take off, so there was no way Cade could talk to me until after. Well, fan-fucking-tastic. I rested my hands against the armrest and looked straight ahead, doing my best to ignore Cade's glare.

Okay, this conversation was coming sooner than planned, but I needed to have it. *Cade. I'm in love with your sister.* No, that sounded desperate. *Cade, your sister and I had a moment.* Not a moment that I want to share with him.

"Have you figured out what's going on with her?" Cade asked loud enough to hear over the engine noises. "She was cozying up to Aiden and Adam at the game last night, so I thought you got some insight when you walked her home? Good move by the way. Not letting her go to Covey's Cantina with them."

So, he didn't suspect me. Maybe I could just leave my confession for another day then.

I was going to hell for this.

"Madison?" I leaned my head back onto the seat and clicked my tongue, pretending to think about it. Maybe I *should* tell him now and get the beating I was no doubt due, over with. He had been in a fight last night, so he'd be tired, which meant I'd have more of a chance of coming out of it alive at least.

"Yeah, which one is she dating? Because if I had to pick, I'd take Adam. Not that either is a good option, but Aiden is something else, and if the rumors are true, then I know far too much about his body parts for my *sister* to be with him."

"She isn't dating either of them."

He looked unconvinced. Or at least, what I could see of him did. "Really? Then why's she hanging out with them so much?"

"I think it's because she's trying to branch out of your shadow. She mentioned something about trying to make her own friends outside of the hockey realm." I inwardly cursed myself because I couldn't think of a better lie than that.

"So, she picks a bunch of football players?" he asked, surprised. "Wouldn't she want to make friends with girls in her dorm before hanging out with a bunch of guys? A football team, no less. I've met smarter rocks." He blew out a whistle. "What does she even talk about with those guys? It's not like she knows a thing about football."

"You know your sister. She's more of a guy's girl." The lie was building, but unless I was going to tell him the truth right now, then there was no point in stopping. "I did see her speaking to Henry after the game. Who knows, she might be trying to make him jealous."

"Henry?" Cade cracked his knuckles, sounding intrigued and much less annoyed than usual. Interesting. He hated Henry, so why the change of heart? And where did those matching bruises come from? "You don't think she's still pining over him, do you?"

"She's definitely not pining over Henry." I could say that with the utmost certainty, but I had no idea if Henry was into her. It was obvious he was disappointed when he saw me last night, and if Madison was telling the truth, then he might have been shooting his shot with her right before I showed her who she belonged to.

"Good to know. Henry doesn't have a chance with her, anyway." That sounded like he knew something I didn't.

"Is he trying to get one?"

Cade laughed with ease. "Doubt it. Unless he's thinking another broken nose will straighten it out, then he knows to stay far away from her."

"Did he speak to you about Madison?" Did I look angry? Because I was feeling a fire burning through my veins at the mere thought of Madison and Henry together.

"Why are you so interested?" Cade took me in, and I just had to go with it, at this point.

"Because maybe you're looking at this all wrong. Maybe *he's* why she's been acting strange. Maybe they're having a relationship behind your back."

"Uh, Cade." Before Cade could answer, Alex said his name about two pitches higher than his usual tone. Peering at us from behind, he gripped my seat as he glanced between us. Then, clearing his throat, he said, "Cade," much deeper now.

"Yes?" With his sunglasses on, Alex couldn't see Cade's bruises, but I doubted he'd ask about them anyway since something seemed to be bothering him. He was sweating and gulping constantly like he was a fish out of water.

"I couldn't help overhearing your conversation about Madison." Oh, no. Had I underestimated my teammate? Was Alex about to out me? Had he finally figured out what was actually going down at the diner?

Cade raised a brow, so it was visible over the rim of his sunglasses. "Yes?"

Running a shaky hand through his hair, Alex looked like he was about to faint.

"I told you not to do this," Scotty murmured from the seat next to Alex, flicking through his phone instead of watching him. Now I definitely knew it was about me because Scotty sounded disinterested, and he'd made it clear he wanted nothing to do with my current dilemma.

"Madison and I had a moment."

Silence.

Oh, that was where he was going with this?

Cade didn't move for a second and he seemed surprisingly calm about the confession. That might have to do with the abnormal amount of sweat on Alex's forehead, though.

"A moment?"

Cade dropped his chin so he could look at Alex from above the rim of his glasses. I was shaking my head in disbelief because I told Alex it wasn't a big deal the other day, and yet here he was, spilling his guts out, waiting for his punishment.

"I asked Madison out."

"You did what?"

Alex raised his hands. "It was completely by accident." Then he pointed at me. "Dash was there."

Cade immediately drew in a sharp breath and looked at me. Even though I couldn't see his eyes, I noticed the edges of his lips had turned up as though he was finding this funny. "Dash? And you didn't tell me?"

I was embarrassed for Alex, but what could I do without outing myself? "It wasn't a moment. Alex is exaggerating," I explained.

"You sure? Because from what it sounds like, we might have just figured out why she's been acting so strange. Alex and my sister have been secretly dating."

"No. No. That's not what happened. Madison and Dash were together."

I wanted to sink into my seat and pretend I wasn't listening because Alex was just digging a deeper and deeper hole.

"They were?"

"Yeah, they're throwing you a..." Alex shook his head, realizing he had said too much. "Never mind."

"What are you and my sister throwing me, Dash?" That smile was now in full force, and all I could think about was that stupid inflatable dinosaur bounce house. I needed to accept that was in my future.

"Doesn't matter," I responded gruffly.

"You're right. It doesn't. What matters is that she and I flirted, and I asked her out as a joke, but I don't think she took it that way. Now I think I might be dating your sister, and I didn't want you to find that out through anyone else but me."

Cade was still very calm for a guy who had anger issues. "Okay, well, thanks for letting me know. You've got nothing to worry about, but I appreciate you coming to give me the heads-up."

Alex's shoulders relaxed, and just as he started to dip down back into his seat, he popped up again. "Wait. There's more."

"Oh no," Scotty grumbled, pushing his baseball cap lower.

"It wasn't just her usual flirting."

"Alex," I warned. Didn't he realize we were currently in flight and there was nowhere for him to hide?

He raised his hand, stopping me from speaking. "No. Please. I need to get this out." With eyes closed, Alex breathed in to gain some confidence. "She played with my dick."

Fucking hell. He was going there. Idiot.

"She what?" Cade groused, standing so he was face-to-face with Alex.

"She didn't play with his dick," I interrupted, knowing this wouldn't end well if I didn't intervene. "She was playing footsie under the table, and her foot strayed a little higher than she realized."

"Playing footsie?" Cade said. "With Alex?" Okay, now we were getting the slightly more unhinged Cade.

"It's not a big deal." I waved off, trying to act nonchalant. "She played footsie with me too."

"She did?" Alex asked with wide, surprised eyes. "Why didn't you say anything at the time?"

"Did she also accidentally brush your dick?" Cade asked, unamused.

"No. Of course not. That's why it was clearly an accident with Alex. She was just taunting us. You know, the way she always does." I was annoyed that I was having to defend Madison against her brother considering the only reason she was flirting with Alex in the first place was because she was trying to tease me. I guess I'd just have to punish her later, although all the punishments I could think about involved her tied to my bed, screaming in pleasure. Not sure how much torture that involved.

With pressed lips, Cade pointed at Alex. "Do you like my sister?"

"No. No. She's hot. Shit." He crushed his eyes shut, pinching his nose. "I didn't mean it like that. She's a good-looking girl. Much like you're a good-looking guy."

"Alex," Scotty mumbled, pulling at his arm to try to get him to sit.

"But I wouldn't go there. Never. You're my teammate, and trust is the most important thing between us. That's why I decided to be honest with you."

Honesty. Teammates. Trust.

All things I should have been worried about too, but my dick had taken over my thinking a long time ago.

Cade seemed to relax with Alex's admission, but I gulped, realizing just how far I'd screwed up. It wasn't like I could take back escalating things with Madison, or that I'd want to, but how the hell was I supposed to admit to Cade that I went behind his back like this?

I piped up to mute my own thoughts. "I don't think it's that big a deal, Alex. You joked around, and although Madison accidentally brushed things she shouldn't have, she was in on the joke too."

Cade clasped Alex's shoulder. "You know what? I had a really long night last night. My head hurts, and it sounds like you got the wrong end of the stick. It's fine, Alex. I'll have a word with my sister, so she won't harass you anymore." His shoulders visibly dropped. "However, if you are considering asking my sister on a date, I would strongly suggest you move on. Madison's not the girl for you."

He nodded. "Understood. I'm sorry," he mumbled before turning around, obviously completely embarrassed by his outburst. Scotty side-eyed me as everyone sat back in their seats.

"It was nothing," I whispered. "I was there, and I can assure you, it was all innocent. Nothing happened."

Cade grunted in nonchalance before pulling out some earbuds and sticking them in his ears. He crossed his arms over his chest and rested his head against the back of the chair. "Whatever. It's not true. Madison isn't stupid enough to try to date another one of my teammates."

"You think?" I shut my mouth and clenched my teeth together, but I could feel the sweat trickling down my forehead. Cade was going to kill me.

"No. Henry was an asshole, and she knew how much it screwed up the team dynamic. She gets it. This is my team. I let her get away with flirting because there's an unspoken rule between us. She knows how important this is to me."

I gulped, feeling really shitty.

"That's why I think she's trying to date a football player, and I've heard things about that team that I can't erase. So, if she really is secretly dating one of them, I'm going to nip it in the bud before she gets her heart broken again."

"Makes sense."

"Which is why I'm still waiting on you to tell me what's up with her."

"I'm working on it."

"Well, you need to work harder," he said pointedly before lying back and closing his eyes. "Now, if you don't mind, I need to get some sleep before anyone else starts talking to me about things I don't care about."

Cade had pretty much switched off our conversation, but I couldn't stop thinking about it. Did they actually have an unspoken rule? It would make sense that he would think that, but Madison sought me out, and didn't let me go until it was too late.

I needed to speak to Madison. I wanted to text her, but the risk of Cade opening his eyes and side-glancing at our text exchange was too much. It wasn't until I heard a steady rhythm of snoring from him that I dared to pull my phone out of my pocket. After turning on the plane Wi-Fi, I was hit with several unread messages.

Madison: I can't believe it's five hours to New York. What am I supposed to do while I wait for you to turn your phone on?
Madison: Oh...wait, I've got a few ideas.
Madison: *Photo Attached*

I clicked on the picture, and unsurprisingly, it was zoomed-in like all the other ones she sent me. It was pink and blurry, but this time it had a little shimmer to it. My jaw clenched, and I swallowed, thinking about what that could be based on the other things she'd sent me.

Madison: That's better. Can you figure out what it is a picture of?
Madison: Oh, that's right. You're in the air. I guess I'll leave you a full shot, so you have something fun to look at when you've landed.
Madison: *Photo Attached*

My thumb hesitated over the download button for a minute. Did I want to know what she sent me? Her brother was sleeping to my right and he'd just said she was off-limits. Yet, here I was, his best friend and teammate betraying him. And I wasn't going to stop. This could only end in disaster, but he wasn't going to wake up anytime soon, so I accepted my fate and clicked the button. It took a few minutes but when the picture opened up, I had to close my eyes and take a deep breath, hoping that it would calm me. Nope. That did nothing. How could I expect it to? Madison had just sent me a picture of three of her fingers. Three of her very wet fingers.

Madison: I thought about you the entire time. Thanks for the O.

I scratched my palm across my face and hit the back of my head against my seat methodically. How the fuck was I supposed to concentrate on anything when she was sending me shit like that? All I wanted to do was go to her dorm and give her everything I had, but I couldn't.

Dash: I cannot believe you sent me that.
Madison: Oh, you're back. Still in the air, I presume. How are

things?

Dash: I'm sitting next to your brother, hoping to hell he's sleeping, and he hasn't just seen that message.

Madison: What's wrong? I was just merely sending my friend a couple pictures.

Dash: You're going to be the death of me, I swear.

Madison: I've got a solution for you. Just wake my brother up and tell him that we're dating. Boom. Problem solved.

Dash: I wish it were that simple.

As I looked over at Cade, I cursed the fact that Madison was his sister. If it were any other girl, I'd be able to date her freely and not have guilt gnawing in my stomach. Things were so damn complicated between us. The reality was that I wasn't close to many people. Cade was my one confidant, and he helped me through the toughest time of my life. Losing him would be a big blow, even if it meant gaining Madison. There had to be a way to have both. I just needed to take it slow and figure it out.

CHAPTER 20

Madison

"So, when do you plan on telling Cade that you've been sleeping with his best friend?"

"Tiff," I whispered sharply down the phone, looking around campus as if anyone else was actually interested in this conversation. "Haven't you been listening for the last thirty minutes?"

"I have, but honestly, I don't have time for games these days. I'm either changing a diaper or dealing with a tantrum, so you need to get to the point."

"Fine. We haven't told Cade because we aren't official yet."

"But he took your V-card like a month ago?"

"Yes."

"And you fooled around in a janitor's closet a couple of days ago."

"The equipment closet if you want to be nitpicky about it."

"And he claims he wants to take you out again just to make sure you're feeling each other? It sounds like you've felt a lot of each other already."

We may have been on the phone, but I could hear my cousin's disbelief loud and clear. I wasn't expecting her to roll around on the floor and start dancing over the news about Dash and me, but I was expecting a lot more than this. Tiff couldn't hide the bitterness, not that she tried very hard. She had guy issues—that much was for sure—but that sometimes clouded her judgment.

I wanted to say just that, but Ella shrieked so loudly that I had to pull the phone away from my ear. "Be right back," Tiff said, and I rounded the corner, heading to the library while I waited for her.

"Okay," she breathed out. "I'm here."

"Um, who possessed Ella this morning? She's normally a sweet little princess. I've never heard her shriek like that."

Tiff sighed, and I could only imagine how she looked right now. Her hair was probably a mess, and I had no doubt that she hadn't slept in days. My once fun-loving and vibrant cousin had been drained like a used battery because of her one-year-old, which made me feel awful for sharing my drama. Yes, finally getting my biggest crush to notice me was huge, but in the grand scheme of things, it didn't really matter, and paled in comparison to her issues. But Tiff was always willing to listen because she said it made her feel like we were back in high school, and her life hadn't changed as much.

"I have no idea. She's just constantly shrieking. I've tried everything. The doctor says she's probably teething, but it's been months and there are no teeth coming in. How is that even possible?"

"I'm sorry. I know less about babies than I do football, and that's nothing, so I think you're asking the wrong person." It sucked. I wanted to help her through this just like she'd been helping me, but I didn't know how. Not when I was across the country and couldn't just offer to take over for her at any point.

"Yeah," she exhaled. "I'll figure it out. I always do."

"I'll keep praying for you, cuz."

"Thanks." I felt shitty flaunting the fact that I was going to our dream school while she was stuck in Indiana attending a community college because her cousin from her dad's side offered to pay for her accommodation.

I cringed when I heard another shriek but waited patiently for Tiff to calm her daughter again. I was the lucky one in all of this. I didn't have to deal with sleepless nights and tantrum-filled days. Not to mention the shit her baby daddy was putting her through.

With my phone in one hand and a couple of books in the other, I continued walking to the library, patiently waiting for Tiff.

"Okay, I'm back again," she said, sounding somewhat relieved.

"All good?"

"Yup, *Baby Shark* is back on. Now, tell me before Ella has another meltdown. If you're not in a relationship with Dash, are you fudge bunnies or something?"

"Fudge bunnies?" I questioned but then shook my head, remembering the child in the room and that she meant fuck buddies. "No. Definitely not fudge bunnies." Although I wouldn't say no to another orgasm.

"You sure? Because what you've described sounds really casual, and you're the least casual person I know. You pretty much saved yourself for him, and now you're happy to just sit back and have spontaneous sex until he deems you worthy enough to tell your brother?"

"He's my brother's best friend. He wants to make sure that we're in it for the long haul before he tells Cade and potentially screws up their relationship."

"Don't you think that by not telling him, you're guaranteeing that outcome?"

I contemplated that for a minute.

"Look, I'm not trying to yuck your yum. I just want to remind you what happened last time Cade found out you were fooling around with his teammate in high school. What was that guy's name again? Dirtbag Von Trash?"

"Henry, and that situation doesn't count. Things were completely different. You know, I saw him the other day. He transferred here and apologized. Two years too late, but I think it helped."

"Really?"

"Yeah. Who knows, we could end up friends."

"So, you're just casual Maddie now? Guys can walk all over you, take what they want, and you don't mind?"

"The two situations bear no resemblance."

"You sure? Because from here, they sound almost identical. Secret relationship. Brother's teammate. I'm not trying to put a damper on things; I'm just being realistic."

"I know. I get it, and that's why I need you in my life. You're my reality check, but Dash isn't Henry."

Tiff was quiet for a second. "Look, Mads, I get it. You like him, and you want to see the best in your situation, but I'm just offering my opinion as a casual observer. It sounds like you've agreed to be secret fudge bunnies, and I'm worried he's going to drop you the minute you've had your fun, and you push to tell Cade. He'll dump you, and he knows you won't say anything because you'll be too embarrassed to admit you made the same mistake."

"No. That's not what's going to happen."

I hated that was a potential scenario for us. I wasn't the type of girl who had a fuck buddy. Yes, I liked to flirt, but that was because it was non-committal and fun. This thing with Dash wasn't non-committal. In fact, it was probably the biggest commitment I was willing to make. He was a serious guy, and if things didn't work out, I'd still have to see him because he would always be around Cade. That was why I was so desperate for him to see me kissing him in the equipment room for what it was. I wouldn't have done it if I didn't want him for the long-haul.

Slowing, I waited for the automatic library doors to open and strolled in. "We're more than that," I said, noticing a few heads turning, so I dropped my gaze to the floor and kept my mouth shut.

"You can tell me that all you want, but I think it's Dash you've got to convince. If you really want to be with him for the long haul, then I'd suggest getting out of whatever situationship you're in now because it might become the norm."

Situationship?

I sighed because she had a point. I knew it when Dash suggested we try things out before telling Cade, but I went with it because I always assumed it was going to lead to a relationship. Dash hadn't given me any reason to question his narrative, but the more I thought about it, and how naïve I was last time, the more concerned I became.

A guy cleared his throat so loudly, he startled me. Standing right in front of me was Ralph Higgins, the head librarian, glaring at me like I stole his puppy. With his brow raised, he tipped his chin to my phone, and that was when I knew I was in trouble. Clearly, I was being too loud.

Swallowing, I said, "Umm, you know what, Tiff? I've got to go."

"But wait, we aren't done with this—"

I hung up before she could finish and flashed Ralph a flirty smile to try to stop his pressed lips and scowling brows.

"No cell phones in the library," he said, unimpressed.

"Oh, yes. I'm so sorry about that. I only came in to return these." I raised the books as though they were a good excuse to talk, but Ralph's face remained the same. "I'm sorry. I'll, uh, make sure I don't do it again." With folded arms, he narrowed his eyes as he turned away and muttered something inaudible.

"Sor-ry," I sassed under my breath, knowing that he couldn't hear me but feeling like a badass, anyway.

While returning the books, Dash's name flashed on my phone, and I couldn't help myself. I wanted to see what he had sent me.

Quickly, I pushed my books through the return slot, and looked for somewhere private. There was a little nook by the working desks, so I decided to quickly check my messages there.

Big Man: I'm back on campus in ten minutes. Where are you?

I bit my bottom lip, refraining from squealing because that would no doubt get me in trouble with Ralph again, but I couldn't help but be a little excited. It wasn't just the fact that Dash wanted to see me. It was that I was the first person he wanted to see when he got back from his three-day trip. Little old me.

Grinning, I pointed my phone to the stack of shelves and took a zoomed-in picture of one of the books. It was blurry and perfect, so I attached it to a message.

Madison: Can you guess?
Big Man: Don't toy with me, woman.
Madison: But I like toying with you.

Big Man: I'm five minutes away now. If you don't tell me where you are, I'll be forced to go to the gym with the guys instead.
Madison: And stretch with your foam roller?
Big Man: There will be some foam roller stretching, yes.
Madison: *sigh* What's a girl got to do to be treated like that?
Big Man: Tell me where you are, otherwise, you'll never find out.
Madison: That's a good point. I'm in the library.
Big Man: Perfect. Go to the third floor and meet me in the Ancient History aisle. I've just arrived on campus, so I'll see you soon.
Madison: *thumbs-up emoji* Can't wait.

Dropping my phone into my purse, I made my way up the stairs, looking for the Ancient History aisle, which took me forever because it was in an obscure corner that had barely any lights. How the hell did he even know about this place?

With my finger on the books, I paced up and down the aisle in an attempt to calm my nerves. Unfortunately, it didn't work. I was still anxious, and that nagging feeling in the pit of my stomach wouldn't go away. Maybe it was just because I hadn't seen Dash in a few days, and I wasn't exactly dressed to entice him. Or maybe it was something worse.

The conversation with Tiff came to mind. *Fudge bunnies.* Was that it? Was I worried about the potential of just being a little fun to Dash? I tipped on my toes, and my heart started racing at just the thought of it. Yes. I guessed I was. Because Tiff was right, something felt off, and I wasn't sure if it was the fact that we hadn't told my brother about us yet or if it was something else.

"Madison." I nearly melted in my shoes because Dash's deep voice made me feel like every bone in my body had turned to liquid.

"Dash?" I spun on my heels only to come face-to-face with the guy I'd been crushing on for as long as I could remember.

Tall and still brooding, he was wearing a long-sleeved, white T-shirt with gray sweatpants. I swallowed down my thoughts because he looked good enough to eat. I hesitated walking over to him because we were in public.

Dash seemed to notice my hesitancy and swallowed the distance between us so quickly that I instinctively took a few steps back, hitting the wall.

Grinning, he used his strong arms to cage me in.

"You seem to like this position, don't you, Big Man?"

Hungry and dark. Okay, I could now confirm that look wasn't because he wanted to kill me. He definitely wanted to eat me...again.

Funny. I'd been around him since high school, but this was the first time I'd seen him look at me like he wanted to throw me over his shoulder, take me to his dorm, and strip me of every earthly belonging. Something I'd happily oblige to if my brother didn't live two doors down. Although, come to think of it, that didn't stop me before.

As I took a breath in, my breasts rubbed against his chest, and his face was inches away from mine. Neither one of us wanted to speak, and as we stood mere inches apart, all I could feel was this hot tension building between us. The library was quiet, but I couldn't relish in it because my heart was rioting in my chest.

For the first time, the thrill of the chase wasn't there. It was just us. Alone together with no one trying to find us.

Twisting my head to the side, I was in awe at just how many books surrounded us. "How did you know about this place?" I raised my hand and winced. "No wait. I probably don't want to know the answer to that."

He chuckled and I felt that deep in my soul. "I've never been here before. It's just a few of the hockey guys have told me it's a good place to bring girls if you want a little privacy."

This was a hockey make-out spot. My stomach wretched, and I pushed Dash away. "Please. Please. Please don't tell me this is where Cade brings girls?"

"No." It was a short answer, but enough to make me relax. "Cade prefers to hang out..." He shook his head. "Never mind."

I wasn't about to push him, because frankly, I didn't want to know.

"It was Brooks. The guy has a thing for book nerds."

I couldn't help but think about Tiff's words on my current situationship. Dash asked me to meet him in a make-out spot. It was a great place for privacy, but was it because he only viewed me as a short-term hookup? As *fudge bunny* material?

Was he pushing off the idea of telling Cade because he didn't actually want to date me but use me? Was I falling into the same trap I did with

Henry? Why was it that when he looked at me with his deep, intense eyes, I almost didn't care?

Dash stepped closer, resting his palm on my cheek, and I took in a sharp breath, melting at the touch.

All the wayward thoughts left my mind because something else took over. Something much more carnal.

He leaned in, and I closed my eyes, waiting for his lips to meet mine. Only, that didn't happen. His breath fanned across my face, and my chest was heaving, but he just stood there, taking me in. I tipped my chin, trying to tempt him, but he didn't move.

Was he waiting for me?

Sighing, Dash took a step back.

No. Wait. That wasn't what I wanted.

Without thinking, I grabbed his shirt and pulled him right back in, kissing him hard.

Magic. Was it supposed to feel like magic when you kissed a guy? My body was tingling all over, and that only intensified when Dash's hands dropped to my waist, pressing into my skin.

As our kiss deepened, his fingers gripped me tighter, and he made sure to swallow my every gasp and sigh. Even though I was in jeans, when he pushed his hips into mine, I could feel his hardness rubbing my center, teasing me. Dash dragged one of his hands down to the back of my knee and lifted my leg, letting it rest around his hip so he could grind into me like he was fucking me.

His body moved against mine at an unrelenting pace. Wave after wave of pleasure followed each and every thrust, and I was almost certain I was going to embarrass myself like the first time we did this and come from the friction alone. It was sad and somewhat pathetic, but as much as I didn't want to admit it, I was addicted to his touch. I didn't think anything would feel as good as this.

Dash's lips dragged down my chin, and he kissed my jawline, trailing more kisses down my neck as he made his way to my collarbone. Closing my eyes, I threw my head back in pleasure because it was definitely going to happen again. I was going to climax on nothing but Dash's touch.

"Ahem."

Dash stopped moving when he heard the soft voice, and I slowly dropped my leg from his hip, feeling the mood dampen.

Busted.

"Not again," Dash grumbled, and he looked over his shoulder at the woman interrupting us. I appreciated that he was careful to keep me hidden, but the minute she took a few steps closer, and I saw the flaming red hair, I burrowed into Dash's chest.

"If you're going to do that in here, could you at least book a study room? They don't have windows or books that people might want to read." Her nose was tipped up and her offer might have been sarcastic, but I'd make a note of it since that was a good idea for the future.

"Wait. Madison? Is that you?"

My shoulders slumped as Dash's eyes widened. Standing on my tiptoes, I popped my head over his shoulder and waved.

"Oh, hey, Aster." I played dumb, skirting around Dash as I dusted off my jeans, hoping that my hair was still in the presentable half updo that I put it in before Dash got here. "Sorry about that," I said as I wiped my bottom lip, almost certain I had lipstick smeared across my face. "It's my fault. I got a little overexcited because I haven't seen Dash in a few days, so when he came to pick me up, I couldn't resist."

With flat lips, she looked at us blankly, clearly unimpressed. "Doesn't mean you have the right to ruin the books behind you. Some of them are over one hundred years old, you know?"

"If they're that precious, why are they out here?" I winced at Dash's question, wondering why he would consider prolonging this torture and poking the proverbial bear. Aster stood up straighter and shook her head in annoyance. Judging by Dash's face, he realized his mistake.

"You want the library to put all their books under lock and key so your make-out sessions don't get interrupted?"

"No. You're right. I'm sorry," I said, just to get this over with. "We won't do it again. Promise."

"Good." Aster narrowed her eyes, still watching us as she slowly walked away. When the clicking of her heels was only a distant echo, I looked at Dash and bit my lip, suppressing a giggle because it felt like we were back in high school. When I couldn't hold it back and started laughing, he did too.

"You know she doesn't even work here?" I said lightly, pointing my thumb in the direction she came.

"She doesn't?"

"Nope. She's just always here because she's a tutor."

"How do you know her?"

"I live with her."

"What? Is she a new roommate? I thought you had a single dorm." Interesting that he'd been thinking of my setup.

"I do. She lives opposite."

"Is she that pleasant in the dorms?"

I waved him off. "She's not that bad. As long as you have your music turned off after ten, you wouldn't even notice her there. She's barely around because she and her roommate Marissa don't get along."

Dash bent his knees and kissed me quickly before leaving a lingering kiss behind my ear and resting his forehead against mine. Chuckling lightly, he looked at me as his fingers toyed with the belt loop of my jeans.

"You know, I just wanted to come see you after being away for a few days. I didn't mean to maul you in the library."

"Maul away, Big Man. I'm all yours." I opened my arms out, making my chest push out, grazing his. Dash let out a low grumble before brushing his nose across mine.

"Don't tempt me, Madison. I swear I'm going to have issues walking out of here if you're not careful."

I took a sharp breath. "Because of your boner?"

He rolled his eyes. "I'm not flashing you in the library."

I pouted my bottom lip out. "Why not?"

"Because I like my scholarship," he grumbled before looking up at me with a glint in his eyes. "And you'll most likely see it later."

Fudge bunny alert.

As I looked at Dash, Tiff's words echoed through my mind, and I knew I should have probably talked to him about it instead of kissing him like he was my only oxygen. I couldn't help it, though. The feeling I got with Dash was different. With Henry, I was riddled with anxiety, pushing him to try to get a reaction. I knew Dash better than Henry, and in my mind the situations were completely different. I could trust Dash. I knew it.

"Come to my dorm," I said breathlessly and without thinking, because I didn't want our time together to end.

"Your dorm?"

"Yeah. It's the middle of the day. No one's around. Let's hang out." I sunk my teeth into his bottom lip, playing with the fabric of his shirt. He let out an uneasy sigh because he knew the innuendo behind it. I couldn't help myself. Now that I had him, I wanted to feel him all over again.

"I'm not sure that's a good idea." His eyes dragged down my body, and I tried not to take his hesitancy personally. "I've got a game in a few hours." Ah, yes. How could I forget? I had Cade's hockey schedule plastered on my wall.

"Fine. Then come back to mine for a few more minutes. I just want to spend some time with you. Alone."

Still uncertain, I pushed up on my tiptoes and kissed the light stubble across his chin. His muscles relaxed. Then I kissed the corner of his mouth, moving away when he tried to make it a full-on kiss. Gripping my hands on his shoulders, I pulled him down so I could whisper in his ear. "Pretty please?"

"How the hell am I supposed to say no to that?"

"You're not. That's the point."

"Fine." I grinned, and he pointed at me in warning. "But I can't stay long."

I raised my hands and nodded. "Sure."

Dash held out his large hand, and I eagerly accepted it. I wasn't sure why, but that move made me feel like there was something a little more 'official' about our relationship. He was going to walk out of the library hand in hand with me. Anyone could see us. This was a huge move.

Leading me across the floor, it took two of my steps to keep up with his, but he slowed the minute I heard voices. That was when he dropped my hand and adjusted the bill of his Covey U baseball cap.

With his gaze planted firmly on the floor, he walked ahead of me and out of the building.

Okay then.

I'd clearly read that situation wrong.

Once outside, it took Dash a few of his large strides to realize I was lagging behind him, and although I didn't want to pout in public, this little game between us didn't feel fun right now. I wanted to shout from the rooftops that Dash and I were together, but we still weren't there yet, and I was starting to wonder if he was using the concern over my intentions as a convenient excuse.

"You coming?" he asked, stuffing his hands in his pockets, throwing me a small smile. If I blinked, I would have missed it. I didn't have the heart to throw a scene in public, so I shuffled forward, leaving a comfortable distance between us, but making sure I didn't touch him. His elbow brushed against my arm as he side-stepped a little closer to me, but I stepped away, keeping my gaze to the floor. This wasn't how I wanted Dash, and I was starting to feel like the same dirty little secret Henry was trying to keep.

"You know, I really feel like we should be waiting until tomorrow, after our date, before I go to your dorm," he whispered as we walked through the quad.

I looked at him from the corner of my eye and answered with a small, placid smile. His lips twitched in return and my heart fluttered. Just like the night he took my virginity, that electric energy was flying between us even though we weren't touching.

This had to be real. I refused to believe otherwise.

CHAPTER 21

Dash

"Well, at least this is more appropriate than the library," Aster snarked as she walked past us. When she got to her dorm door, she turned and looked at Madison. "I'm going to put some music on, but could you please spare me the graphic details and at least try to keep it down?"

"Sure thing," Madison said quickly.

I rolled my eyes, wanting to push back on the request, but honestly, that girl kind of scared me, and I didn't want to waste the little time I had out here arguing.

When Madison opened the door to her dorm, I wrapped my arms around her hips, kissing her hard as I walked her in. Admittedly, it probably wasn't my smartest move since I'd never been in her dorm before, so I had no idea where I was going, but once I was far enough in to clear the door, I kicked it shut.

Walking backward, Madison pulled me in until she hit the back of her bed. Then, she dragged me down and we crashed into her bedding. I stopped kissing for a second, admiring her sheets.

"Covey Crusher bedding? Are you a superfan?"

She rolled her eyes, turning her face to hide the pink in her cheeks. "My brother bought them for me as a joke." She playfully pushed me, but she couldn't move me. "Should have changed my sheets. I didn't realize you'd be more interested in inspecting them than having me lying underneath you. Guess I'll just have to do something a little more drastic."

This time, when she pushed me off, I moved back so she could sit up and pull her sweatshirt off.

Her shirt was loose, but I could see her pert nipples through the thin fabric. She wasn't wearing a bra. Fuck. What I wouldn't give to suck on her perfect tits again. I was concentrating so hard on her breasts that it took me a few seconds to notice the emblem stretched across it.

North Central Hockey.

My brows crossed. Was that my shirt? Sure enough, a small number thirty was printed in the center.

Fuck.

She was wearing one of my high school shirts, and I growled in appreciation, remembering all those times I thought about her like that over the years. How, I wished it was me she was cheering for in the stands.

"Where'd you get this?"

I asked as I gently pushed her back onto the bed and rolled the fabric up. I didn't want to take it off her because there were more things I wanted to do with her in it, but that didn't mean I wanted to miss what was underneath.

She hummed lightly. "I may have swiped it from your room as a souvenir that night."

I raised my brows in surprise. "Why would you do that? If you wanted a shirt, all you had to do was ask."

"I guess I thought you were going to tell me it was one night."

I was barely taking in her words, too enamored with the view before me. As suspected, Madison wasn't wearing anything underneath. Without thinking, I bent down and swiped her nipple with my tongue, smiling when she gasped and arched her back into my touch.

"You mean." *Swipe.* "To tell me." *Swipe.* "That you've been wearing this shirt all day, when you weren't even sure you'd see me?"

Her hands threaded through my hair, giving me no other option but to keep toying with her breasts. Her fingers pressed into my scalp as her body followed my moves. "What can I say? It smelled like you, so I thought I'd wear it."

Letting out a low grumble of approval, I dropped my hips, so they connected with hers, and kissed her languidly. When things started to get too hot, I sat back on my haunches and pulled her jeans off, only to find out that she was wearing a tiny, purple G-string.

"You seriously didn't think you'd see me?"

She shook her head with a smile on her face. I bit down on my bottom lip, taking her in. With her legs wide, and her chest heaving, she was better than I could ever imagine.

I dropped down, kissing her on the lips as I let my hand brush against the side of her body until I got to her hip, then I toyed with the string there, ready to go under.

"Na-uh," she teased and pushed me down until my back was on the bed. Throwing a leg over mine, she straddled me, and a wry smile grew on her lips when she could feel my erection.

I gave her a look of warning. She didn't heed it. She just smirked and worked her hips faster. With my shirt now draped over her beautiful body, and her center rubbing against my erection, I knew I wouldn't last long.

"Madison, let's stop."

She wasn't listening to me, but that wasn't new for her. She knew what she wanted and she was ready to take it.

Gripping her hips, I stopped them from moving, forcing her attention back to me. Disappointed, she glanced down at me with flushed cheeks and red lips. Her eyes were dark, filled with a lust she couldn't disguise. It was the sexiest I'd ever seen her. I pulled her down, kissing her, hoping that would satiate her appetite, but the longer we kissed, the more frantic her hands became and the more malleable I felt. Fuck it. Would coming in my pants really be that bad?

She was moving her hips again, so instead of stopping her, I clasped one of my hands on the back of her neck and held her in place, kissing her with all I had.

Madison whimpered into my mouth, and I felt her body shiver from the touch.

Damn. This was better than the first night, and I put it down to the fact that our relationship had grown since then. We'd been able to touch and talk in ways that made it feel less awkward and more real.

Her hands moved from my chest, and she dipped them lower until she was at the hem of my shirt. She drew her lips away from mine but stayed close enough that our noses were still touching.

"Can I?" she asked as her fingers tickled the edges of my shirt, only venturing under once I nodded.

I drew in a sharp breath when her nails skimmed across my skin as they traveled up my chest. When she pulled my shirt off and took me in, I couldn't help but notice her face flush and her breathing quicken.

Was she nervous?

It sure felt like it.

Even though she was the one to suggest that we come here, I didn't want to push her into anything she wasn't ready for.

"Madison?" I didn't get a response. Her eyes were just darting from side to side. Bringing my hand to her chin, I tipped it up to get her attention on me. "Look at me, Madison. We don't have to do anything more, you know? We can just keep kissing or talking."

Madison smiled faintly before shaking her head. "That's not what I want. I wouldn't have invited you up if I was having doubts." Well, that was good to hear. She bit down on her bottom lip and as she fixated on the space between her thighs, I knew something was up, and it wasn't just my dick. Finally, she confessed, "I guess I just can't believe we're here. Like this. I've been thinking about it for so long."

I brought her closer to me, threading my arms under her shirt to pull it up and off. Skin to skin, the only thing blocking us from being completely naked were my sweats and her underwear.

"Madison. What's wrong?" I brushed my nose against hers, feeling her breath fan across my face.

"I don't want to be fudge bunnies," she blurted out, pulling back.

"Fudge bunnies?"

"No," she cried out, crushing her eyes shut as she leaned her head on my chest. I stroked her hair, waiting for her to get it out. "I can't believe I just said that out loud." Drawing her head back, she calmed herself before opening her eyes and looking at me. "What I wanted to say was that I'm all in with you. I'm ready to tell Cade about us because I want the entire world to know that you're mine."

I couldn't help by smile, liking her possessiveness. Pushing a piece of her hair behind her ear, I kissed her before saying, "Believe me, I want to do the same."

"Really? Then why haven't we? We've been texting for days. We've already had sex. It's not like we need to get to know each other. It feels like the last piece of the puzzle would be to tell my brother, so everyone else can know about us too."

I shifted my body, taking hold of Madison and pulling her toward the headboard so I could relax against it since it felt like this might be a long conversation.

As she gnawed at her bottom lip, a rock formed in my stomach because she was so desperately beautiful. So hopeful and eager. I wanted to give her everything.

"I want you to be my boyfriend," she said confidently. "I know you, Dash. You know me. You saw me on my worst day and threw a punch to make me feel better. You see me in ways no one else does. I feel like I do the same for you. I've known forever that you're more than a one-night thing. Hell, I knew the night I suggested it that you were more than that, but I was desperate for you." She swallowed, her eyes darting around my face as she gauged my reaction. "I want to be in the crowd rooting for you. I want to wear your jersey at every single game so everyone knows I'm yours. More importantly, I want you to be the one to peel that jersey off me when you get home. I want to be by your side when you want some peace and quiet. I want to be there when you're frustrated and need to talk it out. I just want you. Every single part."

She'd hardly taken a breath as she uttered all the words I'd only imagined she'd say, because that was exactly how I felt. Officially dating Madison Bright would certainly help to rid the guilt of hiding something so monumental from Cade, even if it meant I'd get a broken nose for it.

But the big question for me was, would it end in a broken nose? I deserved more than that. Especially after I'd heard the way he talked about people dating his sister. We'd been like brothers growing up and we're supposed to be teammates beyond college. Would officially doing this ruin everything? Did I care?

No.

The reality of the situation was that Madison meant so much to me. I wanted her to be happy. No, scratch that. I wanted her to be happy *with* me. Cutting a look at Madison, I could see the same future she did, and it was something I wasn't willing to give up.

"I want every single part of you too, and I want to tell Cade."

"But." She raised a brow because she thought she knew what was coming.

"But nothing. Your words sound like you're serious, and I believe you." I gave her another long, lingering kiss. One that may have involved me dipping my hand between the strings of her underwear so I could grip her ass and move her against me.

She looked wanton and delirious when I pulled away. "I want to tell your brother and get it out in the open. However…"

She groaned. "You do realize that however is just another way to say but?"

"Let me finish. However, I'd really like to take you on one date on Friday before we do it."

"Why?"

"Because the minute everyone knows about us, I'm going to be monitored by every single member of the hockey team. I just want it to be you and me for a little bit. Not because I want us to be 'fudge bunnies,' but because I want to enjoy you for a little longer. I promise we'll tell your brother after our date, but please let me just have a little alone time with you first."

"You and me?" I nodded, and a small smile formed on her lips. "That sounds like a good idea."

Her shoulders visibly relaxed, and that heady smile from earlier returned. "Well, you know it's just you and me right now?"

I swallowed as I felt her fingers tickling up my arm. "It is."

"So, there are a few more things I'd like to learn about you." Her nails scraped down my chest, and I growled, squeezing her ass again, feeling like I was drunk on Madison.

"Do whatever the hell you want."

She nodded, and I instantly regretted giving her free rein because she shimmied her hips down, so her ass was resting on the edges of my knees and her gaze fell straight to my crotch.

I knew what she was thinking, and I wasn't sure she was entirely ready for it. Scratch that, I wasn't sure I was entirely ready for it.

She dropped her hand to my sweats, right across my erection, causing me to cry out.

"Oh, no. I'm sorry. I didn't mean to hurt you."

"You didn't," I said through a wince because, yeah, she was a little rough, but that didn't mean I wanted her to stop. I placed my hand on top of hers, pushing her into my erection, showing her how I liked it. "Just keep doing what you think feels right."

Watching me like it was an exam, she pulled my sweats down, all the way off, before tossing them across the room. I'd worry about where later since I couldn't keep my eyes off her.

She bit back her smile as she took in my boxers before she ventured under the waistband, pulling the fabric down and setting my cock free.

My dick was standing at attention between us, and there was a moment of silence as she frowned down at it. "Oh...my..." She trailed off, staring at my cock like it was a science experiment. Seriously, with her brows furrowed, I almost felt like there was something wrong with it.

"Look at the size of that thing." She scooted her butt a little forward, glared at my cock, and then at her stomach. "How did that not puncture a lung when you were inside me?"

I didn't answer, too amused by her reaction. Then she flicked it and watched it bounce. Well, that was one way to clear my head enough to speak.

"Is this the first time you've seen a dick, Madison?"

"Up close and hard...yes. I told you that the other day, don't you remember?" It was kind of hard to remember much when she was on my lap half-naked, inspecting my dick. She gave it another flick, clearly testing its...bounciness?

"Yeah, but I guess I thought you would have at least passed a few bases in high school with…" It was my turn to trail off because merely thinking about Madison with Henry had completely ruined the mood.

She bit her bottom lip and shifted with a smile. "It's only been you." I wish I could say the same, but it wasn't like I had a huge back catalogue of girls in my history. "Dash, can I, can I taste you?"

I swallowed because that got my dick springing to attention again. With big doe eyes, how was I supposed to say no to the girl I'd imagined doing this with multiple times?

Her shaky hand wrapped around my shaft, and I closed my eyes, because even though she was a little haphazard with it, it felt damn good. Madison's nails grazed my skin ever so slightly, and I liked it.

"Is this the right way?" she asked before she started to move her hand up my shaft, giving it a little squeeze. In all honesty, Madison could breathe in my direction, and I'd be hard, so to have her like this was blowing my mind.

I wrapped my hand around hers and squeezed slightly, coaxing her to add a tiny bit more pressure. When she began to maintain a steady pace, I loosened my grip and closed my eyes. Her little hand felt so good around me, I didn't want it to end.

My hips bucked suddenly when I felt her kiss the tip. Opening my eyes, I looked at her, shocked. "Shit, Madison. I wasn't expecting that."

"Do you want me to stop?" she asked. With her hand still holding me in place, she swiped her tongue across the slit, and I couldn't breathe for all of two seconds.

"No. No. Please. Do. Not. Stop," I said through labored breaths.

"Okay," she said with a smile. Then, she opened her mouth and took me in. Fuck. This was the best moment of my life. Her tongue tickled against my shaft, and when it hit the back of her throat, I tried to pull out, but she gripped my cock tighter, keeping me in place while she flicked her tongue across the top.

Her lips looked perfect with my cock wrapped around them. Combine that with the fact that she was still wearing my shirt and I was so ready.

"Fuck," I hissed. "I'm going to come if you don't stop. Seeing you like this is better than I'd ever imagined."

Still holding my shaft, she popped my dick out of her mouth to say, "Oh yeah? Did you imagine it a lot?"

Her hand was pumping my cock, and I could barely get the words out because her tits were jiggling right along with the movement.

"Ye-Yes."

"What did you imagine?"

Trust Madison to ask questions at the most inappropriate times. "This, but way less hot." It took several labored breaths and a lot of focus to get those five words out, and thankfully, it seemed to satisfy her.

Licking her lips, she asked, "Do you like it when I suck your cock? Or is it the deep-throating that's getting you off?"

Breathe in. Don't come on her face. But imagine what it would look like?

Heat burned behind my eyes because I had no idea Madison was a dirty talker, or that I so badly wanted to see how far I could take it.

"It's the best view in the world, baby."

"Ugh, I swear I could come just from that," she joked before bringing me back into her mouth. Moving faster, she dropped one hand to my balls and scratched her nails across them. All the while, her tongue was tickling the top of my shaft when she wasn't deep-throating me.

Shaking, I threaded my fingers through her hair, grasping a clump of it so I could guide her to the right spot. She kept up with the unrelenting pace, and I was so close. "Madison, I'm going to come." I gripped her hair, ready to pull her off me, so she didn't have to take any of my cum, but she wouldn't let me.

She just made a disgruntled noise and kept sucking. That was more than enough to make me see stars even though it was daylight. I couldn't think because I was too lost in the way Madison made me feel.

She swallowed every last drop of me, and when she popped me out, she licked her lips clean of me. "Delicious," she said, visibly swallowing.

It was the hottest thing I'd ever seen.

I fell back onto the bed, and she crawled up beside me, trying to curl her body into mine. "That was the most amazing experience of my life," I said, and she hummed, snuggling into me with a contented smile. Did she think we were done?

Rolling over, I encased her body with mine and kissed her. Then, sitting on my haunches, I took her in. "You're beautiful." Madison smiled but looked almost embarrassed by the admission. I couldn't have that. I made a mental note to tell her she was beautiful every day I got the chance to from now on.

I toyed with the sides of her G-string, following the edge of the underwear all the way to the back, so I forced her to open her legs for me. Just a tiny piece of string was in the way of me having my fun, and I couldn't wait to touch her.

Shivering with anticipation, she was catching her breath and I just watched, happy knowing that it was me doing it to her. Just as my fingers grazed the side of her panties, I dipped down and kissed her mid-thigh.

"Da-sh." She could barely say my name, she was so lost in the feeling. I ignored her plea and kissed her all the way up her thigh until I reached the edge of her panties. She was right there, ready for me to taste, but I liked the idea of making her wait for it.

I backed up, letting my fingers tickle her knees, and when Madison realized what I was doing, she growled, pushed her hands through my hair, and pulled my face down until my nose skated across her center. She yelped when I pressed my nose down before lightly biting her panties.

"You like that?" I smiled, so tempted to lick her through the panties.

"Don't be a pussy tease. Just touch me already."

"As you wish."

I picked up the edge of her underwear and shifted it to the side. Giving her no time to feel the cool air across her center, I kissed her clit. French kissing, to be precise. Licking, sucking, kissing. I was watching her body tremble, doing my best to coax out as much pleasure as I could from her.

With her hands still in my hair, she closed her eyes and squeaked out something inaudible. I was flicking my tongue quickly across her clit now, watching her try to hold back.

"Your tongue," she panted out, scratching her nails across my scalp. Her legs were twitching, trying to shut, so I knew she was close.

Pushing her thighs down, I tickled her entrance with my index finger, causing her to lift her knees up and curl her toes. She was holding back, but I wouldn't let her. When her eyes opened and she was watching me eat her out, I pushed my finger into her.

"Dash," she breathed out. It was all it took before her pussy clenched around my finger, and her body convulsed. Her hips were pushing into me. Holding my finger in place, I let her ride out her orgasm while I gently lapped at her clit.

I might have just said that watching her give me a blowjob was the best experience of my life, but apparently, I was wrong. Watching her face while I made her come easily surpassed that.

When her legs fell to the bed and she was regaining her composure, I made my way to her, and lay next to her.

Finally, with wild hair and a satisfied smile, she looked at me.

"That was the best experience of my life." I kissed her, skating my tongue across her lips before dipping it into her mouth, making sure she could taste herself on me. "I'm still hungry."

Even in her delirious haze, her eyes nearly bugged out at the suggestion. "Um, what?"

I chuckled. "You tasted so good, I think I need seconds."

"How can you still be hungry? You just ate me out like I was your last meal."

"I'll never lose my appetite for you." I kissed her again and towered over her ready for another round. She gripped my hair, stopping me from venturing south.

"As much as I'd love to do that again, I need a break. It's a little too sensitive down there, if you know what I mean."

"I promise, the second one will feel even better."

"Maybe, but let's try it next time. You've got to go soon, right?" I nodded, for the first time in my life annoyed that I had a hockey game to get to. "Then, can you hold me for a little bit? Just until I've gotten over the epic orgasm you just gave me."

"Sure." I grinned, loving the fact that it was me that just made her feel that good.

Drawing her body into mine, I rested my chin on the top of her head, spooning her.

"I like this," she said, almost shyly as her ass rubbed against my crotch.

"Madison. Don't. That's too tempting."

She stopped, and I left a kiss on the top of her head, relaxing on the pillow as I held her close. This was perfect, and I had no intention of leaving.

CHAPTER 22
Dash

When I opened my eyes, my head was throbbing, my mouth was dry, and through the tired haze, all I could hear was an incessant buzzing.

Where am I?

Squinting, I tried to move, only to feel the weight of Madison's mostly naked body on top of me. With no covers on, she was curled up on my chest, doing her best to keep warm. I relaxed back down for a second, gently playing with strands of her hair and stroking her back in an attempt to wake her, but she wasn't budging. Lightly snoring, she was exhausted. I was too, but I needed to turn my phone off to stop it from buzzing before it woke her up.

Ever so gently, I slipped out from underneath her and draped a fluffy, white throw blanket over her to keep her warm. As she snuggled into the bed, my body yearned to join her again because she looked so tiny in it without me.

This was it.

I could feel it.

She was the one. The one I was always supposed to be with. The one I didn't want to be without. Now, I just had to take her on that date and tell her brother all about us. Simple. I inwardly groaned because if it were that easy, I would have told him already.

My phone was still buzzing, but finding my pants seemed impossible after Madison tossed them across the room earlier. When I finally found them behind the chest of drawers, I pulled my phone out, only to be met with a burst of messages from my teammates.

"Fuck," I whispered sharply.

I had no time to read through any of the messages because I was already thirty minutes late for warm-up. Coach was going to kill me.

"Fuck. Fuck. Fuck," I repeated like an annoying mantra and shoved my clothes on as quickly as possible. If I left right now, I might just get there in time for the start of the game, but that didn't mean I'd be ready to play.

I had to get to the rink, either way. I couldn't let my team down.

Holding on to the doorknob, I looked over my shoulder at Madison's still-sleeping form and felt guilt slithering through my veins. I didn't want to leave her like this, but I didn't want to wake her either. Scanning the room, I smiled when I saw the pink Post-it notes on her desk. Grabbing the pad and a pen, I quickly wrote a message to her, inviting her to the game tonight. When I put the pen down, I took one final look at Madison, and my chest constricted.

I didn't want to leave. Madison looked beautiful, but I promised myself I'd be straight back in her bed once this game was finished.

Gently closing the door behind me, I ran as fast as I could to the rink. Unfortunately, by the time I got there, the team was already out on the ice.

Shit.

I wasn't just late. Goodman, our backup goaltender, was out on the ice. I'd been replaced and I couldn't blame them. I was always early for games because of the stretching I needed to do, so missing warm-up entirely didn't look good.

Coach was going to kill me, and I deserved it. I knew going to Madison's dorm was a mistake. I should have gone to my room and stretched straight after the flight, but I just couldn't help myself. I needed to see her, and planned to talk to her about everything, but as per usual, that went out the window the minute I saw her in my T-shirt.

After twenty minutes of trying to convince Coach I was ready to go out there, I was sitting in the locker room, stewing with anger, because I wasn't even allowed on the bench. I blew out an annoyed breath, looking around at the empty wooden benches and only hoped that I'd somehow be called into the game, but I knew it was unlikely. Coach wanted me dead. Drawn and quartered, then skewered onto a kebob, was the exact way he wanted me to go. I knew because he told me. I was an idiot and let my dick do the thinking today.

Dammit.

My game was being affected by all this sneaking around, and I hated to admit that Cade might have been right. Maybe having a girlfriend really did make me a terrible goalie. Or maybe it was karma punishing me because I'd gone behind my best friend's back and slept with his sister. Either way, I was pissed off that I'd somehow screwed myself and the team over because I couldn't keep my dick in my pants for a couple of hours before the game.

"So, are you just going to sit there acting all broody instead of acknowledging that we're sitting here together?" Henry said from across the locker room, looking at me like I was an idiot, which to his defense was the truth.

Glaring at him, I held back what I really wanted to say, which would be something along the lines of, *"stay the hell away from Madison, or I'm going to add to those black eyes."* I still had no idea where he'd gotten them from or why he and Cade were suddenly okay with each other, but I had my own things to worry about.

"Why bother? I have nothing to say to you."

Henry let out an amused breath and shook his head. "Really? You don't think we have anything to talk about at all?"

Scratching my chin, I resigned myself to the fact that Henry wasn't going to shut up. "Fine. What's this about? Amy?"

"Amy?" Henry raised his eyebrows in surprise. "Oh, really? That's what you think I want to talk about?"

"What else is there that we need to address? The cost of a nose job, maybe?" I groused. I could admit I was being an ass, but I was annoyed, and Henry deserved it.

Henry's nose twitched at the mere mention of it. "Typical goaltender. Guarding the shit out of things that don't need guarding."

"What are you even talking about?"

"This team. You don't need to be so protective of it. I'm not here to try to take down anything or anyone. I just want to play hockey."

"Then why'd you come here knowing Cade and I play here?"

"I told you already, because we make a good team on the ice, and it's been years. I didn't think you cared about Amy while you were dating her, so how the hell was I supposed to know you'd still be holding a grudge about it now?"

"I don't care about Amy."

That made Henry laugh again. He stood, made his way to my side of the locker room, and took a seat on the bench opposite. This was why I hated people. The minute you interacted with them, they thought it was okay to come closer and talk about their feelings.

"No, you're right. That much was obvious in high school, but you still won't admit the real reason you hate me, will you?"

"And why exactly do you think I hate you?"

"You're going to make me say it, aren't you?"

"Say what?"

"Madison."

When her name fell out of his mouth, I held back the urge to knock him out because that would be proving his point. "Not sure what you're talking about."

In his full gear, Henry leaned forward and whispered, "Ask me what I'm studying."

"What are you studying?"

He pushed his tongue out, wetting his lips, clearly amused by the whole situation. "Computer science."

Madison's course.

"You know, I tried to speak to her the first day of my lectures, but as she walked out of the room, I couldn't help but notice you were dragging her over to the corner, hiding away with her. Then you leaned in like you were about to kiss her. Almost like she was your girlfriend."

"Well, she's not," I spat out because I didn't trust Henry with any information about Madison and me. Not when Cade was still in the dark about it. He had to hear it from me first.

"Really?" With another raise of his brow, he mulled over my words. "Because I could have sworn I saw you chasing Madison into the equipment room earlier this week. Don't you remember?"

I knew that would come back to haunt me eventually, but I couldn't control myself that day.

"Look, I get it. She's cute and really nice, but coming from someone who's been in your position before, I'd probably tell Cade sooner rather than later. I wasn't his friend, and he held a grudge for two years. Kind of like you." He pushed out a laugh. "Sometimes I wonder if the two of you are attached by the umbilical cord."

"What makes you think he doesn't know about Madison and me?"

"Because you're walking straight," he joked, but pursed his lips when I didn't laugh. "I know you think you're being discreet when you're checking your phone or looking in her direction but, Dash, you're a big guy. You trying to be inconspicuous is like a giraffe trying to hide in an ant museum. It's so obvious you've got a girl on your brain." He held his hand out and pointed at me. "Look at you right now. In all the years I've known you, you've never been late for a game, but here we are."

I clenched my jaw, mulling over his words because I knew he was right. Scotty knew, Henry knew, and I had no doubts that if Alex thought about it long enough, he'd see right through it too. The only person who didn't know was Cade, and it was because I let him believe that I was fucking Sienna instead.

"You're screwing up because you're trying to keep a secret that's not worth keeping."

"What do you mean she's not worth keeping?" I stood, feeling the same rage I did when he arrived. I knew I'd just openly admitted to him that there was something going on with Madison and me, but what did it matter? He already suspected it.

"Whoa. Whoa. Whoa. Calm down. I didn't mean Madison wasn't worth keeping. I meant the secret wasn't. You and Cade have been buddies for years. I really don't think he'll be ticked off that you're making his sister happy. Seeing the way her face lit up when she saw you before Hockeyfest made it obvious how much she likes you. She seems a lot less anxious too."

"Probably because she isn't worried about her boyfriend cheating on her," I muttered, ready to punch him at the mere memory of him doing that. What a douche.

He just gave me a wry smile. "Boyfriend, huh?"

"Why are you telling me all this? Are you planning on blackmailing me or something?" I changed the subject because having a heart-to-heart with Henry was not on my bingo card tonight.

"Blackmail? Wow, you really think badly of me, don't you?" I grumbled as a response. "I'm not going to blackmail you. Honestly, what are you going to do for me? Try to help convince Coach to put me out there instead of Erik? I doubt that will help since you're back here with me."

My fists clenched, frustrated at how easy it was for Henry to annoy me without trying.

"I'm telling you this because I want to prove to you that you can trust me. I don't want to get involved in any drama. All I want is to play hockey and win games so I can be seen by scouts."

"So, you're not going to tell Cade?"

He shook his head. "I'd have nothing to gain. It's going to screw up the team dynamic, and like I said, I'm not here to create any drama. I'm just letting you know that I'm going to feign ignorance to the whole thing."

"Thanks," I mumbled, not sure how to respond. I was angry at myself today, and it was coming out in all kinds of ways.

Henry sighed before standing and walking back to his locker.

"Henry."

He looked over his shoulder but didn't turn around.

"You're a great player. I have no doubt you'll get drafted at the end of the season." I fully expected my words to taste like poison, but they didn't. Maybe I wasn't as angry at Henry as I thought. I had Madison now, so what was the point in holding a grudge against him?

He rolled his head to the front and huffed out a sarcastic breath. "Thanks. Now, if only I could convince Coach to play me."

"He'll play you in the next game."

"Oh, yeah? What makes you think that?"

"It's against Southern Collegiate, and you hate them, right?"
"Yeah."
"That's how Coach Hansen works. He's just warming you up by letting you stew in your anger. Do well in that game, and you'll be fine."
"If you say so."

Leaning against my locker, I watched the players walk in, celebrating their win. One I had no part in because I didn't get called up. The idea of doing post-game stretches felt moronic, so I decided to check my phone to see if Madison had woken up yet.

No messages.

Surprising. That orgasm must have knocked her out cold. Maybe I could somehow subtly sneak away from the guys later and give her another one. That would definitely help my mood.

Just as I was about to type out a message to her, I noticed Scotty making his way to me, so I dropped my phone and started taking my gear off.

"How you doing, Sasquatch?"

I rolled my eyes and grumbled out something so incoherent, even I didn't know what it was.

"Uh oh. Angry Dash is back. Are you annoyed about not playing, or did you have a fight with Baby B?"

"Neither," I said, pulling off my gloves and putting them back in my bag.

"Then why do you look so angry?"

"I'm just tired. That's all."

"Well, I just came over here because I wanted to warn you."

"About?"

He glanced over his shoulder and then leaned down so he could talk to me. "Rumors are starting to spread."

"About?"

Scotty gave me no other explanation except a glare, and I knew exactly what it meant. There were rumors about Madison.

"Who's talking?" I asked gruffer than I intended. Had Henry played me just now? Was he the one starting those rumors?

Scotty shrugged, taking his gloves off casually so he didn't draw attention. "After Alex's little show on the plane the other day, people have started talking about Madison and who she might be dating."

"In the context of Alex, why is that a problem?"

Scotty rolled his eyes. "Because Erik mentioned the other day that the only time they see her now is when it's with you."

I paused, knowing that I was getting in too deep. People were getting suspicious, and eventually someone was going to tell Cade. But could I hold out for one more day just so I could take Madison on that date?

"Cade seems to be immune to any suggestion, though. When someone asks him about it, he plays it off like you and Madison hanging out isn't a big deal."

"That's because he doesn't think it is." Scotty raised a brow in question, and I rolled my eyes, feeling stupid for having to mention this. "It's because he thinks I'm dating Sienna, and a couple of weeks ago he asked me if I'd talk to Madison and find out why she was acting so strange."

"Wait a minute. Are you telling me that Cade thinks you're spending time with his sister to *help* him, but you're actually sleeping with her?"

"Shh."

"Dude, no one can hear me over the cheering going on over there."

He had a point. The rest of the team were either in the showers or still out on the ice, celebrating our performance because we were now seven wins away from qualifying for the Frozen Four.

"Don't say anything to Cade. I'm going to speak to him."

Scotty laughed sarcastically. "Believe me, I won't." Clasping my shoulder, he looked at me seriously. "But for your own sake, you need to tell Cade. Screwing with his sister when he thinks you're helping him is a new level of betrayal. You get how bad that is, right?"

I paused, trying to think of something that would make it sound better than it did. "He didn't unintentionally bring us together. He asked me to help him after things had already progressed with Madison."

Scotty blew out a sarcastic whistle and chuckled. "This gets better and better every time I speak to you, I swear. So, what you're telling me is that he asked you to help him find out what guy she was dating, and you're just avoiding the answer while sleeping with her?" I blinked and gave him the slightest of nods as my response. "This is going to blow up in your face so badly, and I want to be there when it does."

"It won't be that bad."

"If you say so."

Just as Scotty started to take his boots off, Cade walked into the locker room, laughing about something with Brooks.

Traitor. Traitor. Traitor.

Dammit. The word echoed in my brain again because Scotty was right. I was the worst kind of friend, and I shouldn't have kept this from him for as long as I had. I still had the taste of Madison on my lips. Hell, she nearly sucked the soul out of my body before I came here. Things were getting serious between us, and neither one of us was built to hide things. Especially from her brother and my best friend.

Cade tipped his chin when he saw me looking at him. "Coming over to you in a second, Bridges. I need to talk to you."

I froze. Scotty did too. "Fuck," he whispered under his breath.

I nodded in response and bumped Scotty on the shoulder to make sure he moved a little, so we didn't look so suspicious before turning back to my locker. As I put my pads away, Scotty did the same. "What are you going to do?"

Letting a breath out, I thought about my options, but I knew what I had to do. Throwing the final pad in my locker, I put my shirt on and said, "I'm going to tell him the truth."

"Now?"

"There's no time like the present. Things aren't changing between Madison and me anytime soon. He's my best friend. He needs to know."

It was like I'd suddenly had an epiphany. The sooner I told her brother, the sooner I could kiss her on campus without anyone caring. Madison wasn't a girl who was going to be gone in a day or a week. She wasn't someone I'd forget about, either. She'd been in my life since I could remember, and frankly, I only imagined that trending in a more positive direction in the future. Yes, Cade might beat me down, but if he did it now, at least I'd have time to recover before the Frozen Four—if we were lucky enough to get there.

"Well, just so you know, I'm going to act as shocked as everyone else in the locker room when you tell him because there's no way in hell I'm going to let Cade break my nose for *your* indiscretions. My father would probably pay for some Hollywood dude to redo it, and I don't want to end up in some tabloids over a botched nose job."

"Are you done?"

"Yes."

"Good. Don't worry. I started this; it's only right I finish it on my own."

I considered messaging Madison to ask her if she'd be okay with me telling Cade, but at this point, it almost felt like that would be stalling. She probably wouldn't answer and then I'd have to wait to get her approval.

As Cade made his way over to me, I'd never felt his presence more in my life. Sure, I was a grumpy asshole, but Cade had this menacing aura about him that gave off a vibe of, *"I'm going to beat the living shit out of you, and then set you on fire."* With his eyes dark, it was the first time I was concerned that I might be the recipient of his wrath.

Sitting on the bench in front of me, Scotty was chewing on his granola bar inconspicuously. "Hey, C. What's up?"

Cade didn't say a word, he just kept his focus on me. Scotty's chews slowed as he looked between the two of us, seemingly getting the hint that Cade wanted to talk to me alone. "You know what? I've got to check on Erik and Alex."

When Scotty was out of earshot, Cade finally started to talk to me. "Are you and Reporter Girl having problems or something? Because she's fucking with you, and I don't like it."

I was taken aback by his abruptness, and honestly, the way he was looking at me made me think he had something else on his mind. His leg was bouncing, and his hands were jittery. When I didn't immediately answer, he looked down and cursed under his breath.

"Is, uh, everything okay?"

He ran a hand through his buzzed hair and sighed. "It's nothing. It's just this stupid shit."

"Stupid shit involving *Behind Closed Doors*?"

"Maybe," he drawled out. "But that's not why I'm here. Why were you late today?"

The confidence I had to tell Cade about my relationship with his sister suddenly dwindled because this was going to hit him like a freight train.

"Umm, yeah. About that. There's something I need to tell you. I saw Madison." Saying her name was at least a start.

"Oh no. This doesn't sound good. Did you find out who she's dating? It's Aiden Matthews, isn't it?"

"Nope. She's not secretly dating Aiden." It was all I managed to get out before Cade's phone started ringing, and he pulled it out of his pocket, cursing again.

Holding his finger up, he kept his eyes on his phone. "Give me a minute. I've got to get this. Sorry."

I nodded, and he walked out of the room, speaking in hushed whispers. Judging by the way he was talking, I didn't think he'd be back any time soon.

"You're not dead?" Scotty assessed the parts of me he could see as he strolled back, now chomping on a crisp, green apple. Where did he get that? He dropped his arm, looking disappointed. "You didn't tell him, did you?"

"I was about to, but he got a phone call."

"Convenient," he said with a quirked lip.

"I'm going to tell him once he's back."

"Sure, you are," he drawled out, taking a large bite of his apple.

"I will. I told you; I don't care if I get beaten up. This has gone on too long. He needs to know."

"Party tonight," Cade hollered as he walked back in the room with an edacious grin on his face. People who didn't know him as well as me would mistake that look for happiness, but it wasn't. You didn't grow up with someone for the better part of eleven years and not know when he was hiding something. Someone pissed him off on that phone call, and he was just masking the problem by partying.

There were a few grumbles, but since no one questioned him, I decided to. "We just finished a game. We've got another one in two days. We need to rest."

With a smirk drawing across his face, Cade said, "We can rest when we're dead."

When he looked around the locker room, he realized there was a lackluster response to his party idea, so he held up his phone. "Message has already been sent out. There's a party at the hockey dorm tonight. If you don't want to be part of it, then you don't have to come home until we're finished, which will be tomorrow morning."

"Asshole," I said under my breath and grabbed my foam roller, begrudgingly planning on doing my non-post-game stretches. "See you at the dorm when I'm done with this."

"Wait, you're going to the party?" Scotty asked, surprised. "I thought you'd be sneaking over to a certain someone's dorm."

"I think that certain someone is still sleeping. Besides, last time I wasn't home for one of Cade's parties, my door got a hole punched through it. I refuse to let that happen again."

"You're almost guaranteeing that outcome if you tell him about Madison tonight."

I pursed my lips, pushing them out as I thought about it. "You're right. I'll feel him out, and if there is something going on with him, I'll wait until the morning, but that's it. He needs to know."

"If you say so." Scotty couldn't hide his disbelief, and I couldn't blame him. I'd been talking a big game for the last twenty minutes but still hadn't made a move.

That was all going to change tonight.

Chapter 23

Dash

No new messages

I sighed because there was still no message from Madison. It'd been over six hours since I'd left her, and I was starting to get concerned. She couldn't still be sleeping, could she? Gripping my water, I had an urge to go to her dorm and check, but there was no way I was leaving this party anytime soon.

Cade was drunk.

Living up to his party boy reputation, he was standing on the wooden coffee table, shirtless. Drinking a beer via a tube connected to a keg while random partygoers cheered him on, he looked ridiculous, and was far too drunk to think rationally, which was putting me off having to speak to him about anything rational.

I couldn't leave him alone because I wasn't sure what he'd do, and I was hoping there'd be a way that I could distract him enough to somehow lock him in his room, but with every chug of his beer, the possibility was becoming less likely.

Taking a drink of my water, I contemplated whether I should call Madison and get her to come over. Maybe if we were both here together, and he saw how much we liked each other, he'd take it easy on me.

"Stop overthinking." Scotty shunted my shoulder as he stood next to me. "It makes that wrinkle in the middle of your eyebrows more pronounced, and if it gets any bigger, people are going to start thinking you have a unibrow."

"Why do you think Cade's drinking so much tonight?"

Cade was sitting on the table now, and weirdly, Henry was by his side amongst the puck bunnies, looking like a kid brother that was finally getting to hang out with his sister's friends at a pajama party. He was almost acting like he'd never touched a girl before.

"Are you using Cade's drunkenness as a distraction to get out of talking to your best friend about the shitshow relationship the two of you now have?"

"What do you mean? Our friendship isn't a shitshow."

"You sure? Because Cade's clearly going through something, but your head is too far up your own ass and your new secret relationship to ask. Gotta admit, if you were my best friend, I'd be hurt."

"Cade doesn't do feelings. Talking it out isn't his thing, and as his friend, I respect that. If he wants to talk to me, he knows I'm here."

"And he's handling it so well." Cade's tongue was out, and he was showing the rest of the team that he'd finished his drink. "Did you ever find out why he and Henry showed up with matching bruises earlier this week?"

"Was I supposed to be finding out?"

"You're the only one Cade would tell."

"Well, he didn't tell me anything."

With Cade's arm around Henry's shoulder, I realized Scotty had a point. Something happened between them, and I didn't know. I also didn't know who was calling him or why he was hanging out at *Behind Closed Doors* so often. I was the one who usually kept Cade in check and stopped him from doing outlandish things, but I'd been so busy thinking about his sister that

I'd put our friendship on the back burner. I knew nothing about what was going on in Cade's life, and it sucked.

"Daniel," Sienna said sharply, and I could have sworn her voice had the ability to make a boner flaccid.

"I'm out," Scotty said, sneaking away before Sienna could talk to him.

When I turned to face her, she was glaring at me "Sienna? What are you doing here?"

"I'm just trying to enjoy the party like everyone else." She held her hand out, trying to look like any other college kid, but, as per usual, failed miserably. With her thick glasses and a pencil skirt, she was making it too obvious that she wasn't here to party.

She had her eyes on Cade, watching as he sauntered around the room, making a show of himself. I wondered if he was her new target, but she was barking up the wrong tree there. Drinking a keg at a party wasn't enough for a story, and that was all she'd get. Cade was a private guy. He did shady shit all the time, but no one knew what that shady shit was because he kept himself to himself. Like I said before, he tells me nothing, and if I, as his best friend, couldn't get the information out of him, then there was no way Sienna would.

"Sienna."

She couldn't help herself. She whipped her head in my direction, her smile so wide that she looked like the Joker. "Have you got a story for me? Give me all the deets. Please, please be about substance abuse."

I shook my head. This girl was insufferable, and there was a moment that I thought I could just let this all go. That was until Sienna grabbed my arm and held me in place. Surprisingly, for a small girl, she was pretty strong. "Dash. If you don't tell me what you know, I'll find someone who will, and getting the story from them won't do you any favors."

I glared at her with a furrowed brow. "Is that your way of asking if I'm taking performance-enhancing drugs?"

She puffed out a breath obnoxiously. "I know you're not, but I'm pretty sure you'll have an idea who is."

"Wait, how do you know I'm not?"

She looked at me with the tiniest hint of amusement marring her lips. "Come on, Dash. You're a goalie."

"And?"

"What are performance-enhancing drugs going to do for you? You just stand there and squat for the entire game."

Wow. If Sienna were a guy, I'd have decked her for that comment. "They could do a hell of a lot, thank you very much. How about helping the accuracy of my hand-eye coordination or heightening my attention span?"

She smiled, watching me with amusement as I listed out all the ways drugs could help. It wasn't until a few seconds later that I realized that was her plan all along. She was trying to get me to admit to something I hadn't done, and I was the stupid sap falling for it.

"Look. I'm not doing drugs. None of my friends are doing drugs either. I don't have a story for you. I've got nothing to talk about."

"I think Madison Bright might be a little offended by that," she teased, and when I turned to glare at her, she just smiled and winked. "You know, if you want to keep that relationship hidden, you should probably try to stop your eyebrow from quirking every time her name is mentioned. It's such an obvious tell."

I shook my head, shaking my hair forward so it was harder to make out my eyebrows. For the first time, I was happy I had curtains.

"How do you know that?"

"Did you forget she nearly cried when she saw me walking out of your room? I may have followed you guys around for a little bit the next few days. It's a boring, unimaginative story, but since there seems to be nothing else interesting to write about with the hockey team, I'm considering writing an article about it."

"You're not going to write a story about Madison and me."

She clicked her tongue across her teeth. "So touchy, but don't worry, Daniel. Don't worry, I'm not here for your lame story. Sleeping with your best friend's sister is idle gossip compared to what I found out about Cade."

My spine straightened, and I moved closer toward her in an act of intimidation. Sienna moved back, but she didn't stop looking at me with a challenging glare. If she thought she could ruin Cade's college career, she was mistaken.

"What do you know about Cade?"

Her smile grew, and she stood a little bit taller because for the first time in this conversation, she seemed to have the upper hand. "Does the name Savannah Barnett mean anything to you?"

Savannah Barnett? I racked my brain, trying to think of anywhere I'd heard it, but I was drawing a blank. I didn't want her to know that, though, so I played along. "What about Savannah Barnett?"

She grinned at my answer. "You don't know, do you?"

"Hard to know what I don't know when you're talking to me in riddles."

"Adley Barnett?"

I pursed my lips together because this was getting harder to lie about.

She shook her head, laughing. "Nope. You don't know." Her chin tipped up. "That means this story will break the internet when I publish it."

Standing dumbfounded, I was trying to figure out if Cade had mentioned this Savannah girl before, but I couldn't remember. I also couldn't remember the last time I spoke to him without it involving Madison.

Sienna tapped me on the shoulder and smiled. "That's all I needed to know," she hummed out.

Turning on her heel, she was about to skip away from me, but I gripped her arm, stopping her. "You're going to tell me everything you know right now."

Glaring at my hand, Sienna's smile dropped as she looked up at me in anger. "Or what?"

"Dash. Reporter Girl." Cade drawled out her nickname seductively, but he was staring at me with a smirk on his face as he wiggled his eyebrows. His eyes were bloodshot now, and that keg had clearly gone to his head because he couldn't walk straight. Well, that wasn't exactly helping Cade's reputation.

I took a subtle glance at her. With her brows furrowed, she looked genuinely concerned, which was odd for her. She was usually a pit bull but maybe she was softening toward us. No. That wasn't it. She hated me, so maybe the softness was only toward Cade because of the things she found out.

She reached out her hand, holding on to Cade's bicep. "I think you might need to sit down."

Cade blew out his breath and laughed. "Will you sit on my lap if I do?

Oh, wait, sorry. I know you're Dash's girl. I would never steal a girl from my main man," he said with pride, and that guilt I was feeling earlier came straight back to the pit of my stomach. I was a dick. I already knew that, but this was making me feel worse.

Taking a step in front of Sienna because I didn't want him doing anything he might regret, I forced him to focus on me. "C, is everything okay?"

With hazy eyes and a drunken smile, he said, "I'm fine, D. Why wouldn't I be?"

"I know you like to drink, but I think you've gone a little too far tonight." I could tell he didn't like the challenge in my voice. His blue eyes said as much as they stared into mine. Even drunk, the guy was a force that you didn't want to mess with.

"Hey, Reporter Girl," he said, staring at me. "Did you know the last time you were in Dash's room, you were so loud that you woke up the team cat?"

"Team cat? We don't have a team cat."

Cade cackled and pointed at me. "Ha, but you didn't deny it was Reporter Girl in there with you, did you? You're too easy to fool." He pushed past me so he was directly in front of Sienna. "Will you just admit you're dating Dash because you're looking for a story?"

"I'm not."

Cade didn't let her finish talking. "Because he already told me you were a mistake the first time you left his dorm, and you've been fucking up his game ever since you walked in here in those platform heels." Sienna's eyes grew wide in surprise. "You might think he's the easiest one of us to crack because he doesn't let many people in, but he's not. You've been dating him for a few weeks now, which makes me think he cares about you, and I don't want to have to deal with a broken-hearted Dash. Last time, he broke a guy's nose and got suspended, and I don't want that for my big, burly best friend."

He was talking garbage, and as I looked at Sienna with unease from over Cade's shoulder, he wrapped his arm around my neck, pulling me close enough to kiss me on the cheek. "I love this guy. He deserves the best, and if that's not you, then you can get the hell out."

It was official. I was going to hell for everything I put my best friend through.

"Don't worry, I have no intention of hurting Dash. You're right, he's a pretty good, upstanding guy. I wouldn't want to break his heart," she said with a smile as we both tried to calm my overly affectionate drunk friend, who swooped his other arm over Sienna's shoulder. "He's a good guy."

"A good guy who deserves to get his dick sucked!" Cade yelled, and I pushed him off me.

"Cade!"

He opened his arms wide and cackled. "What? I'm just saying what we're all thinking. Maybe it would help you loosen up."

Okay, this wasn't working, there were two things I needed to do. Get Cade in his bed, and make sure that whatever story Sienna had on him stayed out of print. Looking over at Scotty, I motioned for him to come over.

"Can you take care of Cade until I'm back?" He looked between Sienna and me. "It won't take long."

"Okay," he said and made his way over to our teammate. I didn't waste time watching them, I was too intent on making sure Cade's private life remained private.

Sienna yelped when I grabbed her arm and started dragging her to my room. "Hey! Get off me. What are you doing?" When I didn't answer, she kept talking. "Where are you taking me?"

"Somewhere we can talk," I gritted out.

Chapter 24

Madison

Frozen, I stood in the middle of the hockey common room because my legs felt too heavy to move. My entire body did too, for that matter.

"MB!" my brother called, making his way over to me with a noticeable sway in his step. Scotty was right behind him, scowling. I didn't take too much notice of them, though, because I was too confused about what was happening in front of me.

Cade smothered me in a hug, and the only thing I could muster was a gentle pat on his arm.

This wasn't happening. There had to be another explanation.

As Cade pulled away, he poked his bottom lip out. "What's wrong?" His breath stank of alcohol, but that still wasn't enough to draw my attention away from them. When he followed my gaze, he burped and said, "Ah, have you met hockey's newest golden couple?"

"Go-golden couple?" What was he talking about? My heart was beating wildly because I was currently watching the guy I was sleeping with drag another girl into his bedroom.

"Dash finally has a girlfriend."

I raised my brow, looking into my brother's bloodshot eyes for the first time. He was obviously drunk, so maybe he was making this up. "He does?"

"Yeah, Reporter Girl."

Okay. Breathe.

Cade had mentioned Sienna before, and Dash brushed it off. He didn't know about us, so maybe he was wrong about this. I shouldn't jump to conclusions, but it was hard not to when those conclusions were staring me in the face. Swallowing down my embarrassment, I gave my brother a forced smile. My head was spiraling with questions. *Had Dash been lying to me the entire time? Was Tiff right about him? Had he been playing me when he told me he was going to tell my brother about us after our date?*

I blinked away tears as the reality of the situation started to sink in. Looking between Scotty and my brother, my eyes were burning as I desperately tried to hold back my emotions. I couldn't cry here. Not in front of these guys.

"I need some air," I said before taking a few steps back.

"Madison," Henry drawled, accidentally bumping into me, and I crushed my eyes shut because I just had to bump into him, didn't I? We might have been on good terms now, but that didn't mean I wanted him to see me like this. "Good to see you again."

"Henry," Cade said in warning.

At this point, Scotty was standing beside Cade, and even though I knew he was there, I didn't have the courage to look up and acknowledge him. There was too much going on in my brain.

"Do you remember what we talked about?"

Henry raised his hands. "Relax. Your sister doesn't want me. She's in love with Dash."

I gasped. When I looked at Scotty, he stilled. What the hell did Henry know?

"Dash?" Cade said, and my blood ran cold because, even though he was drunk, his voice sounded menacing. "Still?"

That last word forced me to look at him because what did he mean, *"still?"*

Cade's eyes dripped with pity as I asked, "What are you talking about?"

Cade sighed. "I'm sorry, Madison. I thought you were over that and

THE DRAFT

dating some football player. I wouldn't have flaunted Dash's new relationship in front of you if I thought there was any hint that you were still into him."

New relationship? Did he have to keep using words like that? Didn't he see it was making me want to crumble to dust? Everyone was watching me, and I was too busy trying to tamper down my reaction to think.

"You know what? I'm going to go." I pointed my thumb at the door. I felt like the pin cushion of an overly enthusiastic seamstress. Punctured to the point that the stuffing was coming out and everyone could see the damage. What was I doing with Dash? Fooling around? Giving him everything, all the while, he was giving his everything to someone else. To Sienna, of all people. They didn't fit. Dash had respect. He was quiet. He didn't like being in the limelight, and Sienna *was* the limelight. She literally reported on the team all the time.

"Oh, I hope you're not leaving on my account." Henry looked genuinely concerned, but it wasn't like I could answer him with the truth. That seeing him had only solidified that I was a dumb girl, chasing after my brother's teammates, looking for validation where I shouldn't.

How could I have been so naïve to think that Dash ever wanted me? I wasn't his type. I was an obnoxious, flirty girl that people didn't get serious with.

Just as I was about to run out, an arm draped over my shoulder and the familiar woody cologne hit my senses.

"Let me take you home, Baby B," Scotty said, looking down at me with a placid smile. Scotty? He was the one who came to my rescue. The guy who barely spoke to me because he was too busy chasing after some random girl I didn't know. Not Dash. The guy I thought was chasing after me.

Henry looked between me and Scotty and then pointed his finger at us. "Wait, are you interested in Madison, too?" he asked, surprised.

That was when Cade took a step forward. "You are not going anywhere near Madison again, Newman."

Henry raised his hands, looking between Cade and Scotty. "Woah, I'm not trying to start anything, it's just...uh, never mind." He was holding back on saying something, but I had no idea what it was.

"I'm not dating Madison," Scotty said, pushing his chest out and making a point with the inflection in his voice. He'd seen I was a wreck, thinking it was over Henry, and he was swooping in to try to make me look less pathetic. "Cade put a veto on that a long time ago," he joked, giving me a playful wink. He was trying to cheer me up, but I doubted anything would make me feel better.

"Watch it," Cade said, looking around the room with narrowed eyes.

My face was blooming red because being present for this conversation was humiliating, and I didn't know where to look at this point, so I just stared at my feet.

"Madison is off-limits, and you should all know that by now. Henry hasn't had a straight nose since high school because of Dash, and I'm more than happy to see if I can punch it back into place."

"You ready to go?" Scotty squeezed my shoulder, and when I looked up to him, he gave me a calming smile. He moved his hand to my back and started to guide me to the door. Without another word, I followed him, ready to get away from all the drama.

Standing in the elevator, I glanced up for all of two seconds and regretted it immediately. Everyone was watching, and it was all starting to come together. Dash lied. He never planned on telling my brother, and he just used me for a quick round of sex.

"Smile," Scotty said through his teeth, and I did my best to muster up an "I don't give a fuck" look, but I was seconds away from crumbling into nothing. Thankfully, the elevator doors shut, so I could drop my head, in a vain attempt to get my thoughts together.

Scotty didn't say anything; he just stood next to me as the comforting presence I didn't know I needed. When we were out of the building, he stuffed his hands in his pockets and looked at me with a sigh. "Come on, Baby B. It's cold."

"What on earth was that back there?"

"Madison." Scotty looked at me with more sympathy than I could handle, confirming everything I thought. It was all he had to say. I was in his arms, bawling and feeling just as raw as when I was sixteen and the first guy I liked cheated on me. With Scotty's arms tightly around me, he stood there, saying nothing. Not that I'd be able to hear him, anyway. My crying was obnoxiously loud, and if the music wasn't blasting from the hockey dorm upstairs, I had no doubts that they'd be able to hear it.

He stroked my back, and when I finally calmed down, I backed away, wiping my tears. Scotty pursed his lips together, sympathy dripping across his features.

"I'm sorry. I have no idea what's going on, but I couldn't sit back and watch you crumble in front of the hockey team."

"Was it that obvious I was about to break down?" I tried to make it sound like I wasn't affected by his words, but Scotty could see right through it.

Shaking his head, Scotty said, "I don't know what the fuck is going on with Dash, but you don't deserve to be treated like that. Frankly, he needs to get his head out of his ass and figure out what he wants before he screws everything up with you *and* Cade."

Sucking in a harsh breath, I tried to give him a small smile because he was trying to be nice, but damn, those words hurt because he was essentially confirming the reality that I'd played out in my head. Dash was playing me, and Scotty found out the same time I did.

Swallowing, I asked, "How'd you find out about us?"

"It's been pretty obvious for anyone who's willing to look that Dash has a thing for you. I noticed it the first day you arrived on campus and came to the hockey dorm to see Cade. Dash was looking at us like he was ready to pounce on anyone that looked at you. Then...well, his antics at The Draft confirmed it." He shrugged, and I'd almost forgotten he was there, it had happened so long ago.

"And yet, you're the one standing here, saving me when it matters."

"Honestly? I think you need to hear Dash out. I only stepped in because he wasn't there to. I'm pretty sure he was planning on telling your brother about you guys tonight. I just have no idea why he's suddenly speaking to Sienna."

"No," I quipped, operating on emotion more than anything. *Planning. Intending.* Dash threw all these words around like they were nothing. Like they didn't mean something to me. "Dash and I are over."

That statement was said with so much conviction, I almost believed it. But were we over? Could we ever really be over when we never really started? I wanted to give him my virginity. Just like I wanted to with Henry.

268

Would the painful feeling of being crushed from the inside ever subside? Maybe Dash wasn't the one. Maybe there was someone better out there for me. I didn't know, but all I knew was that looking at Scotty wasn't making things better. In fact, it was making things worse because it was a constant reminder that I'd been embarrassed in front of his teammates.

"I'm going to go home."

"I'll walk you." He didn't let me take a step before he was matching my stride.

I stopped and turned to face him. "No, really. Don't worry. I'm fine." I wanted to shake him off because I wanted to call my cousin Tiff and tell her she was right. All men were trash, and I would never try to make a connection with a hockey player ever again. It was a conversation I couldn't have with Scotty standing there.

"Madison, I'm not leaving you to walk home on your own when you're this fragile."

"It's ten minutes away. I'll be fine."

Scotty winced. "Yeah, no offense, but you look like a panda that fell out of a tree backward. It's not happening. I'm walking you home."

I bit down a response because there was no point in fighting him. This whole conversation was just taking up more time.

"Look, I understand. I wouldn't want to be around any hockey players either, but I'm not leaving. You don't have to talk to me. I'll walk five paces behind if that helps, but I'm not letting you walk home alone because one of my best friends fucked up. Cade is too drunk to realize what's going on, but neither he nor Dash would want you walking home on your own."

I pushed out a laugh. "Maybe I should have told Cade then and there. I could have watched Dash get his balls barbecued. It might have made me feel better."

"You don't mean that."

I hung my head and didn't answer because he was right. I didn't want Dash to lose his balls, but I was annoyed that I played with them earlier today, knowing what I know now.

"Dash is just as crazy about you as you are him. Don't ever think otherwise. There's something else going on with Sienna which has nothing to do with a relationship. All I ask is that you listen to him when he comes to talk to you because the guy is a moody asshole on a good day, and losing you will most certainly make him worse."

I nodded but had no intention of speaking to Dash for a long time. I needed space.

"Come on. Let's go." Scotty wrapped his arm around me, and I followed him blindly, walking in silence. There was nothing left to say because all I wanted to do was go to my room and talk to Tiff while I cried. Sure, it sounded pathetic, but I needed to do it for my own sake.

When we got to my dorm, Scotty offered to walk me up, but I politely declined and gave him a hug to show how much I appreciated him. He wasn't the knight in shining armor I was expecting, but he was there for me, and that said something about his character.

When I finally got to my room, Aster was walking to hers. "Is, uh, everything all right?" I could tell in her tone that she only asked because she felt like she had to.

"Everything's fine," I tried to say confidently, but the crack in my voice wasn't helping. I sucked in a breath, holding back my emotions, and opened my door. "If anyone comes here tonight, can you tell them I'm not here?"

She nodded and gave me the same sympathetic look as Scotty.

Sighing, I walked into my room and locked the door. Leaning my forehead against it, I took a deep breath and held back the tears, cursing myself for ever leaving this room because the only thing it brought me was heartache.

Chapter 25
Dash

I threw my dorm door open in aggravation. I should have known speaking to Sienna was a waste of time. She knew nothing. Just a couple of names that she was hoping I'd accidentally let something slip about. The only good thing about interrogating her was that I now knew Cade was her target and I needed to get to the bottom of this story before she did.

When a hand grabbed my ankle, I stopped, only to find Cade sitting beside the door, looking bleary-eyed and exhausted.

"Ugh!" Sienna cried as she hit me in the back. "You're like a brick wall." She walked around me, rubbing her nose, but I ignored her because finding out what was going on with Cade was more important to me.

"Cade?" I bent down so we were face-to-face.

He looked up at me in surprise, as though his hand wasn't currently clutching my ankle. "You're back already? I guess I shouldn't be surprised. You did tell me you only last thirty seconds."

"Is everything okay?"

He pushed out a breath, laughing. "Everything is fine. Why? Do I seem upset?"

His hand flew up in the air for no apparent reason, and I glanced over my shoulder, noting Sienna's judgmental gaze. Yeah, I needed to get Cade out of here before she found anything out. Cade had loose lips when he was drunk, and I didn't want her knowing that little fact.

"Where's Scotty?" I looked around the room, noticing how quiet it had become. There were only a few people on the couch watching tv. I didn't know any of them. There was no Erik, no Scotty. No one. "He was supposed to be looking after you."

Cade waved me off with a chortle. "Scotty's gone. He left a while ago."

"Come on." I offered my hand to Cade, and he glared at my palm, refusing to take it.

"Did you know your lifeline is really long? Like freakishly long," he said, completely entranced. I pulled my hand away and stuffed it in my pocket.

"I need to talk to you in there." I used my eyebrows to point to his room. Side-eyeing Sienna, I said, "You can go now."

"Fine," she sighed, which surprised me since I expected her to push back. Maybe she'd had enough of the drama as I had today. Looking around me, she raised her hand to Cade. "Good seeing you again, C. I hope you don't have a headache in the morning."

Without looking or moving anything other than his hand to salute her, Cade said, "Goodbye, Little Miss Pop My Cherry."

Deadpanned, she glanced at me for answers, and I shook my head. "Long story. Don't ask."

My phone vibrated in my jeans, but I ignored it. Cade was more important, and I was determined to make him my priority. When I reached for my door, Cade slapped my opened hand, giving me a high-five I didn't ask for. Sighing, I slung one of his arms over my shoulder and dragged him to his bedroom.

Pushing the door open, I rolled him onto the bed and sat on the black leather office chair beside it.

Cade moved around a little before throwing an arm over his eyes and growling.

"So," I started. "Are you going to tell me what's wrong, or are you just going to keep growling like a bear over there?"

With no way to see me, he replied, "That's rich coming from you. You've got one of the hottest girls on campus chasing after you, and you're still the grumpiest shit I've ever met."

"I can't help you if you don't tell me what's going on."

"Nothing. I'm fine."

"You sure about that, because when you're fine, you usually take your aggression out in the rink."

"I believe your door would have other opinions on that."

I let out a small laugh because, even in his drunk state, he had a way of being obtuse. I was getting nowhere with him tonight. He wasn't going to tell me anything in this drunk state, but I couldn't exactly just up and leave him. My best friend needed me, and it was high time I started acting like one myself.

"I don't know what's going on with you, C, but I do want you to know that I'm here and willing to help you."

Cade lifted his arm just enough to open one eye. Surprisingly, it was less bloodshot than earlier. "You can't help me. Not with this problem."

"Why not? You in financial trouble or something?"

"No. Nothing like that. I'm just…"

He closed his eyes, trailing off, and I had no idea what his issue was. "Spit it out, Bright."

"I'm in love, okay?"

Well, shit. That wasn't where I was expecting this to go.

"You are?" I swallowed, watching as my friend's face morphed from nonchalance to aggravation. Was this one of the girls that Sienna mentioned?

"Yes, and she hates me. It doesn't matter who I beat up for her or how much I pay to see her, she doesn't want anything to do with me."

Constantly checking his phone, going out straight after games, throwing parties after losses. How had I not figured out sooner that there was a girl involved with all his weird behavior? I frowned because I knew why. Madison. I was focusing so much on her that I'd been completely oblivious to my friend's needs. Even now, I'd been thinking about her all night instead of stopping my friend from getting into such an intoxicated state.

"It's fucked up, and it pisses me off."

"Because she doesn't like you?"

"Because she has a boyfriend."

"Ah, that could be a problem."

"Yeah, and you don't know her, but she's a good girl. She's not going to cheat. Not with me, at least."

"That's admirable. If she cheated *with* you, then she'd probably cheat *on* you in the future, and that's not something you'd want."

He pushed himself up, glaring at me as though I had just insulted the King of England, and he was imagining all the ways he could chop my head off. "People only cheat when they aren't getting what they want out of their relationship. She wouldn't cheat on me because I'd give her everything."

"But she doesn't want it?"

He chuckled, nodding to himself. "Oh, she wants it. She just doesn't want to admit she wants anything to do with me."

"Give it time. I'm sure you can wear her down."

My phone continued to buzz in my jeans, but I kept ignoring it. The noise seemed to inspire Cade to pull his own phone out and start to swipe through messages. Ones I presumed were from the girl he was in love with.

"Maybe you should talk to her."

"You don't think that was the first thing I did? She doesn't want me. It's fine. I'll move on." He raised his hand, rolling over dramatically.

"Sure, seems like it."

"Don't act all high and mighty with me, Dash. You may think you and Reporter Girl have your shit together, but she's fucking up your game."

"So you keep saying," I mumbled and ran a hand through my hair. I was fucking up because I was lying to my best friend, which had to stop. Cade had rolled over, so he was facing the wall. Since he wasn't looking at me, I'd gained some of that courage I had earlier, and it all started to make sense. Cade had opened up to me, and it was only fair that I opened up about me and Madison. He had a right to know, and Madison deserved to be more than a secret.

"About that. Cade, there's something I've been meaning to tell you."

I took my phone out of my pocket and pulled up the note that I'd been editing constantly for the last few weeks. Clearing my throat, I looked over at Cade, who was lying on his bed, grumbling something, and started reading off my note.

"I would appreciate it if you would let me finish everything I have to say before talking." Taking a deep breath, I continued. "Cade. I remember the first day I met you. We were ten years old, on the ice. I was tiny back then, and some older kids pushed me, making me lose my balance. I was being laughed at, but you didn't let it last for long. You beat the shit out of them even though they were double your size. From that moment forward, I knew you'd be like a brother to me, and over a decade later, I can say you still are. Every big life event, you've been there, and I don't plan on that changing anytime soon."

I took a break because my hand was shaking. He was finally going to learn about Madison and me, and I really wanted it to go well. "But with all that said, it wasn't just you I built a relationship with. It was with your family. With your dad, who took me to hockey games when mine couldn't. It was with your mom, who made me all the homemade dinners I'd missed out on. It was with Madison. The girl who was always there, trying to be just like her brother but usually failing miserably. I watched her go from gawky and awkward to heartbroken and beautiful. I don't know when exactly it happened, but at some point, I started to fall in love with your sister. Who could blame me? She's vivacious, caring, and sweet."

Cade let out another grumble, but at least he was letting me finish.

"I know you hate the idea of her dating one of your teammates, and I completely understand if you don't want me to date your sister, but know this, I can't stop. I love you like a brother, and maybe one day we'll get to the point where I'm the lucky bastard that gets to legally call you that, but that's not what I wanted to tell you today. What I want to tell you is that I'm in love with your sister, and I fully intend on treating her like she's the best goddamn thing that's ever happened to me, because she is. I love Madison, and I'll happily let you break my nose for it, but just know, bones can heal. My heart won't if I can't be with Madison."

There. I got it out, and I had to admit that I suddenly felt lighter. I hadn't even told Madison just how much she meant to me, but telling someone made me realize how hard I'd fallen for her. She was everything. Always would be. Cade hadn't said anything yet, but he had moved a little in his bed, so I figured he was just taking it all in since there was a lot to process.

After a few minutes of silence, I said, "Cade? What do you think?"

Still no answer. So I stood up and walked over to the bed, grabbed his shoulder, and shook him.

"Fuck."

He was sleeping, snoring loudly as I rolled him onto his back. Well, shit. Had he heard any of my speech? I assumed not because telling him that would be like a bucket of cold water poured over him. Unless the beginning was too long and I'd bored him into slumber. I dropped my head on a sigh because I'd worked myself up for a confession that meant nothing.

"Dash!" I heard my name being called from the common room.

"Dash? Are you here? I swear I'm going to beat your ass if you don't get out here soon."

Was that Scotty?

I quietly walked out of the room, only to find Scotty searching for me under the sofa cushions with a scowl. "What's wrong?"

"You're a fucking idiot, that's what's wrong." He stomped over to me, getting all up in my face.

"What are you talking about? You're the one that left Cade drunk on his own."

"Oh, don't you dare blame this mess on me."

"What mess?"

"Madison."

My body stilled at the mention of her name. "What happened?"

He shook his head. "She saw you." I waited for more of an explanation, but that seemed to be all that Scotty was willing to give until I raised my brow. "With Sienna. She saw you dragging her into your room, and Cade told her that you were dating."

"Fuck."

"Yes. Fuck. Now, if you ever want a chance in hell with Madison again, you need to go and fix this right now."

I didn't have to think about my next move. I ran to the elevator, and as I pressed the call button, I said, "Watch over Cade."

Scotty nodded. "Good luck."

The elevator doors shut, and I could feel it in my bones. I was going to need a lot more than luck this time.

"Pick up your phone, Madison," I muttered to myself, cursing when my call went through to her voicemail again. I'd called her at least twenty times since leaving the dorm, but she'd ignored every single attempt, which was starting to tick me off.

How the hell was I supposed to explain anything to her when she wouldn't let me?

I took another shot at calling, and yet again, I was ignored. She was pissed, and I'd somehow screwed up badly.

I might have inadvertently let her waltz out of the hockey dorm, but I wasn't going to let her waltz out of my life, or my bed, for that matter. Not without forcing her to hear me out. If talking to Cade had taught me anything, it was to keep fighting for what was yours, no matter what got in the way.

Madison's dorm may have only been a few minutes away, but it felt like I'd been walking for hours. I was going to have to explain myself but every time I walked through the conversation in my head, it sounded ridiculous. It didn't help that I had no idea what Cade had said to make Madison believe I was dating Sienna, so trying to refute those claims would be impossible. It felt like I was standing on quicksand, and I had no idea how to get out of it.

When I was standing outside her dorm, I tried to call Madison one more time. Unsurprisingly, I got no answer. The building was shut down for the evening, and the only way in now was by using a keycard or someone letting you in. I had neither option open to me.

"Dammit!" I huffed out as cold air billowed around my face. It was getting colder now, not that I noticed or cared. I was used to cooler weather at this point.

Taking several steps back, I counted the floors, and then the windows. Third floor. Fourth window. At least that was where I thought her room was. The lights weren't on in any of the rooms on that floor. Strange. Madison probably left my dorm about an hour or two ago. Surely, she wouldn't be sleeping yet. Knowing her, she'd be bitching about me to Tiff.

Did Scotty walk her home or take her somewhere else?

I doubted it. But after all her escapades with football players, I wasn't sure what she'd get up to if she was mad at me; so I decided to double check.

Dash: Did you drop Madison off at her dorm?

What a ridiculous message that I had to send my friend who acted more like Madison's protective boyfriend than me. I was an idiot, and I needed to make it up to her, but that wouldn't be possible if she wouldn't let me try.

Scotty: Yes, but I doubt she'll talk to you tonight. She was heartbroken and looked exhausted when I left her.

Heartbroken?

My stomach lurched because that was the last thing I wanted her to feel when it came to our relationship. I tried to call her again, and this time, when I was forwarded to her voicemail, I decided to leave a message. "Madison. We need to talk. I don't know what you saw, but it's not what it looked like. I was trying to figure out what Sienna knew about Cade. You can't let something as trivial as this stop what's going on between us. Madison, I can't let you go. I-I—"

God, I wanted to tell her that I loved her so badly. That the day I broke Henry's nose was the day I vowed to myself that I'd never let anyone upset her again, but she'd probably delete the message before listening to the entire thing. No. It wasn't the right time to grovel. The right time to do it would be just after I'd given her the best orgasm of her life to make up for it, only for her to realize that no one could make her feel as good as me.

"I need to talk to you. I'm outside your dorm, and I'm not leaving until you let me up." I was well aware that it was past visiting hours for this place, but I'd sneak in if I had to.

When I heard some high-pitched voices laughing in the distance, I rolled to the side of the door and waited for the girls to approach because I assumed they lived in the dorm.

When they got close enough, I stepped out and raised my hand. "Excuse me." The girls were startled by my presence but seemed to relax when I smiled—something I only did with strangers when I was desperate. "Sorry, I didn't mean to scare you. My girlfriend is on the third floor. I was supposed to meet her tonight, but she's fallen asleep on me and left me no way to get up there." I pointed to the third floor, and the two girls followed my finger as though that would help check out my story. It didn't help that none of the lights were on in any of the rooms. "Would you mind letting me in?"

One of the girls glared at me while the other elbowed her friend. "Sorry, I'm not sure I believe you."

I ground my teeth because it would have been better if I could just sneak in behind them, but I wasn't small enough for that. I'd make a scene, and the girls would no doubt scream, thus, I'd get banned from this dorm for life, and I needed access here.

"Come on, Ati. Let's get inside."

Okay, they thought I was a creep, and I couldn't blame them. It was dark, and I looked shady as fuck popping out of the darkness asking to be let in. As the girls shifted away, I closed my eyes and took a breath because I was about to do something that I vowed I never would.

"Do either of you know Scotty Hendricks?"

Yup. I just name-dropped my teammate.

The shorter girl laughed. "You're joking, right? Who doesn't know him on this campus? Wasn't he voted the most eligible athlete at Covey U or something?"

"Do either of you like him?" I asked with raised brows.

"Yes. I think he's a good guy." The shorter one smiled, trying to act cool. I wasn't surprised that I'd managed to find a hockey fan between them because when Scotty committed to Covey U, the female applications apparently increased by twenty percent.

"That's an understatement," the other one, Ati, I think, mumbled.

Thinking fast, I pulled out my phone, unlocked it, and swiped through my gallery until I found a picture of him. I flipped my phone over, showing the girls Scotty and me at The Draft. Okay, it wasn't my best shot. I looked angry as hell and like I wanted to kill someone, but that wasn't far from the truth.

"Scotty is one of my best friends." They were still studying the picture. "And my teammate."

"You're on the hockey team? I don't recognize you."

"That's because I'm the goaltender. I don't like to take my helmet off."

"Wait a minute, are you the one that does all those fancy warm-ups?" Her lips curled, and I wanted to roll my eyes because Scotty did say that would come back to haunt me.

"Yes," I answered curtly, which seemed to be enough to warm them up to me. "How about this? I will invite you to the next party at the hockey dorm if you let me in."

Okay, maybe I'd made that offer too quickly because both of their smiles turned, and they looked at each other wearily.

"Look, I'm sure you're a nice guy and everything, but really, I've seen far too many slasher movies to think that it would be okay to let you into a dorm full of girls when I don't actually know you. Besides, you might have just photoshopped those pictures with Scotty."

Fuck. Why was the universe conspiring against me on this? Name-dropping Scotty didn't work, and they were backing away. I was losing them, so I needed to take a different tactic.

Glancing back at my phone, I flicked through my gallery and showed them a picture of Madison. It was from the other day. I was kissing her on the cheek, and she was smiling.

"This is the girl I need to see. Do you know her?"

The taller girl examined the picture. "I think I've seen her in here before."

"Her name is Madison Bright. She's the love of my life, and I screwed things up earlier. I need to talk to her and let her know just how much she means to me."

"Aww," the short one cooed, giving me a far more sympathetic look. Was this going to work?

"Come on, Ati. Maybe we should let him up."

"No," she replied quickly. "We are not going to be responsible for a death on campus. Sorry, dude. You're just going to have to wait until the morning." She opened the door, letting her shorter friend through, before shutting it and locking me out of the building.

Well, shit. I was out of ideas, so I called Madison again. When there was no answer, I scoured the ground, grabbed a few pebbles and tried to throw them at her window. Or, at least, the one I thought was her window.

After six attempts, I threw the rest of the pebbles at the ground because I'd missed every single shot.

"Fuck!" I yelled so loudly that I knew the entire dorm block heard me. I didn't care. Maybe it would wake her up. Trudging over to the door, I leaned against the window and slid down until I was sitting next to it. She'd have to walk out of her building eventually, and I was going to be here when she did.

Bringing my knees up, I relaxed my head against the glass and closed my eyes. I could feel myself drifting to sleep, but I wasn't doing anything to stop it. It'd been a long day and I was exhausted. Just as my eyes shut, there was a loud banging against the window, causing me to jump.

When I looked around and saw Aster pointing at me from behind the glass, I knew I was in trouble. Pushing the door open, she had no qualms about walking out here in her bathrobe. "This is the guy, Todd. He won't leave the dorm, he's throwing rocks at windows, and constantly swearing like a drunk."

I held back from laughing upon seeing the look Aster was giving Todd. Glad it wasn't just me who she thought was an imbecile. "Can't you see him?"

Todd rolled his eyes before looking at me. "Yes, I see him, Aster. He's the only person out here."

"Well, then you need to do your thing." She flailed her hands in his direction. "Because, frankly, I'm tired of doing your job for you. Why haven't you gotten rid of him already?"

I tipped my chin as I stood, recognizing Todd as one of the more motivated Crusher fans at this college. He'd always sit in the first row, banging on the plexiglass, wearing a polar bear's head with purple body paint. "Todd."

"Dash, what are you doing here?" Todd gave me an uneasy look, but I could tell that he wanted to give me the benefit of the doubt. He glanced at Aster, who clearly didn't believe or trust me at this point. For a small thing, she was pretty damn feisty.

"He needs to leave, Todd. It's past visiting hours, Madison's not here, and I've got a ton of work I need to do, which is impossible with him screaming at the windows."

Todd sucked in a breath and looked at me with unease. "There's not much I can do, Aster. He's not in the building. He's not currently shouting, and he's standing on campus. Something he's allowed to do because he's a student here."

"Are you serious? But he's stalking a resident."

Todd rolled his neck so he was looking at me. "Are you stalking Madison Bright?" Maybe it was because he was a sucker for the Crushers, but man, Todd made a weak security guard.

"No. She's my teammate's sister, and I need to talk to her."

"Can it wait until morning?"

"Not really. Can you let me up to speak to her?"

Aster tipped on her toes, piping up, "I already told you, she's not in there." She flailed her arms in Todd's face. "Do something."

"Sorry, Dash, but I think you'll need to try again in the morning."

"Sure," I drawled out, taking a few steps back. They might not have wanted me here, but I wasn't leaving. I strolled over to the bench across the path and took a seat.

"Todd! Look, he's sitting there."

"It's a bench on campus, Aster. I can't force him to move. Unless he starts acting up, then there's nothing I can do."

"Well, then you better stand right there and watch him," Aster huffed out before stomping her way back into the dorm. Todd sighed, but followed behind her, nonetheless.

I wasn't going to leave. Madison was too important for that.

Standing outside of the dorm, I looked at the window that I thought was her room one last time and decided to call her again. I could have sworn I saw the flicker of a light, but it could have just been my wishful thinking.

"Madison. This isn't over between us."

I left my message at that. Yes, it was mildly threatening, but it was the truth. If she thought she could be done with me over a misunderstanding, then she was about to be very disappointed.

Chapter 26

Madison

With my head hung low, I tentatively stepped out of my bedroom and into the dorm hallway. Thankfully, it was still early enough that no one was around. I needed the quiet to get out of here with no one seeing my red, raw eyes from crying myself to sleep last night.

I glanced at my phone on the desk before closing my door. I turned it off before going to sleep and planned on leaving it like that for the rest of the day because I didn't see the point in taking it with me.

Why have it when the only person I wanted to talk to was also the only person I was too afraid to get a message from?

Dash had been hounding me with calls and texts, and if I were a better person, I would have answered and heard him out. Scotty raised a lot of good points during our chat, and after some thinking, I decided I needed to focus on myself for a hot second instead of everyone else. I'd been so hell-bent on getting Dash's attention that I'd failed to see the bigger picture with all of this. I failed to remember who I was.

So that was what I was doing right now.

Focusing on myself because no one else was.

I needed to take a breath, and make sure that I was doing the right thing for me.

Putting my sunglasses on, I pushed through the doors and walked out of the building before tucking my hands in my sweatshirt. With my head down, I hoped I could get a coffee and walk to class without anyone seeing me.

"Madison."

Really? I stopped and huffed out an annoyed breath because I couldn't even make it two feet out of my dorm before Dash found me.

"Madison's not home right now," I said with pointed annoyance, refusing to look back at him because I knew the minute I did, I'd fall into his arms, and he'd see I'd been crying the entire night.

Walking faster, I hoped I could shake him off and maybe hide in a bush before he could see, but unfortunately, the campus was impeccably landscaped, and I couldn't see a bush big enough for me to hide in.

My eyes were red-rimmed, my body felt exhausted, and all I wanted to do was stay in my dorm for at least two weeks. Having to see Dash wasn't something I wanted to deal with.

His heavy footsteps loomed closer, so I picked up my pace, refusing to look back.

"Madison. Stop."

His voice was urgent, but I obviously ignored it because he had a hell of a lot of explaining to do. It wasn't until I looked over my shoulder that I slowed, realizing that running from Dash was pointless. The guy's stride was at least three normal steps, and he seemed to have a knack for chasing me down. It didn't matter where I hid, he'd always find me.

Sill staring at the ground, I accepted my fate and turned to face him. I needed to get this over with. There was always a feeling in the back of my mind that Dash and I could only end in disaster. I'd just hoped I was wrong. But now that I'd seen the truth, there was no point in delaying the inevitable heartbreak that was coming my way.

When his feet came into view, I tipped my chin, surprised to see that his hair was a mess and he had obvious dark circles under his eyes. He looked just as exhausted as me.

"Madison," he said when he finally got close enough, and surprisingly, he bent forward, wheezing from the chase.

"Wow, Big Man. Really? Chasing after a five-foot-four girl has winded you? Aren't you supposed to be an elite athlete?"

Still taking deep breaths, he shook his head, laughing. "Don't start with me, Madison. You know speed isn't one of my strong points."

"That I do," I mumbled sarcastically.

Dash lifted his head, looking at me with bloodshot eyes for the first time. I didn't want to admit it, but there was a smell lingering between us. My nose twitched as I took in his rumpled clothing, and I couldn't let it linger. "Dash, you stink."

He laughed bitterly. "Hard to take a shower when you're sleeping outside on a bench."

My brows furrowed, and I looked into the distance, seeing the small bench just outside my dorm. "Wait, you actually slept on the bench? I thought Todd and Aster were exaggerating when they told me you wouldn't leave last night."

"You weren't answering my calls or texts. What else was I supposed to do?"

"Oh, I don't know, maybe wait for me to contact you like any other normal person would do?"

"I think we've established that I'm not a normal person when it comes to you, Madison. Besides, I know you. You were never planning on calling me back again."

I pouted my lips out and tipped my chin up, trying to seem defiant, but feeling like I was about to crumple into nothing. "You're right. I have no reason to call my brother's playboy best friend." I took him in, curling my lips with disgust. "I should have known that you were seeing other people. It was just so obvious, but I was blinded by how much I liked you." I pushed him a little, trying to get my anger across. "You told me Sienna was just a girl looking for a story. I didn't realize that story was in your pants."

He stepped back, surprised at my outburst. "She is looking for a story, and she found one."

"Oh, let me guess... she found out you have a twelve-inch cock?"

"I don't—" He shook his head, growling in frustration. "You're not going to make this easy, are you?"

He got his answer when he saw my angry scowl.

"She couldn't find anything on me, so she found a story on your brother instead."

I rolled my eyes in disbelief. "Sure. I bet that's exactly why you were dragging her into your room last night, too."

"It was," he refuted. "I was dragging her in there because she was refusing to tell me what she knew about Cade. I needed to threaten her but couldn't exactly do that in front of the rest of the hockey team."

With my arms now folded, I watched Dash's expression change. There was something in his eyes that I hadn't seen before. Desperation, maybe? Exhaustion was probably more likely.

"What did you do? Threaten her with your sword because, frankly, that thing could poke an eye out if you're not careful."

Dash grumbled, running a hand through his hair before shaking his head. "You make me crazy, Madison. I have no interest in Sienna. You're all I've ever wanted, and I had you right in the palm of my hand, but I somehow fucked it up because I was trying to protect your brother."

"Protect him from what? Cade's a big boy, he can take care of himself."

"Scotty told me that you spoke to Cade last night, so I'm sure you understand how incapacitated he was. There was no way he could deal with Sienna on his own. I urgently needed to find out what she knew because there's a very real chance it could be about his extra-curricular activities."

He didn't need to elaborate. I knew what my brother did in his spare time when he thought no one was watching. I also knew that it could get him in huge trouble with the NHL if he was ever found out.

"Did she know anything?"

Dash shook his head. "I don't think so. She mentioned a couple of names, but that was it. I think she's still trying to figure out the story, which means Cade and I have time to stop it or find something else for her to focus on."

I raised my brow, my lips turning up. "That's an awfully convenient excuse, isn't it?"

"Madison, think about it for a second. If I was trying to hide something, don't you think I would have been able to do it? I've managed to hide us pretty well."

"Is that supposed to make me feel better? That if you were cheating on me, I wouldn't know because you're better at hiding it?"

He growled, dropping his head. "What can I do to get you to believe me?"

I thought back to Scotty's words from last night. He told me to hear Dash out and had essentially vouched for him. Scotty had nothing to gain by asking me to do that, so why was I still reluctant to listen?

"Don't you get it? You're the only person in this world that I want to be around. I hate the fact that I didn't try to date you in high school. I hate that you ever thought dating Henry would make you happy. I hate it that you can so easily flirt with every other guy on campus and not see that it makes me want to kill them. I hate that whenever I look at you, all I want to do is kiss you until you can't remember your own name."

Well, that reluctance was starting to fade. Dash's harsh breaths were all I could hear as he looked around, making sure we were still alone. My mouth dropped, but I didn't know what to say. That was the most Dash had ever spoken about anything, let alone his feelings, and out in public no less.

"You're the only reason I broke Henry's nose. It was all for you because you deserved so much more than him. You deserve more than me, but I'm too selfish to let you go."

"Why does it feel like you're going to rip your shirt off and turn green in a minute?" I tried to soften the tension with a joke because I'd never seen him so intense.

"Madison." It was another growly warning, which seemed to be all he did with me these days. "I just want to talk to you."

"Isn't that what we're doing right now?"

"Yes, but sometimes it feels like we're not saying anything." He reached his hands out to touch me, but I took a step back. He sighed, dropping his arms, and seemingly giving up. "Look, I just want to have a conversation with my girlfriend. Alone."

With pinched lips, I looked at him, confused. "Girlfriend? Thought you didn't want to do that until you told Cade about us. Which you've been too chickenshit to do, might I add."

"So, we're having this conversation here? In front of everyone?"

"There's no one around, Big Man. It's just you and me."

"I wasn't chickenshit. The minute I finished with Sienna—"

I raised my hand and cringed at the mere mention of her name. She made me feel desperate and stupid, and I hated that. "Can we please stop talking about Sienna?"

"Absolutely." Dash pulled his phone out, showing me a note on his screen. "I'd been planning all the things I was going to say to your brother for weeks. I finally cut it down to a few minutes, and after having a heart-to-heart with Cade, I told him."

The words took a few minutes to process, but when they did, I yelled, "What?! You *told* my brother about us?"

I took a step forward, and for some reason I raised my hand, ready to slap him in the chest, but Dash caught it with ease, holding my hand in the air as he looked down at me. "I thought that's what you wanted me to do?"

"Yes, *before* Sienna."

Dash growled. "Stop talking about her. She means nothing. When are you going to realize that there is no one else? There never has been. No other girl compares to you because, for some asinine reason, my heart only beats when it sees you smile."

I shut my mouth, staring at Dash with confusion. "Have you been drinking?" This wasn't like him. Not at all.

"No." Dropping our hands to his heart, Dash pulled me closer. "I told Cade about us, but he was so drunk, he'd fallen asleep before he heard it."

Again, I couldn't help but feel disappointment at those words. "Why does every part of this story lead to another convenient reason for Cade still not knowing about us?"

"No. It's actually very inconvenient, because I decided I really wanted to surprise you on our date tonight with that news."

I pushed out a laugh, looking to the side. "You still think we're going on a date tonight?"

"Do you really think I'm going to give you any other choice?"

With our hands still resting on his chest, he interlaced our fingers, and dropped his forehead to rest on mine.

"Dash, we're in public."

"I know."

He dipped down so his lips ghosted mine.

"Then you might want to back away."

"I'm never backing away from you again, Madison." He caught my lips with his, and when he kissed me, I felt it all the way down to my toes. I knew at that moment that he wasn't lying. I could feel it with every swipe of his tongue and every squeeze of his fingers. This was it. *I* was it.

As he pulled away from me, his dark eyes took me in. "It's always been you," he whispered. "I've never seen another girl except for you, and I never will."

"Ditto." I rolled my eyes and shook my head a little. I'd always want Dash, and the idea of holding back to make a point felt ridiculous considering how he just laid out his feelings to me. "Guy, of course. I've never seen another guy except for you. Well, unless you want to count Henry, which I still view as a severe lack in judgment during my teen years. Or Tate Sorenson, but I guess you'd call him a celebrity crush more than a reality thing. Also, I think he's like ten years older than me, so it's not like it would work out, anyway."

Dash's hands cupped my face, forcing me to stop talking and focus my attention on him. "Madison, will you please let me take you on our first date tonight?"

That was all he had to say to take my breath away.

"Yes," I said without hesitation.

"Great, then I need you at the hockey dorm at seven."

I looked at him quizzically. "The hockey dorm? What about the rest of the guys?"

"They're going out for some surprise birthday party for Scotty."

"And you're not? Won't they be angry if you miss it?"

"No. I've attended too many parties over the last few months. Scotty will understand. He probably won't even notice I'm not there once he realizes that Erik managed to convince the girl he likes to come."

"He has?! And you don't want to be there to see how that goes down?"

"Like I said before, Madison, you're all I want to see."

My lips quirked the tiniest bit as I tried to hold back my smile, but it wasn't working. There was just something about the way he talked, all gruff yet assertive, that made me melt.

"Okay. I'll come over tonight, but until then, I've got class. Care to walk me?"

"Gladly."

Unlike yesterday, Dash offered me his arm, and I looped my hand through it, happy that it felt like he was almost proud to show us off to the rest of campus.

When we passed other students, he didn't hide or cower away from anyone, and I liked that feeling. This was his apology, and I was happily accepting it.

Standing in the hockey common room, it was the first time I'd ever felt out of place. Usually, I was here to see my brother, but tonight, I was here to have a date with Dash, and it was just us.

Well, I thought we were on a date, at least. It didn't feel like the kind of date I was expecting. I couldn't lie. I'd just assumed when Dash invited me up here that we were going to have filthy, dirty sex all night, so I didn't bother wearing panties. Now, as I admired the perfectly set dinner table, I was feeling bad for completely misreading his intentions, and a little cold.

With the kitchen island acting as a barrier between us, I didn't know what to do with myself. Dash was standing on the other side, reading off a handwritten recipe, making me dinner, which was in itself swoon-worthy, but he was also wearing this black leather apron that was doing things to me it shouldn't.

I was hot, and Dash didn't help the situation when he licked some sauce off his thumb.

Rubbing my thighs together, I pushed the fabric of my miniskirt down and made my way over to the kitchen. Taking a seat on one of the barstools opposite Dash, I leaned over and watched him tend to the rice. "Smells delicious," I drawled out, and he responded with a usual grumble.

"So, are you sure you're okay with missing Scotty's party?"

"Yes." Short and to the point. I was getting the distinct feeling that he didn't want to talk, which was fine. He probably needed the quiet to concentrate, and I didn't want to get in the way.

Pushing myself off the barstool, I let my hand brush across the countertop as I explored the room while Dash was busy. A large wicker basket caught my interest, so I strolled over and opened the lid. "What's this basket for?" I asked, pulling out a rubber duckie and making it squeak.

He looked up and shook his head, letting out a low rumble of laughter. "Scotty introduced it when we moved in. He calls it the basket of doom. He hates messes, and it's the only way to keep this place looking good. We shove everything in there that's found out here, and if it isn't claimed in two weeks, it's thrown out."

Just as he finished, I pulled out a purple lacy bra and cringed. "Guessing no one is going to claim that."

"You don't want to know where that was found, but I'm guessing it's a friend of Erik's since most of the girls he sleeps with like being watched," he said before stirring the rice.

I raised my brows and dropped the bra back in the basket before placing the lid on top. That explained why I saw Erik out here sleeping on the couch that last time. Wincing, I really hoped I hadn't walked in on a freshly fucked Erik. I shivered, trying not to think about it as I walked away from the basket.

Strolling around the couch, I let my fingers dance across the fabric as I made my way to the TV. It wasn't on, but there was a little picture beside it, and it was the first time I'd gotten close enough to see that it was a team photo from last year. Dash was in the back, towering over everyone and scowling. The uniform made him look menacing, and his height only added to it.

"Dinner's ready," he said, and by the time I'd gotten to him, the food was already on the table and Dash was holding out a chair for me. Pushing my skirt down one more time, I gave him a small smile before sitting. He kissed the top of my head as he tucked me in. "I hope you like it." His breathing was jagged, and he let out another low, almost anxious chuckle. Was Dash nervous?

As if my heart couldn't warm any more for this man, it almost felt like it was melting from his behavior. I was the one causing his nervousness and that was something I never thought possible. With Dash Bridges, no less.

"I'm sure I will. It looks delicious."

Dash seemed calmer now as he sat opposite me, reaching for his fork.

"Cheers." I raised a glass, and although surprised by my gesture, he dropped his fork and followed along. Bringing his glass to mine, they clinked together. "To us."

He tipped his chin in acknowledgment, and after taking a sip of his wine, he went straight to eating as if I weren't here. He was hoovering up his dinner, and just as I was about to take my first bite, I dropped the fork onto the plate because I wanted to say something.

With my hands braced on top of the table, I let them dance across the wood before asking, "Do you think this is weird?"

"What?" He stopped himself from taking a bite and looked at me.

"You and me being on a date."

He coughed, seemingly annoyed at my question. "No. Why? Do you?"

"No. Um, it's just…" I was squirming in my seat, not really sure how to broach the subject. "You're not talking."

"I don't talk much."

That made me feel bad. I wasn't trying to suggest Dash should change. I knew who he was when I first approached him, but I guessed I was just expecting something a little different.

"I know, but you went to all this effort to cook for me, and you're even skipping Scotty's party to be here, so it kind of feels like you might want to talk more instead of just getting to the point." He kept staring at me and it made me nervous. I couldn't help myself; I kept talking. "But if getting to the point is what you want, I'm not wearing panties, because I kind of assumed you'd want quick and easy access. Just so you know."

He closed his eyes and breathed in, and I knew I had struck a nerve. "You aren't wearing panties?"

"Nope," I popped out with a big smile.

He pinched his nose between his thumb and forefinger. "I knew I should have taken you out to a restaurant for dinner. That shit is too tempting."

I instinctively crossed my legs, sitting up straighter. "But you didn't take me to a restaurant. Why?"

"I didn't because I wanted it to be just us. Like you said. I wanted to get to know you out of the context of everything else."

"Well, I'm here now, Big Man. I'm yours for the taking, so take me."

Lifting my fork, I took a bite of the risotto and let out a hum of approval.

He paused, then shook his head with a smile. I loved that I could break the tension between us so easily. I playfully knocked his foot with mine from under the table, and when I moved my foot back, he followed, leaving his leg in between mine. Like he didn't want to stop our connection.

"Later. Let's enjoy our meal first."

"Oh, I agree." I took another bite and closed my eyes to savor the taste. "This is the best dish anyone has ever cooked for me."

"Thanks," he grumbled, chewing the risotto with little enthusiasm. What was wrong with the compliment? "It's my mom's recipe."

Oh.

Keep it together. I didn't know much about Dash's mom, but I knew she passed away right before he moved to Connecticut, and that it was a topic he never talked about.

"Did she teach you to cook?" I asked as I took another bite, hoping that hid my nervousness about asking.

"Kind of," he said quietly. "After she died, every Sunday, my dad and I would try to make one of her recipes." He gestured to the handwritten note on the countertop in the kitchen. "Dad said it didn't matter how hard we tried, it never tasted the same, but sometimes having the smells in the house made us feel like she was still around."

My chewing slowed because that was the most heartbreaking sentence I'd ever heard. Dash usually hid his feelings, but he opened up so quickly about this. With me, no less. I felt this burning desire to go over and hug him, but I didn't think he was done yet, and I wanted to give him the freedom to talk for once.

"She passed away right before I met Cade." Dash didn't look at me, he was just staring at his food as though it would have all the answers. "When I moved to Connecticut, it was for a fresh start, so I didn't tell him about her at first."

"Why not?"

"Because I didn't want him to know. People change when they find out you've been hit with a tragedy. We ended up becoming *that* family in our town. You know, the ones with the tragic story, and people are so thankful that it didn't happen to them. I was treated as this poor little kid who would never grow up under a mother's influence because mine got cancer. I was that story parents told their kids at night, reminding them to be grateful for what they had because poor Daniel Bridges just lost his mom."

"Dash," I breathed out, my heart feeling heavy.

He glanced up, his eyes dark and serious. "That was when I started hating people. No one understood me, and I couldn't figure out how they didn't get that. We just wanted to grieve on our own and not be reminded of our tragedy every day."

"I'm sorry." Tears threatened to fall, but I held them back because I didn't want him to think I was just as bad as those people. I wasn't upset over what happened to Dash, I was upset over the little kid that everyone seemed to forget was just that. A little kid.

"Don't be. My dad and I moved to Connecticut for that very reason. We didn't want people to feel sorry for us. We needed a fresh start." There was a whisper of a smile on his face. "And Cade was that for me. I still remember the first day I met him. I was on the ice, trying to practice my skating because I was so slow, but I couldn't catch a break because there were two older guys circling me. At one point, they tripped me up, and I was lying on the ice, ready to go home. But then brother glided over, knocked those two guys out like it was nothing, and then held his hand out to me. Once I was back on my skates, he berated me and told me I should get in the hockey net because that was the only way I was ever going to make it onto a hockey team."

"What an idiot."

"No. It was the best thing that ever happened to me. He was the first person to treat me like I was just any other kid, and I liked that the only reason he wanted to help me was because he wanted us to get into the NHL together. I never thought it would actually happen, but I guess his determination pushed me to want it too. I had no drive at that age, and my dad was busy with work or grieving. It was your parents that drove me to games and kept my life going while we tried to repair ours."

I swallowed because the gravity of the situation started to take hold. This was the reason why he didn't want to betray Cade. Their bond ran much deeper than I realized. Still staring at his risotto, I noticed the fork in his hand was shaking.

Instinctively, I pushed my chair out, walked over to him and sat on his lap. Dash's breathing was slow and methodical as I brushed the hair out of his face. "I didn't meet your mom, but I'm sure she would have been proud of the man that you've become. You're dedicated, strong, determined, and you treat people right. I've never met someone I look up to more than you, and not just because you're ridiculously tall."

He couldn't look at me for a second, but when he did, I saw raw sadness in his eyes.

"You think?" He cracked a smile, trying to break the heaviness in the room.

"Definitely. You're caring and focused, and when you care for someone, you put everything you can into making them happy."

"Thanks." He flicked his gaze down, taking a minute before looking back at me. "I think she'd like you too."

"Really?" I said, cringing. I'd never met a boyfriend's mother before, but I always figured I wouldn't make a good impression. "I bet she'd think I talk too much."

His smile grew wider, and those deep brown eyes of his started to lighten. "Nah. She'd like you. You make me smile."

Resting a hand on my chest, I said dramatically, "I do?"

He chuckled and squeezed my thigh. "Yeah, I love the way you ramble."

"Oh, thanks." I sat up straight, trying really hard not to be offended because Dash had just spilled his guts out to me, but geez. Couldn't I have gotten one compliment? Like he could have said my hair looked nice, or something, but rambling? No one wants to be told they ramble.

"Hey." He kissed the side of my neck, drawing my attention back to him. "It's a good thing. You make it so I don't have to talk to people."

"Oh, so, you like me talking?"

He smiled with a side smirk. "I love it. You fill the silence with something I want to hear."

My heart fluttered, and if it were possible, it would have fluttered out of my chest at all the things Dash was saying to me. I just couldn't believe I was here.

Dash leaned in and kissed me, long and slow, and that did everything to confirm that he was telling me the truth.

Pulling away, he rested his forehead against mine. "I still remember the first day I met you, you know?"

"You do?"

"How could I forget? Isn't that what you called a core memory before? It's etched in my brain forever. Your mom invited me for dinner, and you were there, talking about some TV show you were obsessed with."

"Sharks." It was all I had to say to confirm that I remembered that day too. "I loved sharks."

"I know. The goblin shark was your favorite, right?"

"You remember?"

"Oh, yeah. I remember every single fact about sharks you said that day. No one else was listening, probably because they'd heard it a thousand times, but I did. You had this light, airy way of talking that made me feel comfortable, and completely forget about everything bad going on in my life. Even then, there was something about you that intrigued me. I just didn't know what it was. At the time, I assumed it was to do with your unabashed confidence."

My eyebrows drew together. "Unabashed confidence? I wouldn't say I had that then."

"You did. When it came to school, you and Tiff were taking classes above your grade, and outperforming people like me. It was only after Henry was an asshole that you decided to show everyone else what a badass you were. You gave no fucks after that and just did whatever the hell you wanted. That was when I knew I was wrecked for any other girl because who else could be as good as you?"

Pushing him gently, I laughed and turned away, trying to hide my blushing cheek. "Oh, Big Man. You're a charmer when you want to be."

Dash took the opportunity to kiss the spot right behind my ear. I melted. He just felt so good. So right. His breath skated across my ear when he said, "And you're sitting on my lap, not wearing panties."

His hand grasped my thigh as he worked his way up to the edges of my skirt. I swatted him away and moved off his lap. "As much as I want to have some fun tonight, my risotto is getting cold, and it's too good to go to waste."

He watches me as I skipped back to my seat, plucked my fork from the table and started to eat.

When I finished chewing a bite, I said, "I also want to apologize to you."

"For what?"

"Kissing you at The Draft and teasing you until you had no choice but to go behind my brother's back. I realize now the gravity of your friendship, something I'd never really appreciated before, and I wouldn't have pushed so hard if I'd known how important Cade was to you." I rolled my eyes to the ceiling, holding back a smile. "Well, I should say probably, because I know I would've gotten drunk at some point this year and asked to make out with you, anyway."

"You didn't *make* me do anything. I could have said no."

"I'm not so sure. I was all over you at The Draft. I was worse after it, and I kind of tricked you into sleeping with me a couple of weeks later." I sucked in a breath, really starting to evaluate how bad my actions were.

"How did you trick me?"

"I told you it was just one night, knowing full well I'd want more."

"And I accepted the one night, knowing full well that I was going to try to get another round in the morning."

"You were?" I raised my brows in surprise. "Well, crap. Now I feel bad that I left you."

"No, you shouldn't. You needed to leave." He swiped his napkin across his lips and placed it on the table. "We wouldn't be here if you hadn't."

"What makes you think that?"

He shrugged. "I figured I got my taste, and that was it. That was all a guy like me deserved."

"A guy like you deserves everything. Like I said before, you're loyal, dedicated, and your calf muscles are huge. I mean, seriously, what do you do to make them look like that? It's not normal."

"Tend a goal every day of the week."

"Well, that's not something I'm going to do. Maybe I could tend your bed instead?" I popped the last forkful of food in my mouth.

"Your brother might have something to say about that," Dash muttered. He had a habit of bringing up Cade at the most inappropriate times, but I'd lay off him for now since we were still eating. "Do you want seconds?"

he asked.

"Nope. I'm full." Standing, I pushed the chair in and walked over to the couch, toying with my dress straps.

"What are you doing?" Dash asked, watching me curiously.

"Getting ready for my dessert." I winked, pulling one of the straps down, revealing my shoulder. Without another word, Dash followed me. His mouth immediately dropped to my collarbone so he could kiss my now exposed skin.

I thought he might push me onto the couch, but when his hands wrapped around my waist, and he hauled me over his shoulder, I squealed, desperately trying to keep my skirt from riding up.

"Dash! Where are you taking me?"

His palm rested on my fabric-covered butt as he squeezed my left cheek and walked to the other side of the dorm. "Taking you to my room because I don't want anyone spoiling *my* dessert."

I squealed again when he managed to push the fabric of my skirt up so high that my ass was on show. He playfully slapped one of my cheeks and then kicked his door open.

This was going to be the start of a long, fun night.

CHAPTER 27
Dash

Kissing Madison's neck, my hands roamed her naked body as I lavished her with attention for just giving me the best blowjob of my life. Taking advantage of the empty dorm, we'd made a serious dent in my condom supply, and that didn't look like it was stopping any time soon.

Licking Madison's skin, I dipped down to her breasts, showing her how much I admired her body with my hands. This girl was everything, and I wanted to make sure she knew it.

She threaded her hands through my hair, pulling a little before using it to drag my attention to her eyes. Light blue and wanton, I could stare into them for hours. "Why'd you stop me? I was just about to get another taste." She shivered when I licked my lips, still tasting her from last time.

"I've, uh, got something to ask you." She bit her bottom lip, trying to hide the smile from tugging at the edges.

"Anything." I crawled over her and kissed her. When I finished, I bit into her bottom lip and then kissed it better.

Madison pushed me to the side and rolled off the bed. I watched her naked ass as she sauntered over to my gym bag and growled when she bent down to go through it. Was she trying to kill me with that view?

"Where is it? I could have sworn you kept it in here," Madison grumbled as she threw towels and clothes out of the bag. I didn't care that she was making a mess, or that all the stuff in there was dirty because I was so satiated by her touch. "Ah ha. Here it is."

She pulled out my foam roller, or Bertha as some of the team had affectionately named it, and walked back to the bed. I couldn't think straight because I wanted to memorize every curve of Madison's body so I could remember it anytime I was alone.

Standing next to me, she placed it on the bed and smiled. "That's my foam roller."

"Yes. It is."

"And?" Was I missing something?

She frowned but didn't stop swaying her hips. "I want you to fuck me the way you fuck your foam roller."

Silence.

I took in her words and her overeager expression and said, "But I don't fuck my foam roller."

"Are you sure about that? Because I've seen you in the gym a few times, and well..." She fanned herself, letting her blonde hair flutter over her shoulders. "I've got to say, I've had many sessions on my own where I've thought about how it would feel to be under you while you roll your thigh on that damn thing."

And I was getting hard again, just thinking about Madison touching herself while thinking about me.

Grabbing the foam roller, I rested it on the other side of the bed before taking Madison's hand and guiding her back to the mattress.

"Is that a no?" She sounded disappointed, and I chuckled.

When she was lying on the bed, I lay on top of her and kissed her. "It's an *I can think of something*." I kissed her jaw, then made my way down her neck and to the middle of her chest. I kept going until I got to just under her belly button. Madison opened her legs so that I could slip in between them, and as I dragged my body down, I made sure my skin brushed against hers. She winced as her hips involuntarily shifted. I wasn't surprised. It was probably uncomfortable having my breath fanning across her pussy, knowing I wasn't going to touch her yet.

Kissing the skin just above her slit, I slipped my hands under her thighs until my arms were hooked around them, then I pushed up, so she was forced to place her feet on the bed and have herself completely open to me.

I couldn't deny how much I loved seeing her like this. Quivering and wet as she eagerly waited for me to touch her. I was more than ready to skate my tongue across her slit, but I wanted to fulfill her request first.

Moving back, I tapped her thighs and said, "Lift up." She did as I said, raising her hips into a bridge position, and I tucked the foam roller under the small of her back before instructing her to rest on it.

Perfect.

With her bottom half shifted and her legs wide open, I had a much better angle to make her scream while I ate her out.

Wrapping my arms back around her legs, I kissed her inner thighs one side at a time, ignoring the way her body was bucking just to get me to pay attention to her center.

"Dash, please," Madison whined, and I looked up at her, grinning.

"Good things come to those who wait."

Then I shocked her by swiping my tongue from the bottom of her slit all the way to the top. When I got there, I feasted on her clit as though I hadn't eaten in years, flicking it so she was lashing at the pillows.

She couldn't decide whether she wanted to get away from me or if she wanted me to keep going. Thankfully, with my firm grip on her thighs, she didn't have a choice. I was in control, and that was just the way I liked it.

"Dash," she drawled out as her hands threaded through my hair and her feet started to slip. I kept on with my assault, licking and eating her until she was vibrating with pleasure. It wouldn't be long until she came, I knew that much.

My fingers very slowly caressed her thighs as my tongue continued lapping at her center. Her nails dug into my scalp and pushed down until I was fucking her with my tongue. I knew what she was trying to do. She was trying to delay the pleasure, so I pushed myself back up and lapped at her clit one more time.

That was all it took.

Her feet were almost off the bed at this point, and I couldn't see her face because her back was arched so high, but when she came, I was happy no one else was in the dorm but us tonight. Apparently, she was a screamer. With her legs shaking, I held my tongue in place, letting her ride out her orgasm.

Her chest was heaving, and she looked exhausted as she wiped her brow. "What are you doing to me?"

I didn't give her an answer. I just took another condom from my bedside drawer, rolled it on, and held her legs wide open. On my knees, I looked down at her beautiful body and pushed inside her slowly.

"Dash."

She drew in a breath, and I stayed inside her, enjoying the moment before taking both of her ankles and placing her feet on my chest. Then I started moving, hoping the foam roller underneath would help with the motion. I thrust into her a few times before I noticed Madison was wincing and stopped.

"Are you okay? Am I hurting you?"

Her face softened as she gave me an uneasy smile. "No. It's not that. It's, uh, the foam roller." She pointed to the bed. "It's just digging into my back, that's all."

I nodded, immediately knowing how to help that out. "Be a good girl and roll over." She paused in surprise, but I didn't stop looking at her until she did as I asked. Madison's ass was a beautiful sight. It was an even better one when my fingerprints were on it. Grappling with her hips, I pulled her ass up in the air so I could move the foam roller into position. Unfortunately, I got distracted by her wet pussy. She just looked so…tasty. So why wouldn't I go for another round?

With my hands still resting on both sides of her ass, I parted her lips and dipped down. She squealed when she felt the unexpected intrusion of my tongue but didn't back away. Good, because I wasn't going to stop until I felt her squeezing my fingers and crying out in pleasure again.

Madison groaned, dropping her head to the pillow and breathing heavily. When I pushed my finger inside her, I curled it, waiting until I heard that little mewl coming from her. "Do you like when my fingers are inside you?"

"Mhmm." I stopped moving, and that was when she looked over her shoulder at me, exhausted.

"I need more of an answer than that," I said, still teasing her G-spot with my finger, watching how she was affected by it.

"I-I like it." Her face was red, and she was clenching around my fingers, which only made me want another taste.

"What do you like?"

With her eyes closed, she bit her bottom lip and said, "I like it when you finger fuck me from behind."

"Good girl."

She turned her head, so her face was smashing into the pillow, and I added another finger, loving how tight she felt. "I don't think I can come again, Dash."

I laughed. "That's the point. I'm pushing you to your limits to see if I can make something happen."

"Wh-what are you trying to do?"

"I'm trying to give you an orgasm that will make you see stars and drench my face in your arousal. Now, are you going to be a good girl and do it for me?"

She answered by pushing her pussy in my face, and I laughed, giving one of her cheeks a gentle slap before getting back to work. After a few more swipes, I blew my breath over her heated flesh, making her shudder. Good. She liked this almost as much as I did. I knew she would come, and I was going to prove it to her. With a few more flicks of my tongue, I was pretty much holding her up with one hand by the ass, but I could tell she was close by the way her body was moving.

"Dash. I—"

That was when I pulled away, and she gasped in surprise because I didn't think she expected me to edge her like that. Adjusting the foam roller under her hips, I made sure it was tilting her ass up in my direction before I climbed over her and entered her tight, soaked pussy.

So warm and tight. I wanted to live inside her and never leave. She felt so good, and I could feel her clenching around me.

Taking her hand, I intertwined our fingers, and slowly fucked her, letting the foam roller move her body so I could go deeper and harder—watching her moan while her fingers pressed into my hand.

Thanks to eating her out, I wasn't far from coming, but I needed to give her another orgasm before that happened.

Her head fell back and she cried out in pleasure, and that was when I felt her legs stiffen and her back arch.

"Dash, I want you to come," she whined with her eyes shut.

Giving her hand one final squeeze, I said, "I will when you do."

A few short breaths later, she bit down on her bottom lip and moaned. I quickly lifted myself up so I could splay my hands across her ass, and pulled her cheeks apart so I could watch as I entered her. That was all it took for me to see stars.

Falling on top of her, I rested my head on her back. We were a sticky mess, both overstimulated at this point, but I couldn't wait to do it again. "I think you're going to have to sanitize your foam roller before you bring it to the gym with you," she sighed, patting my sticky shoulder.

Ding.

Fuck. That was the elevator door. Bringing my hand to her mouth, I brought my fingers to my lips in a shushing motion. She was confused at first, but once she heard the voices of my roommates, she got it.

I couldn't make out what they were saying, but I definitely heard Scotty and Erik, which meant that I'd lost track of time with Madison. We should have stopped before the foam roller, but I couldn't help myself. She asked, and all I wanted to do was give her everything.

"Looks like you'll have to stay here tonight," I whispered in her ear with my hand still on her mouth. "I can't risk you sneaking out when I don't know who's going to be in that common room. I'll set an alarm for five a.m. We'll see if the coast is clear by then."

She nodded, so I removed my hand from her mouth, and as I reached to get my comforter, she pulled the foam roller out and tossed it across my room before turning around.

Draping the throw over both of us, I lay down next to her, leaving a little kiss on her lips.

Madison looked exhausted as she drew lazy circles across my chest with the tiniest frown on her face. "I know they're back, but does that mean we've got to stop what we're doing?"

Unbelievable. This girl was unbelievable, and I was insatiable for her. "No, but it does mean you've got to be quiet."

"I'm sure you can think of many ways to help with that. Maybe you could cover my mouth with your hand like you did when you took my virginity?" She rolled her eyes to look at the ceiling. "Or you could stuff my mouth full of your cock."

Yup, it was official. Madison Bright was going to be my downfall, but maybe it didn't count as one if I was going down with her willingly.

I woke up with a nearly numb arm because Madison was lying on top of it, using my bicep as a pillow while her blonde hair was sprawled across the bed. The fresh scent of strawberries floated through the room, and memories of last night stirred in my mind. Madison Bright was in *my* bed, wearing *my* shirt as she soundly slept next to *me*. It was everything. She was mine. I was hers, and we were making it official today. Once she was out the door, I'd talk to her brother, and then she'd be free to come here whenever she wanted to.

Kissing the top of her head, I brought her body closer. Madison lazily rubbed her cheek against my arm, slowly waking and leaving little kisses as she wiggled her ass to snuggle into me further. My body was reacting, and I was sure she could feel the erection through my boxers, but I couldn't act on it. Not with people potentially getting up.

"Good morning," she said groggily, kissing my forearm.

As I tried to shift my hips away from hers, she shimmied her body closer. At first, I thought the stroke of her ass against my dick was an accident because she wanted to keep warm, but as her booty moved slower, languidly taking in the feel of my cock, I realized she was doing it on purpose. She was trying to entice me, which wasn't hard.

What was hard now was my dick, so I pulled her in tighter, hoping that would stop her squirming since I didn't want to waltz into practice with a raging erection. Apparently, that move only served to encourage her. She took my hand, which was on the bed and laced our fingers together before moving them to her chest, over her heart. It was sweet, and I felt like we could stay like this for hours and still be happy.

But then she slid our hands down the front of her body, all the way until they were at the edge of the shirt she was wearing. Fuck. I wanted to keep touching her. So. Damn. Badly.

I glanced at the door, and that cardboard-covered hole glared at me because the risk factor had just increased twofold. I checked the time on my phone, noting it was five a.m., and the boys would be up soon.

"Morning," I griped because although it wasn't unusual for me to be awake at this time, I was exhausted. Staying up until three to play with Madison's delectable body would do that to you.

Madison turned in my arms, and her hand immediately dropped to my dick. Unbelievable. She was ready for another round, and even though my cock might have fooled her into thinking I was too, I wasn't.

"Madison."

"What? We're up. No one else is. Isn't this the perfect time to have some fun?"

"No, because we're only up so we can get you out of here before anyone sees you."

"Do I have to go? I was thinking we could just tell Cade this morning."

"You think your brother will be accepting of our relationship if he finds out you slept over and I gave you at least eight orgasms last night?"

"It was actually nine."

I shook my head at her antics. "I'm going to tell him, but I want to do it alone. I don't want any blowback on you."

"You sure? Because I like to blow you."

"Madison. This is serious. I want to make sure we do this right."

She sighed and removed her hand from me reluctantly. "If you say so."

Kissing her on the lips, I patted her cute little ass. "Come on. Go take a shower, and I'll come back with a coffee for you."

"Yes, please," she murmured with a lazy smile. She languidly moved out of the bed, and when she was standing in just my shirt in front of me, my dick stood, too. "Care to join me in the shower?"

"Next time." It felt like I was stabbing myself in the foot saying no, but I knew that if I joined her, we wouldn't be leaving this room until the evening, and I didn't want Madison thinking that all she was to me was a fuck buddy. She was so much more, and the way to prove that was to finally tell her brother about us.

Rolling her eyes, she said, "Fine," and skipped to my shower.

Damn. I really was a lucky asshole.

After dragging myself out of bed, I threw on a pair of basketball shorts and a sweatshirt and made my way to the common room, assuming no one would be out there yet.

Shutting my door fully, I made my way to the kitchen, happy that I was right with my assumption. All the dorm doors were shut, and no one was up. Looked like my plan was going to work. Madison could leave before anyone saw her. Dropping a coffee capsule into the machine, I yawned as I waited for it to heat.

"You're up early. Guess that's what happens when you miss out on a party."

I gulped down my yawn and glanced over my shoulder. Shit. "Hey, Cade. What are you doing up?"

He pointed to his temple. "Last night was crazy, and I'm wired. I can't sleep. I haven't been able to for a while."

"Cade. That's not normal. I think you might have a problem."

"I think you do too." He gestured to the coffeepot with his eyes. "You're getting domesticated. You better watch out."

"I have no idea what you are talking about."

He pointed to the cup that was now filling with the brown liquid. "You hate coffee, so I know that mug's not for you. Must be for Reporter Girl."

Whelp, if I needed any confirmation that he hadn't heard my declaration of love the other night, I just got it. Maybe I should go into my room and pull up my speech, so he'll never mention me and Sienna again. Although Madison is still in my room, so I should probably wait.

"By the way, have you heard from Madison?"

That perked me up. Was he reading my thoughts? "Um. Why?"

With his brows crossed, he was swiping his phone, looking annoyed. "I've been trying to call her, but she hasn't answered."

"It's five a.m. She's probably sleeping like the rest of campus. We're the only idiots awake right now."

"Yeah, but that doesn't explain why she didn't text me last night. She always checks her phone before she goes to bed."

Unless she was being eaten out by me, apparently. I had no idea where her phone even was. I hadn't seen it all night, so it must have still been in her sweatshirt.

I scratched the back of my neck, trying to think of another excuse for her. "Maybe she hasn't gone to sleep yet. It's Saturday morning. She probably went out and had a good night with her friends."

Cade looked up in shock. Wrong thing to say. "You don't think she's out with those football guys, do you?"

"No. No, of course not. I bet she's out with some other friends."

"She doesn't have any other friends."

Shit. I didn't think this through.

"Cade, do you hear yourself? Madison is fine. I bet she just fell asleep before she could text you back. That's all."

"Madison's a light sleeper, though. Don't you remember when she blackmailed me for sneaking out of my window to a party in high school? She would have heard any of my texts or calls."

"Not if her phone is on silent."

"You know what? I'm going to go over to her dorm. I think it opens at six."

"Wait. How about I come with you?" I said as he started walking to the elevator. We were in too deep because if he went to Madison's room and she wasn't there, he would freak the hell out, so I needed to distract him and give her some time to get there before he did. "The security guard, Todd, and I go way back. He might let me in early."

"How do you know his name?" Thankfully, he was too concerned about Madison to think about it for long enough to draw conclusions.

"He's a big Crushers fan. That's all." Taking the two drinks, I walked past Cade, trying to act casual. "Look, I'm sure she's fine and she'll text back in a minute, but if you want to check, let me just put some clothes on and I'll come with you."

I gestured to the door as I walked backward to my room so I could watch Cade's facial expression. He wasn't going to let this go. Not that I blamed him. It was his little sister, and if he thought she was in danger, he'd do anything to protect her. "How about I try to call her before we go? Maybe you ticked her off, and she's ignoring you," I joked.

"No. If you call her, she might get suspicious about why you're suddenly all over her. She'll probably think that you've got a crush on her or something." He chuckled, but I didn't find it funny. I tried to keep my smile from dropping as I nodded.

"I'll just call her." He had the phone to his ear before I could stop him, and I turned, wincing as I waited to hear her ringtone, only sighing in relief when there was no noise.

Thank goodness.

"Still no answer," he said, glaring at his phone like it was the phone's fault Madison was ignoring him.

"My phone is just in there." I used my elbow to point at my door because I was holding the coffee and orange juice. "Let me see if she answers, and I'll let you know."

There. Easy way out of this conversation. No need to go into any more detail and I could still hide the fact that Madison was here.

I stepped toward my room, feeling good that I'd come up with something, but just as I was about to open my door, Cade said, "That's weird."

Ignore it. Go into your room and fix this thing by getting Madison to text him. That was what I needed to do, but I wasn't thinking straight, and for some reason, was having trouble leaving Cade outside my room.

"It says her phone is here."

"Here?"

"Yeah, you know, the tracker app that we have. It says her phone is here."

Fuck. Fuck. Fuck.

"Maybe she came over last night looking for you and dropped it in between the sofa cushions." I walked over to the couch, already feeling my demise because I knew her phone wasn't there.

"But the signal isn't saying it's there."

His phone started beeping like a fucking metal detector as he moved his hand around. What the fuck kind of app was this? He took a few steps, and my heart was beating faster than I ever thought it could. What a way to go, dying of a heart attack because your best friend's sister was naked in your room.

"Cade, there's something I've got to tell you." He wasn't listening, even though I was willing to confess everything right now and accept the beating I'd get for it. As Cade stood behind me, I knew this was it. The tension in my shoulders was building, and I was doing everything I could to try to remain calm.

"Weird. The signal is showing that the phone is in *your* room."

He still sounded confused. Of course he would be, because why would I have lied about anything?

I swallowed. "How about I go and check?"

Standing next to me, I felt it. For the first time in our friendship, he didn't trust me. He knew I was hiding something, and unfortunately, when Madison started singing Taylor Swift's "I Knew You Were Trouble" in the shower, we were all but done.

"Is that Reporter Girl?" His lips were flat, and his face was stone cold. I couldn't figure out what he was feeling, so I took a step back and cursed the pizza box taped to my door. It was the only reason he could hear her, after all.

"Cade, there's something I've got to tell you."

Without asking, he opened the door, and as if on cue, Madison strolled out of the bathroom with one of my towels wrapped around her body and a beautiful smile on her face.

Damn, that was a sight that would never bore me.

"Madison. What the *fuck* are you doing in Dash's room naked?"

She jumped, grabbing the top of her towel as she looked at her brother in shock. "Cade. I-I-I…what are you doing here?"

"I could ask you the same thing." Cade glared over his shoulder, looking at me in a way I never expected. Disgust. He was disgusted with me, and I couldn't say that I blamed him. "Or do I need to ask you, Dash?"

He turned, staring me down fully now, and I closed my eyes, taking a deep breath, ready to admit everything.

"I'm in love with Dash," Madison blurted out before I could take one for the team. Her words replayed in my head, making my stomach drop. It was the first time she'd said she was in love with me, and although it felt nice, it wasn't exactly the best way to hear it.

Cade let out a sarcastic laugh, pointing at me with his thumb. "You're in love with this idiot?"

"He's not an idiot."

Cade had taken several steps forward, but I didn't move. A part of me knew exactly what was coming and didn't want to leave. In a way, I knew I deserved a punch in the face.

"Oh, Madison. Can't you see it? He's cheating on you."

Cheating? Wait, what?

Before I could deny anything, Cade's fist met my jaw first, and my chin was pushed up into the air. The hot coffee I was holding spilled all over my shirt, and I heard the crack of the orange juice glass as it hit the floor.

"Cade!" Madison shouted.

I couldn't see what was happening because my head was spinning. My mind went blank, and the only thing I could feel was the excruciating pain in my jaw. I knew Cade was strong, but I didn't realize he could throw a punch like that without trying.

I felt Madison's arms wrap around me as her hand rested on my cheek. "Dash, can you see me? Shit. His nose is bleeding, and there's blood coming out of his mouth. Get me a towel."

"You still want to help him?"

"I swear to God, Cade, if you don't get me a towel right now, I'm going to take the one I'm wearing off and use it to clean Dash."

"Fine."

The pain in my jaw started to subside, only to push through to my brain. "Ouch," I muttered as I lifted my hand and rubbed my head.

"Dash." Her voice was frantic but had a soft edge to it. "Thank goodness."

As I opened my eyes, she had one of my gray towels and dabbed it across my forehead before placing it under my nose. The towel wrapped around her body was covered in blood, so I could only assume my clothes were just as messy.

"I can't believe you did that, Cade." Madison refused to look at her brother as she shook her head in annoyance and kept her blue eyes focused on me.

"You can't believe I'd do that? He's been sleeping with that reporter girl for the last two months, and you're getting angry at me for protecting your honor?"

"I was never dating Sienna." The relief I felt from getting that off my chest was short-lived because I was still in so much pain. Sitting up, I rested my hand against the wall, using the connection to stabilize me as I edged myself up to a stand. "I just went along with the Sienna stuff so you wouldn't suspect I was with Madison."

Cade immediately took a step toward me, but Madison purposely stood in his way.

"So you decided to sleep with my sister after I asked you to figure out who she was dating?"

Jesus, this whole thing was a mess.

"Cade. Stop. I've been in love with Dash since eleventh grade."

"I know that. I just didn't think Dash would use you like that."

"Use her? I would never use her."

"Please. You dated that chick, Amy, for years and showed nothing but a passing interest in her. The only thing I've seen you show any amount of affection for is your foam roller."

"Cade, I've been in love with Madison for years, too."

"Aw, you have?" She sounded shocked, but I couldn't understand why since I'd pretty much told her this yesterday.

Without warning, Cade threw another punch, this time to my stomach.

"So you've been lying to me and sleeping with my sister behind my back? Didn't even have the decency to tell me you were in love with her? Selfish asshole."

"Cade. We didn't tell you because we thought you'd react like this."

"Madison, dear sweet sister, would you mind leaving?"

"No." She pushed him. "I'm not leaving you to hurt my boyfriend."

Cade threw his head back in a laugh. "Well, I need to talk to your *boyfriend*."

"What the—" In just boxers, Scotty came running through the door and kneeled in front of me. "Dash, are you okay?"

"He's fine." Cade waved off Scotty's concern. "He's been hurt worse on the ice."

"Shit, D. I think you need to go to the hospital. Your nose looks broken."

"Not the nose!" Madison sighed dramatically.

"That would explain why I'm finding it hard to breathe."

"I think that's more to do with the blood coming out of it. Come on." Scotty hoisted me up and dragged me through my door. "Alex!" he called into the common room, immediately rousing the rest of the team. "Can you help me carry Dash? Erik," he grumbled out our teammate's name reluctantly.

Unbeknownst to me, Erik was under a blanket on the sofa and had only just woken up. He looked between us, and his eyes grew wide. "What the?"

"Don't ask," Scotty muttered.

"Oh, no. Did Cade find out about Dash and Madison?"

"Wait, you knew, too?" Scotty said with surprise.

Erik rubbed his eyes, too tired to censor himself. "Yeah, I saw Madison sneaking out of his room a few weeks ago."

"And you didn't tell me?" Cade groused.

Erik raised his hands, his gaze flicking over to Scotty. "I have my own problems to deal with."

"Go downstairs and bring a car to the front of the building. Madison, you stay here," Scotty said, taking control of the situation.

Alex rushed over to us and raised my other arm over his shoulder, so I was effectively being dragged out of the room by the two of them.

"No. I'm not leaving Dash."

"You're staying here, Madison," Cade said sternly. "We need to talk."

As we got to the elevator, Madison came toward me and kissed me on the cheek. Looking up at me with her big blue eyes, she said, "I love you."

Swallowing blood, I smiled. "I love you too."

"Stop," Cade wailed. "I'm going to be sick."

When the elevator opened, Scotty and Alex dragged me in, only turning me to face the common room when the doors were about to shut. "No one tells Coach," Scotty yelled before they did.

"I told you fucking around with Madison would get you in trouble," Scotty mumbled under his breath, but Alex just laughed.

"I still can't believe it took Cade this long to figure it out," Alex said.

"You knew, too?" Scotty asked, leaning so he could see over me.

"Yeah. Took me a minute, but when you start looking, it's pretty fucking obvious that the two of them are hot for each other."

That was the last thing I heard before the wooziness took over.

CHAPTER 28

Madison

As I watched the elevator doors shut with my boyfriend behind them, I was fuming. Cade and I were the only ones left, so I turned on my heels and headed straight for him, flailing my arms and screeching so loud that I was sure the entire building heard.

"How dare you?"

He seemed surprised when I came at him, ready to punch him in the face. Somehow, he'd managed to catch my wrists and keep me in a tight hold. That didn't stop me from desperately trying to make him feel some kind of pain. When I couldn't break my arms free, I kicked my legs out, hoping to hurt him the same way he hurt me.

"I hate you, Cade."

He didn't say anything, which only infuriated me more and forced me to lash out further. "I hate everything about you."

"You don't hate me," he said almost casually, which ticked me off because it didn't sound like he was breaking a sweat. Then he brought my arms over my head to turn me around. I was stuck in his hold with no way out.

"Right now, I do."

"Well, I gotta be honest with you, MB. I'm not your biggest fan either right now. I mean, seriously, Madison. You're in a towel in my dorm. Go put some clothes on so I can take you home."

"No. I hate you. I hate you. I *hate* you." Letting all my aggression out, I screamed, kicked, and punched until my limbs were aching. I hadn't managed a single blow because Cade was so much stronger than me. My head was hung low, and I stared at our bare feet because I couldn't bear to look at him. With my chest heaving, tears pooled in my eyes. Why did it feel like everything was over before it could truly start? This was exactly what Dash was afraid of, and he was right. We never had the chance when I had an overprotective asshole for a brother. "Why?" I asked with a meek voice.

"Why what?"

"Why'd you beat Dash up? He's your best friend."

"Really? You want me to answer that? Doesn't the towel you're wearing give you enough of a clue?"

"I like him, Cade."

"I like him too. He's my best friend." Cade dropped my hands and walked over to the kitchen where his jacket was draped over one of the barstools. He took it and tossed it at me. I accepted it and put it on, feeling much less exposed. "He should have told me about his feelings before even thinking about acting on them."

"It's not his fault. It's mine. I was the one that kissed him at The Draft."

Cade's head whipped up in disgust. "The Draft? You kissed him at The Draft?" I nodded. "This has been going on for over a month?" Then he dropped his head and thought about it. "Oh god. Were you Little Miss Pop My Cherry the whole time?" My mouth hung open because I didn't know what to say, but he closed his eyes and raised his hand, stopping himself from retching. "Don't answer that. I don't want to know. I'm already going to have to pretend my best friend doesn't have a functioning dick to survive this."

"I love him, Cade."

"I know you do." Cade ran a hand across his face and growled out in frustration. "I've always known that you've had a crush, I just never expected you to act on it, much less for him to want you back."

"Why?" I straightened up. "What's wrong with me? You make it sound like I'm the ugliest person in the world." He looked down. "Clearly, I'm not that bad if Henry wanted to date me, and your best friend does too. What's so wrong with me that I don't deserve to be happy like everyone else?"

Cade looked surprised, but his features softened. "There's nothing wrong with you, MB. It's just you're my baby sister, so I'm always going to want the best for you. After everything that happened with Henry, I thought you'd want a nice, nerdy guy who would treat you well. Not some knucklehead hockey player."

"He's not just a knucklehead hockey player, though. He's Dash. Your best friend and the guy that defended me when he found out Henry was playing me."

"Exactly, my best friend. That you've been sneaking around with. Why does your happiness always seem to involve my teammates?"

I closed my eyes because he just wasn't getting it. "It doesn't. Henry was the biggest mistake of my life. Dash is the best thing that ever happened to me. I love him." Cade's jaw clenched as he looked at the floor. "Dash is a gentleman, and you know it. He's much better than any hockey or football player out there."

"Dash or a football player? Are those the only options because you're not giving me much of a choice there?"

"Frankly, Cade, you don't get a choice. This is my life and my relationship. I get to choose who I date, not you. You can complain all you want, but you can't stop me from being with Dash. You can either stand in the way and lose your sister and your best friend in the same day, or you can try to be happy for us like we'd be for you."

Silence fell between us because what was I supposed to say now? Cade knew, and he wasn't happy about it. Dash was in the hospital because they thought he had a broken nose. Word would get out and everyone would know soon. I just hoped this wouldn't be the end for us. But as I looked at how angry my brother was, I felt like it could be.

I could see how it was going to play out. Cade was going to give Dash an ultimatum, and Dash would always pick Cade. I knew that when I kissed him the first night; I just didn't think he would ever have to choose. Salty tears started to well up in my eyes, and I took a deep breath, doing my best to hide my emotions because I didn't want Cade to see just how upset I was over everything.

Sighing, Cade looked over at me. Resigned, he said, "Come on, MB. Go get dressed."

I tried to bite back my words, but the more I thought about everything Cade had done, the angrier I got.

"You know what?" I started, and Cade looked shocked by my outburst. "I am not that naïve sixteen-year-old anymore, Cade. You can't wrap me in bubble wrap and still expect me to breathe. I'm nineteen. I know what I want, and you should let me make up my own mind. I'm happy and in love with Dash. If you don't like it, well, screw you, but I'm damn well not going to let you ruin the only good thing that's going on in my life."

"That's not what I was trying to do."

"You sure about that? Because that's exactly what it feels like."

"I'm sorry if I ever made you feel like you couldn't make your own decisions, but that doesn't give you the right to sleep with my best friend behind my back. Now, will you hurry up and get dressed?" He stalked toward me, but I stepped away from his touch. He was trying to kick me out, and, in a way, I deserved it. He was right. I should have learned my lesson with Henry. I should have kept my hands to myself.

"No. I'm not leaving here with you pretending like nothing happened."

"I'm not asking you to."

Standing firm, I realized that we were at an impasse. There was nothing that either of us could say that would change the other's mind. I hung my head as I walked over to Dash's room. The mood was frosty, and I knew it would be a long time before Cade and I could fix our relationship, especially if I did keep dating Dash, which I planned to do.

"Come on, MB. Hurry up. We need to get going."

"And where exactly are we going?"

"To see Dash." My eyes widened, but Cade's face remained expressionless. "I'm not going to hurt him, even if he deserves it. I need to talk to him, and you need to check on him." Raising his hands, he eased out an unamused smile. "Hey, if you and Dash love each other like you say you do, then who am I to stand in the way?"

What the hell just happened?

Was this Cade's way of offering me an olive branch?

"But you just said you didn't want me to date him."

"That's not what I said. I actually said I didn't think you'd want to date an idiot like him, but as I'm turning over a new leaf, I'm going to let you make your own decisions and decide what's best for you. So, if you do want to date an idiot like him, go right ahead."

"Cade." I smiled, not knowing what to say. That was the closest I was going to get with his blessing.

"Besides, I know Dash wouldn't act on his feelings with you unless he was serious. Don't hurt him. He's been through a lot." I tipped on my toes, holding back a squeal of excitement because his words sounded a lot like acceptance. Raising his finger, he said, "That does not mean I'm happy with the way any of this went down or that you can come gallivanting in here whenever you want. In fact, you're banned. I only want to see you outside or at games. No sleepovers because I will vomit if I have to hear things. I already need to look into how to bleach my ears because I'm pretty sure I've already heard things I didn't want to."

I bit down on my bottom lip, holding back a smile. "Okay. That sounds like a reasonable request."

"Good." Tight-lipped, he closed his eyes. "Now, get changed. Let's go."

Chapter 29

Dash

"I seriously can't believe that happened," Erik said, recounting the story as if we all weren't there. The dude loved drama, and this entire morning was satiating his appetite. "Honestly, out of all the guys on the team, I really thought Madison would have boned Brooks before Dash."

"Watch it," I warned. Sure, my teeth might have felt a little out of line, and I wasn't able to breathe properly, but I was ready to fight anyone if I needed to. Especially if they were trying to pass my girlfriend off to other teammates.

Erik raised his hands and laughed nervously. "Sorry, man. I didn't mean to say anything. It's just, well, you know Brooks. Everyone loves him, and no one knows you. You just sit in the net with so much padding you look like a giant grizzly bear."

"Brooks never had a chance. Madison's been in love with Dash since she was a kid," Scotty explained, whacking him upside the head. "Now, if you're not going to say anything useful, you can go out in the waiting room. I didn't drop my name to get VIP treatment so we could hear you gossiping all day."

"How much longer do you think it will be?" Alex asked. "We've been waiting three hours, and there's still no sign of a doctor."

"That's because my injuries aren't that bad," I grumbled. "I didn't need to come here. My face would have healed on its own."

Scotty sucked in a breath. "I mean, if that's the nose placement you want moving forward, who am I to judge?"

Alex sighed. "It's just that I can't stay much longer. I'm going to be late for my tutor, and she loves roasting people's balls for tardiness."

"Then go. We'll take it from here."

As Alex walked out, he slowed down and let out a sarcastic chuckle. "Looks like you might not need me anyway. Dash, you've got some more visitors."

When Madison stepped in the doorway, I could have sworn my heart nearly dropped. I wasn't worried that Cade would do anything to her, but I didn't think he'd ever allow me to be alone with her again. So, the fact that she was here probably meant that she'd somehow evaded him.

"Dash." Her voice immediately made the pain go away, and when she rushed in to hug me, I let her. Sweet strawberries. Madison was here, but how? She didn't drive, and everyone who knew what happened was in the room with me. "I'm so glad to see you." She drew back from our hug, and her eyes darted across my face as she took me in. "You look like shit," she said with a smile on her face and glanced over at Scotty and Erik. "Why haven't either of you offered to get him a paper towel from the bathroom so he could at least wipe the blood off his face?"

Erik shrugged. "I guess we thought the doctor needed to see what his injury looked like in its entirety. Cleaning him up might give them the wrong impression."

She shook her head and rolled her eyes. "Idiot."

"Are we talking about Dash? Because yes, I can confirm he's an idiot. The biggest one I've met, actually." Cade walked into the room with his hands in his pockets, looking annoyed to be here. "Hey, guys. Did I miss anything?"

Scotty and Erik immediately stood in front of my hospital bed, acting as a barrier between me and Cade.

"Cade, if you're here for anything other than an apology, then you need to leave right now." Scotty pointed at the door and used his height to try to intimidate him. "Because there is no way I'm letting you anywhere near our goaltender again when we are so close to playing Southern Collegiate. Who fucking beats up their goalie during a Frozen Four run?"

"Relax," he said, pulling his hands out of his pockets and raising them. "I come in peace." He glanced over at me and smiled. "Dash, I'm not sorry for hitting you. You deserved it, but I promise I won't do it again. Unless you deserve it, of course."

Cade was telling the truth, I could tell from his voice, but his facial expression was a mix of nonchalance and pissed, so I didn't know what to think.

Without looking at me, Madison gripped my hand and squeezed it in an act of reassurance. The fact that Cade hadn't growled at the move suggested that they'd talked about things.

"Madison, we've confirmed he's alive, now can you and the rest of the guys please give Dash and I some privacy? We need to have a little chat."

Everyone turned to look at me, seemingly wanting to get my permission. I sat up on the bed and pulled my feet over the edge, so they were on the floor. Even though I believed that Cade wouldn't do anything, that didn't mean I wanted to be in a vulnerable position if he did. "It's fine. Cade and I need to talk."

Madison's thumb rubbed across my palm, and she kissed my cheek, ignoring the dried blood that flaked off as she moved away. "I love you," she whispered so only I could hear.

"Aww," Erik said. "That's so cute."

I pinned him with a glare, but with a face that bore a striking resemblance to a charcuterie board, I assumed I looked less than menacing.

"Erik," Scotty griped, knocking him gently as he ushered him out of the room.

"What? How can you not be rooting for them? It's like Romeo and Juliet with hopefully a happier ending," Erik continued as he walked out of the room.

"Madison, I won't be long," Cade said.

She looked over at me with an overprotective edge, but I didn't need her to be concerned for me, so I squeezed her hand. "Go. I'll be fine."

THE DRAFT

"And I'll be just outside." Madison stood and glared at her brother as she walked past him, and just as she was standing in the doorframe, she looked over her shoulder and winked.

Man, did I love her. And shit, it felt so good to be able to think that without hearing Cade's voice haunting me. I loved Madison. She loved me, and everyone now knew about it.

When she was out of sight, it was just me and Cade. Strange. We'd been friends for so long that I couldn't remember the last time we were in a room and had nothing to say to each other. Potentially never. This was the first time in our lives that we had to deal with something less than kosher.

He blew out a long breath before moseying over to the bed and sitting next to me. We both stared straight ahead at the now-shut door.

More silence.

Not awkward at all.

"So, you and my sister?" He gently clapped his hands together, rubbing them as he stared at the door, still refusing to look at me.

"Yeah," I sighed out. "Me and Madison."

"How long?"

"It's been a little over a month." He deserved the truth.

"No. I know that. Madison told me it started at The Draft."

"Okay," I drawled out, confused.

"How long have you been secretly pining over her?"

Fuck. I should have known this would come up.

"Since I found out about Henry and Amy. I, uh, always thought she was cute, but I didn't really think of her as anything other than your kid sister. Not until that day, then I saw her in a different light. She's the reason I broke his nose, because I wanted to make sure I never saw her that upset again."

"Figured. I always thought it was strange that you fought so passionately for Amy when you barely mentioned her name in high school." He shook his head and bit his bottom lip. "Not to mention how you were always the one to tell me when guys were approaching Madison. I even got you to see who she was dating here." He laughed bitterly to himself. "I was really stupid not to see this coming, wasn't I?"

"No. I never intended to act on it. Ever. But it just kind of happened."

"I'm guessing that wasn't a dream I had the other night, then?" I looked at him quizzically. "I had a dream you told me you were in love with Madison. Thought it was because I'd been drinking, and then when I saw her in your room today, I thought I'd somehow predicted the future."

I laughed nervously. "No. You weren't dreaming. I wrote an entire speech, knowing full well I'd been an ass and expecting to be reprimanded as such. It was only after I finished that I realized you were asleep."

"Figures. Look, I know you're a serious guy, and you wouldn't be going near my sister unless you felt like she was equally serious about you, but I just wanted to say, she's always had a thing for you, so please don't break her heart."

"I never intend to."

"Good."

Holding his hand out, he looked at me expectantly. I shook it as he offered me a curt smile. Was that it? No more punching? No more anger about betraying him? Had I missed something?

"Are *we* still good?"

He nodded. "You're my friend and teammate. We have to be good. Do I like that you're dating my sister? Not particularly, but you're better than a football player." I nodded, and then he clasped my shoulder. "Do I like that you snuck around behind my back? Not at all, but we're clear that will never happen again, right?" He squeezed my hand, making me wince from the pain.

"Right," I said, and I let out a breath when he let go.

"Good." I watched Cade stand, making his way to the door, and the little pinches of pain where his fingertips left my shoulder were a reminder that he was serious.

"Oh, and Dash," Cade said, turning to look at me again. I raised my brows in acknowledgment. "If I ever find out you've lied to me again, or if you hurt Madison, I will kill you. I will literally handcuff you to a fence with bike chains and torch your dick off." Well, that wasn't where I was expecting this conversation to go. He raised his hands, tipping his chin in amusement. "I don't want to do it, but I'll have to. To defend her honor."

I pursed my lips together because, what the hell do you say to that? "Good to know."

"Welcome to the family," he said with a wicked smile, and I gulped, wondering what the hell I got myself into but realizing I didn't give a shit. Cade could threaten me all he wanted. I wasn't going anywhere.

"So," Madison drawled out once Erik dropped us off at her dorm.

Even though my face looked like a conceptual art piece, I was lucky that Cade hadn't broken my jaw or nose, which meant I could still play hockey and help the team get through to the Frozen Four. Once the swelling reduced, of course.

"How did it go with my brother?"

She was perched on her desk as she looked down at me sitting on her bed. It was the first time we'd been alone since our relationship had been put out in the open. We were a couple now, and it felt freeing, yet somewhat constricting at the same time. Cade asked Erik to drive so he could sit between us on the car ride home, and I knew that would only be the start of the team's monitoring of our relationship.

"Better than I expected. He threatened to burn my balls off before pleasantly welcoming me to the family," I laughed.

Madison's jaw dropped. "He didn't?" She covered her face in embarrassment and shook her head. "I'm going to kill him. He drove me here after I told him he had no right meddling in my relationships, and here he is, meddling in them."

"It's fine. He was just looking after you, and the more people that are on your side, the better. He's not going to stop us being together because he knows I'm serious about you, but he's not thrilled with the situation either. The only good thing is that I'm certain we're past the point of him giving me another black eye over you. Unless I hurt you, of course. Then it's warranted."

Madison smiled, but it quickly dropped. "Wait. Is that your way of saying you're not getting any more black eyes?"

"Yup. No more black eyes from Cade, at least."

"That's too bad." With a smirk on her face, she c

rossed her arms and sauntered over to me. "Because I've got to admit, your purple and black face really is kind of sexy." She crinkled her nose, taking me in. "You got beaten up for little old me." She fanned herself overdramatically.

I glared at her, but I was pretty sure she couldn't tell since my face was that swollen. "Really?"

Madison moved over to me and sat on my lap. When she was comfortable enough, she wrapped her arms around my neck and kissed me. "Definitely. All you need now are a couple of your front teeth knocked out, and then you'll be my wildest dream."

I shook my head before resting it against hers. "You're a weirdo, you know that?"

"What can I say? Hanging out with those pretty football players has made me realize just how much I like a ruggedly aggressive goaltender who tends to my needs." She wiggled her eyebrows and bit down on her bottom lip. "Do you get it?"

I shook my head, kissing her cheek. "We need to talk about this budding friendship you've got with those guys. I'm not sure I like it."

"You should love it. They're the only reason I even spoke to you about the kiss after The Draft. If my friendship with them didn't happen, then we might not be here."

"Good point. Maybe I'll watch a game or two to thank them. They need all the ticket sales they can get." She cackled, wrapping her arms around me, scooting herself further into my lap. "So, do you still want me? After all the shit with your brother?"

"Of course. I think the bigger question is if you still want me, after all the shit with my brother?"

I paused, pretending to think about it.

"Dash?"

"There's no one I'd rather be fighting the world with than you."

A sly smile drew across her lips. "Oh, Dash. Look at you. I knew you were the brooding type, but I didn't realize you were the 'fight for your girl type,'" she said with a husky drawl. "How can I not swoon?"

When she kissed me on the lips, I winced. "Oh, sorry. I guess that's probably going to hurt."

The Draft

Clasping her jaw in my hand, I brought her forward and kissed her passionately, letting her know that no amount of pain would stop me from kissing her. Ever. "Kiss me all you want. It makes me feel better."

It was technically a lie since the heavy meds were probably the thing helping ease my pain, but I felt like it reduced the throbbing more than anything, and I didn't want to bother Madison with the details. Mainly because I didn't want her to ever stop kissing me.

With a mischievous glint in her eyes, she pushed me down and straddled me. "I can think of a few places to kiss you that would make you feel a lot better." She wiggled her eyebrows and dropped her hand to my waistband, but I stopped her from going under.

"Before you do that, I've got something to ask you."

"Yes?"

"Do you maybe want to move off me before I ask?"

"Nope, I'm perfectly content right here." She wiggled a little, rubbing her center across my crotch. What a tease.

"Will you be my girlfriend? Officially?"

"Um, yeah? I kind of thought we were already there."

Squeezing her sides, I smiled. She was now dry humping me, and I wasn't stopping her. "Okay, fine. How about this? Will you wear my jersey at our game against Southern Collegiate next week?"

I should have started with that because that made her squeal in excitement. "Yes, please! You are going to get two blowjobs for that."

I couldn't wait.

She dropped to her knees, giving me one more long, passionate kiss before pulling my shirt over my head. Kissing my chest, she made her way back to my shorts. "Thank you." She kissed my abs and circled her tongue around my belly button. A move I remembered using on her once or twice.

Closing my eyes, I lay back and let my girlfriend ease my pain.

EPILOGUE
Dash

Protecting the goal, I watched the puck flit between two Southern Collegiate players. Back and forth. The only thing that was important to me at that moment was making sure the puck stayed far away from the back of my net.

Closer. Closer. SoCol's center was coming for me, and just as he lifted his stick for a slapshot, Cade barged into him, bringing him down. I couldn't relax for long because their right winger was right there, snatching the puck before Scotty could get anywhere near it and shooting it in my direction.

I dropped, landing on the ice in a split, feeling the puck hit against my pads. I kept it out, but the right winger was beside me now, pushing up into me, trying to force me to move or make a mistake so he could flick the puck over me. Brooks was by my side, pushing their team out of the way.

When the whistle blew, I relaxed for a second while the refs tried to untangle Cade from a SoCol player, which wasn't going well since he had him in a headlock. Admittedly, I knew I wasn't Cade's favorite person right now, but he would do anything to ensure the goal was tended.

With the break in play, I took the opportunity to look into the crowd and smiled when I saw Madison sitting in the front row, right next to Todd, who just so happened to be dressed as our mascot, Crushie the polar bear. The poor people behind him had no chance of seeing the game.

Madison blew me a kiss, and I subtly pretended to catch it. Yeah, I'd become a sap for her, but it was the least I could do considering she was out there wearing my jersey tonight.

When the ref finally pulled Cade off the opposing player, Cade skated around my net in an attempt to cool down, but instead, he glared at me, annoyed that he had to step in. Getting back into position, Cade brought two of his gloved fingers to his hockey mask and then pointed them at me, in a gesture that said, *"eyes on the game, not my sister."*

Yeah. I remembered.

Cade and I had a way to go before we were besties again, and I couldn't blame him. I slept with his sister behind his back. I'd betrayed him in a way no other person could, and it wasn't like he could get rid of me. He lived with me; he trained with me. We were going to Atlanta together, whether he liked it or not. He was going to have to put up with me for a long time, and I was hell-bent on making sure I atoned for my sins. I didn't care how long it took; I was determined to make us friends again.

When play recommenced, Scotty had snatched the puck and taken it across the ice. I took my eyes off the puck for one second, only to see Henry get boarded by one of the SoCol players. I pointed to him, trying to get the ref's attention for the illegal body check, but no one was watching me, and that was only amplified when Scotty scored.

4-0.

We were winning this game with ease, but that didn't mean Henry should take a beating for it. He was quick to get off the board and back into the game, but I wasn't going to stop watching him. We weren't best friends, or even friends, for that matter, but he was my teammate, and we looked out for each other.

Within the next few seconds, SoCol attempted to score again, but I blocked it easily. I was on fire tonight, which I put down to wanting to impress Madison and my teammates. There was no denying that my game had been poor over the last few weeks because I was trying to keep such a monumental secret. Now that everything was out in the open, I was able to concentrate on what was important. The game. So far tonight, I was proving I was worthy of starting for the Covey Crushers. With eight blocked attempts and only five minutes left in the game, it was my best performance in a while.

Scotty passed the puck to Henry, and SoCol immediately took the opportunity to surround him, stealing the puck with ease. I didn't have time to see Henry's reaction because the puck was coming my way. Passing it between each other, there was no way our defense could stop them this time, so it was down to me. When they took a shot, I raised my glove, guessing it was the top left corner, and somehow managed to stop it.

The player threw his stick down, swearing, and just as I was passing the puck to Scotty, I saw it again.

SoCol was charging Henry, and the refs were doing nothing about it. What the hell happened to Henry's fight from our practice games? As suspected, Coach waited until today to debut him, but that wasn't doing Henry any favors. He wasn't playing with his usual cockiness. There was no attack.

Scotty rounded the net, and just as he skated past, I motioned to Henry and then to my eyes. He nodded, getting that I wanted him to watch Henry as he skated toward the puck. The next time Henry was illegally bodychecked, Scotty intervened, causing a fight on the ice, which got him ejected from the rest of the game.

With one minute left, we were still up by four, so SoCol decided to swap their goalie out for an extra player, meaning SoCol had a huge advantage against us with Scotty out.

Henry seemed to find a newfound vigor, and with him, Cade, Alex, and Brooks helping me to guard the goal, we managed to last the last few seconds of the game without a hitch.

When the final whistle blew, and we were celebrating our win, I looked over at Madison, who was jumping in her seat, hugging the polar bear like we'd just won the Frozen Four. We were still five wins away from that, but I didn't care because she was out there celebrating for me, and that was the biggest win I had all year.

I pushed my helmet up, popping my mouth guard out and playing with it in my mouth when Henry came over. He held his hand out, and I took it as we slapped each other's backs in congratulations.

"Thanks," he said curtly.

"For?" I played dumb. He knew what I did with Scotty.

"Watching out for me."

I shrugged. "Didn't do much."

"Still, I know you brought it to Scotty's attention. Surprised Cade didn't notice. He always wants an excuse to hurt someone."

"Don't I know it. What's going on with you two, by the way? Just a few weeks ago, he was saying he didn't want you in our dorm, then the next day, you show up with matching black eyes."

Henry shook his head and chuckled. "It's an incredibly long story. I'm sure Cade will tell you sometime."

"I won't hold my breath," I whispered.

"But I hope this game proves that I'm here to play and not fuck with the team. Just because I played with a bunch of cheats at SoCol doesn't mean I'm one too." I nodded, knowing that I was wrong. "I'm also sorry I was an asshole to you and Madison when I was sixteen. I was young, stupid, and equated being popular with being successful. I've learned that's not always the case."

"That's all water under the bridge. We're teammates now." It was the truth. I didn't care about anything that happened in high school, much less Henry's reasons for being here. As long as he was a good teammate, that was all I wanted.

"Maybe even teammates in Atlanta," he joked, and I pushed him as he headed to the gate.

"I hope not."

As the crowd was filtering out, I glanced back into the stands, and Henry followed my gaze, knowing exactly who I was looking at before he found the object of my affection. Madison had made her way to the player's box and was talking to her brother now. Throwing her head back and laughing, she was at ease with Cade, and I was happy this entire thing hadn't ruined their relationship. It had been a week since he found out about us, and although it took him a few days to talk to us again, he was now back to normal. With Madison, at least.

"Take care of her," Henry said, drawing my attention back to him. Okay, we might have bonded over the game, but I wasn't interested in his advice. "Don't make the same mistake I did."

I grunted in response. "On that note, I'm going to go and see her."

I skated over to my estranged best friend and his sister, or, should I say, *my* girlfriend, and smiled. Sliding up next to Cade, Madison immediately moved over to me and wrapped her arms around my neck, hugging me. "You played amazing today," she said. As we pulled out of the hug, she cupped my cheeks and kissed me fully on the lips.

"Yeah, I could have lived a happy life without seeing that," Cade joked, pushing himself off to the side, making his way to the locker room. "See you later, MB." Leaving Madison and me together, the rink was quieter now as the crowd had filtered out.

I picked Madison up over the barrier and skated around the ice with her in a bridal carry. Her hands gripped my neck as I kept skating, waiting for everyone else to leave so we could be on our own. She seemingly knew what I was waiting for so she dropped her head on my chest and closed her eyes. Gliding across the ice, her blonde hair flicked with the motion, throwing that strawberry scent around again.

"I still can't believe you're mine," I whispered in awe when the place was quiet.

"I still can't believe you can hold me with all this padding on."

I lifted her a little higher, causing her to squeal and then giggle as I switched her position. Her legs were wrapped around my waist now, but I didn't think she'd be able to hold on like that for long since my pads doubled my size, and her thighs could barely get a grip around my waist. I drifted over to the net, placing her on the top so she could sit.

With my hands on either side of her, I said, "You know you're the only person I can stand in this world, right?" I kissed her forehead, rubbing her thigh.

"That's not true. You like Cade."

"I put up with Cade because he's Cade. He's like an annoying brother you know you can't get rid of, so you have to love him."

"He *is* my annoying brother that I can't get rid of."

"Exactly, which is why you're still the only one I *want* to spend time with. Everyone else can go and fuck themselves for all I care."

She giggled at that, throwing her arms back around me as she placed a small kiss on my lips. I could kiss her all day, and it still wouldn't be enough. She leaned back, pulling me into her so much that I had to hold on to the net for balance.

"Bet you say that to all the girls," she joked, but that didn't mean I liked it. Madison knew that she was the only girl for me, so whenever she said something like that, it felt like she was trying to mask some hidden insecurity that I was ready to leave her at any minute. I wasn't. Now that I had her, she was going to have to forcibly remove me if she wanted me out of her life.

"Erik, I already told you. Outside of games and practice, I don't want to talk to you." Scotty's voice echoed through the rink as he walked out of the locker room with a shaking head and an annoyed look etched across his face.

Madison and I immediately stilled, watching the scene before us.

"I've already apologized. What else do you want me to do?" Erik followed closely behind him, but the minute Scotty saw us, he clamped his lips shut. "How was I supposed to know that was going to happen?" Erik said through a clenched jaw.

"Just leave me alone because I need to figure out how to get out of the shit that you started." Scotty pushed past Erik, who looked at us confused. He hunched his shoulders before following Scotty back into the locker room.

"What was that about?" Madison asked, toying with the hair at the nape of my neck.

"Not sure. Scotty is ticked off about something from his birthday party."

"And you haven't asked what?" Madison said, surprised.

I shrugged. "I don't care." My gaze dragged down to her lips, and I could already feel myself getting excited. "And we've been a little busy."

"Still. I'd really like to know, so I'd appreciate it if you could find out what exactly happened. You know, to reduce the chances of me putting my foot in it at a later junction."

"Sure thing." I knew that wasn't the reason she wanted to know. Madison loved the gossip, and I would happily supply it once I figured it out for myself.

I took her in my arms again, knowing that I had to take her off the ice. She clung to me tightly before saying, "Dash, I've got something to ask you."

"Shoot."

"I know everything is new, and we just got together, but I was wondering what's going to happen between us?"

"You mean tonight? Well, since you're banned from coming to mine, I was thinking I could take you out for dinner, then we could hang out at yours. I hear there's a new season of *Baseball Wives* that is gearing up to be the most ridiculous season ever, and that sounds like something you'd watch."

"Not tonight. I mean to us later." She bit down on her bottom lip. "What's going to happen when you go off to play with Atlanta at the end of the year and I'm still here?"

"Oh." I slowed my skating down but didn't let go of her. "I thought we'd just keep doing what we're doing."

"Do you think that would work? You'll be across the country, and there will be so many girls after you."

"What makes you think I'm looking at anyone else but you? I've already told you that you're all I want, but I'm happy to prove that to you every day if I need to."

She rolled her eyes. "You don't need to do that. I guess I just feel a little like you might not need me anymore. You'll be out starting your own life, and I'll still be here."

"Working on yours," I finish for her. "I want you here because I know you'll be happy. You can attend every and any game you want, and you can come live with me when you're on break from classes."

She grinned. "Live with you? We might want to ease Cade into that."

"Yeah, because easing him into the idea of us dating worked so well last time."

She barked out a laugh but then pulled herself high enough that she could leave a lingering kiss on my lips. "I love you, Big Man," she said so softly that only I could hear.

The Draft

"I love you too, Madison, and I can't wait to see where this life takes us."

"Me, either." She rested her head against my chest, and I skated with her in my arms until the facility manager kicked us out.

Life couldn't get better than this.

THE END

EXTENDED EPILOGUE

Madison

Summer

"Go away," I said to a fly sitting on the head of the dinosaur cake that I made last night. Okay, it was supposed to be a dinosaur, and everyone here was acting like I'd done an awesome job on it, but I hadn't. With pointy ears and a long tail, the thing looked more like a green cat than a T. rex. Not that Cade cared. He was just bemused at the fact that Dash and I had gotten together to throw him a surprise birthday party in the first place. After outlining the entire event with Alex, it seemed ridiculous to not throw it.

The music was playing in the background, drifting across an unusually empty backyard, but I figured the guys were taking a break inside. There were at least thirty college hockey players here who were using the event as their last celebration with Cade and Dash before they moved on to playing with the Atlanta Anglerfish.

The NHL. I still couldn't believe my brother and boyfriend were heading there in a week. It seemed unreal, but I couldn't wait to be in the crowd during their first game in a couple of months.

I plucked a food net from the opposite end of the table, and just as I was about to put it over the cake, I noticed something didn't look right in the back. "What the?"

Standing on my tiptoes, I inspected the back of the dinosaur and cursed. Sure enough, some drunk hockey player had walked past and bitten a chunk out of the tail. Admittedly, it looked much more like a dinosaur with the now shorter tail, but that wasn't the point. "Idiots," I grumbled, putting the net in place, but what was the point in protecting it now? We'd already sung Happy Birthday, and now some drunk hockey hooligan had left his mark on my beautiful creation.

I frowned when I noticed there were only two dinosaur cupcakes left. Strange. I made eighteen, and no one had gone for the desserts yet, except for Erik, of course. My guess was that he'd been slowly pinching cupcakes throughout the day, thinking no one would notice if they reduced in size. Not that I cared about the cupcake count. It was Cade's birthday after all, and I just wanted them to have a good time.

"What are you doing back here all alone?" Dash's deep voice asked as his arms wrapped around me.

Closing my eyes, I leaned into his touch before kissing his bicep and resting my cheek on it. Was it weird to say days like today made me feel like my life was perfect? Everything felt so right with Dash, even after being with each other for close to six months.

"Protecting my cake from wild insects," I said, snarling at another fly that was hovering over the cupcakes. "Where did everyone else go?"

Dash stepped back and leaned his hip against the food table so he could look at me. Tipping his chin in the house's direction, he said, "They're all still in that inflatable laser tag arena we hired out front. There's a heated game going on between Cade and Brooks, and honestly, I don't think it's going to end until someone's crying."

I raised my hand. "That'll be me because you're leaving in two days," I said, looking over at the dinosaur bounce house. I had to admit, it was everything I wanted it to be. Huge and super bouncy with hidden areas inside. Dash said it was gaudy and atrocious, but I didn't think he really understood that was the point. Because if you were going to have a dinosaur bounce house, you better have the best one. The best part about it was trying to watch hockey players who'd had a little too much to drink make it through without falling.

Dash groaned at my remark, not taking my bait but staring at me expectantly. I ignored it, tending to the napkins and paper plates instead. They were also dinosaur-themed but maybe a little too young for Cade. Since they didn't have twenty-one, I used a mix of things for ages two and one, which Cade didn't find as funny as I expected.

"You're so dramatic, Madison. Did you forget that you have two bags in your bedroom packed because you're also coming to Atlanta to see Cade in a few days?"

I rolled my head back to look at Dash, doing everything in my power to tame down my smirk, but I couldn't. See Cade. Yeah, right. Like anyone believed that was the reason I was going to spend three weeks out in Atlanta. Cade had more important things to do than entertain his little sister, but it just so happened that Dash lived right across the hall.

Pulling me into a hold, I leaned back so I could look at my boyfriend. "We all know you're going to be spending more of your time with me," he said so confidently that it came off as smug.

Pushing my lips out, I didn't like it, so I decided to teach him a lesson. I kissed Dash to distract him from the fact that I swiped a cupcake from the table and hid it behind my back.

I backed away from him with a hum. "You really think highly of yourself, don't you?"

Dash leaned in, ready for another kiss. "Nope. I just know you. When you want something, you go out and get it. You want me, so it only makes sense."

"Is that so?" Dash nodded, and as I stood on my tiptoes, I let him believe that I was just about to kiss him. When he closed his eyes, and our lips were inches apart, I smashed a cupcake against the side of his face, smushing it until the cake stuck without my force.

When Dash opened his eyes and touched his cheek, he growled as he examined the sticky icing on his fingers.

Shrieking, I ran because I knew I was about to be punished, but since there weren't many places to hide, I ended up jumping into the mouth of the dinosaur bounce house, hoping he wouldn't follow. On my hands and knees, I took hold of the rope that acted as the dinosaur's tonsils. (Side note: Did T. rex's have tonsils? It was something I'd have to look up when I wasn't running for my life.)

Pulling myself up the slide-slash-mouth, I made it to the end of his throat and fell down. Thankfully, there was a ball pit below to break my fall. "Ah," I said to myself, trying to drown in the balls as I attempted to make ball pit angels.

"Madison." My eyes popped open in shock when I heard Dash calling my name because I didn't think he'd be able to get his giant frame inside the mouth. Turning on my front, I swam through the balls to the end where there were a few steps to climb into the next section.

When I got to the top, I smiled because I was met with a mass of inflatable columns, which I assumed acted as the dinosaur intestines. It didn't matter either way. What did matter was that Dash wouldn't be able to find me if I hid in just the right place.

Slithering in between the columns, I held a hand over my mouth, stopping myself from laughing because that would give the game away.

"Did you really think you could hide from me?" His voice was menacing, and I jumped away, almost falling into the columns. Dash took me in his arms before I could fall and dragged me to the side of the wall. The bounciness of the floor was making it difficult for Dash to keep a firm grip on me, so I tried using that to my advantage and bounced away.

As if he knew my plan, he grabbed me by the waist and pushed me to the ground so he was lying on top of me. With the green inflated floor to catch my fall, the only thing uncomfortable about this position was the six-foot-six hockey player smothering me.

Dash started tickling me, and I swatted his hands, only really looking at him for the first time when he braced his hands on either side of my head. Catching our breath, we were breathing so loudly that we couldn't hear the fan inflating the bounce house.

"You've still got cake on your face." I lifted a finger, swiping a tiny bit of icing off his jaw, licking it seductively.

Apparently, Dash didn't like my teasing. "Lick it off," he commanded. My finger was still in my mouth, my lips surrounding it in a way that was annoying Dash.

"I just did," I popped out before trailing my tongue across my fingers, watching Dash the entire time.

"No. Lick all of it off my face, now."

I fell silent, and even though we were bouncing to the rhythm of the music playing outside, there was a thick tension brewing between us. Lick it off. Those words were very reminiscent of the fun time we had in the equipment closet before we became official, and as I looked up at Dash, I realized he was thinking the same thing.

Placing my hands on his shoulders, I pulled my body up so that I was close to Dash's ear. "Gladly," I whispered before gently licking off the cake left on his cheek. He didn't make a noise, so I drew myself back to look him in the eyes. Dark heat was burning behind them, which encouraged me to continue. I licked at his temple, getting rid of all the cupcake that was left. Even when there was nothing there, I kept slowly lapping at his skin, making sure that he could feel my body squirming under his.

When I moved back to look him in the eyes again, he stopped me with a searing kiss. One I'd been waiting for. My fingers dug into his shoulder as I tried to get closer, but the unstable floor underneath me was making that task a little difficult.

Evidently, it was ticking off Dash, too, because he stood up and dragged me back to the ball pit, which had a hard floor once you got the plastic balls out of the way. Dash made sure his butt was on the ground before sitting me on his lap.

I threw one of my legs over so I was straddling him, and we continued kissing. This time, it was so much easier. I was clawing at him, dry humping him because I was trying to get as close as I could. With harsh breaths, we were both enjoying the motion, and I knew Dash was getting as hot as me.

As his hand drifted from the small of my back to my breast, I pulled away from the kiss, giggling.

"We can't do anything in here." I looked around at our green surroundings. With only four inflatable walls separating us from the rest of the party, there was no way we could do anything without getting caught.

"Why not?" he said, his palm now cupping my fabric-covered breast as his thumb swiped over my nipple. I took in a sharp breath, trying to hide how good it made me feel. "There's no one here but us."

"Yeah, but for how long? You know once the guys have finished laser tag, they're going to come in here."

"They won't be able to get in." I tilted my head in confusion. Dash just shrugged and smiled. "Did I forget to tell you that when I realized you were out here on your own, I locked all the entrances?"

My eyes widened in surprise. "You did what?"

"I may have also blocked the entrance for laser tag, so they can't get out until I help them."

"You're so bad." I laughed, swatting him in the chest. He took my hand, kissing each knuckle as he pushed a few errant balls away.

"And you're so hot. Especially in this damn dress." He fiddled with the fabric of my paisley dress, and I wanted to blush. It wasn't often that I got to dress like this, so hearing him compliment me made me feel good. "Besides, this party has been going on for hours, and I wanted to spend some time with my girlfriend and less time with teammates."

"I will never tire of hearing you say that." I rewarded him with a kiss and didn't bother swatting his hand away this time. I just let him touch me the way he wanted.

When his hands pushed my dress up, revealing my underwear, he groaned, but I pushed him back. "Okay, I'm all for fondling, but we aren't having sex in here. We can't." My voice was shaking with nervousness because I was all for having fun, but there were just certain things I couldn't do. Fucking in a giant inflatable T. rex was apparently one of them.

"No. You're right, but a little taste wouldn't be so bad, would it?"

"Dash." I swatted him playfully, but his fingers were still dancing at the edges of my panties, and I had no intention of moving them.

Biting down on my bottom lip, I shunted my hips forward in an attempt to encourage him. Dash gently peeled my underwear to the side and pushed his fingers inside me. I threw my head back and gasped, immediately enjoying the feeling of his thick fingers filling me up.

He pulled them out, bringing them up to his mouth and tasting me. "Delicious," he said as he popped them out, dropping them between us again.

I shivered at the move, knowing I'd never get tired of it. His fingers moved up and down my slit, driving me wild but never actually pushing back inside me. "But I think I need more."

His fingers thrust into me, and I bounced on his lap, chasing the high that only Dash could deliver. His thumb swiped across my clit, rolling the sensitive flesh and making me scream. Thankfully, with the music and the air fan, there was no way anyone could hear me. Dash's other hand was grabbing my ass, guiding me to move against his fingers as he watched. With every thrust, I was losing my inhibitions, ready to pull Dash's jeans down and ride him if he'd let me.

"Dash!" I called out when I was close to coming, making him work his hand faster.

Just as I was on the edge, clawing at the sides of the bounce house to try to gain some balance, I heard a noise.

"I can't believe how badly you suck at laser tag." Scotty's voice was distinctive enough to hear, and with his fingers still inside me, Dash covered my mouth.

"Shh. Let me keep going, and I'll make sure to get you off before anyone finds us."

I nodded as a small thrill worked its way up my spine. I couldn't deny it, the possibility of getting caught was only adding to the excitement.

Dash's fingers worked faster, and I was sure he knew I wasn't far. My hips were bucking, and I was moaning into Dash's palm, chasing my climax.

So close. I was just so, so close.

He brought his mouth to my ear, kissing me on my cheek before whispering, "If you come right now, I'm going to eat your pussy all night."

That was it. With his fingers still inside me, I came crashing down. My body was heated, and Dash held me tight as the pleasure ran through me.

Breathing heavily, I looked at him. "Why do you have to be so good at that?"

He swiped my clit, making my body convulse with the move, before pulling out of me. "What can I say? I just love to watch you come."

I huffed out a breath, feeling flustered. Suddenly, I noticed the tonsil rope from above was moving. With no time to recover from my orgasm, I pushed myself up, adjusting my underwear and dress before moving to the next section of the bounce house with Dash in tow.

The climb was much harder than the first time because my legs were still recovering from the orgasm, but with the incentive to get away from Dash's old teammates, I was able to get through. We pushed through the inflatable columns, and after climbing the makeshift inflatable ladder, we were at the top of a long slide.

Dash shifted his bulky body next to mine, and I held back my laugh because his weight was making the bounce house dip. He held out his hand, and I eagerly accepted it.

"You ready for this?" he asked, and he may have been referring to going down the slide together, but it felt like a hell of a lot more than that.

"I've been ready since the day I kissed you at The Draft."

He just chuckled before we let go of the sides and slid down.

By the time we'd reached the bottom, we'd realized the backyard was now full.

"I thought you said you locked everything, and they couldn't get back here?"

"Yeah, about that...I may have lied."

"What?" I swatted him in the chest.

"You wouldn't have let me touch you otherwise."

I shook my head, hardly annoyed because I'd done something similar to him when we slept together the first time, but I still couldn't believe he'd use my own tricks against me.

"You're so bad," I teased, strutting away from him toward the front of the now-busy backyard.

He didn't let me get far before he linked his hand with mine and kissed me on the cheek.

"And you're so mine."